THE
D0346919

THE HOUSE OF THE DEAD

[Notes from a Dead House]

THE GAMBLER

Fyodor Dostoevsky

Translated by
CONSTANCE GARNETT

With an introduction by
ANTHONY BRIGGS

WORDSWORTH CLASSICS

I

Readers who are interested in other titles from
Wordsworth Editions are invited to visit our website at
www.wordsworth-editions.com

For our latest list and a full mail order service contact
Bibliophile Books, Unit 5 Datapoint,
South Crescent, London E16 4TL
Tel: +44 020 74 74 24 74
Fax: +44 020 74 74 85 89
orders@bibliophilebooks.com

This edition published 2010 by Wordsworth Editions Limited
8B East Street, Ware, Hertfordshire SG12 9HJ

ISBN 978 1 84022 629 4

Typeset in Great Britain by Roperford Editorial
Printed and bound by Clays Ltd, St Ives plc

CONTENTS

Dostoevsky, like Dante, passed through all the circles of human hell . . . more terrible than the mediaeval hell of the *Divine Comedy*.

Konstantin Mochulsky

From the beginning to the end of his artistic career the curse of physical and psychic suffering hung over Dostoevsky.

René Fueloep-Miller

INTRODUCTION

Extremities of human behaviour

Fyodor Dostoevsky's famous novels are well stocked with melodramatic, violent or gruesome incidents. In *Crime and Punishment* (1866), for instance, Raskolnikov goes out on a hot evening and kills an old pawnbroker with an axe, finding it necessary also to chop down her sister, who happens upon the scene. Soon after, the alcoholic Marmeladov is run down and killed by a coach. His widow goes insane and dies in agony. The villain of the piece, Svidrigaylov, a sexual predator not above child-molesting, recalls one of his crimes in a nightmare, and then goes out and shoots himself. Raskolnikov ends up with penal servitude in Siberia.

The saintly hero of *The Idiot* (1868), Myshkin, an epileptic, is saved from being murdered by having one of his fits. Rogozhin, the personification of violence and his would-be killer, eventually murders the leading lady; he too ends up in Siberia. In a weird scene Myshkin and Rogozhin spend the night together over the corpse of the woman they had both loved. Myshkin ends the novel with an apparently irremediable collapse into idiocy. Other characters include a general who suffers a stroke, and a tedious would-be suicide, who sees himself as a condemned man, but never quite succeeds in killing himself.

Devils (1872) is crammed with corpses. This time, Kirillov, another theorist who talks about nothing but suicide, does succeed in killing himself, but his demise is hardly noticeable against a background of misfortune, violence and murder that sees off Lebyatkin and his sister, Lisa, Fedka, Shatov (who is shot and sunk with stones in a pond), his wife and her baby, and yet another suicide – that of Stavrogin. The manner of his dispatch is significant: he hangs himself in just the same way as the eleven-year-old Matryosha hanged herself after being molested by him.

The last novel, *The Karamazov Brothers* (1880), adds to the toll. The father of the family, Fyodor Karamazov, is a man of brutal debauchery, whose excesses drove two wives, Adelaida and Sofya, to their early graves. He is assumed to be the rapist who molested the village idiot girl, Stinking Liza; she dies in childbirth, leaving a son, Smerdyakov, who turns out to be another epileptic with a tendency towards seizure at critical moments. Fyodor is murdered, by Smerdaykov as it turns out, and the latter kills himself by hanging. At the end of the novel, Dmitri, one of the brothers, is wrongly found guilty of his father's murder, and sentenced to hard labour in Siberia.

This scanty survey reveals more than twenty deaths and several recurrent themes which have to do with violence and illness (there will be others that we have overlooked). None of this is surprising, for two closely connected reasons. First, this author had a particular interest in the outer limits of attitude and behaviour. (His second wife said he was 'prone in everything to rush to extremes.) A brief comparison with Charles Dickens will bring out this point. Dickens shows us young people in great travail, exploited, threatened and in danger. His one recurrent theme is that of the wrongs inflicted on children, and his criticism of contemporary life, overt and implied, brought about significant changes for the better. But when you review these children and their destinies, what is remarkable is how well they survive their ordeals. Dickens was a believer in happy outcomes. Nicholas Nickleby marries Madeleine; Oliver Twist is adopted and educated by Mr Brownlow; in *The Old Curiosity Shop* Kit marries Barbara and tells the story of Little Nell to his adoring children. David Copperfield marries his Agnes; Pip ends up with Estella (*Great Expectations*). All of these happy characters have passed through dreadful misadventures, but they have triumphed, and we need not worry about them from now on – their place in middle-class society is secure, and their happiness is guaranteed.

No one would say that this cannot happen. The human spirit is remarkable in its resilience. People can undergo terrible deprivation and suffering, and still survive with their spirit and personality intact. But Dostoevsky's reaction is a simple one: when this happens it is not very interesting. What seizes his imagination is the propensity for excess and brutality that survives and thrives in not a few people, who may or may not have suffered deprivations in childhood similar to those endured by Dickens's young heroes. What makes a murderer? Who can explain an alcoholic? Where does a child-molester come from? How can we best understand a suicidal maniac? These are issues that are worth lingering over. And above them rises one particular question: why did this author become so fascinated with such extremities of human behaviour? The answer is that he experienced them personally, and with an intensity that few people could dream of in their most lurid nightmares.

Extremities of Personal Experience

Nothing in Dostoevsky's work is stranger than the farrago of misfortunes that overtook him in real life. In a chapter entitled 'The Novel of His Life' René Fueloep-Miller puts this point well:

> Although his works deal profoundly with serious questions, their wild and arbitrary occurrences, their often improbable tragic coincidences, their stark contrasts and melodramatic exaggerations, sometimes give them the tone of thrillers or detective stories. But these melodramatic elements were part and parcel of the tragedy of his own life, which reads almost as if Dostoevsky had invented it himself.

He was born in Moscow (11 November 1821) into the family of a physician, but since they lived in a hospital for poor people some of his earliest impressions were of poverty, pain and disease. His father was a cruel man, not unlike the brutish Fyodor Karamazov, who bullied his children, scaring them into submission, and had his serfs flogged for his amusement. Unsurprisingly, one day these serfs rose against him in a gang, and murdered him. The novelist remained tight-lipped about this incident, but it must have inflicted a terrible impact on his young mind.

After an education in engineering, in Moscow and St Petersburg, he cut his traces and went off to live like a typically impoverished would-be writer, starving in a garret. But his first work hit the target in 1846. *Poor Folk,* a short novel in letters, was instantly (and rather generously) accepted by the important critics of the day as a work of genius, and he was already described as 'the new Gogol'. Several more works were planned, and one or two had been written, when disaster struck him down. He had joined a slightly subversive group known as the Petrashevsky Circle, most of whose activities were limited to hot-air discussion, though some members were of a more revolutionary cast of mind, and there was talk of a printing press and a commitment to political activity. The Russian authorities took them seriously, and because of that an entire decade of Dostoyevsky's life (the best one, from thirty to forty) was lost to him. The circle was infiltrated by the secret police, he was arrested, flung into solitary confinement for eight months, given a show trial and sentenced to death for anti-government conspiracy. A grisly charade was arranged whereby the condemned prisoners were lined up in ranks to be shot. The first three were tied to posts, hooded and given the last rites. Only then did the Prison Governor reveal what had been decided days before. This was a mock execution: instead of being shot they were being sent to Siberia for various terms, and this would be followed by a period of enforced exile in the same region. The story of Dostoevsky's incarceration in a Siberian camp is the subject of the first work in this volume, *Notes from a Dead House* (published in 1860). He was imprisoned in Omsk from 1850 to 1854, then exiled as a soldier until 1859.

Many other difficult experiences lay ahead. While in prison Dostoevsky began to display the symptoms of an illness that would turn out to be epilepsy. Uncertain as to its diagnosis, he refrained from telling his wife-to-be before their wedding in 1857, and managed to fall into an epileptic seizure on his wedding night. (This ghastly experience was repeated ten years later on the occasion of his second marriage, when he had two attacks and lay in great discomfort for several hours.) His wife, a widow, was herself sickly, suffering from both tuberculosis and general hypochondria; she was dead within seven years.

Back in Russia, Dostoevsky had picked up his literary career, setting up two literary journals with his brother, Mikhail: one was suppressed, and the other failed. To the stress of editorship was added another huge burden when Mikhail died and Fyodor voluntarily assumed all his considerable debts. Unable to pay them off, he fled abroad, living for five years in Germany and Switzerland. Even here there was little respite from his troubles. He now became afflicted with a serious psychological condition; that is not too grand a name for the gambling mania that took over his spirit. He lost all his remaining money and was impelled to borrow on a large scale. (In this respect he was following in the footsteps of his great literary contemporary, Leo Tolstoy, who lost thousands in the same way and in some of the same places). These misadventures form the basis of the second story in this volume, *The Gambler* (1866). In order to write this work quickly, because money was urgently needed, he took on a stenographer, Anna Snitkina, who, although twenty-five years younger than he, soon became his second wife. She bore him two daughters and two sons, but, more than that, she transformed his life by imposing an orderly existence and some domestic comfort on his previous chaotic way of living. This made it possible for him to continue the serious writing he had just undertaken, and to do so on an extensive scale. When they married in February 1867 *Crime and Punishment* was behind him, but he would go on to produce three more massive, profound masterpieces and a good number of other works – an amazing achievement when we consider that he had less than fourteen years to live. Anna can claim a lot of credit for making this possible, and for bringing her talented husband a degree of day-to-day happiness the like of which he had never known before. Until she took him over, Dostoevsky's life had been overshadowed by every form of misery stemming from direct personal experience of poverty, cruelty, violence, brutality, imprisonment, exile, stress, and illness, both mental and physical. He died in his sixtieth year, having transcribed all this suffering into his books. The two works presented in this volume are deeply autobiographical, and show the writer at important turning-points in this disturbed life.

Prison Literature

No nation is stronger than the Russians on literature about prisons and prison-life. An early contributor to this genre was Archpriest Avvakum, in the seventeenth century. His dates, 1620–82, almost exactly mirror those of Dostoevsky two centuries later, and his career was even more traumatic and tragic. His emergence into manhood coincided with a terrible and tragic split in the Russian Church, with two factions taking up opposite stances on questions of accuracy in the Church's texts, ritual and calendar. Avvakum became the leader of the Old Believers, who challenged the reforms of Archbishop Nikon. To us, nowadays, these may seem trivial (the proposed use of a triple hallelujah and the use of three fingers, rather than two, when making the sign of the cross), but Avvakum resisted them literally to the death, suffering exile, imprisonment and torture until he was burnt at the stake. He left behind numerous written works, including a range of exhortatory epistles and, most importantly, *Life* (1672–73), Russia's first printed autobiography, in which he recounts the deprivations and tortures of exile and imprisonment. One tiny detail may be worth lingering over. The author's sense of close realism and endearing humour despite his travail allowed him to mention a little dog that came to him in prison and licked his wounds. One astute critic has traced this back to a similar incident concerning Lazarus in the New Testament – not the celebrated Lazarus in John's Gospel but the poor man at the rich man's gate (Luke 16.19). But we can also take him forward in time; he will put in further guest appearances in Russia's prison literature. In Dostoevsky's *Dead House*, for instance, he has expanded into three dogs, Sharik, Kultyapka and Belka, whom the writer treats with great compassion, by contrast to his fellow-inmates who would kill any dog for its fur.

This work is constantly referred to as the next significant prison book in Russian literature, but it was soon to be followed by a steady flow that became a veritable torrent, especially in the twentieth century. It comes as no surprise to learn that an enterprising college in upstate New York now puts on an entire course under the title: *Isolate and Punish: Exile, Prison and Hard Labour in Russian Literature*. Set texts number well over twenty, covering the subject from every conceivable angle, and there are others, who did not make it on to the course. At the very end of the nineteenth century, for instance, no less a writer than Leo Tolstoy devoted his last great novel, *Resurrection* (1899), to a savage denunciation of the Russian prison system. (It is exactly contemporary with Oscar Wilde's moving poem on a similar subject, *The Ballad of Reading Gaol* (1898).)

All the Russian writers who tackled this subject, from Avvakum to Solzhenitsyn, shared a common purpose. They wrote not to bemoan their own misfortune, but to expose the injustice, cruelty and uselessness of the system of punishment and correction into which they had been plunged, in the hope that such things could never happen again, that the victims of such oppression would become fewer and fewer until they died out as a species of citizen. Alas, this must count as the slowest-moving campaign ever mounted in defence of human liberty and justice. It did succeed eventually, but it took an awful long time to do so.

As the years went by, things got worse, not better, and the numbers of the oppressed grew exponentially. What had begun with dozens of prisoners in the seventeenth century grew into hundreds by Dostoevsky's time, and thousands by the end of that century. Surely, with so much publicity from gifted writers – Anton Chekhov's most powerful work by far is not one of his plays or stories but his deeply moving sociological study of the maltreatment, torture and killing of Russian prisoners in *Sakhalin Island* (1895) – surely with all of this to go at, the Russian public would simply not stand for any continuation of such barbarity!

But history gave them no choice in the matter. In the twentieth century tens of thousands became tens of millions. The single island depicted by Chekhov proliferated during the first forty years of the Soviet Union into a system of corrective institutions so numerous and so widely-scattered across the vast Russian time-zones that the only way to define it was by thinking of it as a massive grouping of islands large and small, a veritable archipelago. This was the metaphor imposed upon it by Solzhenitsyn. The infamous word 'GULAG' is an acronym standing for Russian words that mean 'Chief Administration of Corrective Labour Camps', hence the *Gulag Archipelago*. This monstrous thing was one of the greatest crimes in human history, with an extent and proportions too vast for us to comprehend. By the time its existence was acknowledged at the 20th Congress of the Soviet Communist Party in 1956 and its dismantling was undertaken, an estimated *twenty-four million souls* had to be accounted for. Eighteen million were released; the six million who had died were 'posthumously rehabilitated'.

Fortunately for the cause of truth, the atrocities of the Gulag have been well documented. Many memoirs and other studies have been published describing the entire system both at large and in close detail. Foremost among them are the celebrated recollections of Alexander Solzhenitsyn, who has set them down at length in several large volumes. His most eloquent statement came, however, in his first published work, the short novel *One Day in the Life of Ivan Denisovich* (1962), which catapulted him to fame partly by its intrinsic quality as a narrative but also because it was one of the first stories to deal with a hitherto forbidden subject – life in the camps. This microcosmic tale, the story of single day in an eight-year sentence, gives a detailed account of personal experience hour by hour while also striving towards epic proportions in the range of characters presented, the historical importance of record laid down and the universality of human experience implied through the hero's memories, encounters and relationships.

But the last word on Russia's prison literature surely belongs to Georgi Vladimov and his *Faithful Ruslan* (1975), a moving allegorical denunciation of Soviet society and the Stalinist regime of terror. Its hero is a hard-working Gulag guard dog (neatly defined by one critic as *canis sovieticus*), intelligent and efficient, committed to the system, but with no understanding of what work he is doing. When his camp closes he is left to fend for himself (lucky not to have been shot by his own guard, who had had no compunction in shooting down their human charges), while living on memories of his past activities, but there is no role for him in the new world. He dies in agony, incomprehension and disillusionment.

> He had nowhere to go back to. His humble, imperfect love for man had died completely . . . he was unfitted for any other form of existence . . . He had learned enough in his waking life about the world of humans, and it stank of cruelty and treachery.

As the numbers of inmates suffering in Russian prison camps have been many times multiplied, the little dogs of St Luke, Avvakum and Dostoevsky have been magnified into a single eponymous canine hero, who brings this sorry scheme of things to its end.

This is the extensive and highly significant literary context into which Dostoevsky's *Notes from a Dead House* must be set. In this work he played his modest part in a process that would one day rid Russia of its most horrible institution, though he would have been shocked to think how long it would take for this to come about, and how many men would suffer worse than he had before it did.

Life in the Dead House

Dostoyevsky arrived at the Dead House on 23 January 1850. He had travelled there by sledge, which is not as easy as it sounds – they drove for ten hours a day, with only a few brief stops, and in freezing conditions (down to -40°), and his legs were fettered with chains that weighed ten pounds. He described the experience as 'almost unendurable', though he did admit to feeling restored to good physical health by the arduous journey.

But it wasn't the journey that mattered. The prison itself was hellish. There was a drunken and sadistic major to be avoided at all costs because of his random rages and vicious punishments for nothing at all. Nicknamed 'eight-eyes', he was hated by all; his aim was 'to increase the bitterness of already embittered men'. But the worst thing to be endured was not the prison-staff, it was the company of Dostoevsky's fellow-prisoners. They seemed like an utterly vile company (before he got to know them) who loathed each other and all humanity, but reserved a special hatred for him because he came from a higher class in society. Dostoevsky felt like a man surrounded by a hundred and fifty dangerous enemies. Here is a description of them sent at a later date to his brother, Mikhail.

> They are rough, angry, embittered men. Their hatred for the nobility is boundless: they regard all of us who belong to it with hostility and enmity. They would have devoured us if only they could. Judge then for yourself in what danger we stood, having to cohabit with these people for some years, eat with them, sleep by them, and with no possibility of complaining of the affronts which were constantly put upon us.

And the living conditions were straight out of Dante's *Inferno*.

> We all lived together in one barrack-room. Imagine an old, crazy wooden building that should long ago have been broken up as useless. In the summer it is unbearably hot, in the winter unbearably cold. All the boards are rotten. On the ground filth lies an inch thick: every instant one is in danger of slipping and coming down. The small windows are so frozen over that even by day one can hardly read. The ice on the panes is three inches thick . . . In the ante-room a great wooden trough for the calls

> of nature is placed: this makes one almost unable to breathe. All the prisoners stink like pigs . . . Fleas, lice and other vermin by the bushel . . .

The hard labour was indeed hard, and not unlike that performed a century later by Ivan Denisovich, humping bricks and preparing mixes for building out of doors in very low temperatures, or turning a huge lathe in the workshop. The food was impossible – bits of stale bread along with cabbage soup swimming with odd bits of sausage instead of the meat that was legally prescribed. They lived in constant fear of attracting a cruel and underserved punishment – the scars of which were visible on many of the men's backs when they crammed into the disgusting bathhouse from time to time. Most prison literature, including this work, contains descriptions of punishment floggings, which were widespread and barbarically cruel, sometimes with the strokes numbered in thousands, not uncommonly ending in the death of the victim. And this occurred in a country that claimed to have abandoned the death penalty. Dostoevsky speaks eloquently about the mental torment suffered by a man about to undergo this form of torture and the unbearable agony that followed it long afterwards.

No aspects of prison life are neglected in this account. It is all there: innumerable portraits of the inmates, their daily routines, occupations, quarrels and even mild amusements, their strengths and illnesses, the heavy drag of their clanking shackles and the tricky business of (rarely) getting undressed with them in the way, the unpredictable brutality and generosity of the guards. There was, of course, virtually nothing to read. And no possibility of ever being alone. And this went on for four interminable years. No wonder Dostoevsky described this life to another brother as being nailed down in his coffin and buried alive.

And yet there is something unusual about Dostoevsky's account of his imprisonment. First, although these are obviously personal recollections from start to finish, they are presented in pseudo-fictional form. This work calls itself a novel, and it has a narrator by the name of Aleksandr Goryanchikov. The course of the narrative is not what you might excpect. Instead of erupting with rage and bile against the injustice of the Russian prison system – the kind of rage that keeps boiling over in, for example, Tolstoy's *Resurrection* – this memoir is remarkably controlled, detached and restrained. One critic, E. H. Carr, calls it 'the least Dostoevskian of all Dostoevsky's work', and another, S. Mackiewicz, goes further.

> *The House of the Dead* [sic] is a most paradoxical book. It contains a description of life in exile in Tsarist Russia, and in nineteenth-century Western Europe the mere mention of the latter words would suffice to make people's eyes brim over with compassion. Yet this is Dostoevsky's most cheerful, mild and peaceful work. One of its episodes was even published in a Christmas edition for children, namely the description of the convicts collectively choosing and buying a new horse to carry water to the prison [Part 2, Chapter 6]. Thus Dostoevsky even succeeded in bringing penal exile and its shackles into the nursery, and putting them down on the floor alongside the innocent toys of children.

Even allowing for a degree of whimsical exaggeration, there is much truth in this. The tone of *Notes from a Dead House* is distinctly unusual. How can it be that a writer as impassioned as Fyodor Dostoevsky, whose works generally seethe with impatient ideas and a restless urgency to understand and improve, discovered an amazing degree of self-control at a point in his life when he was most viciously laid low by adversity that threatened to crush his body and ruin his mind? There is no doubt that his story gains a good deal through its self-restraint, however, and this quality can be explained in several ways.

First, there is a strong hint that, without denying the inhuman cruelty of prison life, we must acknowledge within it a small degree of compensatory relaxation. The men were allowed to circulate fairly freely, and they had enough time to make small objects or perform services to earn a little money, which in turn made life a fraction more comfortable. One can easily imagine prisons in which the following prison practices described by Dostoevsky to Mikhail would not have been tolerated.

> From all this you can see that one couldn't live there without money; if I had had none, I should most assuredly have perished; no one could endure such a life. But every convict does some sort of work and sells it, thus earning, every single one of them, a few pence. I often drank tea and bought myself a piece of meat; it was

my salvation. It was quite impossible to do without smoking, for otherwise the stench would have choked one. All these things were done behind the backs of the officials.

Further hints of relative leniency can be glimpsed in the chapter headings of this work, some of which seem rather surprising in this context: Christmas. Theatricals. The Hospital. Summer Time, Prison Animals. No one would suggest that life in Omsk was a bed of roses, but there was some small amount of toleration on the part of the officials (who were themselves on a desperately unhappy posting out in the wilds of Siberia) that must have helped people to survive from day to day.

It has also been suggested that Dostoevsky's depiction of prison conditions may have been influenced by a desire to avoid offending the censor. But the most important consideration is the question of time-lapse. Although the author, during a spell in hospital, was allowed to jot down, and keep, some notes about prison life, this was all he was able to do while still inside. Even when he resumed some writing while remaining in exile after his gaol-term, Dostoevsky did not take up his prison notes. Years went by, and he started work on *Notes from a Dead House* only in 1859, virtually a decade since the whole story had begun. It is hardly surprising that this has resulted in a feeling of distance between the lived experience and the written record. This does not indicate a loss of immediacy in the writing; he had enough written notes and all too many ineradicable memories for this to be a danger. But the author has clearly stood back from the maelstrom of events and impressions, and taken stock of them with a good measure of objectivity. Where many of us would have exaggerated, he has understated. What could have emerged as an undirected shriek of fury and desperation has been rearranged as an appealing narrative with a generous supply of comments but also much that is left on the level of implication. In this way the possibility of shrill reportage has been transformed into a well-told story. This is what makes it possible for a commentator to claim that *Notes from a Dead House* is 'one of the finest and most moving studies of prison life in any literature' (W. E. Harkins), and another, Victor Terras, to describe it more recently as 'one of the masterpieces in a tradition reaching from Avvakum to Solzhenitsyn and Shalamov'.

Another Kind of Hell

The two stories in this volume, far from being chosen arbitrarily, are closely linked. Despite being thinly disguised as fictional accounts, they are the two most directly autobiographical works that Dostoevsky ever wrote, coming straight out of his personal experience. In any case, he himself linked them in a special way. Writing to the critic N. N. Strakhov in 1863, he said:

> If the *Dead House* attracted the public's attention as a portrayal of convicts whom no one had portrayed *graphically* before, then this story [*The Gambler*] will without fail attract attention as a first-hand and most detailed portrayal of roulette . . . The thing, perhaps, is really not bad at all. Why, the *Dead House* was equally curious. And this is a description of its own kind of hell, of its own kind of prison 'bath-house'; I want to make a picture and will strive to do so.

Both stories are written on a similar theme, that of enslavement. If the *Dead House* shows a man on his long, slow way out of thraldom, *The Gambler* shows his older alter ego on the way in. This latter story was written under unusual circumstances.

Finding himself in dire need of a new novel to satisfy his unscrupulous publisher, F. T. Stellovsky, Dostoevsky panicked when he realised at the beginning of October 1863 that he had only a month to go, and not a word was written. (He had been working hard on *Crime and Punishment*, but that could not be finished off quickly.) A friend of long standing, A. Milyukov, came to his rescue by suggesting that he engage a stenographer to get the job done quickly. The head of a secretarial school recommended his best pupil, and they sat down to work together on October 4th. *The Gambler* was completed in twenty-five days. This was a remarkable achievement; they had invented, written and revised a work of fifty thousand words, at the rate of more than two thousand a day. (The novel was published in 1867, in Stellovsky's edition of Dostoevsky's complete works.) In breaks between sessions the writer (45 years old) had poured out his heart and all the details of his amazing life to this 20-year-old ingénue, who was deeply and massively impressed by him. We have briefly described above the beneficial impact on his life of this remarkable young woman. Just over a week after completing

The Gambler, Dostoevsky proposed to Anna Snitkina, and was accepted. She said she loved him and would continue to do so for the rest of her life, which she did – and well beyond the end of his life. She herself survived for another three decades, dying in 1918.

The story was supposed to work on four different levels. The writer's first and broadest idea was to consider his country's role and reputation in the modern world by depicting Russians abroad, and draw conclusions from their relationships and conversations with foreigners. But at its most sublime level the novel was meant to portray an unhappy product and representative of the distasteful modern world, irredeemably materialistic, godless, amoral and without purpose or direction. There would, of course, have to be narrative interest, which would centre on a love relationship. However, the real problem would arise from the unhealthy psychological state of his hero. 'The chief thing is,' he wrote to Strakhov, 'that all his vital juices, forces, animation and daring have gone into roulette.'

All of this might have worked out if the novel had had time to develop organically over many months. Alas for his plan. The speed of its execution meant that only the last two aims are fully realised. This means that the novel gains in narrative interest and psychological insight what it loses in intended political-economic commentary and spiritual reflection. Hence, it is one of the author's most lively and entertaining stories, but not by any means his most profound work. Konstantin Mochulsky puts this well when he describes the work as 'a brilliant improvisation' with 'all the merits and faults of this genre'.

The story is quite complicated, involving the family of General Zagoryansky, a name curiously similar at its root to that of Goryanchikov, the fictional narrator of *Notes from a Dead House*, and his step-daughter, Polina, a name curiously similar to that of the real-life Apollinariya (Suslova), with whom Dostoevsky had been conducting a tempestuous on-off affair all too recently. Another major figure is the grandmother of the family, Antonina Tarasevicheva, who is rich (and who could therefore save them all from financial ruin), though she will not remain so for much longer. The dynamic Polina is volatile but very attractive, and the protagonist of the story, Alexey Ivanovich (no surname given) falls in love with her as passionately as his author had done with her namesake. (He is not the only one to do so.) The ups-and-downs of this love affair, and others, form what was intended to be the main narrative interest, and the fates of these characters are linked with those of three foreigners, men from Germany, France and England. Readers must sort out these relationships for themselves – they are fast-moving and full of interest – but it will not spoil the story to reveal that Alexey is clearly doomed from the start because his interests are divided between prosecuting his love affair and dealing with his one big obsession – the roulette table. If Alexey had pursued Polina with single-minded devotion he would certainly have won from her full affection rather than flirtatious beguilement, but this is the man whose vital juices have seeped away into the green baize of the casino. Little should be expected from him. Conversely, however, he becomes the most interesting of all the characters in psychological terms. His career as a gambler closely resembles that of the author himself.

Dostoevsky had been unlucky enough to strike it rich in 1863 at a gaming table in Wiesbaden, winning 10,000 francs in a few hours. His easy infatuation with gambling turned instantly into a mania. Worse than that, he knew beyond doubt that he had immediately spotted a method of play that would guarantee winnings. He wrote to his sister-in-law along these lines: 'Please don't think I'm swaggering, out of delight that I did not lose, when I say that I know the secret of how to win and avoid loss. I really do know the secret.' This was simple; all you had to do was keep calm and restrain yourself, not get excited. 'That is the whole thing; and if you stick to that it is simply impossible to lose, and you are bound to win.'

For Fyodor Mikhaylovich (Dostoevsky) read Alexey Ivanovich (unnamed). They are the same person. They suffer from the classic delusions of an inveterate gambler, the illusory certainty that they can control the odds and predict the future, the conviction that he can stop at any time, that any losses so far can be attributed to momentary lapses from the system, and that he only needs a little more time for his luck to turn. Behind it all is a kind of defiant spiritual challenge to destiny itself. By defeating or controlling fate, you can gain mastery over yourself, your life and the entire universe. To the end of his days Dostoevsky never renounced belief in his system; even Anna accepted that it might actually have been profitable, 'but only on condition that it was worked by some cold-blooded Englishman or German, and not by a man like my husband, nervous, easily carried away, and prone in everything to rush to extremes.' In *The Gambler*, we see all of this borne out with some poignancy: the 'hero' is pitted against a German who believes in his country's system of amassing riches by honest toil, and a cool-headed Englishman, Mr Astley, who lends money rather than borrow it, bides his time, and gets the girl.

Biography and fiction were eventually unravelled. Twenty-one-year-old Anna set out to win her gifted husband away from the two forces that threatened to destroy him: the recent memory of a fiery lover with overwhelming sex appeal, and an obsession with the little white ball. Her impossible task was to disentangle the destructive strands of silly passion and gambling mania, and rebraid them into a new man who could live a semblance of normality. Almost miraculously, she succeeded, and his last years were relatively happy.

His fictional alter ego did not fare so well. The last we see of him, he is taking his leave of Mr Astley, who was willing to set him up in a new career with a thousand pounds. But all he hands over is a paltry ten louis d'or because he knows the thousand pounds would go immediately across the table. Sure enough, when even this small sum has disappeared, Alexey Ivanovich is still to be heard parroting the infallibility of his system. He can see where he went wrong, and tomorrow things will be different. 'Tomorrow,' as he says, 'tomorrow it will all be over!'

ANTHONY BRIGGS
Senior Research Fellow, University of Bristol
Professor Emeritus, University of Birmingham

SUGGESTIONS FOR FURTHER READING

Richard Curle, *Characters of Dostoevsky*, London, Heinemann, 1950

Joseph Frank, *The Seeds of Revolt 1821–49*; *The Stir of Liberation 1860–65*; *The Years of Ordeal 1850–59*; Princeton University Press/Robson Books, 1976, 1983 and 1986

R. L. Jackson, *The Art of Dostoevsky: Deliriums and Nocturnes*, Princeton University, 1981

John Jones, *Dostoevsky*, Oxford, 1983

Malcolm V. Jones, *Dostoyevsky: The Novel of Discord*, London, 1976

W. J. Leatherbarrow, *Fedor Dostoevsky*, Boston, Twayne, 1981.

W. J. Leatherbarrow, *Dostoyevsky: A Reference Guide*, Boston, Hall, 1990.

Konstantin Mochulsky, *Dostoevsky: His Life and Work*, Princeton University Press, 1967

Richard Peace, *Dostoyevsky: An Examination of the Major Novels*, Cambridge, 1971

D. S. Savage, 'Dostoevsky: The Idea of The Gambler', in *Dostoevsky: New Perspectives*, ed. R.L.Jackson, Prentice Hall, 1984, pp. 111–25

George Steiner, *Tolstoy or Dostoevsky: An Essay in the Old Criticism*, London, 1960

Victor Terras, *The Young Dostoevsky 1846–49*, Mouton, 1969

Edward Wasiolek, *Dostoevsky: The Major Fiction*, Cambridge, Massachusetts, 1964

NOTES FROM
A DEAD HOUSE

PART I

INTRODUCTION

In the remote parts of Siberia in the midst of steppes, mountains, or impassable forests, there are scattered here and there wretched little wooden towns of one, or at the most two, thousand inhabitants, with two churches, one in the town and one in the cemetery – more like fair-sized villages in the neighbourhood of Moscow than towns. They are usually well provided with police officers, superintendents and minor officials of all sorts. A post in Siberia is usually a snug berth in spite of the cold. The inhabitants are simple folk and not of liberal views; everything goes on according to the old-fashioned, solid, time-honoured traditions. The officials, who may fairly be said to be the aristocracy of Siberia, are either born and bred in Siberia, or men who have come from Russia, usually from Petersburg or Moscow, attracted by the extra pay, the double travelling expenses and alluring hopes for the future. Those of them who are clever at solving the problem of existence almost always remain in Siberia, and eagerly take root there. Later on they bring forth sweet and abundant fruit. But others of more levity and no capacity for solving the problems of existence soon weary of Siberia, and wonder regretfully why they came. They wait with impatience for the end of their three years' term of office, and instantly, on the expiration of it, petition to be transferred and return home abusing Siberia and sneering at it. They are wrong: not only from the official standpoint but from many others, one may find a blissful existence in Siberia. The climate is excellent; there are many extremely wealthy and hospitable merchants; many exceedingly well-to-do natives. Young ladies bloom like roses, and are moral to the last extreme. The wild game-birds fly about the streets and positively thrust themselves upon the sportsman. The amount of champagne consumed is supernatural. The caviare is marvellous. In some parts the crops often yield fifteenfold. In fact it is a blessed land. One need only know how to reap the benefits of it. In Siberia people do know.

In one of these lively, self-satisfied little towns with most charming inhabitants, the memory of whom is imprinted for ever on my heart, I met Alexandr Petrovitch Goryanchikov, a man who had been a gentleman and landowner born in Russia, had afterwards become a convict in the second division for the murder of his wife, and on the expiration of his ten years' sentence was spending the rest of his life humbly and quietly as a settler in the town. Although he was officially described as an inhabitant of a neighbouring village, he did actually live in the town as he was able to earn some sort of a living there by giving lessons to children. In Siberian towns one often meets teachers who have been convicts; they are not looked down upon. They are principally employed in teaching French, of which in the remote parts of Siberia the inhabitants could have no notion but for them, though the language is so indispensable for success in life. The first time I met Alexandr Petrovitch was in the house of Ivan Ivanitch Gvozdikov, an old-fashioned and hospitable official who had gained honours in the service and had five very promising daughters of various ages. Alexandr Petrovitch gave them lessons four times a week for thirty kopecks a lesson. His appearance interested me. He was an exceedingly pale, thin man, small and frail-looking, who could hardly be called old – about five-and-thirty. He was always very neatly dressed in European style. If one talked to him he looked at one very fixedly and intently, listened with strict courtesy to every word one uttered, as though reflecting upon it, as though one had asked him a riddle or were trying to worm out a secret, and in the end answered clearly and briefly, but so weighing every word that it made one feel ill at ease, and one was relieved at last when the conversation dropped. I questioned Ivan Ivanitch about him at the time and learnt that Goryanchikov was a man of irreproachably moral life, and that otherwise Ivan Ivanitch would not have engaged him for his daughters; but that he was dreadfully unsociable and avoided everyone; that he was extremely learned, read a great deal but spoke very little, and in fact it was rather difficult to talk to him; that some people declared that he was positively mad, though they considered that this was not a failing of much importance; that many of the most respected persons in the town were ready to be kind to Alexandr Petrovitch in all sorts of ways; that he might be of use, indeed, writing petitions and so forth. It was supposed that he must have decent relations in Russia, possibly people of good position, but it was known that from the time of his con-viction he had resolutely cut off all communication with them – in fact he was his own enemy. Moreover, everyone in the town knew his story, knew that he had killed his wife in the first year of his marriage, had killed her from jealousy, and had surrendered himself to justice (which had done much to mitigate his sentence). Such crimes are always looked upon as misfortunes, and pitied accordingly. But in spite of all this the queer fellow persisted in holding himself aloof from everyone, and only came among people to give his lessons.

I paid no particular attention to him at first but, I can't tell why, he gradually began to interest me. There was something enigmatic about him. It was utterly impossible to talk freely with him. He always answered my questions, of course, and with an air, indeed, of considering it a sacred obligation to do so; but after his answers I somehow felt it awkward to ask him anything more; and there was a look of suffering and exhaustion on his face afterwards. I remember one fine summer evening, as I was walking home with him from Ivan Ivanitch's, it occurred to me suddenly to invite him in for a minute to smoke a cigarette. I can't describe the look of horror that came into his face; he was utterly disconcerted, began muttering incoherent words, and, suddenly looking angrily at me, rushed away in the opposite direction. I was positively astounded. From that time he looked at me with a sort of alarm whenever we met. But I did not give in: something attracted me to him, and a month later for no particular reason I went to Goryanchikov's myself. No doubt I acted stupidly and tactlessly. He lodged in the very outskirts of the town in the house of an old woman of the working class, who had a daughter in consumption, and this daughter had an illegitimate child, a pretty, merry little girl of ten. Alexandr Petrovitch was sitting beside this child teaching her to read at the moment when I went in. Seeing me, he was as confused as though he had been caught in a crime. He was utterly disconcerted, jumped up from his chair and gazed open-eyed at me. At last we sat down; he watched every look in my face intently, as though he suspected in each one of them some peculiar mysterious significance. I guessed that he was suspicious to the point of insanity. He looked at me with hatred, almost as though asking me: how soon are you going? I began talking about our town and the news of the day; it appeared that he did not know the most ordinary news of the town known to everyone, and what is more, did not care to. Then I began talking of the country and its needs; he heard me in silence and looked me in the face so strangely that at last I felt ashamed of what I was saying. I almost succeeded in tempting him, however, with new books and reviews; they had just come by post, they were in my hands and I offered to lend them, uncut. He glanced eagerly at them but at once changed his mind and declined my offer, alleging that he had no time for reading. At last I took leave of him, and as I went out I felt as though an insufferable weight were taken off my heart. I felt ashamed, and it seemed horribly stupid to pester a man who made it his great aim to shrink as far as possible out of sight of everyone. But the thing was done. I remember that I noticed scarcely a single book in his room, and so it was not true that he read a great deal as people said. Yet passing by his windows once or twice, very late at night, I noticed a light in them. What was he doing, sitting up till daybreak? Could he have been writing? And if so, what?

Owing to circumstances I left the town for three months. Returning home in the winter, I learnt that Alexandr Petrovitch had died in the autumn, in solitude, without even sending for the doctor. He was already almost forgotten in the town. His lodgings were empty. I immediately made the acquaintance of his landlady, intending to find out from her what had occupied her lodger, and whether he had written anything. For twenty kopecks she brought me quite a hamper of manuscript left by her late lodger. The old woman confessed that she had already torn up two exercise books. She was a grim and taciturn old woman from whom it was difficult to extract anything much. She could tell me nothing very new of her lodger. According to her, he scarcely ever did anything, and for months together did not open a book or take up a pen; but he would walk up and down the room all night, brooding, and would sometimes talk to himself; that he was very fond of her little grandchild, Katya, and was very kind to her, especially since he had heard that her name was Katya, and that on St Katherine's day he always had a requiem service sung for someone. He could not endure visitors; he never went out except to give his lessons; he looked askance even at an old woman like her when she went in once a week to tidy up his room a bit, and scarcely ever said a word to her all those three years. I asked Katya whether she remembered her teacher. She looked at me without speaking, turned to the wall and began to cry. So this man was able to make someone, at least, love him.

I carried off his papers and spent a whole day looking through them. Three-fourths of these papers were trifling, insignificant scraps, or exercises written by his pupils. But among them was one rather thick volume of finely written manuscript, unfinished, perhaps thrown aside and forgotten by the writer. It was a disconnected description of the ten years spent by Alexandr Petrovitch in penal servitude. In parts this account broke off and was interspersed by passages from another story, some strange and terrible reminiscences, jotted down irregularly, spasmodically, as though by some overpowering impulse. I read these fragments over several times, and was almost convinced that they were written in a state of insanity. But his reminiscences of penal servitude – 'Scenes from a Dead House' as he calls them himself somewhere in his manuscript – seemed to me not devoid of interest. I was carried away by this absolutely new, till then unknown, world, by the strangeness of some facts, and by some special observations on these lost creatures, and I read some of it with curiosity. I may, of course, be mistaken. To begin with I am picking out two or three chapters as an experiment – the public may judge of them.

CHAPTER ONE

A Dead House

Our prison sttod at the edge of the fortress grounds, close to the fortress wall. One would sometimes, through a chink in the fence, take a peep into God's world to try and see something; but one could see only a strip of the sky and the high earthen wall overgrown with coarse weeds, and on the wall sentries pacing up and down day and night. And then one would think that there are long years before one, and that one will go on coming to peep through the chink in the same way, and will see the same wall, the same sentries and the same little strip of sky, not the sky that stood over the prison, but a free, faraway sky. Imagine a large courtyard, two hundred paces long and a hundred and fifty wide, in the form of an irregular hexagon, all shut in by a paling, that is, a fence of high posts stuck deeply into the earth, touching one another, strengthened by crossway planks and pointed at the top; this was the outer fence of the prison. On one side of the fence there is a strong gate, always closed, always, day and night, guarded by sentries; it is opened on occasion to let us out to work. Outside that gate is the world of light and freedom, where men live like the rest of mankind. But those living on this side of the fence picture that world as some unattainable fairyland. Here there is a world apart, unlike everything else, with laws of its own, its own dress, its own manners and customs, and here is the house of the living dead – life as nowhere else and a people apart. It is this corner apart that I am going to describe.

When you come into the enclosure you see several buildings within it. On both sides of the large inner court run two long log-houses of one storey. These are the prison barracks. Here the convicts live, distributed in divisions. Then at the further end of the enclosure another similar log-house: this is the kitchen, divided in two for the use of two messes. Beyond it another building, where are the cellars, the storehouses and stables, all under one roof. The middle of the courtyard is empty and forms a fairly large level square. Here the convicts fall in, here they are mustered, and their names are called over in the morning, at midday, and in the evening, and on occasion several times a day as well – if the sentries are suspicious and not very clever at counting. A fairly wide space is left all round between the buildings and the fence. Here behind the buildings prisoners of an unsociable and gloomy disposition like to walk in their spare time, to think their own thoughts, hidden from all eyes. Meeting them as they walked there, I used to like looking into their grim, branded faces, and guessing what they were thinking about. There was a prisoner whose favourite occupation in his spare time was counting the posts in the fence. There were fifteen hundred of them, and he had counted and noted them all. Every post stood for a day with him: he marked off one post every day, and in that way could see at a glance from the number of posts uncounted how many days he had left in prison before his term was out. He was genuinely glad every time one side of the hexagon was finished. He had many years yet to wait, but one had time in prison to learn patience. I once saw a convict who had been twenty years in prison and was being released take leave of his fellow prisoners. There were men who remembered his first coming into the prison, when he was young, careless, heedless of his crime and his punishment. He went out a greyheaded, elderly man, with a sad sullen face. He walked in silence through our six barrack-rooms. As he entered each room he prayed to the ikons, and then bowing low to his fellow prisoners he asked them not to remember evil against him. I remember too how a prisoner who had been a well-to-do peasant in Siberia was one evening summoned to the gate. Six months, before, he had heard that his former wife had married again, and he was terribly downcast about it. Now she herself had come to the prison, asked for him, and given him alms. They talked for a couple of minutes, both shed tears and parted for ever. I saw his face when he returned to the barracks . . . Yes, in that place one might learn to be patient.

When it got dark we used all to be taken to the barracks, and to be locked up for the night. I always felt depressed at coming into our barrack-room from outside. It was a long, low-pitched, stuffy room, dimly lighted by tallow candles, full of a heavy stifling smell. I don't understand now how I lived through ten years in it. I had three planks on the wooden platform; that was all I had to myself. On this wooden platform thirty men slept side by side in our room alone. In the winter we were locked up early; it was fully four hours before everyone was asleep. And before that – noise, uproar, laughter, swearing, the clank of chains, smoke and grime, shaven heads, branded faces, ragged clothes, everything defiled and degraded. What cannot man live through! Man is a creature that can get accustomed to anything, and I think that is the best definition of him.

There were two hundred and fifty of us in the prison, and the number scarcely varied. Some came, others completed their sentence and went away, others died. And there were some of all sorts. I imagine every province, every region of Russia had some representative there. There were some aliens, and there were some prisoners even from the mountains of Caucasus. They were all divided according to the degree of their criminality, and consequently according to the number of years they had to serve. I believe there was no sort of crime that had not sent some prisoner there. The bulk of the prison population were exiled convicts or *sylno-katorzhny* of the civilian division (the *silno-katorzhny*, or heavily punished convicts, as the prisoners naïvely mispronounced it).

These were criminals entirely deprived of all rights of property, fragments cut off from society, with branded faces to bear witness for ever that they were outcasts. They were sentenced to hard labour for terms varying from eight to twelve years, and afterwards they were sent to live as settlers in some Siberian village. There were prisoners of the military division, too, who were not deprived of rights, as is usual in Russian disciplinary battalions. They were sentenced for brief terms; at the expiration of their sentence they were sent back whence they had come, to serve in the Siberian line regiments. Many of them returned almost at once to the prison for some second serious offence, this time not for a short term, but for twenty years: this division was called the 'lifers'. But even these 'lifers' were not deprived of all rights. Finally there was one more, fairly numerous, special division of the most terrible criminals, principally soldiers. It was called 'the special section'. Criminals were sent to it from all parts of Russia. They considered themselves in for life, and did not know the length of their sentence. According to law they had to perform double or treble tasks. They were kept in the prison until some works involving very severe hard labour were opened in Siberia. 'You are in for a term, but we go onwards into servitude,' they used to say to other prisoners. I have heard that this class has since been abolished. The civilian division, too, has been removed from our prison also, and a single disciplinary battalion of convicts has been formed. Of course, the officials in control of the prison were all changed at the same time. So I am describing the past, things long bygone.

It was long ago; it all seems like a dream to me now. I remember how I entered the prison. It was in the evening, in January. It was already dark, the men were returning from their work, and they were getting ready for the roll-call. A non-commissioned officer with moustaches at last opened for me the door of this strange house in which I was to spend so many years, and to endure sensations of which I could never have formed the faintest idea if I had not experienced them. I could never have imagined, for instance, how terrible and agonising it would be never once for a single minute to be alone for the ten years of my imprisonment. At work to be always with a guard, at home with two hundred fellow prisoners; not once, not once alone! Yet this was not the worst I had to get used to!

There were here men who were murderers by mischance and men who were murderers by trade, brigands and brigand chiefs. There were simple thieves, and tramps who were pickpockets or burglars.

There were people about whom it was difficult to guess why they had come. Yet each had his own story, confused and oppressive as the heaviness that follows a day's drinking. As a rule they spoke little of their past, they did not like talking about it and evidently tried not to think of bygone days. I knew some among them, even murderers, so gay, so heedless of everything that one might bet with certainty that their consciences never reproached them. But there were gloomy faces, too, men who were almost always silent. As a rule it was rare for anyone to talk of his life, and curiosity was not the fashion; it was somehow not the custom and not correct. Only on rare occasions, from want of something better to do, some prisoner would grow talkative, and another would listen coldly and gloomily. No one could astonish anyone here. 'We are men who can read,' they would often say with strange satisfaction. I remember how a robber began once when he was drunk (it was sometimes possible to get drunk in prison) telling how he had murdered a boy of five, how he had enticed him at first with a toy, led him away to an empty shed, and there had murdered him. The whole roomful of men, who had till then been laughing at his jokes, cried out like one man, and the brigand was forced to be silent; it was not from indignation they cried out, but simply because there is no need to talk *about that*, because talking *about that* is not the correct thing. I may mention in parenthesis that they were 'men who could read', and not in the slang, but in the literal sense. Probably more than half of them actually could read and write. In what other place in which Russian peasants are gathered together in numbers can you find two hundred and fifty men, half of whom can read and write? I have heard since that someone deduces from such facts that education is detrimental to the people. That is a mistake; there are quite other causes at work here, though it must be admitted that education develops self-reliance in the people. But this is far from being a defect.

The divisions were distinguished from one another by their dress: some had half their jackets brown and half grey, and the same with their trousers – one leg dark brown and one grey. One day when we were at work a girl who was selling rolls looked at me intently for some time and then suddenly burst out laughing. 'Ugh, how horrid,' she cried, 'they had not enough grey cloth and they had not enough black!' There were others whose jackets were all grey, and only the sleeves were blackish-brown. Our heads were shaved in different ways too: some had half the head shaved lengthways and others transversely.

At the first glance one could discover one conspicuous trait, common to all this strange family; even the most prominent and original personalities, who unconsciously dominated the others, tried to adopt the common tone of the prison. Speaking generally, I may say that, with the exception of a few indefatigably cheerful fellows who were consequently regarded with contempt by everyone, they were all sullen, envious, dreadfully vain, boastful people, prone to take offence and great sticklers for good form. Not to be surprised at anything was regarded as the greatest merit. They were all mad on keeping up to their standard of good form. But often the most aggressive conceit was followed in a flash by the most cringing feebleness. There were some genuinely strong characters; they were simple and unaffected. But strange to say, among these really strong people there were some who were vain to the most exaggerated degree, to a morbid point. As a rule vanity and regard for appearances were most conspicuous. The majority of them were corrupt and horribly depraved. Slander and backbiting went on incessantly; it was hell, outer darkness. But no one dared to rebel against the self-imposed rules and the accepted customs of the prison; all submitted to them. There were exceptional characters who found it hard and difficult to submit, but still they did submit. Some who came to the prison were men who had lost their heads, had become too reckless when at liberty, so that at last they committed their crimes as it were irresponsibly, as it were without an object, as it were in delirium, in intoxication, often from vanity excited to the highest pitch. But they were quickly suppressed, though some had been the terror of whole villages and towns before they came to prison. Looking about him, the newcomer soon realised that he had come to the wrong place, that there was no one he could impress here, and he gradually submitted and fell in with the general tone. This general tone was apparent externally in a certain peculiar personal dignity of which almost every inmate of the prison was acutely conscious. It was as though the status of a convict, of a condemned prisoner, was a sort of rank, and an honourable one too. There was no sign of shame or repentance! Yet there was an external, as it were official, resignation, a sort of philosophic calm. 'We are a lost lot,' they used to say; 'since we didn't know how to get on in freedom now we must walk the Green Street,* and count the ranks.' 'Since we disobeyed our fathers and mothers, now we must obey the drum tap.' 'We wouldn't embroider with gold,

* The torture of *palki*, or the sticks, described on pages 194–198, is meant. It was a favourite form of punishment under Nicholas I, who was nicknamed Nicholas Palk, or the 'stick'. Why it was called the 'Green Street' I have not been able to discover. – *Translator's note.*

so now we break stones on the road.' Such things were often said by way of moral reflections and proverbial sayings, but never seriously. They were all words. I doubt whether one of the convicts ever inwardly admitted his lawlessness. If anyone, not a prisoner, were to try reproaching the criminal for his crime, upbraiding him (though it is not the Russian way to reproach a criminal), an endless stream of oaths would follow. And what masters of abuse they were! They swore elaborately, artistically. Abuse was carried to a science with them; they tried to score not so much by insulting words as by insulting meaning, spirit, ideas – and that is subtler and more malignant. This science was developed to a higher point by their incessant quarrels. All these people were kept at work by force, consequently they were idle, consequently they were demoralised; if they had not been depraved beforehand, they became so in prison. They had all been brought together here apart from their own will; they were all strangers to one another.

'The devil must have worn out three pairs of shoes before he brought us all here,' they used to say of themselves, and so backbiting, intrigues, womanish slander, envy, quarrelling, hatred were always conspicuous in this hellish life. No old women could be such old women as some of these cut-throats. I repeat, there were strong characters even among them, men who had been accustomed all their lives to go ahead and to dominate, hardy and fearless. These men were instinctively respected; yet though they for their part were often very jealous over their prestige, as a rule they tried not to oppress the others, did not pick quarrels over trifles, behaved with exceptional dignity, were reasonable and almost always obeyed the authorities – not from any principle of obedience, nor from a sense of duty, but as though it were a sort of contract with the authorities for the mutual advantage of both. On the other hand they were treated with consideration.

I remember how one of these convicts, a fearless and determined man, well known to the authorities for his brutal propensities, was once summoned to be punished for some offence. It was a summer day and not in working hours. The officer who was immediately responsible for the management of the prison came himself to the guard-house, which was close to our gate, to be present at the punishment. This major was, so to speak, a fateful being for the prisoners; he had reduced them to trembling before him. He was insanely severe, 'flew at people', as the convicts said. What they feared most in him was his penetrating lynx-like eyes, from which nothing could be concealed. He seemed to see without looking. As soon as he came into the prison he knew what was being done at the furthest end of it. The prisoners used to call him 'eight eyes'. His system was a mistaken one. By his ferocious, spiteful actions he only exasperated people who were already exasperated, and if he had not been under the governor of the prison, a generous and sensible man who sometimes moderated his savage outbursts, his rule might have led to great trouble. I can't understand how it was he did not come to a bad end; he retired and is alive and well, though he was brought to trial for his misdeeds.

The convict turned pale when his name was called. As a rule he lay down to be flogged resolutely and without a word, endured his punishment in silence and got up again quite lively, looking calmly and philosophically at the mishap that had befallen him. He was always, however, handled with caution. But this time he thought himself for some reason in the right. He turned pale and managed, unseen by the guard, to slip into his sleeve a sharp English knife. Knives and all sharp instruments were sternly forbidden in prison. Searches were made frequently and unexpectedly, and they were no joking matter for the penalties were severe; but as it is difficult to find what a thief particularly means to hide, and as knives and instruments were always indispensable in the prison, in spite of searches they were always there. And if they were taken away, new ones were immediately obtained. All the convicts rushed to the fence and looked through the crevices with beating hearts. They all knew that this time Petrov did not mean to lie down to be flogged, and that it would be the end of the major. But at the critical moment our major got into his droshki and drove away, leaving the execution of the punishment to another officer. 'God himself delivered him!' the convicts said afterwards. As for Petrov, he bore his punishment quite calmly. His wrath passed off with the departure of the major. The convict is obedient and submissive up to a certain point; but there is a limit which must not be overstepped. By the way, nothing can be more curious than these strange outbreaks of impatience and revolt. Often a man is patient for several years, is resigned, endures most cruel punishment, and suddenly breaks out over some little thing, some trifle, a mere nothing. From a certain point of view he might be called mad, and people do call him so in fact.

I have said already that in the course of several years I never saw one sign of repentance among these people, not a trace of despondent brooding over their crime, and that the majority of them inwardly considered themselves absolutely in the right. This is a fact. No doubt vanity, bad example, brag, false shame are responsible for a great deal of this. On the other side, who can say that he has sounded the depths of these lost hearts, and has read what is hidden from all the world in them? Yet surely it would have been possible during all those years to have noticed, to have detected something, to have caught some glimpse which would have borne witness to some inner anguish and suffering in those hearts. But it was not there, it certainly was not there. No, it seems crime cannot be interpreted from preconceived conventional points of view, and the philosophy of it is a little more difficult than is supposed. Of course, prisons and penal servitude do not reform the criminal; they only punish him and protect society from further attacks on its security. In the criminal, prison and the severest hard labour only develop hatred, lust for forbidden pleasures, and a fearful levity. But I am firmly convinced that the belauded system of solitary confinement attains only false, deceptive, external results. It drains the man's vital sap, enervates his soul, cows and enfeebles it, and then holds up the morally withered mummy, half imbecile, as a model of penitence and reformation. Of course, the criminal who revolts against society hates it, and almost always considers himself in the right and society in the wrong. Moreover, he has already endured punishment at its hands, and for that reason almost considers himself purged and quits with society. There are points of view, in fact, from which one is almost brought to justify the criminal. But in spite of all possible points of view everyone will admit that there are crimes which always and everywhere from the beginning of the world, under all legal systems, have unhesitatingly been considered crimes, and will be considered so as long as man remains human. Only in prison have I heard stories of the most terrible, the most unnatural actions, of the most monstrous murders told with the most spontaneous, childishly merry laughter.

I am particularly unable to forget one parricide. He was of the upper class and in the service, and had been something like a prodigal son. He was thoroughly dissipated in his behaviour, and made debts everywhere. His father, an old man of sixty, tried to influence and restrain him; but the father had a house, a small estate, and, it was suspected, money, and the son killed the father through greed for his inheritance. The crime was only discovered a month later. The murderer himself gave information to the police that his father had disappeared, he knew not where. He spent all that month in the most profligate way. At last in his absence the police found the body. There was running right across the yard a ditch covered with planks for carrying off refuse water. The body was lying in this ditch. It was dressed and tidy, the grey head which had been cut off had been put on the body, and under the head the murderer laid a pillow. He did not confess, was deprived of his rank and rights, and sent to penal servitude for twenty years. All the time I spent with him, he was in the liveliest, merriest spirits. He was an unaccountable, feather-brained fellow, irresponsible in the highest degree, though by no means stupid. I never noticed any special cruelty in him. The convicts despised him – not on account of his crime, which was never mentioned, but for his foolishness, for his not knowing how to behave. In conversation he sometimes referred to his father. Once talking to me about the healthy constitution hereditary in their family, he added: '*My parent*, for instance, never complained of any illness right up to the end.' Such savage insensibility seems impossible. It is phenomenal; it is not a case of simple crime, but of some constitutional defect, some mental and bodily monstrosity not yet understood by science. Of course I did not believe this criminal's story. But people who came from the same town and must have known every detail of his history told me about the whole case. The facts were so clear that it was impossible not to believe in them.

The convicts heard him cry out one night in his sleep, 'Hold him, hold him! Chop off his head, his head, his head!'

Almost all the convicts raved and talked in their sleep. Oaths, thieves' slang, knives, axes were what came most frequently to their tongues in their sleep. 'We are a beaten lot,' they used to say; 'our guts have been knocked out, that's why we shout at night.'

Forced and penal labour was not an occupation, but a compulsory task: the convict completed his task or worked the allotted hours and returned to the prison. The work was looked upon with hatred. If it were not for his own private work to which he was devoted with his whole mind, his whole interest, a man could not live in prison. And, indeed, how else could all that mass of men, who had had experiences, lived keenly and desired to live, who had been forcibly brought together here, forcibly torn away from society and normal existence, be expected to live a normal and regular life here of their own free will? Idleness alone would have developed in the convict here criminal propensities of which he had no idea before. Without labour, without lawful normal property man cannot live; he becomes depraved, and is transformed into a beast. And so, in obedience to a natural craving and a sort of sense of self-preservation, everyone in the prison had his special craft and pursuit. The long summer day was almost filled up with the compulsory work; there was hardly time in the brief night for sleep. But in the winter the convict had by regulation to be locked up in prison as soon as it got dark. What could he do in the long dull hours of the winter evenings? And so in spite of prohibition almost every prison ward was transformed into a huge workshop. Work, occupation, were not formally forbidden; but it was strictly forbidden to have in one's possession in prison any tools, and without these work was impossible. But they worked by stealth, and I fancy that in some cases the authorities shut their eyes to it. Many convicts came to the prison knowing nothing, but they learnt from others, and afterwards went back into the world skilled workmen. There were cobblers there, shoemakers, tailors, cabinet-makers, locksmiths, woodcarvers and gilders. There was one Jew, Isay Bumshtein, a jeweller and pawnbroker. They all worked and earned something. They got orders for work from the town. Money is coined liberty, and so it is ten times dearer to the man who is deprived of freedom. If money is jingling in his pocket, he is half consoled, even though he cannot spend it. But money can always and everywhere be spent, and, moreover, forbidden fruit is sweetest of all. Even vodka could be got in prison. Pipes were strictly forbidden, but everyone smoked them. Money and tobacco saved them from scurvy and other diseases. Work saved them from crime; without work the convicts would have devoured one another like spiders in a glass jar. In spite of this, both work and money were forbidden. From time to time a sudden search was made at night and all forbidden articles were carried off, and however carefully money was hidden, it was sometimes found by the searchers. This was partly why it was not saved but was quickly spent on drink; that was how vodka came to be brought into prison. After every search the guilty, in addition to losing their property, were severely punished. But after every search all they had lost was immediately replaced, new articles were promptly procured, and everything went on as before. The authorities knew this and the convicts did not grumble at the punishments, though such a life was like living on Vesuvius.

Those who did not know a craft carried on some other sort of trade. Some ways of doing so were rather original. Some, for instance, were only occupied in buying and retailing, and they sometimes sold things which it would never occur to anyone outside the walls of the prison to buy or sell, or, indeed, to consider as things at all. But the prisoners were very poor and had great commercial ability. The poorest rag had its price and was turned to account. They were so poor that money had quite a different value in prison. A great and complicated piece of work was paid for in farthings. Some practised moneylending with success. Convicts who had been extravagant or unlucky carried their last possessions to the moneylender and got from him a few copper coins at a fearful rate of interest. If the articles were not redeemed at the time fixed, they were sold without delay or remorse; the moneylending flourished to such an extent that even prison property liable to inspection was accepted as a pledge; for instance, the prison clothes, boots, and so on – things which were essential for every convict at every moment. But such transactions sometimes took a different though not altogether unexpected turn: the pawner after receiving the money would sometimes, without further talk, go straight to the senior sergeant in command, and inform him of the pawning of prison property, and it would be immediately taken back from the pawnbroker without even a report on the subject to the higher authorities. It is a curious fact that sometimes this was not followed by a quarrel: the moneylender returned what was required in sullen silence, and seemed even to expect what had happened. Perhaps he could not help admitting that in the pawner's place he would have done the same. And so even if he sometimes swore afterwards, it would be without malice, simply to appease his conscience.

Generally speaking, they stole from one another dreadfully. Almost everyone had a box of his own, with a lock on it to keep his prison belongings in. This was allowed; but boxes were no security. One may imagine that there were skilful thieves among them. A convict who was sincerely attached to me (this is no exaggeration) stole from me a Bible, the only book which one was allowed to have in the prison; he confessed it to me himself the same day, not from repentance, but feeling sorry for me because I spent such a long time looking for it.

There were convicts who traded in vodka and soon grew rich. Of this trade I will speak more in detail later: it was rather remarkable. There were many convicts who were in prison for smuggling, and so it was scarcely to be wondered at that vodka was brought into the prison in spite of guards and supervision. Smuggling, by the way, is a crime of a peculiar character. Would it be believed, for instance, that gain is only a secondary consideration with some smugglers, and is never in the foreground of their minds? Yet there are cases of this kind. A smuggler works from inclination, from passion. He is on one side an artist. He risks everything, runs terrible dangers; he is cunning, invents dodges, and gets out of scrapes, and sometimes acts with a sort of inspiration. It is a passion as strong as gambling. I knew a convict in the prison, of colossal proportions physically, but so quiet, gentle and meek that it was impossible to imagine how he had got into prison. He was so mild and easy to get on with that all the while he was in prison he never quarrelled with anyone. But he was a smuggler who came from the western frontier, and, of course, he could not resist smuggling vodka into the prison. How often he was punished for doing this, and how he dreaded the lash! And for bringing in the vodka he was paid the merest trifle. No one made money out of it but the dealer. The queer fellow loved art for art's sake. He was as lachrymose as a woman, and how often after being punished he swore and vowed not to smuggle. He manfully controlled himself sometimes for a whole month, but yet in the end he broke down . . . Thanks to men like him, there was no stint of vodka in the prison.

Finally there was another source of income for the convicts, which, though it did not enrich them, was constant and very welcome. This was charity. The higher classes in Russia have no idea how deeply our merchants, tradespeople and peasants concern themselves about 'the unfortunates'. Almsgiving is almost continual, usually in the form of bread, fancy loaves and rolls, far more rarely in money. But for these gifts, in many places prisoners, especially those who are awaiting trial and are much worse treated than convicts, would fare badly. The alms are divided with religious exactitude among the convicts. If there is not enough for all, the loaves are cut up equally, sometimes even into six portions, and every prisoner invariably receives his piece.

I remember the first time I received money alms. It was soon after my arrival in the prison. I was returning from my morning work alone with the guard. There came to meet me a mother and her child, a little girl of ten, pretty as an angel. I had seen them once already, the mother was the widow of a soldier. Her husband, a young soldier, had died in hospital in the convict ward while awaiting his trial, at the time when I, too, was lying ill there. The mother and daughter came to say goodbye to him; both cried terribly. Seeing me the little girl flushed and whispered something to her mother. The latter at once stopped short, found a farthing in her bag and gave it to the child. The latter flew running after me. 'There, poor man, take a farthing, for Christ's sake!' she cried, overtaking me and thrusting the coin into my hand. I took her farthing, and the girl returned to her mother quite satisfied. I treasured that farthing for a long time.

CHAPTER TWO

First Impressions [1]

The first month and all the early days of my prison life rise vividly before my imagination now. My other prison years flit far more dimly through my memory. Some seem to have sunk completely into the background, to have melted together, leaving only one collective impression – oppressive, monotonous, suffocating.

But all I went through during my first days in Siberia is as vivid to me now as though it had happened yesterday. And this is bound to be so.

I remember clearly that from the first step what struck me most in this life was that I found in it nothing striking, nothing exceptional or, rather, nothing unexpected. It seemed as though I had had glimpses of it in my imagination when, on my way to Siberia, I tried to conjecture what lay in store for me. But soon I began to find a mass of the strangest surprises, the most monstrous facts awaiting me at every step. And it was only later, after I had been some time in the prison, that I realised fully the exceptional, the surprising nature of such an existence, and I marvelled at it more and more. I must confess that this wonder did not leave me throughout the long years of my imprisonment; I never could get used to it.

My first impression on entering the prison was most revolting, and yet strange to say it seemed to me that life in prison was much easier than on the journey I had fancied it would be. Though the prisoners wore fetters, they walked freely about the prison, swore, sang songs, did work on their own account, smoked, even drank vodka (though very few of them) and at night some of them played cards. The labour, for instance, seemed to me by no means so hard, so *penal*, and only long afterwards I realised that the hardness, the penal character of the work lay not so much in its being difficult and uninterrupted as in its being *compulsory*, obligatory, enforced. The peasant in freedom works, I dare say, incomparably harder, sometimes even all night, especially in the summer; but he is working for himself, he is working with a rational object, and it makes it much easier for him than for the convict working at forced labour which is completely useless to himself. The idea has occurred to me that if one wanted to crush, to annihilate a man utterly, to inflict on him the most terrible of punishments so that the most ferocious murderer would shudder at it and dread it beforehand, one need only give him work of an absolutely, completely useless and irrational character. Though the hard labour now enforced is uninteresting and wearisome for the prisoner, yet in itself as work it is rational; the convict makes bricks, digs, does plastering, building; there is sense and meaning in such work. The convict worker sometimes even grows keen over it, tries to work more skilfully, faster, better. But if he had to pour water from one vessel into another and back, over and over again, to pound sand, to move a heap of earth from one place to another and back again – I believe the convict would hang himself in a few days or would commit a thousand crimes, preferring rather to die than endure such humiliation, shame and torture. Of course such a punishment would become a torture, a form of vengeance, and would be senseless, as it would achieve no rational object. But as something of such torture, senselessness, humiliation and shame is an inevitable element in all forced labour, penal labour is incomparably more painful than any free labour – just because it is forced.

I entered the prison in winter, however, in December, and had as yet no conception of the summer work, which was five times as hard. In winter compulsory work was generally scarce in our prison. The convicts used to go to the River Irtish to break up old government barges, to work in the workshops, to shovel away snow-drifts from government buildings, to bake and pound alabaster and so on. The winter day was short, the work was soon over and all of us returned early to the prison, where there was scarcely anything for us to do, if one did not happen to have work of one's own. But only a third of the prisoners, perhaps, were occupied in work of their own. The others were simply idle, wandered aimlessly all over the prison, swore at one another, got up intrigues and rows, got drunk if they could scrape up a little money, at night staked their last shirt at cards, and all this from boredom, from idleness, from having nothing to do. Later on I realised that besides the loss of freedom, besides the forced labour, there is another torture in prison life, almost more terrible than any other – that is, *compulsory life in common.* Life in common is to be found of course in other places, but there are men in prison whom not everyone would care to associate with and I am certain that every convict felt this torture, though of course in most cases unconsciously.

The food too seemed to me fairly sufficient. The convicts used to declare that it was not so good in disciplinary battalions in European Russia. That I cannot undertake to pronounce upon: I have not been in them. Moreover, many of the convicts were able to have food of their own. Beef cost a halfpenny a pound, in summer three farthings. But only those who always had money used to buy food for themselves; the majority of the convicts ate only what was provided. But when the convicts praised the prison fare they referred only to the bread and they blessed the fact that it was given us all together and was not served out in rations. The latter system horrified them; had the bread been served out by weight, a third of the people would have been hungry; but served in common there was plenty for everyone. Our bread was particularly nice and was celebrated throughout the town. It was ascribed to the successful construction of the prison oven. But the cabbage soup was very unattractive. It was cooked in a common cauldron, was slightly thickened with grain and, particularly on working days, was thin and watery. I was horrified at the immense number of cockroaches in it. The convicts took absolutely no notice of them.

The first three days I did not go to work; it was the custom with every prisoner on arrival to give him a rest after the journey. But I had to go out next day to have my fetters changed. My fetters were not the right pattern, they were made of rings, 'tinklers', as the convicts called them. They were worn outside the clothes. The regulation prison fetters that did not prevent the prisoner from working were not made of rings, but of four iron rods almost as thick as a finger, joined together by three rings. They had to be put on under the trousers. A strap was fastened to the middle ring and this strap was fastened to the prisoner's belt which he wore next to his shirt.

I remember my first morning in the prison. In the guardhouse at the prison gates the drum beat for daybreak and ten minutes later the sergeant on duty began unlocking the prison wards. We began to wake up. By the dim light of a tallow candle the prisoners got up from their sleeping platform, shivering with cold. Most of them were silent and sleepily sullen. They yawned, stretched and wrinkled up their branded foreheads. Some were crossing themselves, others had already begun to quarrel. The stuffiness was awful. The fresh winter air rushed in at the door as soon as it was opened and floated in clouds of steam through the barracks. The prisoners crowded round the buckets of water; in turns they took the dipper, filled their mouths with water and washed their hands and faces from their mouths. Water was brought in overnight by the *parashnik* or slop-pail man. In every room there was by regulation a prisoner elected by the others to do the work of the room. He was called the *parashnik* and did not go out to work. His duty was to keep the room clean, to wash and scrub the platform beds and the floor, to bring in and remove the night pail and to bring in two buckets of fresh water – in the morning for washing and in the daytime for drinking. They began quarrelling at once over the dipper; there was only one for all of us.

'Where are you shoving, you roach-head!' grumbled a tall surly convict, lean and swarthy with strange protuberances on his shaven head, as he pushed another, a stout, squat fellow with a merry, ruddy face. 'Stay there!'

'What are you shouting for? Folks pay for their stay, you know! You get along yourself! There he stands like a monument. There isn't any *fortikultiapnost* about him, brothers!'

This invented word produced a certain sensation. Many of them laughed. That was all the cheery fat man wanted. He evidently played the part of a gratuitous jester in the room. The tall convict looked at him with the deepest contempt.

'You great sow!' he said as though to himself. 'He's grown fat on the prison bread. Glad he'll give us a litter of twelve sucking pigs by Christmas.'

The fat man got angry at last.

'But what sort of queer bird are you?' he cried, suddenly turning crimson.

'Just so, a bird.'

'What sort?'

'That sort.'

'What sort's that sort?'

'Why, that sort, that's all.'

'But what sort?'

They fixed their eyes on each other. The fat man waited for an answer and clenched his fists as though he meant to fall to fighting at once. I really thought there would be a fight. All this was new to me and I looked on with curiosity. But afterwards I found out that such scenes were extremely harmless; that they were played by way of a farce for the general entertainment and hardly ever ended in fights. It was all a fairly typical specimen of prison manners.

The tall convict stood calm and majestic. He felt that they were looking at him and waiting to see whether he would discredit himself by his answer or not; that he must keep up his reputation and show that he really was a bird and what sort of bird he was. He looked with inexpressible contempt at his opponent, trying to insult him to the utmost by looking down upon him as it were over his shoulder, as though he were examining him like an insect, and slowly and distinctly he brought out: 'Cocky-locky!'

Meaning that that was the bird he was. A loud roar of laughter greeted the convict's readiness.

'You are a rascal not a cocky-locky!' roared the fat man, feeling he had been done at every point and flying into a violent rage.

But as soon as the quarrel became serious the combatants were at once pulled up.

'What are you shouting about!' the whole room roared at them.

'You'd better fight than split your throats!' someone called from a corner.

'Likely they'd fight!' sounded in reply. 'We are a bold, saucy lot; when we are seven against one we are not frightened.'

'They are both fine fellows! One was sent here for a pound of bread, and the other is a plate-licking jade; he guzzled a country woman's junket, that's what he got the knout for!'

'Come, come, come, shut up!' cried the veteran soldier who had to be in the room to keep order and so slept on a special bedstead in the corner.

'Water, lads! Old Petrovitch has waked up. Good morning, old veteran Petrovitch, dear brother!'

'Brother . . . brother indeed! I never drank a rouble with you and I am brother, am I!' grumbled the old soldier, putting his arms into the sleeves of his overcoat.

They were making ready for inspection; it began to get light; a dense, closely packed crowd had gathered in the kitchen. The convicts in their sheepskins and particoloured caps were crowding round the bread which one of the cooks was cutting up for them. The cooks were chosen by the prisoners, two for each kitchen. They kept the knife, one only for each kitchen, to cut up the bread and meat.

In every corner and all about the tables there were convicts with their caps and sheepskins on, their belts fastened, ready to go out to work at once. Before some of them stood wooden cups of kvas. They crumbled the bread into the kvas and sipped that. The noise and uproar were insufferable; but some were talking quietly and sensibly in the corners.

'A good breakfast to old man Antonitch, good morning!' said a young convict sitting down by a frowning and toothless prisoner.

'Well, good morning, if you mean it,' said the other, not raising his eyes and trying to munch the bread with his toothless gums.

'I thought you were dead, Antonitch, I really did.'

'No, you may die first, I'll come later.'

I sat down beside them. Two steady-looking convicts were talking on my right, evidently trying to keep up their dignity with one another.

'They won't steal from me, no fear,' said one. 'There's more chance of my stealing something from them.'

'I am a prickly customer too.'

'Are you though? You are a jail-bird like everyone else; there's no other name for us . . . She'll strip you and not say thank you. That's where my money went, brother. She came herself the other day. Where could I go with her? I began asking to go to Fedka-Hangman's, he's got a house at the end of the town, he bought it from the Jew, Scabby-Solomon, the fellow who hanged himself afterwards.'

'I know. He used to sell vodka here three years ago and was nicknamed Grishka Black Pot-house. I know.'

'No, you don't know. That was another fellow, Black Pothouse.'

'Another! You know a fat lot. I'll bring you ever so many witnesses.'

'You'll bring witnesses! Where do you come from and who am I?'

'Who are you? Why, I used to beat you and I don't boast of it and you ask who are you!'

'You used to beat me! Why, the man's not born who'll beat me, and the man who did is underground.'

'You Bender pest!'

'Siberian plague take you!'

'And I hope a Turkish sabre will have something to say to you!'

A storm of abuse followed.

'Come, come! They are at it again!' people shouted round them. 'They couldn't live in freedom; they may be glad they've bread to eat here . . . '

They quieted them down at once. Swearing, 'wagging your tongue', is allowed. It is to some extent an entertainment for all. But they don't always let it come to a fight, and it is only rarely, in exceptional cases, that enemies fight. Fights are reported to the major; investigations follow, the major himself comes – in short, everyone has to suffer for it, and so fights are not allowed. And indeed the combatants swear at one another rather for entertainment, for the exercise of their linguistic powers. Often they deceive themselves: they begin very hot and exasperated; one fancies they will fall on one another in a minute. Not a bit of it: they go on to a certain point and then separate at once. All this surprised me immensely at first. I have intentionally quoted here a typical specimen of convict conversation. I could not imagine at first how they could abuse one another for pleasure, find in it amusement, pleasant exercise, enjoyment. But one must not forget their vanity. A connoisseur in abuse was respected. He was almost applauded like an actor.

The evening before, I had noticed that they looked askance at me.

I had caught several dark looks already. On the other hand some of the convicts hung about me suspecting I had brought money with me. They began making up to me at once, began showing me how to wear my new fetters, got me – for money of course – a box with a lock on it, for me to put away the prison belongings already served out to me, as well as some underclothes I brought with me into the prison. Next day they stole it from me and sold it for drink. One of them became most devoted to me later on, though he never gave up robbing me at every convenient opportunity. He did this without the slightest embarrassment, almost unconsciously, as though fulfilling a duty, and it was impossible to be angry with him.

Among other things, they told me that I ought to have tea of my own, that it would be a good thing for me to have a teapot too, and meanwhile they got me one on hire, and recommended a cook, saying that for thirty kopecks a month he would cook me anything I liked if I cared to eat apart and buy my own provisions . . . They borrowed money from me of course, and every one of them came to borrow from me three times the first day.

As a rule, convicts who have been gentlemen are looked at with hostility and dislike.

In spite of the fact that they are deprived of all the rights of their rank and are put on exactly the same level as the other prisoners, the convicts never consider them their comrades. This is not the result of conscious prejudice but comes about of itself, quite sincerely and unconsciously. They genuinely looked upon us as gentlemen, though they liked to taunt us with our downfall.

'No, now it's time to pull up! In Moscow, Pyotr drove like a lord, but now Pyotr sits and twists a cord,' and similar pleasantries were frequent.

They looked with enjoyment at our sufferings, which we tried to conceal from them. We used to have a particularly bad time at work because we had not as much strength as they had and could not do our full share in helping them. Nothing is harder than to win people's confidence (especially such people's) and to gain their love.

There were several men belonging to the upper classes in the prison. To begin with there were five or six Poles. I will speak of them separately later on. The convicts particularly disliked the Poles, even more than those who had been Russian gentlemen. The Poles (I am speaking only of the political prisoners) were elaborately, offensively polite and exceedingly uncommunicative with them. They never could conceal from the convicts their aversion for them, and the latter saw it very clearly and paid the Poles back in the same coin.

I spent nearly two years in the prison before I could succeed in gaining the goodwill of some of the convicts. But in the end most of them grew fond of me and recognised me as a 'good' man.

There were four other Russians of the upper class besides me. One was a mean abject little creature, terribly depraved, a spy and informer by vocation. I had heard about him before I came to the prison, and broke off all relations with him after the first few days. Another was the parricide of whom I have spoken already. The third was Akim Akimitch; I have rarely met such a queer fellow as this Akim Akimitch. I have still a vivid recollection of him. He was tall, lean, dullwitted, awfully illiterate, very prosy and as precise as a German. The convicts used to laugh at him, but some of them were positively afraid to have anything to do with him, owing to his fault-finding, his exactingness and his readiness to take offence. He got on to familiar terms with them from the first, he quarrelled and even fought with them. He was phenomenally honest. If he noticed any injustice he always interfered, though it might have nothing to do with him. He was naïve in the extreme; when he quarrelled with the convicts he sometimes reproached them with being thieves and seriously exhorted them not to steal. He had been a lieutenant in the Caucasus. We were friendly from the first day, and he immediately told me about his case. He began as a cadet in an infantry regiment in the Caucasus, plodded on steadily for a long time, was promoted to be an officer at last, and was sent as senior in command to a fortress. One of the allied chieftains burnt his fortress and made a night assault upon it. This was unsuccessful. Akim Akimitch was wily and gave no sign of knowing who had done it. The attack was attributed to the hostile tribes, and a month later Akim Akimitch invited the chieftain to visit him in a friendly way. The latter came, suspecting nothing. Akim Akimitch drew up his company, proved the chieftain's guilt and upbraided him before them all, pointing out to him that it was shameful to burn fortresses. He discoursed to him in great detail on the way allied chiefs should behave in the future, and, in conclusion, shot him and at once sent in a full report of the proceedings to the authorities. For all this he was court-martialled and condemned to death, but the sentence was commuted and he was sent to Siberia to penal servitude in the second division for twelve years. He fully recognised that he had acted irregularly. He told me he knew it even before he shot the chieftain, he knew that an ally ought to be legally tried; but, although he knew this, he seemed unable to see his guilt in its true light.

'Why, upon my word! hadn't he burnt my fortress? Was I to say thank you to him for it?' he said to me in reply to my objections.

But, although the convicts laughed at Akim Akimitch's foolishness, they respected him for his preciseness and practical ability.

There was no handicraft which Akim Akimitch did not understand. He was a cabinet-maker, a cobbler, a shoemaker, a painter, a gilder, a locksmith, and he had learnt all this in the prison. He was self-taught in everything; he would take one look at a thing and do it. He used to make all sorts of little boxes, baskets, lanterns, children's toys, and sold them in the town. In that way he made a little money and he immediately spent it on extra underclothes, on a softer pillow or a folding mattress. He was in the same room as I was, and was very helpful to me during my first days in prison.

When they went out from prison to work the convicts used to be drawn up in two rows before the guard-house; in front of them and behind them the soldiers were drawn up, with loaded muskets. An officer of the Engineers, the foreman and several engineers of the lower rank, who used to superintend our work, came out. The foreman grouped the convicts and sent them to work in parties where they were needed.

I went with the others to the engineers' workshop. It was a low-pitched stone building standing in a large courtyard which was heaped up with all sorts of materials; there was a smithy, a locksmith's shop, a carpenter's, a painter's and so on. Akim Akimitch used to come here and work at painting; he boiled the oil, mixed the colours and stained tables and other furniture to look like walnut.

While I was waiting for my fetters to be changed, I was talking to Akim Akimitch about my first impressions in prison.

'Yes, they are not fond of gentlemen,' he observed, 'especially politicals; they are ready to devour them; no wonder. To begin with, you are a different sort of people, unlike them; besides, they've all been serfs or soldiers. Judge for yourself whether they would be likely to be fond of you. It's a hard life here, I can tell you. And in the Russian disciplinary battalions it's worse still. Some of these fellows come from them and they are never tired of praising our prison, they say it's like coming from hell to paradise. It's not the work that's the trouble. There in the first division they say the authorities are not all military, anyhow they behave very differently from here. There they say the convicts can have little homes of their own. I haven't been there, but that's what they say. They don't have their heads shaved, they don't wear a uniform, though it's a good thing they do wear a uniform and have their heads shaved here; it's more orderly, anyway, and it's pleasanter to the eye. Only they don't like it. And look what a mixed rabble they are! One will be a Kantonist,* another will be a Circassian, a third an Old Believer, a fourth will be an orthodox peasant who has left a wife and dear little children behind in Russia, the fifth will be a Jew, the sixth a gypsy, and the seventh God knows who; and they've all got to live together, they've all got to get on together somehow, eat out of the same bowl, sleep on the same bed. And no sort of freedom. If you want an extra crust you must eat it on the sly; every farthing you've to hide in your boots, and nothing before you but prison and more prison . . . You can't help all sorts of nonsense coming into your head.'

But I knew that already. I particularly wanted to question him about our major. Akim Akimitch made no secret of things and I remember my impression was not altogether agreeable.

But I had to live for two years under his rule. All that Akim Akimitch told me about him turned out to be perfectly true, with the only difference that the impression made by the reality is always stronger than that made by description. The man was terrible, just because being such a man he had almost unlimited power over two hundred souls. In himself he was simply a spiteful and ill-regulated man, nothing more; he looked on the convicts as his natural enemies and that was his first and great mistake. He really had some ability, but everything, even what was good in him, came out in a distorted form. Unrestrained and ill-tempered, he would sometimes burst into the prison even at night, and if he noticed that a convict was sleeping on his left side or on his back he would have him punished next day: 'You've to sleep on your

* Kantonists were soldiers' sons brought up in a military settlement and bound to serve in the army – a special class no longer existing. – *Translator's note.*

right side, as I've ordered you.' In the prison he was hated and feared like the plague. His face was purplish crimson and ferocious. Everyone knew that he was completely in the hands of his orderly, Fedka. What he loved most in the world was his poodle, Trezorka, and he almost went mad with grief when Trezorka fell ill. They say he sobbed over him as though it had been his own son; he drove away one veterinary surgeon and, after his usual fashion, almost beat him. Hearing from Fedka that one of the convicts in the prison was a self-taught 'vet' who was very successful in curing animals, he called him in at once.

'Help me! I'll load you with gold, cure Trezorka!' he shouted to the convict.

The man was a Siberian peasant, crafty, clever, really a very skilful vet, though a peasant in every sense of the word.

'I looked at Trezorka,' he told the convicts afterwards, long after his visit to the major, however, when the whole story was forgotten. 'I looked – the dog was lying on a white cushion on the sofa and I saw it was inflammation, that it ought to be bled and the dog would get well, yes indeed! And I thinks to myself – what if I don't cure it, what if it dies? "No, your honour," said I, "you called me in too late; if it had been yesterday or the day before, I could have cured the dog, but now I can't." '

So Trezorka died.

I was told in detail of an attempt to kill the major. There was a convict in the prison who had been there several years and was distinguished for his mild behaviour. It was observed, too, that he hardly ever spoke to anyone. He was looked upon as a bit queer in the religious way. He could read and write and during the last year he was continually reading the Bible, he read it day and night. When everyone was asleep he would get up at midnight, light a church wax candle, climb on to the stove, open the book and read till morning. One day he went up and told the sergeant that he would not go to work. It was reported to the major; he flew into a rage, and rushed into the prison at once himself. The convict threw himself upon him with a brick he had got ready beforehand, but missed his aim. He was seized, tried and punished. It all happened very quickly. Three days later he died in the hospital. As he lay dying he said that he meant no harm to anyone, but was only seeking suffering. He did not, however, belong to any dissenting sect. In the prison he was remembered with respect.

At last my fetters were changed. Meanwhile several girls selling rolls had come into the workshop. Some of them were quite little girls. They used to come with the rolls till they were grown up; their mothers baked them and they brought them for sale. When they were grown up they still came, but not to sell bread; this was almost always the case. There were some who were not little girls. The rolls cost a halfpenny and almost all the convicts bought them.

I noticed one of the convicts, a grey-headed but ruddy cabinet-maker, smiling and flirting with the baker girls. Just before they came in he had tied a red handkerchief round his neck. A fat peasant woman whose face was covered with pock-marks put her tray on his bench. Conversation began between them.

'Why didn't you turn up yesterday?' said the convict with a self-satisfied smile.

'Upon my word I did, but not a sign to be seen of you,' answered the lively woman.

'I was wanted, or you may be sure I'd have been there . . . The day before yesterday all your lot came to see me.'

'Who did?'

'Maryashka came, Havroshka came, Chekunda came, Two-penny-halfpenny came.'

'What does it mean?' I asked Akim Akimitch. 'Is it possible?'

'It does happen,' he answered, dropping his eyes discreetly, for he was an extremely chaste man.

It certainly did happen, but very rarely, and in spite of immense difficulties. On the whole, men were much more keen on drinking, for instance, than on that sort of thing, in spite of its being naturally difficult for them to live in the way they were forced to do. Women were difficult to get hold of. The time and place had to be found, arrangements had to be made, meetings had to be fixed, seclusion had to be sought, which was particularly difficult, the guards had to be won over, which was still more difficult, and altogether a sum of money – immense, relatively speaking – had to be spent. Yet I happened sometimes, later on, to be a witness of amatory scenes. I remember one day in the summer we were three of us in a shed on the bank of the Irtish, heating some sort of kiln;

the guards were good-natured fellows. At last two 'frillies', as the convicts called them, made their appearance.

'Well, where have you been so long? I bet you've been at the Zvyerkovs,' was how they were greeted by the convict whom they had come to see and who had been expecting them a long time.

'I've been so long? Why, I haven't been there longer than a magpie on a pole,' the girl answered gaily.

She was the dirtiest girl imaginable. She was the one called Chekunda. With her came Twopenny-halfpenny. The latter was beyond all description.

'I've not seen you for a long time, either,' the gallant went on, addressing Twopenny-halfpenny; 'how is it you seem to be thinner?'

'Maybe. I used to be ever so fat, but now one would think I'd swallowed a needle.'

'Always being with the soldiers, eh?'

'No, that's a lie that spiteful tongues have told you; though what of it? Though I'm thin as any rake, the soldier-lads I'll ne'er forsake!'

'You chuck them and love us; we've got cash . . . '

To complete the picture, imagine this gallant with a shaven head, in parti-coloured clothes, guarded and in fetters.

I took leave of Akim Akimitch, and hearing that I might go back to the prison, I went back escorted by a guard. The convicts were already coming home. The men on piece-work are the first to return. The only way of making a convict work hard is to put him on piece-work. Sometimes huge tasks are set them, but they always do the work twice as quickly as when they are working by the day. When he finishes his task the convict goes home without hindrance and no one prevents his doing so.

They don't dine all together, but as they come in, just as it happens; indeed, there would not have been room for them all at once in the kitchen. I tried the soup, but not being used to it I could not eat it, and I made myself some tea. We sat down at the end of the table. With me was a comrade of the same social class as myself.

Convicts kept going and coming. There was plenty of room however; they were not yet all in. A group of five men sat down together at the big table. The cook poured them out two bowls of soup and put on the table a whole dish of fried fish. They were keeping some sort of fête and eating their own food. They cast unfriendly glances in our direction. One of the Poles came in and sat down beside us.

'I've not been at home, but I know all the news,' a tall convict shouted aloud as he walked into the kitchen and looked round at everyone present.

He was a thin, muscular man of fifty. There was something sly, and at the same time merry, about his face. What was particularly striking about him was his thick, protruding lower lip; it gave a peculiarly comic look to his face.

'Well, have you had a good night? Why don't you say good morning? Hullo, my Kursk friends!' he added, sitting down beside the group who were eating their own food. 'A good appetite to you! Give a welcome to a friend.'

'We are not Kursk men, brother.'

'Tambov, then?'

'But we are not from Tambov either. You'll get nothing from us, brother. You go and ask a rich peasant.'

'I've colliwobbles and rumble-tumbles in my belly today. And where is he living, your rich peasant?'

'Why, Gazin yonder is a rich peasant, you go to him.'

'Gazin's having a spree today, lads, he is drinking; he is drinking all his money.'

'He's worth a good twenty roubles,' observed another. 'It's a good business, lads, selling vodka.'

'Well, won't you welcome a friend? I must have a sup of regulation fare, then.'

'You go and ask for some tea. The gentlemen there have got some.'

'Gentlemen? There are no gentlemen here. They are the same as we are now,' a convict sitting in the corner brought out gloomily. He had not said a word till then.

'I should like some tea, but I am ashamed to ask; we have our pride!' observed the convict with the protruding lip, looking good-naturedly at us.

'I'll give you some, if you like,' I said, inviting the convict to have tea; 'would you like some?'

'Like it? To be sure I'd like it.'

He came up to the table.

'At home he ate broth out of a shoe, but here he's learnt to like tea; and wants to drink it like the gentry,' the gloomy convict pronounced.

'Why, does no one drink tea here?' I asked him. But he did not deign to answer me.

'Here they are bringing rolls. Mayn't we have a roll, too?'

Rolls were brought in. A young convict brought in a whole bundle and was selling them in the prison. The baker girl used to give him one roll out of every ten he sold; he was reckoning on that tenth roll.

'Rolls, rolls!' he cried, entering the kitchen. 'Moscow rolls, all hot! I'd eat them myself, but I haven't the money. Come, lads, the last roll is left; surely someone, for his mother's sake?'

This appeal to filial affection amused everyone and several rolls were bought.

'I say, lads,' he announced, 'Gazin will get into trouble, the way he's carrying on! Upon my word, he has pitched on a time to drink! Ten to one, Eight-Eyes will be round.'

'They'll hide him. Why, is he very drunk?'

'Rather! He is wild, he is pestering everyone.'

'Oh, it will end in a fight, then . . . '

'Of whom are they talking?' I asked the Pole, who had sat down beside me.

'It's Gazin, a convict. He does a trade in vodka here. When he's saved up money enough, he spends it in drink. He is spiteful and cruel; when he is sober he is quiet, though; when he is drunk it all comes out; he flies at people with a knife. Then they have to restrain him.'

'How do they restrain him?'

'A dozen convicts fall upon him and begin beating him horribly until he loses consciousness, they beat him till he is half dead. Then they lay him on the bed and cover him with a sheepskin.'

'But they may kill him!'

'Anyone else would have been killed by now, but not he. He is awfully strong, stronger than anyone in the prison and of the healthiest constitution. Next day he is perfectly well.'

'Tell me, please,' I went on questioning the Pole; 'here they are eating their own food while I drink my tea. And yet they look as though they were envious of the tea. What does it mean?'

'It's not because of the tea,' answered the Pole. 'They are ill-disposed to you because you are a gentleman and not like them. Many of them would like to pick a quarrel with you. They would dearly like to insult you, to humiliate you. You will meet with a lot of unpleasantness here. We have an awfully hard time. It's harder for us than for any of them. One needs to be philosophical to get used to it. You will meet unpleasantness and abuse again and again for having your own food and tea, though very many of them here frequently have their own food, and some have tea every day. They may, but you mustn't.'

He got up and went away from the table; a few minutes later his words came true.

CHAPTER THREE

First Impressions [2]

M—y (the Pole who had been talking to me) had scarcely gone out when Gazin rolled into the kitchen, hopelessly drunk.

This convict, drunk in broad daylight, on a working day when all were bound to be out at work, under the rule of a stern officer who might come into the prison at any moment, under the control of the sergeant who never left the prison, with guards and sentries about – in short, in the midst of severity and discipline – threw into confusion all the ideas I had begun to form of prison life. And it was a long time before I could explain to myself all the facts which were so puzzling to me during my early days in prison.

I have mentioned already that the convicts always had private work of their own and that such work was a natural craving in prison life; that, apart from this craving, the prisoner is passionately fond of money, and prizes it above everything, almost as much as freedom, and that he is comforted if he has it jingling in his pocket. On the other hand, he becomes dejected, sad, uneasy and out of spirits when he has none, and then he is ready to steal or do anything to get it. But, though money was so precious in prison, it never stayed long with the lucky man who had it. To begin with, it was difficult to keep it from being stolen or taken away. If the major discovered it in the course of a sudden search, he promptly confiscated it. Possibly he spent it on improving the prison fare; anyway, it was taken to him. But much more frequently it was stolen; there was no one who could be relied upon. Later on, we discovered a way of keeping money quite securely: it was put into the keeping of an Old Believer who came to us from the Starodubovsky settlements.

He was a little grey-headed man of sixty. He made a vivid impression on me from the first minute. He was so unlike the other convicts, there was something so calm and gentle in his expression that I remember I looked with a peculiar pleasure at his serene, candid eyes, which were surrounded with tiny wrinkles like rays. I often talked to him and I have rarely met a more kindly, warm-hearted creature in my life. He had been sent there for a very serious offence. Among the Starodubovsky Old Believers, some converts to the Orthodox Church were made. The government gave them great encouragement and began to make great efforts for the conversion of the others. The old man resolved with other fanatics to stand up for the faith, as he expressed it. An orthodox church was being built and they burnt it down. As one of the instigators, the old man was sent to penal servitude. He had been a well-to-do tradesman and left a wife and children behind him, but he went with a brave heart into exile, for in his blindness he considered it 'martyrdom for the faith'. After spending some time with him, one could not help asking oneself how this meek old man, as gentle as a child, could have been a rebel. Several times I talked to him of 'the faith'; he would never yield an inch in his convictions, but there was no trace of anger or of hatred in his replies. And yet he had destroyed a church and did not deny doing it. It seemed that from his convictions he must have considered his action and his suffering for it a glorious achievement. But, however closely I watched him and studied him, I never detected the faintest sign of pride or vanity in him. There were other Old Believers in the prison, mostly Siberians. They were very well-educated people, shrewd peasants, great students of the Bible who quibbled over every letter, and great dialecticians in their own way; they were a crafty, conceited, aggressive and extremely intolerant set. The old man was absolutely different. Though perhaps better read than they, he avoided argument. He was of a very communicative disposition. He was merry, often laughing, not with the coarse cynical laugh of the other convicts, but with a gentle candid laugh, in which there was a great deal of childlike simplicity that seemed peculiarly in keeping with his grey hair. I may be mistaken, but I fancy that one can know a man from his laugh, and if you like a man's laugh before you know anything of him, you may confidently say that he is a good man. Though the old man had gained the respect of all throughout the prison, he was not in the least conceited about it. The convicts used to call him grandfather, and they never insulted him. I could partly imagine the sort of influence he must have had on his fellow believers. But in spite of the unmistakable courage with which he endured his punishment, there was also a deep inconsolable melancholy in his heart, which he tried to conceal from all. I lived in the same room with him. One night I woke up at three o'clock and heard the sound of quiet, restrained weeping. The old man was sitting on the stove (the same stove on which the Bible reader who threw the brick at the major used to pray at night). He was saying his prayers over his manuscript book. He was weeping and I could hear him saying from time to time, 'Lord, do not forsake me! Lord, give me strength! My little ones, my darling little ones, I shall never see you again!' I can't describe how sad it made me.

It was to this old man that almost all the convicts began by degrees to give their money, for him to take care of it. Almost all the prisoners were thieves, but suddenly for some reason the belief gained ground that the old man could not steal. They knew that he hid the money given into his keeping in some place so secret that no one could find it. In the end he explained his secret to me and some of the Poles. On one of the posts of the fence there was a twig apparently adhering firmly on the trunk. But it could be taken out, and there was a deep hollow in the wood. Here 'grandfather' used to hide the money and then insert the twig again so that no one could ever find anything.

But I am wandering from my story. I was just saying why money never stayed long in a convict's pocket. Apart from the difficulty of keeping it, life in prison was so dreary, a convict is a creature by nature so eager for freedom, and from his social position so careless and reckless, that to 'have his fling for all he is worth', to spend all his fortune carousing with noise and music and so to forget his depression, if only for the moment, naturally attracts him. It was strange to see how some of them would work unceasingly, sometimes for several months, simply to spend all their earnings in one day, leaving nothing, and then to drudge away for months again, till the next outbreak. Many of them were very fond of getting new clothes, which were never of the regulation pattern: black trousers unlike the uniform, tunics, coats. Cotton shirts and belts studded with metal discs were also in great demand. They dressed up on holidays, and then always paraded through all the prison wards to show themselves to all the world. Their pleasure in fine clothes was quite childish, and in many things the convicts were perfect children. It is true that all these fine things soon vanished from the owner's possession – sometimes they pawned or sold them for next to nothing the same evening. The outbreak of drinking developed gradually, however. It was put off as a rule till a holiday or till a nameday: on his nameday the convict set a candle before the ikon and said his prayers as soon as he got up; then he dressed in his best and ordered a dinner. He bought beef and fish, Siberian patties were made; he would eat like an ox, almost always alone, rarely inviting his comrades to share his meal. Then vodka was brought out; the hero of the day would get drunk as a lord and always walked all over the prison, reeling and staggering, trying to show to everyone that he was drunk, that he was 'jolly' and so deserving of general respect. Everywhere among the Russian people a certain sympathy is felt for a drunken man; in prison he was positively treated with respect. There were certain aristocratic customs connected with prison revelry. The carousing convict always hired music. There was a little Pole in prison, a runaway soldier, a nasty little fellow who played the fiddle and had an instrument – his one possession in the world. He had no sort of trade, and his only way of earning money was by playing lively dances for convicts who were having a spree. His duty was to follow his drunken employer from room to room and to play the fiddle with all his might. Often his face betrayed boredom and dejection. But the shout of 'Play on, you're paid to do it!' made him go on scraping away. The convict can always feel confident when he begins drinking that, if he gets too drunk, he will certainly be looked after, will be put in bed in time and hidden away if the authorities turn up, and all this will be quite disinterested. The sergeant and the veteran guards, who lived in the prison to keep discipline, could have their minds at rest too: the drunken convict could not create any disorder. All the prisoners in the room looked after him, and if he were noisy or unmanageable they would quickly restrain him and even tie him up. And so the inferior prison officials winked at drunkenness and were unwilling to notice it. They knew very well that if vodka were not allowed it would make things worse. But how was vodka obtained?

It was bought in the prison itself from the so-called 'publicans'. There were several of them, and they carried on their trade successfully and unintermittently, though the number of those who drank and 'made merry' was small, for merry-making costs money and the convicts' money is hardly earned. The publicans' operations were begun, managed and carried on in a very original way. Suppose a convict knows no trade and is not willing to exert himself (there were men like this), but is keen on getting money and of an impatient disposition, in a hurry to make his pile. If he has a little money to start with, he makes up his mind to trade in vodka: it's a bold and risky enterprise involving considerable danger. He may have to pay for it with a flogging, and lose his stock and his capital all at once. But the publican takes the risk. He begins with a small sum, and so at first he smuggles the vodka into the prison himself, and, of course, disposes of it to great advantage. He repeats the experiment a second and a third time, and if he does not get caught he quickly sells his stock and only then builds up a real trade on a large scale: he becomes an entrepreneur, a capitalist, employs agents and assistants, runs far less risk and makes more and more money. His subordinates risk themselves for him.

There are always in the prison lots of men who have wasted all they have on cards or drink, wretched ragged creatures who have no trade but have a certain pluck and daring. The only asset such a man has left is his back; it may still be of some use to him and so the spendthrift profligate decides to turn it to profit. He goes to the publican and offers his services for smuggling vodka; a well-to-do publican has several such working for him. Somewhere outside the prison there is some person – a soldier, a workman, sometimes even a woman – who for a comparatively large commission buys vodka at a tavern with the publican's money and conceals it in some out-of-the-way place where the convicts go to work. Almost always the intermediary tests the quality of the vodka to begin with, and ruthlessly fills up the measure with water; the publican may take it or leave it – a convict is not in a position to make his own terms. He must be thankful that he has got the vodka, however poor the quality, and has not lost his money altogether. The publican introduces his agents to the intermediary beforehand, and then they go to the latter carrying with them the guts of a bullock, which have been washed and then filled with water to keep them supple and fit to hold vodka. When he has filled the guts with vodka the convict winds them round himself where they will be least conspicuous. I need not say that this calls forth all the ingenuity, all the thievish cunning of the smuggler. His honour is to some extent involved: he has to deceive both the guards and the sentries. He does deceive them: the guard, often a raw recruit, is never a match for a clever thief. Of course the guard is the subject of special study beforehand; besides, the time and place where he is working is all carefully considered, too, by the smuggler. The convict may be building a stove; he climbs on to the stove; who can tell what he is doing there? A guard cannot be expected to climb after him. On his way to the prison he takes some money in his hand, fifteen or twenty silver kopecks, in case of need, and waits for the corporal at the gate. The corporal examines every convict returning from work, and feels him over before opening the prison door to him. The man smuggling in vodka usually reckons on the corporal's scrupling to handle him too minutely in some parts. But sometimes the wily corporal does not stand on ceremony and discovers the vodka. Then there is only one thing left to do: the smuggler, unseen by the guard, silently slips into the corporal's hand the coin he has been keeping concealed in his own. It sometimes happens that, thanks to this manoeuvre, he gets successfully into the prison with the vodka. But sometimes this method does not answer, and then he has to pay with his last asset, his back. It is reported to the major, the asset is flogged, and cruelly flogged, the vodka is confiscated and the agent takes it all on himself without giving away his employer, and, be it noted, not because he scorns to tell tales, but simply because it does not pay him to do so. He would be flogged anyway; his only consolation would be that the other man would be flogged too. But he will need his employer again, though in accordance with custom and previous agreement the smuggler gets nothing from his employer to compensate him for the flogging. As for telling tales in general, it is very common. In prison the man who turns traitor is not exposed to humiliation; indignation against him is unthinkable. He is not shunned, the others make friends with him; in fact, if you were to try and point out the loathsomeness of treachery, you would not be understood. The convict with whom I had broken off all relations, a mean and depraved creature who had been a gentleman, was friendly with the major's orderly, Fedka, and served him as a spy, while the latter reported all he heard about the convicts to the major. Every one of us knew this, yet no one ever dreamed of punishing the scoundrel or even reproaching him for it.

But I am wandering from my subject. It happens, of course, that vodka is smuggled in successfully. Then the publican takes the guts, pays for them, and begins to count the cost. It turns out when he reckons it that the stuff has cost him a great deal, and so to increase his profit he dilutes the vodka once more, adding almost an equal bulk of water, and then he is ready for his customers. On the first holiday, sometimes even on a working day, the customer turns up: this is a convict who has been working like an ox for some months, and has saved up his money in order to spend it all on drink on some day fixed beforehand. Long before it arrives, this day has been the object of the poor toiler's dreams at night and happy day-dreams over his work, and its fascination has kept up his spirits through the weary routine of prison life. At last the happy day dawns in the east; his money has been saved, not taken away, not stolen, and he brings it to the publican. To begin with, the latter gives him the vodka as pure as possible, that is, only twice diluted; but as the bottle gets emptier he invariably fills it up again with water. A cup of vodka costs five or six times as much as in a tavern. You can imagine how many cups of such vodka must be drunk, and what they will have cost before the point of intoxication is reached. But from having lost the habit of drinking, and having abstained from it so long, the convict readily gets drunk and he usually goes on drinking till he has spent all his money. Then he brings out all his new clothes; the publican is a pawnbroker as well. He first gets hold of the newly acquired personal possessions, then the old things and finally the prison clothes. When he has drunk up everything to the last rag, the drunken convict lies down to sleep, and next day, waking up with the inevitable splitting headache, he vainly entreats the publican to give him just a sip of vodka as a pick-me-up. Mournfully he endures his sad plight and the same day sets to work again, and works again for several months unceasingly, dreaming of the happy day of debauch lost and gone for ever, and by degrees beginning to take heart again and look forward to another similar day, still far away, but sure to come sometime in its turn.

As for the publican, after making a huge sum of money – some dozens of roubles – he gets the vodka ready for the last time, adding no water to it, for he means it for himself – he has done enough of trading, it is time for him to enjoy himself too! Then begins an orgy of drinking, eating and music. With such means at his disposal he even softens the hearts of the inferior prison officials. The debauch sometimes lasts several days. All the vodka he has prepared is soon drunk, of course; then the prodigal resorts to the other publicans, who are on the lookout for him, and drinks until he has spent every farthing! However carefully the convicts guard their drunken fellow, he is sometimes seen by a higher official, by the major or the officer on duty. He is taken to the guard-house, stripped of his money if he has it on him and finally flogged. He shakes himself, goes back into the prison, and a few days later takes up his trade in vodka again. Some of the festive characters, the rich ones of course, have dreams of the fair sex, too; for a big bribe to the guard escorting them, they can sometimes be taken in secret to some place in town instead of to work. There in some out-of-the-way little house at the furthest end of the town there is a feast on a huge scale, and really large sums of money are squandered. Even a convict is not despised if he has money. A guard is picked out beforehand who knows his way about. Such guards are usually future candidates for prison themselves. But anything can be done for money, and such expeditions almost always remain a secret. I must add that they are a very rare occurrence; so much money is needed and devotees of the fair sex have recourse to other methods which are quite free from danger.

Before I had been many days in prison my curiosity was particularly aroused by a young convict, a very pretty lad. He was called Sirotkin. He was rather an enigmatic creature in many ways. What struck me first of all was his beautiful face; he was not more than three-and-twenty. He was in the 'special division', that is, of criminals with a life sentence, which means that he was considered one of the worst of the military convicts. Mild and gentle, he talked little and rarely laughed. He had blue eyes, regular features, a clear-skinned delicate face and fair hair. He was such a pretty fellow that even his half-shaven head hardly disfigured him. He knew no sort of trade but he often had money, though not much at a time. One could see that he was lazy, and he was untidy in his dress. But occasionally someone would give him something nice to wear, even sometimes a red shirt, and Sirotkin was obviously pleased at his new clothes and walked about the prison to show himself. He did not drink nor play cards, and hardly ever quarrelled with anyone. He used to walk behind the prison with his hands in his pockets, quiet and dreamy. What he could be dreaming about it was difficult to guess. If one called to him sometimes from curiosity, asked him some question, he answered at once and even respectfully, not like a convict, though always briefly and uncommunicatively; and he looked at one like a child of ten years old. When he had any money he did not buy himself something necessary, did not get his coat mended, did not order new boots, but bought rolls or gingerbread and ate them like a child of seven. 'Ah, you Sirotkin,'* the convicts would say to him sometimes, 'you are an orphan all forlorn!' Out of working hours he used to wander about the prison barracks; almost everyone else would be at work, only he had nothing to do. If anything was said to him, usually a taunt (he and the others in his division were often made fun of), he would turn round and go off to another room without saying a word; sometimes he blushed crimson if he were much ridiculed. I often wondered how this peaceable, simple-hearted creature had come into prison. Once I was in the convicts' ward in the hospital. Sirotkin too was ill, and was in the bed next to mine; one evening we fell into talk. Somehow he got warmed up, and incidentally told me how he had been taken for a soldier, how his mother cried seeing him off, and how wretched he was as a recruit. He added that he could not endure the life of a recruit, because everyone there was so cross and stern, and the officers were almost always displeased with him.

'How did it end?' I asked. 'What brought you here? And in the special division too . . . Ah, Sirotkin, Sirotkin!'

'Why, I was only a year in the battalion, Alexandr Petrovitch, and I came here because I killed my commanding officer.'

'I'd heard it, Sirotkin, but I can't believe it. How could you kill anyone?'

'It happened so, Alexandr Petrovitch. I was awfully miserable.'

* Orphan – in Russian sirota. – *Translator's note.*

'But how do the other recruits manage? Of course it's hard at first, but they get used to it and in the end they become fine soldiers. Your mother must have spoiled you; she fed you on milk and goodies till you were eighteen.'

'My mother was very fond of me, it's true. She took to her bed when I went for a recruit and I've heard she never got up from it . . . Life was very bitter to me at last when I was a recruit. The officer did not like me, he was always punishing me – and what for? I gave way to everyone, was punctual in everything, did not touch vodka, did not pick up any habits; it's a bad business, you know, Alexandr Petrovitch, when one picks up habits. Such cruel-heartedness everywhere, no chance to have a good cry. Sometimes you'd get behind a corner and cry there. Well, I was once on sentry duty. It was at night; I was put as sentry by the gun-rack. It was windy; it was autumn, and pitch-dark. And I felt so sick, so sick. I stood my gun on the ground, I twisted off the bayonet and put it on one side; slipped off my right boot, put the barrel to my breast, leant against it and with my big toe pulled the trigger. It missed fire. I looked at the gun, cleaned the touch-hole, poured some fresh powder into it, struck the flint and put the gun to my breast again. And would you believe it? The powder flashed but the gun did not go off again. I wondered what was the meaning of it. I took my boot and put it on, fixed on the bayonet and walked to and fro, saying nothing. It was then I made up my mind to do what I did: I did not care where I went if I could get away from there. Half an hour later, the officer rode up; he was making the chief round of inspection. He went straight for me: 'Is that the way to stand on sentry duty?' I took my gun in my hand and stuck the bayonet into him up to the hilt. I've come four thousand miles and I am here with a life sentence . . . '

He was not lying. And for what other crime could he have been given a life sentence? Ordinary crimes are punished far more leniently. But Sirotkin was the only good-looking one of these 'lifers'. As for the others in the same case, of whom there were about fifteen among us, it was strange to look at them: there were only two or three tolerable faces among them; the others were all such hideous creatures, filthy-looking, with long ears. Some of them were grey-headed men. If possible, I will describe all this group more exactly later on. Sirotkin was often friendly with Gazin, the convict whom I mentioned at the beginning of the chapter, describing how he staggered into the kitchen drunk and how he upset my preconceived ideas of prison life.

This Gazin was a horrible creature. He made a terrible and painful impression on everyone. It always seemed to me that there could not be a more ferocious monster than he was. I have seen at Tobolsk, Kamenev, a robber famous for his crimes; later on I saw Sokolov, a runaway soldier who was being tried for terrible murders he had committed. But neither of them made such a repulsive impression on me as Gazin. I sometimes felt as though I were looking at a huge gigantic spider of the size of a man. He was a Tatar, terribly strong, stronger than anyone in the prison, of more than average height, of Herculean proportions, with a hideous, disproportionately huge head; he walked with a slouch and looked sullenly from under his brows. There were strange rumours about him in the prison; it was known that he had been a soldier, but the convicts said among themselves, I do not know with what truth, that he was an escaped convict from Nertchinsk, that he had been sent more than once to Siberia and had escaped more than once, had more than once changed his name, and had at last been sent to our prison with a life sentence. It was said, too, that he had been fond of murdering small children simply for pleasure: he would lure the child to some convenient spot, begin by terrifying and tormenting it, and after enjoying to the full the shuddering terror of the poor little victim, he would kill it with a knife slowly, with deliberation and enjoyment. All this perhaps was invented in consequence of the feeling of oppression Gazin aroused in everyone; but all these stories were in keeping with him, and harmonised with his appearance. Yet at ordinary times, when he was not drunk, his behaviour in prison was very orderly. He was always quiet, did not quarrel with anyone, and avoided quarrels, but, as it seemed, from contempt for the others, as though he considered himself superior to all the rest; he spoke very little, and was, as it were, intentionally reserved. All his movements were calm, deliberate, self-confident. One could see from his eyes that he was very intelligent and exceedingly cunning; but there was always something of supercilious derision and cruelty in his face and smile. He traded in vodka, and was one of the richest vodka dealers in the prison. But about twice in the year he would get drunk himself, and then all the brutality of his nature came out. As he gradually got drunk, he began at first attacking people with gibes, the most spiteful, calculated, as it seemed, long-premeditated taunts; finally, when he was quite drunk he passed into a stage of blind fury, snatched up a knife and rushed at people. The convicts knowing his terrible strength ran and hid themselves: he fell upon anyone he met. But they soon found means to get control of him. A dozen men, inmates of the same prison ward as Gazin, would suddenly rush at him all at once and begin beating him. Nothing crueller could be imagined: they beat him on the chest, on the heart, on the pit of the stomach, on the belly; they beat him hard and beat him a long time; they only desisted when he lost consciousness and lay like a corpse. They could not have brought themselves to beat any other convict like that: to beat like that meant killing any other man, but not Gazin. Then they wrapped his unconscious body in a sheepskin and carried it to the bed. 'He'll sleep it off.' And he did in fact get up next morning almost uninjured and went to work, silent and sullen. Every time Gazin got drunk everyone in the prison knew that the day would certainly end in a beating for him. And he knew this himself and yet he got drunk. So it went on for several years; at last it was noticed that Gazin was beginning to break up. He began to complain of pains of all sorts, grew noticeably weaker and was more and more often in the hospital. 'He is breaking up!' the convicts said among themselves.

He came into the kitchen, followed by the nasty little Pole with the fiddle, who was generally hired by the 'festive convicts' to enhance their jollity, and he stood still in the middle of the room, silently and attentively scanning all present. All were silent. At last seeing me and my companion, he looked at us spitefully and derisively, smiled self-complacently, seemed to think of something, and staggering heavily came towards our table.

'Where did you get the money for this little treat may I enquire?' he began (he spoke Russian).

I exchanged silent glances with my companion, realising that the best thing was to hold our tongues and not to answer him. At the first contradiction he would have flown into a fury.

'So you've money, have you?' He went on questioning us. 'So you've a lot of money, eh? Have you come to prison to drink tea? You've come to drink tea, have you? Speak, damn you!'

But seeing that we had made up our minds to be silent and to take no notice of him, he turned crimson and shook with rage. Near him in the corner stood a big tray which was used for the slices of bread cut for the dinner or supper of the convicts. It was large enough to hold the bread for half the prison; at the moment it was empty. He picked it up with both hands and raised it above us. In another moment he would have smashed our heads. A murder, or an attempt at murder, threatened the whole prison with extremely unpleasant consequences: it would be followed by enquiries, searches and greater severity, and so the convicts did their utmost not to let things come to such an extremity. And yet in spite of that, on this occasion all kept quiet and waited. Not one word in our defence! Not one shout at Gazin, so intense was their hatred of us! They were apparently pleased at our dangerous position. But the incident passed off without harm: just as he was about to bring down the tray someone shouted from the passage.

'Gazin! Vodka's stolen!' He let the tray fall crashing on the floor and rushed like mad out of the kitchen.

'Well, God saved them!' the convicts said among themselves.

And they repeated it long after. I could not find out afterwards whether the news of the theft of the vodka was true or invented on the spur of the moment to save us.

In the evening, after dusk, before the prison was locked up, I walked round the fence and an overwhelming sadness came upon me. I never experienced such sadness again in all my prison life. The first day of confinement, whether it be in prison, in the fortress, or in Siberia, is hard to bear . . . But I remember what absorbed me more than anything was one thought, which haunted me persistently all the time I was in prison, a difficulty that cannot be fully solved – I cannot solve it even now: the inequality of punishment for the same crime. It is true that crimes cannot be compared even approximately. For instance, two men may commit murders; all the circumstances of each case are weighed; and in both cases almost the same punishment is given. Yet look at the difference between the crimes. One may have committed a murder for nothing, for an onion; he murdered a peasant on the high road who turned out to have nothing but an onion. 'See, father, you sent me to get booty. Here I've murdered a peasant and all I've found is an onion.' 'Fool! An onion means a farthing! A hundred murders and a hundred onions and you've got a rouble!' (a prison legend). Another murders a sensual tyrant in defence of the honour of his betrothed, his sister, or his child. Another is a fugitive, hemmed in by a regiment of trackers, who commits a murder in defence of his freedom, his life, often dying of hunger; and another murders little children for the pleasure of killing, of feeling their warm blood on his hands, of enjoying their terror, and their last dove-like flutter under the knife. Yet all of these are sent to the same penal servitude.

It is true that there are variations in the length of the sentence. But these variations are comparatively few, and the variations in the same sort of crime are infinitely numerous. There are as many shades of difference as there are characters. But let us admit that it is impossible to get over this inequality, that it is in its own way an insoluble problem, like squaring the circle.

Apart from this, let us look at another inequality, at the difference in the effect of a punishment. One man will pine, waste away like a candle in prison, while another had no notion till he came to prison that such a jolly existence, such a pleasant club of spirited companions was to be found in the world. Yes, there are some in prison like that. Or take the case of an educated man with an awakened conscience, intelligence, heart. The mere ache of his own heart will kill him by its torments sooner than any punishment. He condemns himself for his crime more unsparingly, more relentlessly than the most rigorous law. And beside him is another who has never once all the time he has been in prison thought of the murder he has committed. He positively considers he has done right. And there are men who commit crimes on purpose to be sent to penal servitude, in order to escape from a far more penal life of labour outside. There he lived in the deepest degradation, never had enough to eat and worked from morning to night for his exploiter; in prison the work is lighter than at home, there is bread in plenty and of better quality than he has ever seen before; and on holidays there is beef; then there are alms and there is a chance of earning something. And the company? It consists of shrewd crafty fellows who know everything; and he looks on his companions with respectful astonishment; he has never seen anyone like them before; he looks upon them as the very highest society in the world. Is the punishment equally felt in these two cases? But why trouble oneself with unanswerable questions? The drum beats, it is time to be back in our wards.

CHAPTER FOUR

First Impressions [3]

The last roll-call began. After this call-over the prison wards are locked up, each with its own lock, and the convicts remain shut up till daybreak.

The roll was called by a sergeant and two soldiers. For this purpose the convicts were sometimes drawn up in ranks in the yard, and the officer on duty was present. But more frequently the ceremony was conducted in a more homely fashion. The roll was called indoors. This is how it was on that occasion. The men on duty made many mistakes, were wrong in their reckoning, went away and came back again. At last the poor fellows brought their sum out right and locked our prison room. In it there were as many as thirty convicts, rather closely packed on the bed. It was too early to go to sleep. Obviously, everyone needed something to do.

The only representative of authority in the room was the veteran soldier whom I have mentioned already. There was also in each room a head convict who was appointed by the major himself, on the grounds of good behaviour, of course. It often happened that these head convicts were involved in some serious mischief; then they were flogged, at once degraded and replaced by others. In our room the head convict was Akim Akimitch, who to my surprise not infrequently shouted at other convicts. They usually responded with jeers. The veteran was wiser, he never interfered in any way, and, if he ever did open his lips, it was no more than a matter of form to satisfy his conscience. He sat in silence on his bedstead sewing a boot. The convicts took hardly any notice of him.

On that first day of my prison life I made one observation, and found as time went on that it was correct. All who are not convicts, whoever they are, from those who have the most contact with them such as guards, soldiers on duty, down to all who have ever had any connection with prison life, have an exaggerated idea of convicts. It is as though they were every minute in uneasy expectation of the convicts suddenly flying at them with a knife. But what is most remarkable, the convicts were themselves aware that they were feared, and it gave them a certain conceit. And yet the very best man to look after convicts is one who is not afraid of them. And, indeed, in spite of his conceit the convict likes it much better when one trusts him. One may even win his affection by doing so. It happened, though very rarely during my life in prison, that some superior officer came into the prison without a guard. It was worth seeing how it impressed the convicts, and impressed them in the most favourable way. Such a fearless visitor always aroused their respect, and if any harm had been possible, it would not have been so in his presence. The dread inspired by convicts is found everywhere where there are prisoners, and I really do not know to what exactly it is due. It has, of course, some foundation, even in the external appearance of the convict, who is, after all, an acknowledged malefactor; besides, everyone who comes near the prison feels that all this mass of people has been brought together not of their own will, and that, whatever measures are taken, a live man cannot be made into a corpse; he will remain with his feelings, his thirst for revenge and life, his passions and the craving to satisfy them. At the same time I am convinced that there is no need to fear convicts. A man does not so quickly or so easily fly at another with a knife. In fact, if there may be danger, if there is sometimes trouble, the rarity of such instances shows how trifling the risk is. I am speaking, of course, only of convicted prisoners, many of whom are glad to have reached the prison at last (a new life is sometimes such a good thing!) and are consequently disposed to live quietly and peaceably. Moreover, the others will not let those who are really troublesome do mischief. Every convict, however bold and insolent he may be, is afraid of everything in prison. But a convict awaiting punishment is a different matter. He is certainly capable of falling on any outsider, apropos of nothing, simply because he will have to face a flogging next day, and if he does anything to bring about another trial his punishment will be delayed. Here there is an object, a motive for the attack; it is 'to change his luck' at any cost and as quickly as possible. I know one strange psychological instance of the kind.

In the military division in our prison there was a convict who had been a soldier, and had been sentenced for two years without deprivation of rights, an awful braggart and a conspicuous coward. As a rule boastfulness and cowardice are rarely found in a Russian soldier. Our soldiers always seem so busy that if they wanted to show off they would not have time. But if one is a braggart he is almost always an idler and a coward. Dutov (that was the convict's name) served out his sentence at last and returned to his line regiment. But as all, like him, sent to prison for correction are finally corrupted there, it usually happens that after they have been not more than two or three weeks in freedom, they are arrested again and come back to the prison, this time not for two or three years, but as a 'lifer' for fifteen or twenty years; and so it happened with him. Three weeks after leaving the prison, Dutov stole something, breaking a lock to do so, and was insolent and unruly as well. He was tried and sentenced to a severe punishment. Reduced to the utmost terror by the punishment awaiting him, being a most pitiful coward, he fell, knife in hand, upon an officer who went into the convicts' room, the day before he would have had to 'walk the Green Street'. Of course, he was well aware that by such an act he greatly increased his sentence and his term of penal servitude, but all he was reckoning on was putting off the terrible moment of punishment for a few days, even for a few hours! He was such a coward that he did not even wound the officer, but only attacked him as a matter of form, that there might appear to be a new crime for which he would be tried again.

The minute before punishment is certainly terrible for the condemned man, and in the course of several years it was my lot to see a good number of men on the eve of this fatal day. I usually came across these condemned prisoners in the convict ward of the hospital when I lay there ill, which happened pretty often. It is well known to all the convicts throughout Russia that the people most compassionate to them are doctors. They never make any distinction between convicts and other people, as almost all outsiders do, except, perhaps, the peasants. The latter never reproach the convict with his crime, however terrible it may have been, and forgive him everything on account of the punishment he has endured and his general misery. Significantly the peasants all over Russia speak of crime as a misfortune, and of criminals as the unfortunate. It is a definition of deep import, and it is the more significant because it is unconscious, instinctive. The doctors are truly a refuge for the convicts in many cases, especially for those awaiting punishment, who are kept far more severely than the ordinary prisoners. The convict awaiting punishment, who has reckoned the probable date of the awful ordeal, often gets into hospital, trying to ward off the terrible moment, even by a little. When he is taking his discharge from the hospital, knowing almost for certain that the fatal hour will be next day, he is nearly always in a state of violent agitation. Some try from vanity to conceal their feelings, but their awkward show of swagger does not deceive their companions. Everyone understands how it is, but is silent from humane feeling.

I knew a convict, a young man who had been a soldier, condemned for murder to the maximum number of strokes. He was so panic-stricken that on the eve of the punishment he drank off a jug of vodka, in which he had previously soaked snuff. Vodka, by the way, is always taken just before the flogging. It is smuggled in long before the day, and a high price is paid for it. The convict would rather go without every necessity for six months than fail to have the money for a bottle of vodka to be drunk a quarter of an hour before the flogging. There is a general belief among the convicts that a drunken man feels the lash or the sticks less acutely. But I am wandering from my story. The poor fellow after drinking his jug of vodka was at once taken ill in earnest; he began vomiting blood and he was carried to the hospital almost unconscious. The vomiting so affected his chest that in a few days he showed unmistakable signs of consumption, of which he died six months later. The doctors who treated him for tuberculosis did not know how it had been caused.

But, speaking of the cowardice so often found in the convict before punishment, I ought to add that some, on the contrary, astonish the observer by their extraordinary fearlessness. I remember some examples of courage which approached insensibility, and such examples were not so very rare. I particularly remember my meeting with a terrible criminal. One summer day a rumour spread in the hospital wards that a famous robber, a runaway soldier called Orlov, would be punished that evening, and would be afterwards brought to the ward. While the convict patients were expecting Orlov to be brought in, they asserted that he would be punished cruelly. They were all in some excitement, and I must confess that I, too, awaited the famous robber's arrival with extreme curiosity. I had heard marvellous stories about him long before. He was a criminal such as there are few, who had murdered old people and children in cold blood – a man of a terrible strength of will and proud consciousness of his strength. He had confessed to many murders, and was sentenced to be beaten with sticks.

It was evening before he was brought. It was dark and the candles had been lighted in the ward. Orlov was almost unconscious, horribly pale, with thick, dishevelled pitch-black hair. His back was swollen and red and blue. The convicts were waiting on him all night, constantly bringing him water, turning him over, giving him medicines, as though they were looking after a brother or a benefactor. Next day he regained consciousness completely, and walked twice up and down the ward! It amazed me: he had come into the hospital so very weak and exhausted. He had received at one time half of the whole number of blows to which he was sentenced. The doctor had only stopped the punishment when he saw that its continuance would inevitably cause his death. Moreover, Orlov was small and weakly built and exhausted by long imprisonment before his trial. Anyone who has met prisoners awaiting their trial probably remembers long after their thin, pale, worn-out faces, their feverish looks. But, in spite of that, Orlov was recovering quickly. Evidently the energy of his spirit assisted nature. He was certainly not an ordinary man. I was moved by curiosity to make a closer acquaintance with him, and for a week I studied him. I can confidently say that I have never in my life met a man of such strength, of so iron a will as he. I had already seen at Tobolsk a celebrity of the same kind, formerly a brigand chief. He was a wild beast in the fullest sense of the word, and when you stood near him you felt instinctively that there was a terrible creature beside you, even before you knew his name. But in that case what horrified me was the spiritual deadness of the man. The flesh had so completely got the upper hand of all spiritual characteristics that at the first glance you could see from his face that nothing was left but a fierce lust of physical gratification – sensuality, gluttony. I am convinced that Korenev – that was the brigand's name – would have been in a panic and trembling with fear before a flogging, although he could cut a man's throat without turning a hair.

Orlov was a complete contrast to him. His was unmistakably the case of a complete triumph over the flesh. It was evident that the man's power of control was unlimited, that he despised every sort of punishment and torture, and was afraid of nothing in the world. We saw in him nothing but unbounded energy, a thirst for action, a thirst for vengeance, an eagerness to attain the object he had set before him. Among other things I was struck by his strange haughtiness. He looked down on everything with incredible disdain, though he made no sort of effort to maintain this lofty attitude – it was somehow natural. I imagine there was no creature in the world who could have worked upon him simply by authority. He looked upon everything with surprising calmness, as though there were nothing in the universe that could astonish him, and though he quite saw that the other convicts looked on him with respect, he did not pose to them in the least. Yet vanity and self-assertion are characteristic of almost all convicts without exception. He was very intelligent and somehow strangely open, though by no means talkative. To my questions he answered frankly that he was only waiting to recover in order to get through the remainder of his punishment as quickly as possible, that he had been afraid beforehand that he would not survive it; 'but now,' he added, winking at me, 'it's as good as over. I shall walk through the remainder of the blows and set off at once with the party to Nerchinsk, and on the way I'll escape. I shall certainly escape! If only my back would make haste and heal!' And all those five days he was eagerly awaiting the moment when he could be discharged, and in the meantime was often laughing and merry. I tried to talk to him of his adventures. He frowned a little at such questions, but always answered openly. When he realised that I was trying to get at his conscience and to discover some sign of penitence in him, he glanced at me with great contempt and haughtiness, as though I had suddenly in his eyes become a foolish little boy, with whom it was impossible to discuss things as you would with a grown-up person. There was even a sort of pity for me to be seen in his face. A minute later he burst out laughing at me, a perfectly open-hearted laugh free from any hint of irony, and I am sure that, recalling my words when he was alone, he laughed again to himself, many times over perhaps. At last he got his discharge from hospital with his back hardly healed. I was discharged at the same time, and it happened that we came out of the hospital together, I going to the prison and he to the guard-house near the prison where he had been detained before. As he said goodbye, he shook hands with me, and that was a sign of great confidence on his part. I believe he did it because he was much pleased with himself, and glad that the moment had come. He could not really help despising me, and must have looked upon me as a weak, pitiful, submissive creature, inferior to him in every respect. Next day he was led out for the second half of his punishment.

When our prison room was shut it suddenly assumed a special aspect – the aspect of a real dwelling-place, of a home. It was only now that I could see the prisoners, my comrades, quite at home. In the daytime the sergeants, the guards and officials in general could make their appearance at any moment in the prison, and so all the inmates behaved somewhat differently, as though they were not quite at ease, as though they were continually expecting something with some anxiety. But as soon as the room was shut up they all quietly settled down in their places, and almost every one of them took up some handicraft. The room was suddenly lighted up. Every one had his candle and his candlestick, generally made of wood. One worked at a boot, another sewed some garment. The foul atmosphere of the room grew worse from hour to hour. A group of festive souls squatted on their heels round a rug in a corner to a game of cards. In almost every prison room there was a convict who kept a threadbare rug a yard wide, a candle and an incredibly dirty, greasy pack of cards, and all this together was called the *maidan*. The owner of these articles let them to the players for fifteen kopecks a night; that was his trade. The players usually played 'Three Leaves', 'Hillock', and such games. They always played for money. Each player heaped a pile of copper coins before him – all he had in his pocket – and only got up when he had lost every farthing or stripped his companions. The game went on till late in the night, sometimes lasting till daybreak, till the moment when the door was opened. In our room, as in all the other rooms of the prison, there were always a certain number of destitute convicts, who had lost all their money at cards or on vodka or who were simply beggars by nature. I say 'by nature' and I lay special stress on this expression. Indeed, everywhere in Russia, in all surroundings and under all conditions, there always are and will be certain strange individuals, humble and not infrequently by no means lazy, whose destiny is to be destitute for ever. They are always without family ties and always slovenly, they always look cowed and depressed about something, and are always at the beck and call of someone, usually a dissipated fellow, or one who has suddenly grown rich and risen. And position of respect or anything calling for initiative is a burden and affliction to them. It seems as though they had been born on the understanding that they should begin nothing of themselves and only wait on others, that they should do not what they like, should dance while others pipe; their vocation is only to carry out the will of others. And what is more, no circumstance, no change of luck can enrich them. They are always beggars. I have noticed that such individuals are to be found not only among the peasants, but in every class of society, in every party, in every association, and on the staff of every magazine. It is the same in every room, in every prison, and, as soon as a game of cards is got up, such a beggar always turns up to wait on the party. And, indeed, no card party can get on without an attendant. He was usually hired by all the players in common for five kopecks the night, and his chief duty was to stand all night on guard. As a rule he used to freeze six or seven hours together in the passage in the dark, in thirty degrees of frost, listening to every knock, every clang, every step in the yard. But sometimes the major or the officers on duty visited the prison rather late at night, came in quietly and discovered the men at play and at work, and the extra candles, which could indeed be seen from the yard. Anyway, when the key was grating in the lock of the door that led from the passage to the yard, it was too late to hide what they were doing, put out the lights and go to bed. But as the attendant on duty caught it severely from the card players afterwards, cases of such neglect were extremely rare. Five kopecks, of course, is a ridiculously small sum, even for prison, but I was always struck in prison by the harshness and mercilessness of employers, in this and also in other cases. 'You've had your money, so do your work!' was an argument that would bear no objection. For the trifle he had paid the employer would take all he could take – take, if he could, more than was his due, and he considered that he was conferring a favour on the other into the bargain. The convict who is drunk and making merry, flinging his money right and left, always beats down his attendant, and I have noticed it not only in one prison, not only in one group of players.

I have mentioned already that almost all in the room had settled down to some sort of work: except the card players there were not more than five people quite idle; they immediately went to bed. My place on the bed was next to the door. On the other side of the bed, his head nearly touching mine, lay Akim Akimitch. Till ten or eleven he worked, making some sort of coloured Chinese lantern, which had been ordered in the town for a fairly good price. He made lanterns in a masterly way, and worked methodically, without stopping; when he had finished his work he put it away tidily, spread out his little mattress, said his prayers, and conscientiously went to bed. Conscientiousness and orderliness he carried apparently to the point of trivial pedantry; evidently he must have considered himself an exceedingly clever person, as is usually the case with limited and dull-witted people. I did not like him from the first day, though I remember I thought a great deal about him that first day, and what surprised me most was that such a man should have got into prison instead of making his way in the world. Later on, I shall have to speak more than once of Akim Akimitch.

But I will briefly describe all the inmates of our room. I had many years to spend in it, and these were all my future comrades and associates. It may well be understood that I looked at them with eager curiosity. Next to me on the left were a group of mountaineers from the Caucasus, who had been sent here to various term of imprisonment, chiefly for robbery. There were two Lezghis, one Chechenian and three Daghestan Tatars. The Chechenian was a gloomy and morose person; he hardly spoke to anyone, and was always looking about him from under his brows with hatred and a venomous, malignantly sneering smile. One of the Lezghis was an old man with a long, thin, hooked nose, a regular brigand in appearance. But the second, Nurra, made upon me from the first day a most charming and delightful impression. He was a man still young, of medium height, of Herculean build, with the face of a Finnish woman, quite flaxen hair, light blue eyes, and a snub nose. He had bandy legs from having spent all his previous life on horseback. His whole body was covered with scars, bayonet and bullet wounds. In the Caucasus he had belonged to an allied tribe, but was always riding over on the sly to the hostile mountaineers, and making raids with them on the Russians. Everyone in prison liked him. He was always good-humoured and cordial to everyone, he worked without grumbling and was calm and serene, though he often looked with anger at the filth and loathsomeness of prison life, and was furiously indignant at all the thieving, cheating, and drunkenness, in fact, at everything that was dishonest; but he never picked a quarrel, he merely turned away with indignation. He had never during his prison life stolen anything himself, or been guilty of any bad action. He was exceedingly devout, he religiously repeated his prayers; during the fasts before the Mohammedan holy days he fasted fanatically, and spent whole nights over his prayers. Everyone liked him and believed in his honesty. 'Nurra's a lion,' the convicts used to say, and the name 'lion' had stuck to him. He was firmly persuaded that on the expiration of his sentence he would be sent home to the Caucasus, and only lived on the hope of it. I believe he would have died had he been deprived of it. I got a vivid impression of him on my first day in prison. It was impossible to overlook his good sympathetic face among the surly, ill-humoured and sneering faces of the other convicts. Within my first half-hour in the prison he slapped me on the shoulder as he passed by me, and laughed good-naturedly in my face. I could not make out at first what this meant. He spoke Russian very badly. Soon afterwards, he came up to me again, and smiling gave me another friendly pat on the shoulder. He did it again and again, and so it went on for three days. It meant, as I guessed and found out later, that he was sorry for me, that he felt how hard it was for me to get used to prison, that he wanted to show his goodwill to me, to cheer me up and assure me of his protection. Kind, simple-hearted Nurra!

The Daghestan Tatars were three in number and they were all brothers. Two of them were middle-aged men, but the third, Aley, was not more than two-and-twenty and looked even younger. His place on the bed was next to me. His handsome, open, intelligent, and at the same time good-naturedly simple face won my heart from the first minute. I was so thankful that fate had sent me him as a neighbour rather than any other. His whole soul was apparent in his handsome, one might even say beautiful, face. His smile was so confiding, so childishly trustful, his big black eyes were so soft, so caressing, that I always found a particular pleasure in looking at him, even a consolation in my misery and depression. I am not exaggerating. When he was in his native place one of his elder brothers – he had five of them, two of the others had been sent to some sort of penal factory – ordered him to take his sabre, to get on his horse and to go with them on some sort of expedition. The respect due to an elder brother is so great among the mountaineers that the boy did not dare ask, did not even dream of asking, where they were going, and the others did not think it necessary to inform him. They were going out on a pillaging expedition, to waylay and rob a rich Armenian merchant on the road. And so indeed they did: they killed the escort, murdered the Armenian and carried off his goods. But the affair was discovered; all the six were caught, tried, convicted, punished, and sent to penal servitude in Siberia. The only mercy shown by the court to Aley was that he received a shorter sentence: he had been sent to Siberia for four years. His brothers were very fond of him, and their affection was more like a father's than a brother's. He was their comfort in exile, and sullen and gloomy as they usually were, they always smiled when they looked at him, and when they spoke to him (though they spoke to him very little, as though they still thought of him as a boy with whom it was useless to talk of serious things) their surly faces relaxed, and I guessed that they spoke to him of something humorous, almost childish; at least they always looked at one another and smiled good-humouredly after listening to his answer. He hardly dared to address them, so deep was his respect for them. It was hard to imagine how this boy was able during his prison life to preserve such a gentle heart, to develop such strict honesty, such warm feelings and charming manners, and to escape growing coarse and depraved. But his was a strong and steadfast nature in spite of all its apparent softness. As time went on I got to know him well. He was pure as a chaste girl, and any ugly, cynical, dirty, unjust or violent action in the prison brought a glow of indignation into his beautiful eyes, making them still more beautiful. But he avoided all strife and wrangling, though he was not one of those men who allow themselves to be insulted with impunity and knew how to stand up for himself. But he never had quarrels with anyone, everyone liked him and was friendly to him. At first he was simply courteous to me. By degrees I began talking to him; in a few months he had learned to speak Russian very well, which his brothers never succeeded in doing all the time they were in Siberia. He seemed to me a boy of marked intelligence and peculiar modesty and delicacy, who had in fact reflected a good deal. I may as well say at once that I consider Aley far from being an ordinary person, and I look back upon my meeting with him as one of the happiest meetings in my life. There are natures so innately good, so richly endowed by God, that the very idea of their ever deteriorating seems impossible. One is always at ease about them. I am at ease about Aley to this day. Where is he now?

One night, when I had been some time in prison, I was lying on the bed musing; Aley, always occupied and industrious, happened to be doing nothing at the moment, though it was early to go to bed. But it was their Mussulman holiday, and they were not working. He was lying down with his hands clasped behind his head, pondering on something, too. All at once he asked me: 'Are you very sad just now?' I looked at him with curiosity and it seemed strange to me to hear this rapid direct question from Aley, always so delicate, so considerate, so full of the wisdom of the heart. But looking more intently I saw in his face such sadness, such distress at some memory, that I felt at once that his own heart was heavy at that moment and I told him so. He sighed and smiled mournfully. I loved his smile, which was always warm and tender. Besides, when he smiled he showed two rows of pearly teeth which the greatest beauty in the world might have envied.

'Ah, Aley, no doubt you are thinking how they are keeping this holiday at home in Daghestan? It must be nice there.'

'Yes,' he answered enthusiastically, and his eyes shone. 'But how do you know I am thinking about it?'

'How can I help knowing! It's better there than here, isn't it?'

'Oh, why do you say that! . . . '

'What flowers there must be there now, what a paradise!'

'O-oh, better not talk of it.'

He was deeply stirred.

'Listen, Aley, had you a sister?'

'Yes, but why?'

'She must be a beauty if she is like you.'

'Like me! She is such a beauty, there is no one in Daghestan handsomer. Ah, she is a beauty, my sister! You've never seen anyone like her. My mother was beautiful too.'

'Was your mother fond of you?'

'Ah! What are you saying! She must have died of grieving over me by now. I was her favourite son. She loved me more than my sister, more than anyone . . . She came to me in my dreams last night and cried over me.'

He sank into silence and said nothing more that evening. But from that time forward he sought every opportunity to talk to me, though the respect which he for some reason felt for me always prevented him from speaking first. But he was greatly delighted whenever I addressed him. I questioned him about the Caucasus, about his former life. His brothers did not hinder his talking to me, in fact they seemed to like it. Seeing that I was getting fonder and fonder of Aley, they, too, became much more cordial to me.

Aley helped me at work, did his utmost to be of service to me in the prison, and I could see that he was delighted when he could do anything to please me or make my life easier, and in his efforts to please me there was not a trace of anything cringing or self-seeking, nothing but a warm, friendly feeling for me which he no longer concealed. He had, moreover, a good deal of mechanical ability: he learnt to make underclothes fairly well, and to make boots and later on, as far as he could, to do carpentering. His brothers praised him and were proud of him.

'Listen, Aley,' I said to him one day, 'why don't you learn to read and write Russian? It would be a great advantage to you in Siberia later on, you know.'

'I should like to very much. But of whom can I learn?'

'Lots of men here can read and write! But if you like, I'll teach you.'

'Oh, please do!' And he positively sat up on the bed and clasped his hands, looking at me imploringly.

We set to work the next evening. I had the Russian translation of the New Testament, a book not prohibited in prison. With this book alone and no alphabet, Aley learnt in a few weeks to read excellently. In three months he had completely mastered the language of the book. He learnt eagerly, with enthusiasm.

One day we read together the whole of the Sermon on the Mount. I noticed that he seemed to read parts of it aloud with special feeling.

I asked him if he liked what he had read.

He glanced at me quickly and the colour came into his face.

'Oh, yes,' he answered. 'Yes. Jesus is a holy prophet. Jesus speaks God's words. How good it is!'

'What do you like best of all?'

'Where He says "forgive, love, don't hurt others, love even your enemies." Ah, how well He speaks!'

He turned to his brothers who were listening to our conversation, and began warmly saying something to them. They talked earnestly for a long time together, and nodded their heads approvingly. Then with a dignified and gracious, that is, a typically Mussulman, smile (which I love so much, and love especially for its dignity) they turned to me and repeated that Jesus was a prophet of God, and that He worked great marvels; that He had made a bird out of clay, had breathed on it and it had flown away . . . and that that was written in their books. They were convinced that in saying this they were giving me great pleasure by praising Jesus, and Aley was perfectly happy that his brothers had deigned and desired to give me this pleasure.

The writing lessons, too, were very successful. Aley procured paper (he would not let me buy it with my money), pens and ink, and in about two months he had learnt to write an excellent hand. This actually impressed his brothers. Their pride and satisfaction knew no bounds. They did not know how to show their gratitude to me. If they happened to be working near me, they were continually helping me, and looked on it as a happiness to be able to. I need hardly say the same of Aley. He loved me perhaps as much as he loved his brothers. I shall never forget how he left the prison. He drew me away behind the prison, flung himself on my neck and cried. He had never before kissed me or shed tears. 'You've done so much for me, so much for me,' he said, 'that my father and my mother could not have done more: you have made a man of me. God will repay you and I shall never forget you . . . '

Where is he now, my good, dear, dear Aley?

Besides the Circassians there was a group of Poles in our room, and they made a family apart, and had hardly anything to do with the other convicts. I have mentioned already that their exclusiveness and their hatred of the Russian prisoners made them hated by everyone. There were six of them; they were men broken and made morbid by suffering. Some of them were educated men; I will speak of them more fully afterwards. During my later years in prison I used sometimes to get books from them. The first book I read made a great, strange and peculiar impression upon me. I will speak of these impressions more particularly later; they were most interesting to me, and I am sure that to many people they would be utterly unintelligible. Some things one cannot judge without experience. One thing I can say, that moral privation is harder to bear than any physical agonies. When a peasant goes to prison he finds there the company of his equals, perhaps even of his superiors. He has lost a great deal, of course – home, family, everything, but his environment is the same. The educated man condemned to the same punishment often loses infinitely more. He must overcome all his cravings, all his habits, live under conditions that are insufficient for him; must learn to breathe a different air . . . He is a fish out of water . . . And often a punishment supposed to be equal in law is ten times as cruel for him. This is the truth, even if we consider only the material habits which have to be sacrificed.

But the Poles formed a group apart. There were six of them and they kept together. The only other person they liked in our room was a Jew, and him they liked perhaps simply because he amused them. He was liked indeed by the other convicts too, though every one without exception laughed at him. He was the only Jew among us, and I can't think of him even now without laughing. Every time I looked at him I could not help recalling Gogol's Jew Yankel in *Taras Bulba*, who when he undressed at night and prepared to get into the cupboard where he slept with his wife, looked exactly like a chicken. Isay Fomitch, our Jew, was the very image of a plucked chicken. He was a man about fifty, short and weakly built, cunning and at the same time decidedly stupid. He was impudent and conceited, and at the same time awfully cowardly. He was covered all over with wrinkles, and on his forehead and each cheek bore the marks of having been branded on the scaffold. I could never understand how he had survived sixty lashes. He had been sent here charged with murder. He had hidden away a receipt which his friends had procured from a doctor immediately after his punishment. It was the receipt for an ointment supposed to remove all traces of branding in a fortnight. He dare not make use of this ointment in the prison, and was awaiting the end of his twelve years' term of imprisonment, after which he fully intended to take advantage of the receipt when he could live as a settler. 'Else I shall never be able to get married,' he said to me once, 'and I certainly want to be married.' We were great friends; he was always in excellent spirits; he had not a bad time in prison. He was a jeweller by trade, always had more than enough work from the town, in which there was no jeweller, and so escaped hard labour. Of course he was a pawnbroker at the same time, and supplied the whole prison with money at a percentage and on security. He had come to the prison before me, and one of the Poles gave me a minute description of his arrival. It is a most amusing story which I will tell later on; I shall speak of Isay Fomitch more than once again.

Among the other prisoners in our room were four Old Believers, elderly men and great Bible readers, one of whom was the old fellow from the Starodubovsky settlement. Then there were two or three Little Russians, gloomy fellows; a young convict of three-and-twenty with a lean little face and a sharp little nose, who had already committed eight murders; a group of false coiners one of whom kept all the room amused; and finally several gloomy and sullen individuals, shaven and hideous, taciturn and envious, who looked with hatred about them and meant to look like that, to scowl, to be silent and full of hatred for long years to come, the whole term of their imprisonment. Of all this I had only a glimpse on that first desolate evening of my new life, a glimpse in the midst of smoke and filth, of oaths and indescribable obscenity, of foul air, of clanking fetters, of curses and shameless laughter. I lay down on the bare boards of the bed, and putting my clothes under my head

(I had not a pillow yet), covered myself with my sheepskin; but for a long while I could not get to sleep, though I was utterly worn out and shattered by all the monstrous, unexpected impressions of that first day. But my new life was only just beginning. There was much awaiting me in the future of which I had never dreamed, of which I had no foreboding.

CHAPTER FIVE

The First Month [1]

The first day after my arrival in prison I was ordered to go out to work. That first day of work is very distinct in my memory, though nothing very unusual happened to me in the course of it, except in so far as my position was in itself unusual. But it was still one of my first impressions, and I still looked eagerly at everything. I had spent those three days in the greatest depression. 'This is the end of my wanderings: I am in prison!' I was continually repeating to myself. 'This is to be my haven for many long years, my niche which I enter with such a mistrustful, such a painful sensation . . . And who knows? Maybe when I come to leave it many years hence I may regret it!' I added, not without an element of that malignant pleasure which at times is almost a craving to tear open one's wound on purpose, as though one desired to revel in one's pain, as though the consciousness of one's misery was an actual enjoyment. The idea of ever regretting this hole struck me with horror: I felt even then how monstrously a man may get used to things. But that was all in the future, and meantime everything about me was hostile and – terrible, for though not everything was really so, it seemed so to me. The savage curiosity with which my new comrades, the convicts, stared at me, the extra surliness of their behaviour towards the new member of their community, who had been a 'gentleman' – a surliness which sometimes reached the point of active hatred – all this so tortured me that I was eager to begin work, so as to find out and test all my sufferings as soon as possible, to begin living like all the rest, so as to get into the same rut with all the others without delay. Of course there was a great deal I did not notice then; I had no suspicion of things that were going on in front of me. I did not divine the presence of consolation in the midst of all that was hostile. Yet the few kind and friendly faces I had come across in the course of those three days helped to give me courage.

The kindest and friendliest of all was Akim Akimitch. And among the faces of other convicts that were sullen and full of hatred, I could not help noticing some kind and good-natured ones. 'There are bad people everywhere, and good ones among the bad,' I hastened to console myself by reflecting: 'and who knows? These people are perhaps by no means so much worse than the *remainder* who have *remained* outside the prison.' Even as I thought this, I shook my head at the idea, and yet, my God, if I had only known at the time how true that thought was!

Here, for instance, was a man whom I only came to understand fully in the course of many many years, and yet he was with me and continually near me almost all the time I was in prison. This was the convict Sushilov. As soon as I begin to speak of prisoners being no worse than other men, I involuntarily recall him. He used to wait on me. I had another attendant too. From the very beginning Akim Akimitch recommended me one of the convicts called Osip, telling me that for thirty kopecks a month he would cook my food for me every day, if I so disliked the prison fare, and had the money to get food for myself. Osip was one of the four cooks elected by the convicts for our two kitchens. They were, however, quite free to accept or refuse the appointment and could throw it up at any moment. The cooks did not go out to work, and their duties were confined to baking bread and preparing soup. They were not called 'povars' (*i.e.* male cooks) but 'stryapki' (*i.e.* female cooks), not as a sign of contempt for them – for sensible, and as far as might be, honest convicts were chosen for the kitchen – but just as an amiable pleasantry which our cooks did not resent in the slightest. Osip was, as a rule, elected, and for several years in succession he was almost always cook, and only threw up the job occasionally for a time, when he was overcome with violent melancholy and a craving for smuggling in vodka. He was a man of rare honesty and gentleness, though he was in prison for smuggling. He was the tall, sturdy smuggler I have mentioned already. He was afraid of everything, especially of a flogging, was friendly to everyone, very meek and mild. He never quarrelled, yet he had such a passion for smuggling that he could not resist bringing in vodka in spite of his cowardice. Like the other cooks he carried on a trade in vodka, though, of course, not on the same scale as Gazin, for instance, because he had not the courage to risk much. I always got on capitally with Osip. As for providing one's food, the cost was trifling. I am not far wrong if I say that I hardly spent more than a rouble a month on my board, always excluding bread, which was part of the prison fare, and occasionally soup, which I took if I were very hungry in spite of the disgust it inspired, though that, too, passed off almost completely in time. Usually I bought a pound of beef a day. And in winter a pound cost a halfpenny. One of the old veterans, of whom there was one in each room to keep order, used to go to the market to buy beef. These veterans voluntarily undertook to go to market every day to buy things for the prisoners and charged the merest trifle, next to nothing, for doing so. They did this for the sake of their own peace and comfort, for they could hardly have existed in the prison if they had refused. In this way they brought in tobacco, tea in bricks, beef, fancy bread and so on, everything in fact but vodka. They were not asked to bring in vodka, though they were sometimes regaled with it.

For years together Osip roasted me a piece of beef, always the same cut. But how it was roasted is another question, and indeed is not what mattered. It is a remarkable fact that for several years I hardly exchanged two words with Osip. Several times I tried to talk to him, but he was incapable of keeping up a conversation; he would smile or answer 'yes' or 'no,' and that was all. It was strange to see this Hercules who was like a child of seven.

Another convict who helped me was Sushilov. I did not ask for his services nor seek them. He found me out and placed himself at my disposal of his own accord; I don't remember when or how it happened. He did my washing. There was a large hole for emptying the water at the back of the prison, made on purpose. The washing troughs stood above this hole and the convicts' clothes were washed there. Sushilov invented a thousand different little duties to please me: he got my tea ready, ran all sorts of errands, took my jacket to be mended, greased my boots four times a month; all this he did eagerly, fussily, as though no one knew what duties he was overwhelmed with; in fact he completely threw in his lot with mine, and took all my business on himself. He would never say, for instance, 'You have so many shirts, your jacket is torn,' and so on, but always '*We* have so many shirts now, *our* jacket is torn.' He watched me to forestall every want, and seemed to make it the chief object of his life. He had no trade, and I think he earned nothing except from me. I paid him what I could, that is in halfpence, and he was always meekly satisfied. He could not help serving someone, and pitched upon me, I fancy, as being more considerate than others and more honest in paying. He was one of those men who could never grow rich and get on, and who undertook to act as sentry for card players, standing all night in the freezing cold passage, listening to every sound in the yard, on the alert for the major. They charged five farthings for spending almost the whole night in this way, while if they blundered they lost everything and had to pay for it with a beating. I have mentioned them already. It is the leading characteristic of such men to efface their personality always, everywhere, and before almost everyone, and to play not even a secondary, but a tertiary part in everything done in common. All this is innate in them.

Sushilov was a very pitiful fellow, utterly spiritless and humbled, hopelessly downtrodden, though no one used to ill-treat him, but he was downtrodden by nature. I always for some reason felt sorry for him. I could not look at him without feeling so, but why I was sorry for him I could not have said myself. I could not talk to him either; he, too, was no good at conversation, and it was evidently a great labour to him. He only recovered his spirits when I ended the conversation by giving him something to do, asking him to go somewhere or to run some errand. I was convinced at last that I was bestowing a pleasure upon him by doing so. He was neither tall nor short, neither good-looking nor ugly, neither stupid nor clever, somewhat pockmarked and rather light-haired. One could never say anything quite definite about him. Only one other point: he belonged, I believe, as far as I could guess, to the same section as Sirotkin and belonged to it simply through his submissiveness and spiritlessness. The convicts sometimes jeered at him, chiefly because he had *exchanged* on the way to Siberia, and had exchanged for the sake of a red shirt and a rouble. It was because of the smallness of the price for which he had sold himself that the convicts jeered at him. To exchange meant to change names, and consequently sentences, with some-one else. Strange as it seems, this was actually done, and in my day the practice flourished among convicts on the road to Siberia, was consecrated by tradition and defined by certain formalities. At first

I could not believe it, but I was convinced at last by seeing it with my own eyes.

This is how it is done. A party of convicts is being taken to Siberia. There are some of all sorts, going to penal servitude, to penal factories, or to a settlement; they travel together. Somewhere on the road, in the province of Perm for instance, some convict wants to exchange with another. Some Mihailov, for instance, a convict sentenced for murder or some other serious crime, feels the prospect of many years' penal servitude unattractive. Let us suppose he is a crafty fellow who has knocked about and knows what he is doing. So he tries to find someone of the same party who is rather simple, rather downtrodden and submissive, and whose sentence is comparatively light, exile to a settlement or to a few years in a penal factory, or even to penal servitude, but for a short period. At last he finds a Sushilov. Sushilov is a serf who is simply being sent out to a settlement. He has marched fifteen hundred miles without a farthing in his pocket – for Sushilov, of course, never could have a farthing – exhausted, weary, tasting nothing but the prison food, without even a chance morsel of anything good, wearing the prison clothes, and waiting upon everyone for a pitiful copper. Mihailov accosts Sushilov, gets to know him, even makes friends with him, and at last at some *étape* gives him vodka. Finally he suggests to him, would not he like to exchange? He says his name is Mihailov, and tells him this and that, says he is going to prison, that is, not to prison but to a 'special division'. Though it is prison it is 'special', therefore rather better. Lots of people, even in the government in Petersburg for instance, never heard of the 'special division' all the time it existed. It was a special, peculiar little class in one of the remote parts of Siberia, and there were so few in it, in my time not more than seventy, that it was not easy to get to hear of it. I met people afterwards who had served in Siberia and knew it well, who yet heard for the first time of the 'special division' from me. In the Legal Code there are six lines about it: 'There shall be instituted in such and such a prison a special division for the worst criminals until the opening of works involving harder labour in Siberia.' Even the convicts of this division did not know whether it was a permanent or a temporary institution. No time limit was mentioned, all that was said was 'until the opening of works involving harder labour', so it was meant for convicts who were in for life.

It is no wonder that Sushilov and the rest of his party knew nothing about it, even including Mihailov, who could only form an idea of the 'special division' from the gravity of his crime, for which he had already received three or four thousand blows. He might well conclude they were not sending him to anything very nice. Sushilov was on his way to a settlement; could anything be better? 'Wouldn't you like to exchange?' Sushilov, a simple-hearted soul, a little tipsy and overwhelmed with gratitude to Mihailov for being kind to him, does not venture to refuse. Besides, he has heard already from the others that exchanges are possible, that other people have exchanged, so that there is nothing exceptional or unheard of about it. They come to an agreement. The shameless Mihailov, taking advantage of Sushilov's extraordinary simplicity, buys his name for a red shirt and a silver rouble, which he gives him on the spot before witnesses. Next day Sushilov is no longer drunk; but he is given drink again; besides, it is a mean thing to go back on a bargain; the rouble he has taken has gone on drink, and the red shirt quickly follows it. If he won't keep his bargain he must give back the money. And where is Sushilov to get a whole silver rouble? And if he does not repay it the gang will make him; that's a point they are strict about. Besides, if he has made a promise he must keep it – the gang will insist on that too; or else they will devour him. They will beat him, perhaps, or simply kill him; in any case, they will threaten to.

Indeed, if the gang were once to be indulgent in such a matter, the practice of changing names would be at an end. If it were possible to go back on a promise and break a bargain after taking money, who would ever keep it afterwards? This, in fact, is a question that concerns the gang, concerns all, and therefore the gang is very stern about it. At last Sushilov sees that there is no begging off it and makes up his mind to agree without protest. It is announced to the whole gang; and other people are bribed with drink and money, if necessary. It is just the same to them, of course, whether Mihailov or Sushilov goes to the devil, but vodka has been drunk, they have been treated, so they hold their tongues. At the next *étape* the roll is called; when Mihailov's name is called, Sushilov answers 'here'; when Sushilov's is called, Mihailov shouts 'here' and they go on their way. Nothing more is said about it. At Tobolsk the convicts are sorted: Mihailov is sent to a settlement and Sushilov is conducted with extra guards to the 'special division'. Protest later is impossible; and after all, how could he prove it? How many years would an inquiry into such a case take? Might he not come in for something else? Where are his witnesses? If he had them they would deny it. So the upshot of it is that for a red shirt and a rouble Sushilov is sent to the 'special division'.

The convicts laughed at Sushilov not because he had exchanged (though they feel contempt for all who exchange a lighter sentence for a heavier one, as they do for all fools who have been duped) but because he had done it for a red shirt and a rouble – too trivial a price. Convicts usually receive large sums, relatively speaking, for exchanging. They sometimes charge dozens of roubles. But Sushilov was so submissive, such a nonentity, so paltry in the eyes of all that he was not even worth laughing at.

I got on very well with Sushilov for several years. By degrees he became extremely devoted to me. I could not help noticing it, so that I became quite attached to him too. But one day he did not do something I had asked him, though I had just given him some money and – I can never forgive myself for it – I had the cruelty to say to him, 'Well, Sushilov, you take the money but you don't do your work.' He said nothing, ran to do the job, but became suddenly depressed. Two days passed. I thought to myself, 'Surely it can't be on account of what I said?' I knew that one of the convicts called Anton Vassilyev was worrying him very persistently about a trifling debt. 'Probably he has no money and is afraid to ask me!' On the third day I said to him: 'Sushilov, I think you wanted to ask me for the money to pay Anton Vassilyev? Take it.' I was sitting on the bed at the time; Sushilov was standing before me. He seemed greatly impressed at my offering him the money, at my thinking of his difficult position of my own accord, especially as he had, in his own opinion, been paid too much by me of late, so that he had not dared to hope I would give him more. He looked at the money, then at me, suddenly turned away and went out. All this surprised me very much. I followed him and found him behind the prison. He was standing facing the fence with his head bent down and his elbow leaning on the fence.

'Sushilov, what is it?' I asked him. He did not look at me, and I noticed to my great amazement that he was on the point of tears.

'Alexandr Petrovitch, you think . . . ' he began in a breaking voice, trying to look away, 'that I . . . do for you . . . for money . . . but I . . . e – ech!'

Then he turned to the fence again, even striking his forehead against it – and broke into sobs! It was the first time I had seen a man crying in prison. With great effort I comforted him, and though after that he began to serve me and look after me more zealously than ever – if possible – yet from certain hardly perceptible signs I perceived that his heart could never forgive me that reproach; and yet other people laughed at him, nagged at him on every occasion, and sometimes abused him violently – and he was on amiable and even friendly terms with them, and never took offence. Yes, indeed, it is very hard to understand a man, even after long years!

That is why I could not see the prisoners at first as they really were, and as they seemed to me later. That is why I said that, though I looked at everything with eager and concentrated attention, I could not discern a great deal that was just before my eyes. It was natural that I was struck at first by the most remarkable and prominent facts, but even these I probably saw incorrectly, and all that was left by them was an oppressive, hopelessly melancholy sensation, which was greatly confirmed by my meeting with A., a convict who had reached the prison not long before me, and who made a particularly painful impression upon me during the first days I was in prison. I knew, however, before I reached the prison, that I should meet A. there. He poisoned that first terrible time for me and increased my mental sufferings. I cannot avoid speaking about him.

He was the most revolting example of the depths to which a man can sink and degenerate, and the extent to which he can destroy all moral feeling in himself without difficulty or repentance. A. was that young man of good family of whom I have mentioned already that he reported to the major everything that took place in the prison, and was friendly with his orderly Fedka. Here is a brief account of his story. After quarrelling with his Moscow relations, who were horrified by his vicious conduct, he arrived in Petersburg without finishing his studies, and to get money he gave information to the police in a very base way, that is, sold the lives of a dozen men for the immediate gratification of his insatiable lust for the coarsest and most depraved pleasures. Lured by the temptations of Petersburg and its taverns, he became so addicted to his vices that, though he was by no means a fool, he ventured on a mad and senseless enterprise: he was soon detected. In his information to the police he had implicated innocent people, and deceived others, and it was for this he was sent for ten years to Siberia to our prison. He was still quite young, life was only beginning for him. One would have thought such a terrible change in his fate must have made a great impression on his nature, would have called forth all his powers of resistance, and have caused a complete transformation in him. But he accepted his new life without the slightest perturbation, without the slightest aversion, indeed; he was not morally revolted by it, nor frightened by anything except the necessity of working, and the loss of the taverns and other attractions of Petersburg. It actually seemed to him that his position as a convict set him free to commit even more scoundrelly and revolting actions. 'If one is a convict, one may as well be one; if one is a convict, one may do nasty things and it's no shame to.' That was literally his opinion. I think of this disgusting creature as a phenomenon. I spent several years among murderers, profligates and thoroughgoing scoundrels, but I can positively say that I never in my life met such an utter moral downfall, such complete depravity and such insolent baseness as in A. There was amongst us a parricide, of good family; I have mentioned him already, but I became convinced from many traits and incidents that even he was incomparably nobler and more humane than A. All the while I was in prison A. seemed to me a lump of flesh with teeth and a stomach and an insatiable thirst for the most sensual and brutish pleasures. And to satisfy the most trifling and capricious of his desires he was capable of the most cold-blooded murder, in fact of anything, if only the crime could be concealed. I am not exaggerating; I got to know A. well. He was an example of what a man can come to when the physical side is unrestrained by any inner standard, any principle. And how revolting it was to me to look on his everlasting mocking smile! He was a monster; a moral Quasimodo. Add to that, that he was cunning and clever, good-looking, even rather well-educated and had abilities. Yes, such a man is a worse plague in society than fire, flood and famine! I have said already that there was such general depravity in prison that spying and treachery flourished, and the convicts were not angry at it. On the contrary they were all very friendly with A., and behaved far more amiably to him than to us. The favour in which he stood with our drunken major gave him importance and weight among them. Meanwhile he made the major believe that he could paint portraits (he had made the convicts believe that he had been a lieutenant in the Guards) and the major insisted on A.'s being sent to work in his house, to paint the major's portrait, of course. Here he made friends with the major's orderly, Fedka, who had an extraordinary influence over his master, and consequently over everything and everybody in the prison. A. played the spy amongst us to meet the major's requirements, and when the latter hit A. in the face in his fits of drunkenness he used to abuse him as being a spy and a traitor. It happened sometimes, pretty often in fact, that the major would sit down and command A. to go on with his portrait immediately after beating him. Our major seemed really to believe that A. was a remarkable artist, almost on a level with Brüllov, of whom even he had heard. At the same time he felt himself quite entitled to slap him in the face, feeling probably that, though he was a great artist, he was now a convict, and had he been ten times Brüllov the major was still his superior, and therefore could do what he liked with him. Among other things he made A. take off his boots for him and empty his slops, and yet for a long time he could not get over the idea that A. was a great artist. The portrait lingered on endlessly, almost for a year. At last the major realised that he was being duped, and becoming convinced that the portrait never would be finished, but on the contrary became less and less like him every day, he flew into a rage, gave the artist a thrashing and sent him to hard labour in the prison as a punishment. A. evidently regretted this, and felt bitterly the loss of his idle days, his titbits from the major's table, the company of his friend Fedka and all the enjoyments that Fedka and he contrived for themselves in the major's kitchen. At any rate after getting rid of A., the major gave up persecuting M., a convict whom A. was always slandering to the major.

At the time of A.'s arrival M. was the only 'political' in the prison. He was very miserable, had nothing in common with the other convicts, looked upon them with horror and loathing, failed to observe what might have reconciled him to them, and did not get on with them. They repaid him with the same hatred. The position of people like M. in prison is awful as a rule. M. knew nothing of the crime that had brought A. to prison. On the contrary, seeing the sort of man he had to do with, A. at once assured him that he was being punished for the very opposite of treachery, almost the same thing in fact as the charge for which M. was suffering. The latter was greatly delighted at having a comrade, a friend. He waited upon him, comforted him in the first days of prison, imagining that he must be in great distress, gave him his last penny, fed him, and shared the most necessary things with him. But A. conceived a hatred for him at once, just because he was a fine man, just because he looked with horror on anything mean, because he was utterly unlike himself; and all that M. told A. about the major and the prison A. hastened at the first opportunity to report to the major. The major took an intense dislike to M. in consequence and persecuted him. Had it not been for the governor of the prison, it would have ended in a tragedy. A. was not in the least disconcerted when M. found out later on how base he had been; on the contrary he liked meeting him and looked at him ironically. It evidently gave him gratification. M. himself pointed this out to me several times. This abject creature afterwards ran away from the prison, with another convict and a guard, but that escape I will describe later. At first he made up to me, thinking I had heard nothing of his story. I repeat, he poisoned my first days in prison and made them even more miserable. I was terrified at the awful baseness and degradation into which I had been cast and in the midst of which I found myself. I imagined that everything here was as base and as degraded. But I was mistaken, I judged of all by A.

I spent those three days wandering miserably about the prison and lying on the bed. I gave the stuff that was served out to me to a trustworthy convict recommended to me by Akim Akimitch, and asked him to make it into shirts, for payment, of course (a few halfpence a shirt). I provided myself at Akim Akimitch's urgent advice with a folding mattress made of felt encased in linen, but as thin as a pancake, and also got a pillow stuffed with wool, terribly hard till one was used to it. Akim Akimitch was quite in a bustle arranging all these things for me, and helped to get them himself.

With his own hands he made me a quilt out of rags of old cloth cut out of discarded jackets and trousers which I bought from other convicts. The prison clothes become the property of the prisoner when they are worn out; they are at once sold on the spot in the prison, and however ancient a garment might be, there was always a hope of getting something for it. I was much surprised at first by all this. It was practically my first contact with men of the peasant class. I had suddenly become a man of the same humble class, a convict like the rest. Their habits, ideas, opinions, customs became, as it were, also mine, externally, legally anyway, though I did not share them really. I was surprised and confused, as though I had heard nothing of all this and had not suspected its existence. Yet I had heard of it and knew of it. But the reality makes quite a different impression from what one hears and knows. I could, for instance, never have suspected that such things, such old rags could be looked upon as objects of value. Yet it was of these rags I made myself a quilt! It was hard to imagine such cloth as was served out for the convict's clothing. It looked like thick cloth such as is used in the army, but after very little wearing it became like a sieve and tore shockingly. Cloth garments were, however, only expected to last a year. Yet it was hard to make them do service for so long. The convict has to work, to carry heavy weights; his clothes quickly wear out and go into holes. The sheepskin coats are supposed to last three years, and they were used for that time as coats by day and both underblanket and covering at night. But a sheepskin coat is strong, though it was not unusual to see a convict at the end of the third year in a sheepskin patched with plain hempen cloth. Yet even very shabby ones were sold for as much as forty kopecks at the end of the three years. Some in better preservation even fetched as much as sixty or seventy, and that was a large sum in prison.

Money, as I have mentioned already, was of vast and overwhelming importance in prison. One may say for a positive fact that the sufferings of a convict who had money, however little, were not a tenth of what were endured by one who had none, though the latter, too, had everything provided by government, and so, as the prison authorities argue, could have no need of money. I repeat again, if the prisoners had been deprived of all possibility of having money of their own, they would either have gone out of their minds, or have died off like flies (in spite of being provided with everything), or would have resorted to incredible violence – some from misery, others in order to be put to death and end it all as soon as possible, or anyway 'to change their luck' (the technical expression). If after earning his money with cruel effort, or making use of extraordinary cunning, often in conjunction with theft and cheating, the convict wastes what he has earned so carelessly, with such childish senselessness, it does not prove that he does not appreciate it, though it might seem so at the first glance. The convict is morbidly, insanely greedy of money, and if he throws it away like so much rubbish, he throws it away on what he considers of even more value. What is more precious than money for the convict? Freedom or some sort of dream of freedom. The prisoner is a great dreamer. I shall have something to say of this later, but, while we are on the subject, would it be believed that I have known convicts sentenced for *twenty* years who, speaking to me, have quite calmly used such phrases as 'you wait a bit; when, please God, my term is up, then I'll . . . ' The word convict means nothing else but a man with no will of his own, and in spending money he is showing a will of his own. In spite of brands, fetters and the hateful prison fence which shuts him off from God's world and cages him in like a wild beast, he is able to obtain vodka, an article prohibited under terrible penalties, to get at women, even sometimes (though not always) to bribe the veterans and even the sergeants, who will wink at his breaches of law and discipline. He can play the swaggering bully over them into the bargain, and the convict is awfully fond of bullying, that is, pretending to his companions and even persuading himself, *if only for a time*, that he has infinitely more power and freedom than is supposed. He can in fact carouse and make an uproar, crush and insult others and prove to them that he *can* do all this, that it is all in his own hands, that is, he can persuade himself of what is utterly out of the question for the poor fellow. That, by the way, is perhaps why one detects in all convicts, even when sober, a propensity to swagger, to boastfulness, to a comic and very naïve though fantastic glorification of their personality. Moreover all this disorderliness has its special risk, so it all has a semblance of life, and at least a far-off semblance of freedom. And what will one not give for freedom? What millionaire would not give all his millions for one breath of air if his neck were in the noose?

The prison authorities are sometimes surprised that after leading a quiet, exemplary life for some years, and even being made a foreman for his model behaviour, a convict with no apparent reason suddenly breaks out, as though he were possessed by a devil, plays pranks, drinks, makes an uproar and sometimes positively ventures on serious crimes – such as open disrespect to a superior officer, or even commits murder or rape. They look at him and marvel. And all the while possibly the cause of this sudden outbreak, in the man from whom one would least have expected it, is simply the poignant hysterical craving for self-expression, the unconscious yearning for himself, the desire to assert himself, to assert his crushed personality, a desire which suddenly takes possession of him and reaches the pitch of fury, of spite, of mental aberration, of fits and nervous convulsions. So perhaps a man buried alive and awakening in his coffin might beat upon its lid and struggle to fling it off, though of course reason might convince him that all his efforts would be useless; but the trouble is that it is not a question of reason, it is a question of nerves. We must take into consideration also that almost every expression of personality on the part of a convict is looked upon as a crime, and so it makes no difference whether it is a small offence or a great one. If he is to drink he may as well do it thoroughly, if he is to venture on anything he may as well venture on everything, even on a murder. And the only effort is to begin: as he goes on, the man gets intoxicated and there is no holding him back. And so it would be better in every way not to drive him to that point. It would make things easier for everyone.

Yes; but how is it to be done?

CHAPTER SIX

The First Month [2]

I had little money when I entered the prison; I carried only very little on me for fear it should be taken away, but as a last resource I had several roubles hidden in the binding of a New Testament, a book which one is allowed to have in prison. This book, together with the money hidden in the binding, was given me in Tobolsk by men who were exiles too, who could reckon their years of banishment by decades, and had long been accustomed to look at every 'unfortunate' as a brother. There are in Siberia, and practically always have been, some people who seem to make it the object of their lives to look after the 'unfortunate', to show pure and disinterested sympathy and compassion for them, as though they were their own children. I must briefly mention here one encounter I had.

In the town where our prison was there lived a lady, a widow called Nastasya Ivanoyna. Of course none of us could make her acquaintance while we were in prison. She seemed to devote her life to the relief of convicts, but was especially active in helping us. Whether it was that she had had some similar trouble in her family, or that someone particularly near and dear to her had suffered for a similar* offence, anyway she seemed to consider it a particular happiness to do all that she could for us. She could not do much, of course; she was poor. But we in prison felt that out there, beyond the prison walls, we had a devoted friend. She often sent us news, of which we were in great need. When I left prison and was on my way to another town, I went to see her and made her acquaintance. She lived on the outskirts of the town in the house of a near relation. She was neither old nor young, neither good-looking nor plain; it was impossible to tell even whether she were intelligent or educated. All that one could see in her was an infinite kindliness,

* i.e. political – *Translator's note.*

an irresistible desire to please one, to comfort one, to do something nice for one. All that could be read in her kind gentle eyes. Together with a comrade who had been in prison with me I spent almost a whole evening in her company. She was eager to anticipate our wishes, laughed when we laughed, was in haste to agree with anything we said and was all anxiety to regale us with all she had to offer. Tea was served with savouries and sweetmeats, and it seemed that if she had had thousands she would have been delighted, simply because she could do more for us and for our comrades in prison. When we said goodbye she brought out a cigarette-case as a keepsake for each of us. She had made these cigarette-cases of cardboard for us (and how they were put together!) and had covered them with coloured paper such as is used for covering arithmetic books for children in schools (and possibly some such school book had been sacrificed for the covering). Both the cigarette-cases were adorned with an edging of gilt paper, which she had bought, perhaps, expressly for them. 'I see you smoke cigarettes, so perhaps it may be of use to you,' she said, as it were apologising timidly for her present . . . Some people maintain (I have heard it and read it) that the purest love for one's neighbour is at the same time the greatest egoism. What egoism there could be in this case, I can't understand.

Though I had not much money when I came into prison, I could not be seriously vexed with those of the convicts who, in my very first hours in prison, after deceiving me once, came a second, a third, and even a fifth time to borrow from me. But I will candidly confess one thing: it did annoy me that all these people with their naïve cunning must, as I thought, be laughing at me and thinking of me as a simpleton and a fool just because I gave them money the fifth time of asking. They must have thought that I was taken in by their wiles and cunning, while, if I had refused them and driven them away, I am convinced they would have respected me a great deal more. But annoying as it was, I could not refuse. I was annoyed because I was seriously and anxiously considering during those first days what sort of position I could make for myself in the prison, or rather on what sort of footing I ought to be with them. I felt and thoroughly realised that the surroundings were completely new to me, that I was quite in the dark and could not go on living so for several years. I had to prepare myself. I made up my mind, of course, that above all I must act straightforwardly, in accordance with my inner feelings and conscience. But I knew, too, that that was a mere aphorism, and that the most unexpected difficulties lay before me in practice.

And so, in spite of all the petty details of settling into the prison which I have mentioned already, and into which I was led chiefly by Akim Akimitch, and, although they served as some distraction, I was more and more tormented by a terrible devouring melancholy. 'A dead house,' I thought to myself sometimes, standing on the steps of the prison at twilight and looking at the convicts who had come back from work, and were idly loafing about the prison yard and moving from the prison to the kitchen and back again. I looked intently at them and tried to conjecture from their faces and movements what sort of men they were, and what were their characters. They sauntered about before me with scowling brows or over-jubilant faces (these two extremes are most frequently met with, and are almost typical of prison life), swearing or simply talking together, or walking alone with quiet even steps, seemingly lost in thought, some with a weary, apathetic air, others (even here!) with a look of conceited superiority, with caps on one side, their coats flung over their shoulders, with a sly insolent stare and an impudent jeer. 'This is my sphere, my world, now,' I thought, 'with which I must live now whether I will or not.' I tried to find out about them by questioning Akim Akimitch, with whom I liked to have tea, so as not to be alone. By the way, tea was almost all I could take at first. Tea Akim Akimitch did not decline, and used himself to prepare our absurd, home-made little tin samovar, which was lent me by M. Akim Akimitch usually drank one glass (he had glasses, too), drank it silently and sedately, returning it to me, thanked me and at once began working at my quilt. But what I wanted to find out he could not tell me. He could not in fact understand why I was interested in the characters of the convicts surrounding us, and listened to me with a sort of sly smile which I very well remember. Yes, evidently I must find out by experience and not ask questions, I thought.

On the fourth day, early in the morning, all the convicts were drawn up in two rows at the prison gates before the guard-house, just as they had been that time when I was being refettered. Soldiers with loaded rifles and fixed bayonets stood opposite them, in front and behind. A soldier has the right to fire at a convict if the latter attempts to escape; at the same time he would have to answer for firing except in extreme necessity; the same rule applies in case of open mutiny among the convicts. But who would dream of attempting to escape openly? An officer of engineers, a foreman and also the non-commissioned officers and soldiers who superintend the works were present. The roll was called; those of the convicts who worked in the tailoring room set off first of all; the engineering officers had nothing to do with them; they worked only for the prison and made all the prison clothes. Then the contingent for the workshops started, followed by those who did unskilled work, of whom there were about twenty. I set off with them.

On the frozen river behind the fortress were two government barges which were of no more use and had to be pulled to pieces, so that the timber might not be wasted, though I fancy all the old material was worth very little, practically nothing. Firewood was sold for next to nothing in the town, and there were forests all round. They put us on this job chiefly to keep us occupied, and the convicts themselves quite understood that. They always worked listlessly and apathetically at such tasks, and it was quite different when the work was valuable in itself and worth doing, especially when they could succeed in getting a fixed task. Then they seemed, as it were, inspirited, and although they got no advantage from it, I have seen them exert themselves to the utmost to finish the work as quickly and as well as possible; their vanity indeed was somehow involved in it. But with work such as we had that day, done more as a matter of form than because it was needed, it was difficult to obtain a fixed task and we had to work till the drum sounded the recall home at eleven o'clock in the morning.

The day was warm and misty; the snow was almost thawing. All our group set off to the river-bank beyond the fortress with a faint jingling of chains, which gave a thin, sharp metallic clank at every step, though they were hidden under our clothes. Two or three men went into the house where the tools were kept to get the implements we needed. I walked with the rest and felt a little more cheerful: I was in haste to see and find out what sort of work it was. What was this hard labour? And how should I work for the first time in my life?

I remember it all to the smallest detail. On the road we met a workman of some sort with a beard; he stopped and put his hand in his pocket. A convict immediately came forward out of our group, took off his cap, took the alms – five kopecks – and quickly rejoined the others. The workman crossed himself and went on his way. The five kopecks were spent that morning on rolls, which were divided equally among the party.

Some of our gang were, as usual, sullen and taciturn, others indifferent and listless, others chattered idly together. One was for some reason extraordinarily pleased and happy, he sang and almost danced on the way, jingling his fetters at every caper. It was the same short, thick-set convict who on my first morning in prison had quarrelled with another while they were washing because the latter had foolishly ventured to declare that he was a 'cocky-locky.' This merry fellow was called Skuratov. At last he began singing a jaunty song of which I remember the refrain.

> I was away when they married me
> I was away at the mill.

All that was lacking was a balalaika.

His extraordinary cheerfulness, of course, at once aroused indignation in some of our party; it was almost taken as an insult.

'He is setting up a howl!' a convict said reproachfully, though it was no concern of his.

'The wolf has only one note and that you've cribbed, you Tula fellow!' observed another of the gloomy ones, with a Little Russian accent.

'I may be a Tula man,' Skuratov retorted promptly, 'but you choke yourselves with dumplings in Poltava.'

'Lie away! What do you eat? Used to ladle out cabbage soup with a shoe.'

'And now it might be the devil feeding us with cannon balls,' added a third.

'I know I am a pampered fellow, mates,' Skuratov answered with a faint sigh, as though regretting he had been pampered and addressing himself to all in general and to no one in particular, 'from my earliest childhood bred up – (that is, brought up, he intentionally distorted his words) – on prunes and fancy bread; my brothers have a shop of their own in Moscow to this day, they sell fiddlesticks in No Man's street, very rich shopkeepers they are.'

'And did you keep shop too?'

'I, too, carried on in various qualities. It was then, mates, I got my first two hundred . . . '

'You don't mean roubles?' broke in one inquisitive listener, positively starting at the mention of so much money.

'No, my dear soul, not roubles – sticks. Luka, hey, Luka!'

'To some I am Luka but to you I am Luka Kuzmitch,' a thin little sharp-nosed convict answered reluctantly.

'Well, Luka Kuzmitch then, hang you, so be it.'

'To some people I am Luka Kuzmitch, but you should call me uncle.'

'Well, hang you then, uncle, you are not worth talking to! But there was a good thing I wanted to say. That's how it happened, mates, I did not make much in Moscow; they gave me fifteen lashes as a parting present and sent me packing. So then I . . . '

'But why were you sent packing?' enquired one who had been carefully following the speaker.

'Why, it's against the rules to go into quarantine and to drink tin-tacks and to play the jingle-jangle. So I hadn't time to get rich in Moscow, mates, not worth talking about. And I did so, so, so want to get rich. I'd a yearning I cannot describe.'

Many of his listeners laughed. Skuratov was evidently one of those volunteer entertainers, or rather buffoons, who seemed to make it their duty to amuse their gloomy companions, and who got nothing but abuse for their trouble. He belonged to a peculiar and noteworthy type, of which I may have more to say hereafter.

'Why, you might be hunted like sable now,' observed Luka Kuzmitch. 'Your clothes alone would be worth a hundred roubles.'

Skuratov had on the most ancient threadbare sheepskin, on which patches were conspicuous everywhere. He looked it up and down attentively, though unconcernedly.

'It's my head that's priceless, mates, my brain,' he answered. 'When I said goodbye to Moscow it was my one comfort that I took my head with me. Farewell, Moscow, thanks for your bastings, thanks for your warmings, you gave me some fine dressings! And my sheepskin is not worth looking at, my good soul . . . '

'I suppose your head is, then?'

'Even his head is not his own but a charity gift,' Luka put in again. 'It was given him at Tyumen for Christ's sake, as he marched by with a gang.'

'I say, Skuratov, had you any trade?'

'Trade, indeed! he used to lead puppydogs about and steal their tit-bits, that was all his trade,' observed one of the gloomy convicts.

'I really did try my hand at cobbling boots,' answered Skuratov, not observing this biting criticism. 'I only cobbled one pair.'

'Well, were they bought?'

'Yes, a fellow did turn up; I suppose he had not feared God or honoured his father and mother, and so the Lord punished him and he bought them.'

All Skuratov's audience went off into peals of laughter.

'And I did once work here,' Skuratov went on with extreme nonchalance. 'I put new uppers on to Lieutenant Pomortzev's boots.'

'Well, was he satisfied?'

'No, mates, he wasn't. He gave me oaths enough to last me a lifetime, and a dig in the back with his knee too. He was in an awful taking. Ah, my life has deceived me, the jade's deceived me!'

> And not many minutes later
> Akulina's husband came . . .

he unexpectedly carolled again, and began pattering a dance step with his feet.

'Ech, the graceless fellow,' the Little Russian who was walking beside me observed with a side glance of spiteful contempt at Skuratov.

'A useless fellow,' observed another in a serious and final tone.

I could not understand why they were angry with Skuratov, and why, indeed, all the merry ones seemed to be held in some contempt, as I had noticed already during those first days. I put down the anger of the Little Russian and of the others to personal causes. But it was not a case of personal dislike; they were angry at the absence of reserve in Skuratov, at the lack of the stern assumption of personal dignity about which all the prisoners were pedantically particular; in fact, at his being a 'useless fellow', to use their own expression. Yet they were not angry with all the merry ones, and did not treat all as they did Skuratov and those like him. It depended on what people would put up with: a good-natured and unpretentious man was at once exposed to insult. I was struck by this fact indeed. But there were some among the cheerful spirits who knew how to take their own part and liked doing so, and they exacted respect. In this very group there was one of these prickly characters; he was a tall good-looking fellow with a large wart on his cheek and a very comic expression, though his face was rather handsome and intelligent. He was in reality a light-hearted and very charming fellow, though I only found out that side of him later on. They used to call him 'the pioneer' because at one time he had served in the Pioneers; now he was in the 'special division'. I shall have a great deal to say of him later.

Not all of the 'serious-minded', however, were so outspoken as the indignant Little Russian. There were some men in the prison who aimed at superiority, at knowing all sorts of things, at showing resourcefulness, character and intelligence. Many of these really were men of intelligence and character, and did actually attain what they aimed at, that is, a leading position and a considerable moral influence over their companions. These clever fellows were often at daggers drawn with one another, and every one of them had many enemies. They looked down upon other convicts with dignity and condescension, they picked no unnecessary quarrels, were in favour with the authorities, and took the lead at work. Not one of them would have found fault with anyone for a song, for instance; they would not have stooped to such trifles. These men were very polite to me all the time I was in prison, but they were not very talkative, also apparently from a sense of dignity. I shall have to speak more in detail of them also.

We reached the river-bank. The old barge which we had to break up was frozen into the ice below us. On the further side of the river the steppes stretched blue into the distance; it was a gloomy and desert view. I expected that everyone would rush at the work, but they had no idea of doing so. Some sat down on the logs that lay about on the bank; almost all of them brought out of their boots bags of local tobacco which was sold at three farthings a pound in the market, and short willow pipes of home manufacture. They lighted their pipes; the soldiers formed a cordon round us and proceeded to guard us with a bored expression.

'Whose notion was it to break up this barge?' one observed as it were to himself, not addressing anyone. 'Are they in want of chips?'

'He wasn't afraid of our anger, whoever it was,' observed another.

'Where are those peasants trudging to?' the first asked after a pause, not noticing of course the answer to his first question, and pointing to a group of peasants who were making their way in Indian file over untrodden snow in the distance. Everyone turned lazily in that direction and to while away the time began mocking at them. One of the peasants, the last of the file, walked very absurdly, stretching out his arms and swinging his head on one side with a long peasant's cap on it. His whole figure stood out clearly and distinctly against the white snow.

'Look how brother Peter has rigged himself out!' observed one, mimicking the peasant accent.

It is remarkable that the convicts rather looked down on peasants, though half of them were of the peasant class.

'The last one, mates, walks as though he was sowing radishes.'

'He is a slow-witted fellow, he has a lot of money,' observed a third.

They all laughed, but lazily too, as it were reluctantly. Meantime a baker woman had come, a brisk lively woman.

They bought rolls of her for the five kopecks that had been given us and divided them in equal shares on the spot.

The young man who sold rolls in prison took two dozen and began a lively altercation, trying to get her to give him three rolls instead of the usual two as his commission. But the baker woman would not consent.

'Well, and won't you give me something else?'

'What else?'

'What the mice don't eat.'

'A plague take you,' shrieked the woman and laughed.

At last the sergeant who superintended the work came up with a stick in his hand.

'Hey, there, what are you sitting there for? Get to work!'

'Set us a task, Ivan Matveitch,' said one of the 'leaders' slowly getting up from his place.

'Why didn't you ask for it at the start? Break up the barge, that's your task.'

At last they got up desultorily and slouched to the river. Some of them immediately took up the part of foreman, in words, anyway. It appeared that the barge was not to be broken up anyhow, but the timber was to be kept as whole as possible, especially the crossway beams which were fixed to the bottom of the barge by wooden bolts along their whole length.

'We ought first of all to get out this beam. Set to this, lads,' observed one of the convicts who had not spoken before, a quiet and unassuming fellow, not one of the leading or ruling spirits; and stooping down he got hold of a thick beam, waiting for the others to help him. But nobody did help him.

'Get it up, no fear! You won't get it up and if your grandfather the bear came along, he wouldn't,' muttered someone between his teeth.

'Well then, brothers, how are we to begin? I don't know . . . ' said the puzzled man who had put himself forward, letting go the beam and getting on to his feet again.

'Work your hardest you'll never be done . . . why put yourself forward?'

'He could not feed three hens without making a mistake, and now he is to be first . . . The fidget!'

'I didn't mean anything, mates . . . ' the disconcerted youth tried to explain.

'Do you want me to keep covers over you all? Or to keep you in pickle through the winter?' shouted the sergeant again, looking in perplexity at the crowd of twenty convicts who stood not knowing how to set to work. 'Begin! Make haste!'

'You can't do things quicker than you can, Ivan Matveitch.'

'Why, but you are doing nothing! Hey, Savelyev! Talky Petrovitch ought to be your name! I ask you, why are you standing there, rolling your eyes? Set to work.'

'But what can I do alone?'

'Set us a task, Ivan Matveitch.'

'You've been told you won't have a task. Break up the barge and go home. Get to work!'

They did set to work at last, but listlessly, unwillingly, incompetently. It was quite provoking to see a sturdy crowd of stalwart workmen who seemed utterly at a loss how to set to work. As soon as they began to take out the first and smallest beam, it appeared that it was breaking, 'breaking of itself', as was reported to the overseer by way of apology; so it seemed they could not begin that way but must try somehow else. There followed a lengthy discussion among the convicts what other way to try, what was to be done? By degrees it came, of course, to abuse and threatened to go further . . . The sergeant shouted again and waved his stick, but the beam broke again. It appeared finally that axes were not enough, and other tools were needed. Two fellows were dispatched with a convoy to the fortress to fetch them, and meantime the others very serenely sat down on the barge, pulled out their pipes and began smoking again.

The sergeant gave it up as a bad job at last.

'Well, you'll never make work look silly! Ach, what a set, what a set!' he muttered angrily, and with a wave of his hand he set off for the fortress, swinging his stick.

An hour later the foreman came. After listening calmly to the convicts he announced that the task he set them was to get out four more beams without breaking them, and in addition he marked out a considerable portion of the barge to be taken to pieces, telling them that when it was done they could go home. The task was a large one, but, heavens! how they set to! There was no trace of laziness, no trace of incompetence. The axes rang; they began unscrewing the wooden bolts. Others thrust thick posts underneath and, pressing on them with twenty hands, levered up the beams, which to my astonishment came up now whole and uninjured. The work went like wildfire. Everyone seemed wonderfully intelligent all of a sudden. There was not a word wasted, not an oath was heard, everyone seemed to know what to say, what to do, where to stand, what advice to give. Just half an hour before the drum beat, the last of the task was finished, and the convicts went home tired but quite contented, though they had only saved half an hour of their working day. But as far as I was concerned I noticed one thing: wherever I turned to help them during the work, everywhere I was superfluous, everywhere I was in the way, everywhere I was pushed aside almost with abuse.

The lowest ragamuffin, himself a wretched workman, who did not dare to raise his voice among the other convicts who were sharper and cleverer than he, thought himself entitled to shout at me on the pretext that I hindered him if I stood beside him. At last one of the smarter ones said to me plainly and coarsely:

'Where are you shoving? Get away! Why do you poke yourself where you are not wanted?'

'Your game's up!' another chimed in at once.

'You'd better take a jug and go round asking for halfpence to build a fine house and waste upon snuff, but there's nothing for you to do here.'

I had to stand apart, and to stand apart when all are working makes one feel ashamed. But when it happened that I did walk away and stood at the end of the barge they shouted at once: 'Fine workmen they've given us; what can one get done with them? You can get nothing done.'

All this, of course, was done on purpose, for it amused everyone. They must have a gibe at one who has been a 'fine gentleman', and, of course, they were glad to have the chance.

It may well be understood now why, as I have said already, my first question on entering the prison was how I should behave, what attitude I should take up before these people. I had a foreboding that I should often come into collision with them like this. But in spite of all difficulties I made up my mind not to change my plan of action which I had partly thought out during those days; I knew it was right. I had made up my mind to behave as simply and independently as possible, not to make any special effort to get on intimate terms with them, but not to repel them if they desired to be friendly themselves; not to be afraid of their menaces and their hatred, and as far as possible to affect not to notice, not to approach them on certain points and not to encourage some of their habits and customs – not to seek in fact to be regarded quite as a comrade by them. I guessed at the first glance that they would be the first to despise me if I did. According to their ideas, however (I learned this for certain later on), I ought even to keep up and respect my class superiority before them, that is, to study my comfort, to give myself airs, to scorn them, to turn up my nose at everything; to play the fine gentleman in fact. That was what they understood by being a gentleman. They would, of course, have abused me for doing so, but yet they would privately have respected me for it. To play such a part was not in my line; I was never a gentleman according to their notions; but, on the other hand, I vowed to make no concession derogatory to my education and my way of thinking. If I had begun to try and win their goodwill by making up to them, agreeing with them, being familiar with them and had gone in for their various 'qualities', they would have at once supposed that I did it out of fear and cowardice and would have treated me with contempt. A. was not a fair example: he used to visit the major and they were afraid of him themselves. On the other side, I did not want to shut myself off from them by cold and unapproachable politeness, as the Poles did. I saw clearly that they despised me now for wanting to work with them, without seeking my own ease or giving myself airs of superiority over them. And although I felt sure that they would have to change their opinion of me later, yet the thought that they had, as it were, the right to despise me, because they imagined I was trying to make up to them at work – this thought was very bitter to me.

When I returned to the prison in the evening after the day's work, worn out and exhausted, I was again overcome by terrible misery. 'How many thousands of such days lie before me,' I thought, 'all the same, all exactly alike!' As it grew dusk I sauntered up and down behind the prison by the fence, silent and alone, and suddenly I saw our Sharik running towards me. Sharik was the dog that belonged to our prison, just as there are dogs belonging to companies, batteries and squadrons. He had lived from time immemorial in the prison, he belonged to no one in particular, considering everyone his master, and he lived on scraps from the kitchen. He was a rather large mongrel, black with white spots, not very old, with intelligent eyes and a bushy tail. No one ever stroked him, no one took any notice of him. From the first day I stroked him and fed him with bread out of my hands. While I stroked him, he stood quietly, looking affectionately at me and gently wagging his tail as a sign of pleasure. Now after not seeing me for so long – me, the only person who had for years thought of caressing him – he ran about looking for me amongst all of them, and finding me behind the prison, ran to meet me, whining with delight. I don't know what came over me but I fell to kissing him, I put my arms round his head; he put his forepaws on my shoulders and began licking my face. 'So this is the friend fate has sent me,' I thought, and every time I came back from work during that first hard and gloomy period, first of all, before I went anywhere else, I hurried behind the prison with Sharik leaping before me and whining with joy, held his head in my arms and kissed him again and again, and a sweet and at the same time poignantly bitter feeling wrung my heart. And I remember it was positively pleasant to me to think, as though priding myself on my suffering, that there was only one creature in the world who loved me, who was devoted to me, who was my friend, my one friend – my faithful dog Sharik.

CHAPTER SEVEN

New Acquaintances. Petrov

But time passed and little by little I got used to it. Every day I was less and less bewildered by the daily events of my new life. My eyes grew, as it were, accustomed to incidents, surroundings, men. To be reconciled to this life was impossible, but it was high time to accept it as an accomplished fact. Any perplexities that still remained in my mind I concealed within myself as completely as possible. I no longer wandered about the prison like one distraught, and no longer showed my misery. The savagely inquisitive eyes of the convicts were not so often fixed on me, they did not watch me with such an assumption of insolence. They had grown used to me too, apparently, and I was very glad of it. I walked about prison as though I were at home, knew my place on the common bed and seemed to have grown used to things which I should have thought I could never in my life have grown used to.

Regularly once a week I went to have half my head shaved. Every Saturday in our free time we were called out in turn from the prison to the guard-house (if we did not go we had to get shaved on our own account) and there the barbers of the battalion rubbed our heads with cold lather and mercilessly scraped them with blunt razors; it makes me shiver even now when I recall that torture. But the remedy was soon found: Akim Akimitch pointed out to me a convict in the military division who for a kopeck would shave with his own razor anyone who liked. That was his trade. Many of the convicts went to him to escape the prison barbers, though they were by no means a sensitive lot. Our convict barber was called *the major*, why I don't know, and in what way he suggested the major I can't say. As I write I recall this major, a tall, lean, taciturn fellow, rather stupid, always absorbed in his occupation, never without a strop on which he was day and night sharpening his incredibly worn out razor. He was apparently concentrated on this pursuit, which he evidently looked upon as his vocation in life. He was really extremely happy when the razor was in good condition and someone came to be shaved; his lather was warm, his hand was light, the shaving was like velvet. He evidently enjoyed his art and was proud of it, and he carelessly took the kopeck he had earned as though he did the work for art's sake and not for profit.

A. caught it on one occasion from our major when, telling him tales about the prisoners, he incautiously spoke of our barber as *the major*. The real major flew into a rage and was extremely offended. 'Do you know, you rascal, what is meant by a major?' he shouted, foaming at the mouth, and falling upon A. in his usual fashion. 'Do you understand what is meant by a major? And here you dare to call a scoundrelly convict major before me, in my presence!' No one but A. could have got on with such a man.

From the very first day of my life in prison, I began to dream of freedom. To calculate in a thousand different ways when my days in prison would be over became my favourite occupation. It was always in my mind, and I am sure that it is the same with everyone who is deprived of freedom for a fixed period. I don't know whether the other convicts thought and calculated as I did, but the amazing audacity of their hopes impressed me from the beginning. The hopes of a prisoner deprived of freedom are utterly different from those of a man living a natural life. A free man hopes, of course (for a change of luck, for instance, or the success of an undertaking), but he lives, he acts, he is caught up in the world of life. It is very different with the prisoner. There is life for him too, granted – prison life – but whatever the convict may be and whatever may be the term of his sentence, he is instinctively unable to accept his lot as something positive, final, as part of real life. Every convict feels that he is, so to speak, *not at home,* but on a visit. He looks at twenty years as though they were two, and is fully convinced that when he leaves prison at fifty-five he will be as full of life and energy as he is now at thirty-five. 'I've still life before me,' he thinks, and resolutely drives away all doubts and other vexatious ideas. Even those in the 'special division' who had been sentenced for life sometimes reckoned on orders suddenly coming from Petersburg: 'to send them to the mines at Nerchinsk and to limit their sentence'.

Then it would be all right: to begin with, it is almost six months' journey to Nerchinsk, and how much pleasanter the journey would be than being in prison! And afterwards the term in Nerchinsk would be over and then . . . And sometimes even grey-headed men reckoned like this.

At Tobolsk I have seen convicts chained to the wall. The man is kept on a chain seven feet long; he has a bedstead by him. He is chained like this for some exceptionally terrible crime committed in Siberia. They are kept like that for five years, for ten years. They are generally brigands. I only saw one among them who looked as if he had belonged to the upper classes; he had been in the government service somewhere. He spoke submissively with a lisp; his smile was mawkishly sweet. He showed us his chain, showed how he could most comfortably lie on the bed. He must have been a choice specimen! As a rule they all behave quietly and seem contented, yet every one of them is intensely anxious for the end of his sentence. Why, one wonders? I will tell you why: he will get out of the stifling dank room with its low vaulted roof of brick, and will walk in the prison yard . . . and that is all. He will never be allowed out of the prison. He knows those who have been in chains are always kept in prison and fettered to the day of their death. He knows that and yet he is desperately eager for the end of his time on the chain. But for that longing how could he remain five or six years on the chain without dying or going out of his mind? Some of them would not endure it at all.

I felt that work might be the saving of me, might strengthen my physical frame and my health. Continual mental anxiety, nervous irritation, the foul air of the prison might well be my destruction. Being constantly in the open air, working every day till I was tired, learning to carry heavy weights – at any rate I shall save myself, I thought, I shall make myself strong, I shall leave the prison healthy, vigorous, hearty and not old. I was not mistaken: the work and exercise were very good for me. I looked with horror at one of my companions, a man of my own class: he was wasting like a candle in prison. He entered it at the same time as I did, young, handsome and vigorous, and he left it half-shattered, grey-headed, gasping for breath and unable to walk. No, I thought, looking at him; I want to live and will live. But at first I got into hot water among the convicts for my fondness for work, and for a long time they assailed me with gibes and contempt. But I took no notice of anyone and set off cheerfully, for instance, to the baking and pounding of alabaster – one of the first things I learnt to do. That was easy work.

The officials who supervised our work were ready, as far as possible, to be lenient in allotting work to prisoners belonging to the upper classes, which was by no means an undue indulgence but simple justice. It would be strange to expect from a man of half the strength and no experience of manual labour the same amount of work as the ordinary workman had by regulation to get through. But this 'indulgence' was not always shown, and it was as it were surreptitious; a strict watch was kept from outside to check it. Very often we had to go to heavy work, and then, of course, it was twice as hard for the upper-class convicts as for the rest.

Three or four men were usually sent to the alabaster, old or weak by preference, and we, of course, came under that heading; but besides these a real workman who understood the work was always told off for the job. The same workman went regularly for some years to this task, a dark, lean, oldish man called Almazov, grim, unsociable and peevish. He had a profound contempt for us. But he was so taciturn that he was even lazy about grumbling at us.

The shed in which the alabaster was baked and pounded stood also on the steep, desolate river-bank. In winter, especially in dull weather, it was dreary to look over the river and at the far-away bank the other side. There was something poignant and heart-rending in this wild desolate landscape. But it was almost more painful when the sun shone brightly on the immense white expanse of snow. One longed to fly away into that expanse which stretched from the other side of the river, an untrodden plain for twelve hundred miles to the south. Almazov usually set to work in grim silence; we were ashamed, as it were, that we could not be any real help to him, and he managed alone and asked no help from us, on purpose, it seemed, to make us conscious of our shortcomings and remorseful for our uselessness. And yet all he had to do was to heat the oven for baking in it the alabaster, which we used to fetch for him. Next day, when the alabaster was thoroughly baked, the task of unloading it from the oven began. Each of us took a heavy mallet, filled himself a special box of alabaster and set to work to pound it. This was delightful work. The brittle alabaster was quickly transformed to white shining powder, it crumbled so well and so easily. We swung our heavy mallets and made such a din that we enjoyed it ourselves. We were tired at the end and at the same time we felt better; our cheeks were flushed, our blood circulated more quickly. At this point even Almazov began to look at us with indulgence, as people look at small children; he smoked his pipe condescendingly, though he could not help grumbling when he had to speak. But he was like that with everyone, though I believe he was a good-natured man at bottom.

Another task to which I was sent was to turn the lathe in the workshop. It was a big heavy wheel. It needed a good deal of effort to move it, especially when the turner (one of the regimental workmen) was shaping some piece of furniture for the use of an official, such as a banister or a big table leg for which a big log was required. In such cases it was beyond one man's strength to turn the wheel and generally two of us were sent – myself and another 'gentleman' whom I will call B. For several years whenever anything had to be turned this task fell to our share. B. was a frail, weakly young fellow who suffered with his lungs. He had entered the prison a year before my arrival together with two others, his comrades – one an old man who spent all his time, day and night, saying his prayers (for which he was greatly respected by the convicts) and died before I left prison, and the other quite a young lad, fresh, rosy, strong and full of spirit, who had carried B. for more than five hundred miles on the journey when the latter was too exhausted to walk. The affection between them was worth seeing. B. was a man of very good education, generous feelings and a lofty character which had been embittered and made irritable by illness. We used to manage the wheel together and the work interested us both. It was first-rate exercise for me.

I was particularly fond, too, of shovelling away the snow. This had to be done as a rule after snowstorms, which were pretty frequent in winter. After a snowstorm lasting twenty-four hours, some houses would be snowed up to the middle of the windows and others would be almost buried. Then as soon as the storm was over and the sun came out, we were driven out in big gangs, sometimes the whole lot of us, to shovel away the snowdrifts from the government buildings. Everyone was given a spade, a task was set for all together, and sometimes such a task that it was a wonder they could get through it, and all set to work with a will. The soft new snow, a little frozen at the top, was easily lifted in huge spadefulls and was scattered about, turning to fine glistening powder in the air. The spade cut readily into the white mass sparkling in the sunshine. The convicts were almost always merry over this job. The fresh winter air and the exercise warmed them up. Everyone grew more cheerful; there were sounds of laughter, shouts, jests. They began snowballing each other, not without protest, of course, from the serious ones, who were indignant at the laughter and merriment; and the general excitement usually ended in swearing.

Little by little, I began to enlarge my circle of acquaintance. Though indeed, I did not think of making acquaintances myself; I was still restless, gloomy and mistrustful. My acquaintanceships arose of themselves. One of the first to visit me was a convict called Petrov. I say visit me and I lay special emphasis on the word; Petrov was in the 'special division', and lived in the part of the prison furthest from me. There could apparently be no connection between us, and we certainly had and could have nothing in common. And yet in those early days Petrov seemed to feel it his duty to come to our room to see me almost every day, or to stop me when I was walking in our leisure hour behind the prison as much out of sight as I could. At first I disliked this. But he somehow succeeded in making his visits a positive diversion to me, though he was by no means a particularly sociable or talkative man. He was a short, strongly built man, agile and restless, pale with high cheek-bones and fearless eyes, with a rather pleasant face, fine white close-set teeth, and an everlasting plug of tobacco between them and his lower lip. This habit of holding tobacco in the mouth was common among the convicts. He seemed younger than his age. He was forty and looked no more than thirty. He always talked to me without a trace of constraint, and treated me exactly as his equal, that is, behaved with perfect good-breeding and delicacy. If he noticed, for instance, that I was anxious to be alone, he would leave me in two or three minutes after a few words of conversation, and he always thanked me for attending to him, a courtesy which he never showed, of course, to anyone else in prison. It is curious that such relations continued between us for several years and never became more intimate, though he really was attached to me. I cannot to this day make up my mind what he wanted of me, why he came to me every day. Though he did happen to steal from me later on, he stole, as it were, *by accident*; he scarcely ever asked me for money, so he did not come for the sake of money or with any interested motive.

I don't know why, but I always felt as though he were not living in prison with me, but somewhere far away in another house in the town, and that he only visited the prison in passing, to hear the news, to see me, to see how we were all getting on. He was always in a hurry, as though he had left someone waiting for him, or some job unfinished. And yet he did not seem flustered. The look in his eyes, too, was rather strange: intent, with a shade of boldness and mockery. Yet he looked, as it were, into the distance, as though beyond the things that met his eyes he were trying to make out something else, far away. This gave him an absent-minded look. I sometimes purposely watched where Petrov went when he left me. Where was someone waiting for him? But he would hurry away from me to a prison ward or a kitchen, would sit down there beside some convicts, listen attentively to their conversation and sometimes take part in it himself, even speaking with heat; then he would suddenly break off and relapse into silence. But whether he were talking or sitting silent, it always appeared that he did so for a moment in passing, that he had something else to do and was expected elsewhere. The strangest thing was that he never had anything to do: he led a life of absolute leisure (except for the regulation work, of course). He knew no sort of trade and he scarcely ever had any money. But he did not grieve much over the lack of it. And what did he talk to me about? His conversation was as strange as himself. He would see, for instance, that I was walking alone behind the prison and would turn abruptly in my direction. He always walked quickly and turned abruptly.

He walked up, yet it seemed he must have been running.

'Good morning.'

'Good morning.'

'I am not interrupting you?'

'No.'

'I wanted to ask you about Napoleon. He is a relation of the one who was here in 1812, isn't he?' (Petrov was a Kantonist and could read and write.)

'Yes.'

'He is some sort of president, they say, isn't he?'

He always asked rapid, abrupt questions, as though he were in a hurry to learn something. It seemed as though he were investigating some matter of great importance which would not admit of any delay.

I explained how he was a president and added that he might soon be an emperor.

'How is that?'

I explained that too, as far as I could. Petrov listened attentively, understanding perfectly and reflecting rapidly, even turning his ear towards me.

'H'm . . . I wanted to ask you, Alexandr Petrovitch: is it true, as they say, that there are monkeys with arms down to their heels and as big as a tall man?'

'Yes, there are.'

'What are they like?'

That, too, I explained as far as I was able.

'And where do they live?'

'In hot countries. There are some in the island of Sumatra.'

'That's in America, isn't it? Don't they say that the people in those parts walk on their heads?'

'Not on their heads. You mean the Antipodes.'

I explained what America was like and what was meant by the Antipodes. He listened as attentively as though he had come simply to hear about the Antipodes.

'A-ah! Last year I read about the Countess La Vallière. Arefyev got the book from the adjutant's. Is it true or is it just invented? It's written by Dumas.'

'It's invented, of course.'

'Well, goodbye. Thank you.'

And Petrov vanished, and we rarely talked except in this style.

I began enquiring about him. M. positively warned me when he heard of the acquaintance. He told me that many of the convicts had inspired him with horror, especially at first, in his early days in prison; but not one of them, not even Gazin, had made such a terrible impression on him as this Petrov.

'He is the most determined, the most fearless of all the convicts,' said M. 'He is capable of anything; he would stick at nothing if the fancy took him. He would murder you if it happened to strike him; he would murder you in a minute without flinching or giving it a thought afterwards. I believe he is not quite in his right mind.'

This view interested me very much. But M. could give me no reason for thinking so. And strange to say, I knew Petrov for several years afterwards and talked to him almost every day, he was genuinely attached to me all that time (though I am absolutely unable to say why), and all those years he behaved well in prison and did nothing horrible, yet every time I looked at him and talked to him I felt sure that M. was right, and that Petrov really was a most determined and fearless man who recognised no restraint of any sort. Why I felt this I can't explain either.

I may mention, however, that this Petrov was the convict who had intended on being led out to be flogged to murder the major, when the latter was saved only 'by a miracle' as the convicts said, through driving away just before. It had happened once, before he came to prison, that he had been struck by the colonel at drill. Probably he had been struck many times before, but this time he could not put up with it and he stabbed his colonel openly, in broad daylight, in the face of the regiment. But I don't know all the details of this story; he never told it me. No doubt these were only outbursts when the man's character showed itself fully all at once. But they were very rare in him. He really was sensible and even peaceable. Passions were latent in him, and hot, violent passions, too; but the burning embers were always covered with a layer of ashes and smouldered quietly. I never saw the faintest trace of vanity or boastfulness in him, as in others. He rarely quarrelled; on the other hand he was not particularly friendly with anyone, except perhaps with Sirotkin, and then only when the latter was of use to him. Once, however,

I saw him seriously angry. Something was not given him, something which was properly his share. A convict in the civilian division called Vassily Antonov was quarrelling with him. He was a tall, powerful athlete, spiteful, quarrelsome, malicious and very far from being a coward. They had been shouting at each other for a long time and I thought that the matter would at most end in a blow or two, for at times, though rarely, Petrov swore and fought like the meanest convict. But this time it was not so: Petrov suddenly blanched, his lips suddenly quivered and turned blue; he began breathing hard. He got up from his place and slowly, very slowly with his bare noiseless steps (in summer he was very fond of going barefoot) he approached Antonov. There was a sudden silence in the noisy shouting crowd; one could have heard a fly. Everyone waited to see what would happen. Antonov leapt up as he approached, looking aghast . . . I could not bear the sight of it and left the room. I expected to hear the shriek of a murdered man before I had time to get down the steps. But this time, too, it ended in nothing: before Petrov had time to reach him, Antonov hastily and in silence flung him the object about which they were disputing, which was some old rag they used to put round their legs. Of course, two or three minutes later, Antonov swore at him a little to satisfy his conscience and keep up appearances by showing that he was not quite cowed. But Petrov took no notice of his abuse, did not even answer it; it was not a question of abuse, the point had been won in his favour; he was very well pleased and took his rag. A quarter of an hour later, he was sauntering about the prison as usual with an air of complete unconcern, and seemed to be looking round to find people talking about something interesting, that he might poke his nose in and listen. Everything seemed to interest him, yet it somehow happened that he remained indifferent to most things and simply wandered aimlessly about the prison, drawn first one way and then another. One might have compared him with a workman, a stalwart workman who could send the work flying but was for a while without a job, and meantime sat playing with little children. I could not understand either why he remained in prison, why he did not run away. He would not have hesitated to run away if he had felt any strong inclination to do so. Men like Petrov are only ruled by reason till they have some strong desire.

Then there is no obstacle on earth that can hinder them. And I am sure he would have escaped cleverly, that he would have outwitted everyone, that he could have stayed for a week without bread, somewhere in the forest or in the reeds of the river. But he evidently had not reached that point yet and did not *fully* desire it. I never noticed in him any great power of reflection or any marked common sense. These people are born with one fixed idea which unconsciously moves them hither and thither; so they shift from one thing to another all their lives, till they find a work after their own hearts. Then they are ready to risk anything. I wondered sometimes how it was that a man who had murdered his officer for a blow could lie down under a flogging with such resignation. He was sometimes flogged when he was caught smuggling in vodka. Like all convicts without a trade he sometimes undertook to bring in vodka. But he lay down to be flogged, as it were with his own consent, that is, as though acknowledging that he deserved it; except for that, nothing would have induced him to lie down, he would have been killed first. I wondered at him, too, when he stole from me in spite of his unmistakable devotion. This seemed to come upon him, as it were, in streaks. It was he who stole my Bible when I asked him to carry it from one place to another. He had only a few steps to go, but he succeeded in finding a purchaser on the way, sold it, and spent the proceeds on drink. Evidently he wanted very much to drink, and anything that he wanted very much he *had* to do. That is the sort of man who will murder a man for sixpence to get a bottle of vodka, though another time he would let a man pass with ten thousand pounds on him. In the evening he told me of the theft himself without the slightest embarrassment or regret, quite indifferently, as though it were a most ordinary incident. I tried to give him a good scolding; besides, I was sorry to lose my Bible. He listened without irritation, very meekly, in fact; agreed that the Bible was a very useful book, sincerely regretted that I no longer possessed it, but expressed no regret at having stolen it; he looked at me with such complacency that I at once gave up scolding him. He accepted my scolding, probably reflecting that it was inevitable that one should be sworn at for such doings, and better I should relieve my feelings and console myself by swearing: but that it was all really nonsense, such nonsense that a serious person would be ashamed to talk about it. It seemed to me that he looked upon me as a sort of child, almost a baby, who did not understand the simplest things in the world. If I began, for instance, on any subject not a learned or bookish one, he would answer me, indeed, but apparently only from politeness, confining himself to the briefest reply. I often wondered what the book knowledge about which he usually questioned me meant to him. I sometimes happened to look sideways at him during our conversations to see whether he were laughing at me. But no; usually he was listening seriously and even with some attention, though often so little that I felt annoyed. He asked exact and definite questions, but showed no great surprise at the information he got from me, and received it indeed rather absent-mindedly. I fancied, too, that he had made up his mind once for all, without bothering his head about it, that it was no use talking to me as one would to other people, that apart from talking of books I understood nothing and was incapable of understanding anything, so there was no need to worry me.

I am sure that he had a real affection for me, and that struck me very much. Whether he considered me undeveloped, not fully a man, or felt for me that special sort of compassion that every strong creature instinctively feels for someone weaker, recognising me as such – I don't know. And although all that did not prevent him from robbing me, I am sure he felt sorry for me as he did it. 'Ech!' he may have thought as he laid hands on my property, 'what a man, he can't even defend his own property!' But I fancy that was what he liked me for. He said to me himself one day, as it were casually, that I was 'a man with too good a heart' and 'so simple, so simple, that it makes one feel sorry for you.' 'Only don't take it amiss, Alexandr Petrovitch,' he added a minute later, 'I spoke without thinking, from my heart.'

It sometimes happens that such people come conspicuously to the front and take a prominent position at the moment of some violent mass movement or revolution, and in that way achieve all at once their full possibilities. They are not men of words and cannot be the instigators or the chief leaders of a movement; but they are its most vigorous agents and the first to act. They begin simply, with no special flourish, but they are the first to surmount the worst obstacles, facing every danger without reflection, without fear – and all rush after, blindly following them to the last wall, where they often lay down their lives. I do not believe that Petrov has come to a good end; he would make short work of everything all at once, and, if he has not perished yet, it is simply that the moment has not come. Who knows, though? Maybe he will live till his hair is grey and will die peaceably of old age, wandering aimlessly to and fro. But I believe M. was right when he said that Petrov was the most determined man in all the prison.

CHAPTER EIGHT
Determined Characters. Lutchka

It is difficult to talk about 'determined' characters; in prison as everywhere else they are few in number. A man may look terrible; if one considers what is said of him one keeps out of his way. An instinctive feeling made me shun such people at first. Afterwards I changed my views in many respects, even about the most terrible murderers. Some who had never murdered anyone were more terrible than others who had been convicted of six murders. There was an element of something so strange in some crimes that one could not form even a rudimentary conception of them. I say this because among the peasantry murders are sometimes committed for most astounding reasons. The following type of murderer, for instance, is to be met with, and not uncommonly indeed. He lives quietly and peaceably and puts up with a hard life. He may be a peasant, a house-serf, a soldier or a workman. Suddenly something in him seems to snap; his patience gives way and he sticks a knife into his enemy and oppressor. Then the strangeness begins: the man gets out of all bounds for a time. The first man he murdered was his oppressor, his enemy; that is criminal but comprehensible; in that case there was a motive. But later on he murders not enemies but anyone he comes upon, murders for amusement, for an insulting word, for a look, to make a round number or simply 'out of my way, don't cross my path, I am coming!' The man is, as it were, drunk, in delirium. It is as though, having once overstepped the sacred limit, he begins to revel in the fact that nothing is sacred to him; as though he had an itching to defy all law and authority at once, and to enjoy the most unbridled and unbounded liberty, to enjoy the thrill of horror which he cannot help feeling at himself. He knows, too, that a terrible punishment is awaiting him. All this perhaps is akin to the sensation with which a man gazes down from a high tower into the depths below his feet till at last it would be a relief to throw himself headlong – anything to put an end to it quickly. And this happens even to the most peaceable and till then inconspicuous people. Some of these people positively play a part to themselves in this delirium. The more downtrodden such a man has been before, the more he itches now to cut a dash, to strike terror into people. He enjoys their terror and likes even the repulsion he arouses in others. He assumes a sort of *desperateness*, and a desperate character sometimes looks forward to speedy punishment, looks forward to being *settled*, because he finds it burdensome at last to keep up his assumed recklessness. It is curious that in most cases all this state of mind, this whole pose persists up to the moment of the scaffold, and then it is cut short once for all; as though its duration were prescribed and defined beforehand. At the end of it, the man suddenly gives in, retires into the background and becomes as limp as a rag. He whimpers on the scaffold and begs forgiveness of the crowd. He comes to prison and he is such a drivelling, snivelling fellow that one wonders whether he can be the man who has murdered five or six people.

Some, of course, are not soon subdued even in prison. They still preserve a certain bravado, a certain boastfulness which seems to say 'I am not what you take me for; I am in for six souls!' But yet he, too, ends by being subdued. Only at times he amuses himself by recalling his reckless exploits, the festive time he once had when he was a 'desperate character', and if he can only find a simple-hearted listener there is nothing he loves better than to give himself airs and boast with befitting dignity, describing his feats, though he is careful not to betray the pleasure this gives him. 'See the sort of man I was,' he seems to say.

And with what subtlety this pose is maintained, how lazily casual the story sometimes is! What studied nonchalance is apparent in the tone, in every word! Where do such people pick it up?

Once in those early days I spent a long evening lying idle and depressed on the plank bed and listened to such a story, and in my inexperience took the storyteller to be a colossal, hideous criminal of an incredible strength of will, while I was inclined to take Petrov lightly. The subject of the narrative was how the speaker, Luka Kuzmitch, for no motive but his own amusement had *laid out* a major. This Luka Kuzmitch was the little, thin, sharp-nosed young convict in our room, a Little Russian by birth, whom I have mentioned already. He was really a Great Russian, but had been born in the south; I believe he was a house-serf. There was really something pert and aggressive about him, 'though the bird is small its claw is sharp.' But convicts instinctively see through a man. They had very little respect for him, or as the convicts say, 'little respect to him'. He was fearfully vain. He was sitting that evening on the platform bed, sewing a shirt. Sewing undergarments was his trade. Beside him was sitting a convict called Kobylin, a tall, stalwart lad, stupid and dull-witted but good-natured and friendly, who slept next to him on the bed. As they were neighbours, Lutchka frequently quarrelled with him and generally treated him superciliously, ironically and despotically, of which Kobylin in his simplicity was not fully conscious. He was knitting a woollen stocking, listening indifferently to Lutchka. The latter was telling his story rather loudly and distinctly. He wanted everyone to hear, though he tried to pretend that he was telling no one but Kobylin.

'Well, brother, they sent me from our parts,' he began, sticking in his needle, 'to Ch—v for being a tramp.'

'When was that, long ago?' asked Kobylin.

'It will be a year ago when the peas come in. Well, when we came to K. they put me in prison there for a little time. In prison with me there were a dozen fellows, all Little Russians, tall, healthy, and as strong as bulls. But they were such quiet chaps; the food was bad; the major did as he liked with them. I hadn't been there two days before I saw they were a cowardly lot. "Why do you knuckle under to a fool like that?" says I.

'"You go and talk to him yourself!" they said, and they fairly laughed at me. I didn't say anything. One of those Little Russians was particularly funny, lads,' he added suddenly, abandoning Kobylin and addressing the company generally. 'He used to tell us how he was tried and what he said in court, and kept crying as he told us; he had a wife and children left behind, he told us. And he was a big, stout, grey-headed old fellow. "I says to him: nay!" he told us. And he, the devil's son, kept on writing and writing. "Well," says I to myself, "may you choke. I'd be pleased to see it." And he kept on writing and writing and at last he'd written something and it was my ruin! Give me some thread, Vassya, the damned stuff is rotten.'

'It's from the market,' said Vassya, giving him some thread.

'Ours in the tailoring shop is better. The other day we sent our veteran for some and I don't know what wretched woman he buys it from,' Lutchka went on, threading his needle by the light.

'A crony of his no doubt.'

'No doubt.'

'Well, but what about the major?' asked Kobylin, who had been quite forgotten.

This was all Lutchka wanted. But he did not go on with his story at once; apparently he did not deign to notice Kobylin. He calmly pulled out his thread, calmly and lazily drew up his legs under him and at last began to speak.

'I worked up my Little Russians at last and they asked for the major. And I borrowed a knife from my neighbour that morning; I took it and hid it to be ready for anything. The major flew into a rage and he drove up. "Come," said I, "don't funk it, you chaps." But their hearts failed them, they were all of a tremble! The major ran in, drunk. "Who is here? What's here? I am Tsar, I am God, too." As he said that I stepped forward,' Lutchka proceeded, 'my knife in my sleeve.

'"No," said I, "your honour," and little by little I got closer. "No, how can it be, your honour," said I, "that you are our Tsar and God too?"

'"Ah, that's you, that's you," shouted the major. "You mutinous fellow!"

'"No," I said, and I got closer and closer. "No," I said, "your honour, as may be well known to yourself, our God the Almighty and All Present is the only One. And there is only one Tsar set over us by God himself. He, your honour, is called a monarch," says I. "And you," says I, "your honour, are only a major, our commander by the grace of the Tsar and your merits," says I. "What, what, what, what!" he fairly cackled; he choked and couldn't speak. He was awfully astonished. "Why, this," says I, and I just pounced on him and plunged the whole knife into his stomach. It did the trick. He rolled over and did not move except for his legs kicking. I threw down the knife. "Look, you fellows, pick him up now!" says I.'

Here I must make a digression. Unhappily such phrases as 'I am your Tsar, I am your God, too', and many similar expressions were not uncommonly used in old days by many commanding officers. It must be admitted, however, that there are not many such officers left; perhaps they are extinct altogether. I may note that the officers who liked to use and prided themselves on using such expressions were mostly those who had risen from the lower ranks. Their promotion turns everything topsy-turvy in them, including their brains. After groaning under the yoke for years and passing through every subordinate grade, they suddenly see themselves officers, gentlemen in command, and in the first intoxication of their position their inexperience leads them to an exaggerated idea of their power and importance; only in relation to their subordinates, of course. To their superior officers they show the same servility as ever, though it is utterly unnecessary and even revolting to many people. Some of these servile fellows hasten with peculiar zest to declare to their superior officers that they come from the lower ranks, though they are officers, and that 'they never forget their place'. But with the common soldiers they are absolutely autocratic. Now, of course, there are scarcely any of these men left, and I doubt if anyone could be found to shout, 'I am your Tsar, I am your God.' But in spite of that, I may remark that nothing irritates convicts, and indeed all people of the poorer class, so much as such utterances on the part of their officers. This insolence of self-glorification, this exaggerated idea of being able to do anything with impunity, inspires hatred in the most submissive of men and drives them out of all patience. Fortunately this sort of behaviour, now almost a thing of the past, was always severely repressed by the authorities even in old days. I know several instances of it.

And, indeed, people in a humble position generally are irritated by any supercilious carelessness, any sign of contempt shown them. Some people think that if convicts are well fed and well kept and all the requirements of the law are satisfied, that is all that is necessary. This is an error, too. Everyone, whoever he may be and however downtrodden he may be, demands – though perhaps instinctively, perhaps unconsciously – respect for his dignity as a human being. The convict knows himself that he is a convict, an outcast, and knows his place before his commanding officer; but by no branding, by no fetters will you make him forget that he is a human being. And as he really is a human being, he ought to be treated humanely. My God, yes! Humane treatment may humanise even one in whom the image of God has long been obscured. These 'unfortunates' need even more humane treatment than others. It is their salvation and their joy. I have met some good-hearted, high-minded officers. I have seen the influence they exerted on these degraded creatures. A few kind words from them meant almost a moral resurrection for the convicts. They were as pleased as children and as children began to love them. I must mention another strange thing: the convicts themselves do not like to be treated too familiarly and *too* softly by their officers. They want to respect those in authority over them, and too much softness makes them cease to respect them. The convicts like their commanding officer to have decorations, too, they like him to be presentable, they like him to be in favour with some higher authority, they like him to be strict and important and just, and they like him to keep up his dignity. The convicts prefer such an officer: they feel that he keeps up his own dignity and does not insult them, and so they feel everything is right and as it should be.

* * *

'You must have caught it hot for that?' Kobylin observed calmly.

'H'm! Hot, my boy, yes – it was hot certainly. Aley, pass the scissors! Why is it they are not playing cards today, lads?'

'They've drunk up all their money,' observed Vassya. 'If they hadn't they'd have been playing.'

'If! They'll give you a hundred roubles for an "if" in Moscow,' observed Lutchka.

'And how much did you get altogether, Lutchka?' Kobylin began again.

'They gave me a hundred and five, my dear chap. And, you know, they almost killed me, mates,' Lutchka declared, abandoning Kobylin again. 'They drove me out in full dress to be flogged. Till then I'd never tasted the lash. There were immense crowds, the whole town ran out: a robber was to be flogged, a murderer, to be sure. You can't think what fools the people are, there's no telling you. The hangman stripped me, made me lie down and shouted, "Look out, I'll sting you." I wondered what was coming. At the first lash I wanted to shout, I opened my mouth but there was no shout in me. My voice failed me. When the second lash came, you may not believe it, I did not hear them count *two*. And when I came to I heard them call "seventeen". Four times, lad, they took me off the donkey, and gave me half an hour's rest and poured water over me. I looked at them all with my eyes starting out of my head and thought "I shall die on the spot . . ." '

'And you didn't die?' Kobylin asked naïvely.

Lutchka scanned him with a glance of immense contempt; there was a sound of laughter.

'He is a regular block!'

'He is not quite right in the top storey,' observed Lutchka, as though regretting he had deigned to converse with such a man.

'He is a natural,' Vassya summed up conclusively.

Though Lutchka had murdered six people no one was ever afraid of him in the prison, yet perhaps it was his cherished desire to be considered a terrible man.

CHAPTER NINE

Isay Fomitch – The Bath-house – Baklushin's Story

Christmas was approaching. The convicts looked forward to it with a sort of solemnity, and looking at them, I too began to expect something unusual. Four days before Christmas Day they took us to the bath-house. In my time, especially in the early years, the convicts were rarely taken to the bath-house. All were pleased and began to get ready. It was arranged to go after dinner, and that afternoon there was no work. The one who was most pleased and excited in our room was Isay Fomitch Bumshtein, a Jewish convict whom I have mentioned in the fourth chapter of my story. He liked to steam himself into a state of stupefaction, of unconsciousness; and whenever going over old memories I recall our prison baths (which deserve to be remembered), the blissful countenance of that prison comrade, whom I shall never forget, takes a foremost place in the picture. Heavens, how killingly funny he was! I have already said something about his appearance: he was a thin, feeble, puny man of fifty, with a wrinkled white body like a chicken's and on his cheeks and forehead awful scars left from being branded. His face wore a continual expression of imperturbable self-complacency and even blissfulness. Apparently he felt no regret at being in prison. As he was a jeweller and there were no jewellers in the town, he worked continually at nothing but his own trade for the gentry and officials of the town. He received some payment for his work. He wanted for nothing, was even rich, but he saved money and used to lend it out at interest to all the convicts. He had a samovar of his own, a good mattress, cups, and a whole dining outfit. The Jews in the town did not refuse him their acquaintance and patronage. On Saturdays he used to go with an escort to the synagogue in the town (which is sanctioned by law). He was in clover, in fact. At the same time he was impatiently awaiting the end of his twelve years' sentence 'to get married'. He was a most comical mixture of naïveté, stupidity, craft, impudence, good-nature, timidity, boastfulness and insolence. It surprised me that the convicts never jeered at him, though they sometimes made a joke at his expense. Isay Fomitch was evidently a continual source of entertainment and amusement to all. 'He is our only one, don't hurt Isay Fomitch,' was what they felt, and although Isay Fomitch saw his position he was obviously proud of being so important and that greatly amused the convicts. His arrival in the prison was fearfully funny (it happened before my time, but I was told of it). One day, in the leisure hour towards evening, a rumour suddenly spread through the prison that a Jew had been brought, and was being shaved in the guard-room and that he would come in directly. There was not a single Jew in the prison at the time. The convicts waited with impatience and surrounded him at once when he came in at the gate. The sergeant led him to the civilian room and showed him his place on the common bed. Isay Fomitch carried in his arms a sack containing his own belongings, together with the regulation articles which had been given to him. He laid down the sack, climbed on to the bed and sat down, tucking his feet under him, not daring to raise his eyes. There were sounds of laughter and prison jokes alluding to his Jewish origin. Suddenly a young convict made his way through the crowd carrying in his hand his very old, dirty, tattered summer trousers, together with the regulation leg-wrappers. He sat down beside Isay Fomitch and slapped him on the shoulder.

'I say, my dear friend, I've been looking out for you these last six years. Look here, how much will you give?'

And he spread the rags out before him.

Isay Fomitch, who had been too timid to utter a word and so cowed at his first entrance that he had not dared to raise his eyes in the crowd of mocking, disfigured and terrible faces which hemmed him in, was cheered at once at the sight of the proffered pledge, and began briskly turning over the rags. He even held them up to the light. Everyone waited to hear what he would say.

'Well, you won't give me a silver rouble, I suppose? It's worth it, you know,' said the would-be borrower, winking at Isay Fomitch.

'A silver rouble, no, but seven kopecks maybe.'

And those were the first words uttered by Isay Fomitch in prison. Everyone roared with laughter.

'Seven! Well, give me seven, then; it's a bit of luck for you. Mind you take care of the pledge; it's as much as your life's worth if you lose it.'

'With three kopecks interest makes ten,' the Jew went on jerkily in a shaking voice, putting his hand in his pocket for the money and looking timidly at the convicts. He was fearfully scared, and at the same time he wanted to do business.

'Three kopecks a year interest, I suppose?'

'No, not a year, a month.'

'You are a tight customer, Jew! What's your name?'

'Isay Fomitch.'

'Well, Isay Fomitch, you'll get on finely here! Goodbye.' Isay Fomitch examined the pledge once more, folded it up carefully and put it in his sack in the midst of the still laughing convicts.

Everyone really seemed to like him and no one was rude to him, though almost all owed him money. He was himself as free from malice as a hen, and, seeing the general goodwill with which he was regarded, he even swaggered a little, but with such simple-hearted absurdity that he was forgiven at once. Lutchka, who had known many Jews in his day, often teased him and not out of ill-feeling, but simply for diversion, just as one teases dogs, parrots, or any sort of trained animal. Isay Fomitch saw that clearly, was not in the least offended and answered him back adroitly.

'Hey, Jew, I'll give you a dressing!'

'You give me one blow and I'll give you ten,' Isay Fomitch would respond gallantly.

'You damned scab!'

'I don't care if I am.'

'You itching Jew!'

'I don't care if I am. I may itch, but I am rich; I've money.'

'You sold Christ.'

'I don't care if I did.'

'That's right, Isay Fomitch, bravo! Don't touch him, he's the only one we've got,' the convicts would shout, laughing.

'Aie, Jew, you'll get the whip, you'll be sent to Siberia.'

'Why, I am in Siberia now.'

'Well, you'll go further.'

'And is the Lord God there, too?'

'Well, I suppose he is.'

'Well, I don't mind, then. If the Lord God is there and there's money, I shall be all right everywhere.'

'Bravo, Isay Fomitch, you are a fine chap, no mistake!' the convicts shouted round him, and though Isay Fomitch saw they were laughing at him, he was not cast down.

The general approval afforded him unmistakable pleasure and he began carolling a shrill little chant 'la-la-la-la-la' all over the prison, an absurd and ridiculous tune without words, the only tune he hummed all the years he was in prison. Afterwards, when he got to know me better, he protested on oath to me that that was the very song and the very tune that the six hundred thousand Jews, big and little, had sung as they crossed the Red Sea, and that it is ordained for every Jew to sing that song at the moment of triumph and victory over his enemies.

Every Friday evening convicts came to our ward from other parts of the prison on purpose to see Isay Fomitch celebrate his Sabbath. Isay Fomitch was so naïvely vain and boastful that this general interest gave him pleasure, too. With pedantic and studied gravity he covered his little table in the corner, opened his book, lighted two candles and muttering some mysterious words began putting on his vestment. It was a parti-coloured shawl of woollen material which he kept carefully in his box. He tied phylacteries on both hands and tied some sort of wooden ark by means of a bandage on his head, right over his forehead, so that it looked like a ridiculous horn sprouting out of his forehead. Then the prayer began. He repeated it in a chant, uttered cries, spat on the floor, and turned round, making wild and absurd gesticulations. All this, of course, was part of the ceremony and there was nothing absurd or strange about it, but what was absurd was that Isay Fomitch seemed purposely to be playing a part before us, and made a show of his ritual. Suddenly he would hide his head in his hands and recite with sobs. The sobs grew louder and in a state of exhaustion and almost howling he would let his head crowned with the ark drop on the book; but suddenly, in the middle of the most violent sobbing he would begin to laugh and chant in a voice broken with feeling and solemnity, and weak with bliss. 'Isn't he going it!' the convicts commented. I once asked Isay Fomitch what was the meaning of the sobs and then the sudden solemn transition to happiness and bliss. Isay Fomitch particularly liked such questions from me. He at once explained to me that the weeping and sobbing were aroused at the thought of the loss of Jerusalem, and that the ritual prescribed sobbing as violently as possible and beating the breast at the thought. But at the moment of the loudest sobbing, he, Isay Fomitch, was *suddenly*, as it were accidentally (the suddenness was also prescribed by the ritual), to remember that there is a prophecy of the return of the Jews to Jerusalem. Then he must at once burst into joy, song, and laughter, and must repeat his prayers in such a way that his voice itself should express as much happiness as possible and his face should express all the solemnity and dignity of which it was capable. This sudden transition and the obligation to make it were a source of extreme pleasure to Isay Fomitch: he saw in it a very subtle *künst-stück*, and boastfully told me of this difficult rule. Once when the prayer was in full swing the major came into the ward accompanied by the officer on duty and the sentries. All the convicts drew themselves up by the bed; Isay Fomitch alone began shouting and carrying on more than ever. He knew that the prayer was not prohibited, it was impossible to interrupt it, and, of course, there was no risk in his shouting before the major. But he particularly enjoyed making a display before the major and showing off before us. The major went up within a step of him. Isay Fomitch turned with his back to his table and waving his hands began chanting his solemn prophecy right in the major's face. As it was prescribed for him to express extreme happiness and dignity in his face at that moment, he did so immediately, screwing up his eyes in a peculiar way, laughing and nodding his head at the major. The major was surprised but finally went off into a guffaw, called him a fool to his face and walked away; and Isay Fomitch vociferated louder than ever. An hour later, when he was having supper, I asked him, 'And what if the major in his foolishness had flown into a rage?'

'What major?'

'What major! Why, didn't you see him?'

'No.'

'Why, he stood not a yard away from you, just facing you.'

But Isay Fomitch began earnestly assuring me that he had not seen the major and that at the time, during the prayer, he was usually in such a state of ecstasy that he saw nothing and heard nothing of what was going on around him.

I can see Isay Fomitch before me now as he used to wander about the prison on Saturdays with nothing to do, making tremendous efforts to do nothing at all, as prescribed by the law of the Sabbath. What incredible anecdotes he used to tell me every time he came back from the synagogue! What prodigious news and rumours from Petersburg he used to bring me, assuring me that he had got them from his fellow Jews, and that they had them first-hand.

But I have said too much of Isay Fomitch.

There were only two public baths in the town. One of these, which was kept by a Jew, consisted of separate bathrooms, for each of which a fee of fifty kopecks was charged. It was an establishment for people of the higher class. The other bath-house was intended for the working class; it was dilapidated, dirty and small, and it was to this house that we convicts were taken. It was frosty and sunny, and the convicts were delighted at the very fact of getting out of the fortress grounds and looking at the town. The jokes and laughter never flagged all the way. A whole platoon of soldiers with loaded rifles accompanied us, to the admiration of the whole town. In the bath-house we were immediately divided into two relays: the second relay had to wait in the cold ante-room while the first were washing themselves. This division was necessary, because the bath-house was so small. But the space was so limited that it was difficult to imagine how even half of our number could find room. Yet Petrov did not desert me; he skipped up of his own accord to help, and even offered to wash me. Another convict who offered me his services was Baklushin, a prisoner in the 'special division' who was nicknamed 'the pioneer', and to whom I have referred already as one of the liveliest and most charming of the convicts, as indeed he was. I was already slightly acquainted with him. Petrov even helped me to undress, for, not being used to it, I was slow undressing, and it was cold in the ante-room, almost as cold as in the open air.

It is, by the way, very difficult for a convict to undress till he has quite mastered the art. To begin with, one has to learn how to unlace quickly the bands under the ankle irons. These bands are made of leather, are eight inches in length and are put on over the undergarment, just under the ring that goes round the ankle. A pair of these bands costs no less than sixty kopecks and yet every convict procures them, at his own expense, of course, for it is impossible to walk without them. The ring does not fit tightly on the leg, one can put one's finger in between, so that the iron strikes against the flesh and rubs it, and without the leather a convict would rub his leg into a sore in a day. But to get off the bands is not difficult. It is more difficult to learn how to get off one's underlinen from under the fetters. It is quite a special art. Drawing off the undergarments from the left leg, for instance, one has first to pull it down between the ring and the leg, then freeing one's foot one has to draw the linen up again between the leg and the ring; then the whole of the left leg of the garment has to be slipped through the ring on the right ankle, and pulled back again. One has to go through the same business when one puts on clean linen. It is hard for a novice even to guess how it can be done; I was first taught how to do it at Tobolsk by a convict called Korenev, who had been the chief of a band of robbers and had been for five years chained to the wall. But the convicts get used to it, and go through the operation without the slightest difficulty.

I gave Petrov a few kopecks to get me soap and a handful of tow; soap was, indeed, served out to the convicts, a piece each, the size of a halfpenny and as thick as the slices of cheese served at the beginning of supper among middle-class people. Soap was sold in the ante-room as well as hot spiced mead, rolls and hot water. By contract with the keeper of the bath-house, each convict was allowed only one bucketful of hot water; everyone who wanted to wash himself cleaner could get for a half-penny another bucketful, which was passed from the ante-room into the bathroom through a little window made on purpose. When he had undressed me, Petrov took me by the arm, noticing that it was very difficult for me to walk in fetters.

'You must pull them higher, on to your calves,' he kept repeating, supporting me as though he were my nurse, 'and now be careful, here's a step.'

I felt a little ashamed, indeed; I wanted to assure Petrov that I could walk alone, but he would not have believed it. He treated me exactly like a child not able to manage alone, whom everyone ought to help. Petrov was far from being a servant, he was pre-eminently not a servant; if I had offended him, he would have known how to deal with me. I had not promised him payment for his services, and he did not ask for it himself. What induced him, then, to look after me in this way?

When we opened the door into the bathroom itself, I thought we were entering hell. Imagine a room twelve paces long and the same in breadth, in which perhaps as many as a hundred and certainly as many as eighty were packed at once, for the whole party were divided into only two relays, and we were close on two hundred; steam blinding one's eyes; filth and grime; such a crowd that there was not room to put one's foot down. I was frightened and tried to step back, but Petrov at once encouraged me. With extreme difficulty we somehow forced our way to the benches round the wall, stepping over the heads of those who were sitting on the floor, asking them to duck to let us get by. But every place on the benches was taken. Petrov informed me that one had to buy a place and at once entered into negotiations with a convict sitting near the window. For a kopeck the latter gave up his place, receiving the money at once from Petrov, who had the coin ready in his fist, having providently brought it with him into the bathroom. The convict I had ousted at once ducked under the bench just under my place, where it was dark and filthy, and the dirty slime lay two inches thick. But even the space under the benches was all filled; there, too, the place was alive with human beings. There was not a spot on the floor as big as the palm of your hand where there was not a convict squatting, splashing from his bucket. Others stood up among them and holding their buckets in their hands washed themselves standing; the dirty water trickled off them on to the shaven heads of the convicts sitting below them. On the top shelf and on all the steps leading up to it men were crouched, huddled together washing themselves. But they did not wash themselves much. Men of the peasant class don't wash much with soap and hot water; they only steam themselves terribly and then douche themselves with cold water – that is their whole idea of a bath. Fifty birches were rising and falling rhythmically on the shelves; they all thrashed themselves into a state of stupefaction. More steam was raised every moment. It was not heat; it was hell. All were shouting and vociferating to the accompaniment of a hundred chains clanking on the floor . . . Some of them, wanting to pass, got entangled in other men's chains and caught in their owns chains the heads of those below them;

they fell down, swore, and dragged those they caught after them. Liquid filth ran in all directions. Everyone seemed in a sort of intoxicated, over-excited condition; there were shrieks and cries. By the window of the ante-room from which the water was handed out there was swearing, crowding, and a regular scuffle. The fresh hot water was spilt over the heads of those who were sitting on the floor before it reached its destination. Now and then the moustached face of a soldier with a gun in his hand peeped in at the window or the half-open door to see whether there were anything wrong. The shaven heads and crimson steaming bodies of the convicts seemed more hideous than ever. As a rule the steaming backs of the convicts show distinctly the scars of the blows or lashes they have received in the past, so that all those backs looked now as though freshly wounded. The scars were horrible! A shiver ran down me at the sight of them. They pour more boiling water on the hot bricks and clouds of thick, hot steam fill the whole bath-house; they all laugh and shout. Through the cloud of steam one gets glimpses of scarred backs, shaven heads, bent arms and legs; and to complete the picture Isay Fomitch is shouting with laughter on the very top shelf. He is steaming himself into a state of unconsciousness, but no degree of heat seems to satisfy him; for a kopeck he has hired a man to beat him, but the latter is exhausted at last, flings down his birch and runs off to douche himself with cold water. Isay Fomitch is not discouraged and hires another and a third; he is resolved on such an occasion to disregard expense and hires even a fifth man to wield the birch. 'He knows how to steam himself, bravo, Isay Fomitch!' the convicts shout to him from below. Isay Fomitch, for his part, feels that at the moment he is superior to everyone and has outdone them all; he is triumphant, and in a shrill crazy voice screams out his tune 'la-la-la-la-la', which rises above all the other voices. It occurred to me that if one day we should all be in hell together it would be very much like this place. I could not help expressing this thought to Petrov; he merely looked round and said nothing.

I wanted to buy him, too, a place beside me, but he sat down at my feet and declared that he was very comfortable. Meantime Baklushin was buying us water and brought it as we wanted it. Petrov declared that he would wash me from head to foot, 'so that you will be all nice and clean', and he urged me to be steamed. This I did not venture on. Petrov soaped me all over. 'And now I'll wash your *little feet*,' he added in conclusion. I wanted to reply that I could wash them myself, but I did not contradict him and gave myself into his hands completely. There was not the faintest note of servility about the expression 'little feet'; it was simply that Petrov could not call my feet simply feet, probably because other real people had feet, while mine were 'little feet'.

After having washed me he led me back to the ante-room with the same ceremonies, that is, giving me the same support and warnings at every step, as though I were made of china. Then he helped me to put on my linen, and only when he had quite finished with me he rushed back to the bathroom to steam himself.

When we got home I offered him a glass of tea. Tea he did not refuse; he emptied the glass and thanked me. I thought I would be lavish and treat him to a glass of vodka. This was forthcoming in our ward. Petrov was extremely pleased; he drank it, cleared his throat and observing that I had quite revived him, hurried off to the kitchen as though there were something there that could not be settled without him. His place was taken by another visitor, Baklushin 'the pioneer', whom I had invited to have tea with me before we left the bath-house.

I don't know a more charming character than Baklushin's. It was true that he would not knuckle under to anyone; indeed, he often quarrelled, he did not like people to meddle with his affairs – in short, he knew how to take his own part. But he never quarrelled for long, and I believe we all liked him. Wherever he went everyone met him with pleasure. He was known even in the town as the most amusing fellow in the world who was always in high spirits. He was a tall fellow of thirty with a good-natured and spirited countenance, rather good-looking, though he had a wart on his face. He could contort his features in a killing way, mimicking anyone he came across, so that no one near him could help laughing. He, too, belonged to the class of comic men, but he would not be set upon by those who despised and detested laughter, so they never abused him for being a 'foolish and useless' person. He was full of fire and life. He made my acquaintance during my first days and told me that he was a Kantonist and had afterwards served in the pioneers, and had even been noticed and favoured by some great personages, a fact which he still remembered with great pride. He began at once questioning me about Petersburg. He even used to read. When he came to have tea with me he at once entertained the whole ward by describing what a dressing down Lieutenant S. had given the major that morning, and sitting down beside me, he told me with a look of pleasure, that the theatricals would probably come off. They were getting up theatricals in the prison for Christmas. Actors had been discovered, and scenery was being got ready by degrees. Some people in the town had promised to lend dresses for the actors, even for the female characters; they positively hoped by the assistance of an orderly to obtain an officer's uniform with epaulettes. If only the major did not take it into his head to forbid it, as he did last year. But last Christmas he had been in a bad temper: he had lost at cards somewhere, and, besides, there had been mischief in the prison, so he had forbidden it out of spite; but now perhaps he would not want to hinder it. In short, Baklushin was excited. It was evident that he was one of the most active in getting up the performance, and I inwardly resolved on the spot that I would certainly be present. Baklushin's simple-hearted delight that everything was going well with the theatricals pleased me. Little by little, we got into talk. Among other things he told me that he had not always served in Petersburg; that he had been guilty of some misdemeanour there and had been transferred to R., though as a sergeant in a garrison regiment.

'It was from there I was sent here,' observed Baklushin.

'But what for?' I asked.

'What for? What do you think it was for, Alexandr Petrovitch? Because I fell in love.'

'Oh, well, they don't send people here for that yet,' I retorted laughing.

'It is true,' Baklushin added, 'it's true that through that I shot a German there with my pistol. But was the German worth sending me here for, tell me that!'

'But how was it? Tell me, it's interesting.'

'It's a very funny story, Alexandr Petrovitch.'

'So much the better. Tell me.'

'Shall I? Well, listen, then.'

I heard a strange, though not altogether amusing, story of a murder.

'This is how it was,' Baklushin began. 'When I was sent to R. I saw it was a fine big town, only there were a lot of Germans in it. Well, of course, I was a young man then; I stood well with the officers; I used to pass the time walking about with my cap on one side, winking at the German girls. And one little German girl, Luise, took my fancy. They were both laundresses, only doing the finest work, she and her aunt. Her aunt was a stuck-up old thing and they were well off. I used to walk up and down outside their windows at first, and then I got to be real friends with her. Luise spoke Russian well, too, she only lisped a little, as it were – she was such a darling, I never met one like her . . . I was for being too free at first, but she said to me, "No, you mustn't, Sasha, for I want to keep all my innocence to make you a good wife," and she'd only caress me and laugh like a bell . . . and she was such a clean little thing, I never saw anyone like her. She suggested our getting married herself. Now, could I help marrying her, tell me that? So I made up my mind to go to the lieutenant-colonel for permission . . . One day I noticed Luise did not turn up at our meeting-place, and again a second time she didn't come, and again a third. I sent a letter; no answer. What is it? I wondered. If she had been deceiving me she would have contrived somehow, have answered the letter, and have come to meet me. But she did not know how to tell a lie, so she simply cut it off. It's her aunt, I thought. I didn't dare go to the aunt's; though she knew it, we always met on the quiet. I went about as though I were crazy; I wrote her a last letter and said, "If you don't come I shall come to your aunt's myself." She was frightened and came. She cried; she told me that a German called Schultz, a distant relation, a watch-maker, well-off and elderly, had expressed a desire to marry her – "to make me happy", he says, and not to be left without a wife in his old age; and he loves me, he says, and he's had the idea in his mind for a long time, but he kept putting it off and saying nothing. "You see, Sasha," she said, "he's rich and it's a fortunate thing for me; surely you don't want to deprive me of my good fortune?" I looked at her – she was crying and hugging me . . . "Ech," I thought, "she is talking sense! What's the use of marrying a soldier, even though I am a sergeant?" "Well, Luise," said I, "goodbye, God be with you. I've no business to hinder your happiness. Tell me, is he good-looking?" "No," she said, "he is an old man, with a long nose," and she laughed herself. I left her. "Well," I thought, "it was not fated to be!" The next morning I walked by his shop; she had told me the street. I looked in at the window: there was a German sitting there mending a watch, a man of forty-five with a hooked nose and goggle eyes, wearing a tail-coat and a high stand-up collar, such a solemn-looking fellow. I fairly cursed; I should like to have broken his window on the spot . . . but there, I thought, it's no good touching him, it's no good crying over spilt milk! I went home to the barracks at dusk, lay down on my bed and would you believe it, Alexandr Petrovitch, I burst out crying . . .

'Well, that day passed, and another and a third. I did not see Luise. And meantime I heard from a friend (she was an old lady, another laundress whom Luise sometimes went to see) that the German knew of our love, and that was why he made up his mind to propose at once, or else he would have waited another two or three years. He had made Luise promise, it seemed, that she would not see me again; and that so far he was, it seems, rather churlish with both of them, Luise and her aunt; as though he might change his mind and had not quite decided even now. She told me, too, that the day after tomorrow, Sunday, he had invited them both to have coffee with him in the morning and that there would be another relation there, an old man who had been a merchant but was very poor now and served as a caretaker in a basement. When I knew that maybe on Sunday everything would be settled, I was seized with such fury that I did not know what I was doing. And all that day and all the next I could do nothing but think of it. I felt I could eat that German.

'On Sunday morning I did not know what I would do, but when the mass was over I jumped up, put on my overcoat and set off to the German's. I thought I would find them all there. And why I went to the German's, and what I meant to say, I did not know myself. But I put a pistol in my pocket to be ready for anything. I had a wretched little pistol with an old-fashioned trigger; I used to fire it as a boy. It wasn't fit to be used. But I put a bullet in it: I thought "if they try turning me out and being rude I'll pull out the pistol and frighten them all." I got there, there was no one in the shop, they were all sitting in the back room. And not a soul but themselves, no servant. He had only one, a German cook. I walked through the shop and saw the door was shut, but it was an old door, fastening with a hook. My heart beat; I stood still and listened: they were talking German. I kicked the door with all my might and it opened. I saw the table was laid. On the table there was a big coffee-pot and the coffee was boiling on a spirit lamp. There were biscuits; on another tray a decanter of vodka, herring and sausage, and another bottle with wine of some sort. Luise and her aunt were sitting on the sofa dressed in their best; on a chair opposite them the German, her suitor, with his hair combed, in a tail-coat and a stand-up collar sticking out in front. And in another chair at the side sat another German, a fat grey-headed old man who did not say a word. When I went in Luise turned white. The aunt started up but sat down again, and the German frowned, looking so cross, and got up to meet me.

' "What do you want?" said he. I was a bit abashed, but I was in such a rage.

' "What do I want! Why, you might welcome a visitor and give him a drink. I've come to see you."

'The German thought a minute and said, "Sit you."

'I sat down. "Well, give me some vodka," I said.

' "Here's some vodka," he said, "drink it, pray."

' "Give me some good vodka," said I. I was in an awful rage, you know.

' "It is good vodka."

'I felt insulted that he treated me as though I were of no account, and above all with Luise looking on. I drank it off and said: "What do you want to be rude for, German? You must make friends with me. I've come to you as a friend."

' "I cannot with you be friend," said he, "you are a simple soldier."

'Then I flew into a fury.

' "Ah, you scarecrow," I said, "you sausage-eater! But you know that from this moment I can do anything I like with you? Would you like me to shoot you with my pistol?"

'I pulled out my pistol, stood before him and put the muzzle straight at his head. The women sat more dead than alive, afraid to stir; the old man was trembling like a leaf, he turned pale and didn't say a word.

'The German was surprised, but he pulled himself together.

' "I do not fear you," said he, "and I beg you as an honourable man to drop your joke at once and I do not fear you."

' "That's a lie," said I, "you do!"

'Why, he did not dare to move his head away, he just sat there.

' "No," said he, "you that will never dare."

' "Why don't I dare?" said I.

' "Because," said he, "that is you strictly forbidden and for that they will you strictly punish."

'The devil only knows what that fool of a German was after. If he hadn't egged me on he'd have been living to this day. It all came from our disputing.

' "So I daren't, you think?"

' "No."

' "I daren't?"

' "To treat me so you will never dare."

' "Well, there then, sausage!" I went bang and he rolled off his chair. The women screamed.

'I put the pistol in my pocket and made off, and as I was going into the fortress I threw the pistol into the nettles at the gate.

'I went home, lay down on my bed and thought: "They'll come and take me directly." One hour passed and then another – they did not take me. And when it got dark, such misery came over me; I went out; I wanted to see Luise, whatever happened. I went by the watchmaker's shop. There was a crowd there and police. I went to my old friend: "Fetch Luise!" said I. I waited a little, and then I saw Luise running up. She threw herself on my neck and cried. "It's all my fault," said she, "for listening to my aunt." She told me that her aunt had gone straight home after what happened that morning and was so frightened that she was taken ill, and said nothing. "She's told no one herself and she's forbidden me to," says she. "She is afraid and feels 'let them do what they like'. No one saw us this morning," said Luise. He had sent his servant away too, for he was afraid of her. She would have scratched his eyes out if she had known that he meant to get married. There were none of the workmen in the house either, he had sent them all out. He prepared the coffee himself and got lunch ready. And the relation had been silent all his life, he never used to say anything, and when it had all happened that morning he picked up his hat and was the first to go. "And no doubt he will go on being silent," said Luise. So it was. For a fortnight no one came to take me and no one had any suspicion of me. That fortnight, though you mayn't believe it, Alexandr Petrovitch, was the happiest time in my life. Every day I met Luise. And how tender, how tender she grew to me! She would cry and say, "I'll follow you wherever they send you, I'll leave everything for you!" It was almost more than I could bear, she wrung my heart so. Well, and in a fortnight they took me. The old man and the aunt came to an understanding and gave information against me . . . '

'But excuse me,' I interrupted, 'for that they could not have given you more than ten or twelve years at the utmost in the civil division, but you are in the special division. How can that be?'

'Oh, that is a different matter,' said Baklushin. 'When I was brought to the court the captain swore at me with nasty words before the court. I couldn't control myself and said to him, "What are you swearing for? Don't you see you are in a court of justice, you scoundrel!" Well, that gave a new turn to things; they tried me again and for everything together they condemned me to four thousand blows and sent me here in the special division. And when they brought me out for punishment, they brought out the captain too: me to walk down the "Green Street", and him to be deprived of his rank and sent to serve as a soldier in the Caucasus. Goodbye, Alexandr Petrovitch. Come and see our performance.'

CHAPTER TEN

Christmas

At last the holidays came. The convicts did hardly any work on Christmas Eve. Some went to the sewing-rooms and workshops; the others were sent to their different tasks, but for the most part, singly or in groups, came back to prison immediately afterwards and they all remained indoors after dinner. Indeed the majority had left the prison in the morning more on their own business than for the regulation work: some to arrange about bringing in and ordering vodka; others to see friends, male and female, or to collect any little sums owing to them for work done in the past. Baklushin and others who were taking part in the theatricals went to see certain acquaintances, principally among the officers' servants, and to obtain necessary costumes. Some went about with an anxious and responsible air, simply because others looked responsible, and though many of them had no grounds for expecting money, they, too, looked as though they were reckoning on getting it. In short everyone was looking forward to the next day in expectation of a change, of something unusual. In the evening the veterans in charge who had been marketing for the convicts brought in eatables of all sorts: beef, sucking-pigs, even geese. Many of the convicts, even the humblest and most careful who used to save up their farthings from one year's end to another, felt obliged to be lavish for such an occasion and to celebrate befittingly the end of the fast. The next day was a real holiday, guaranteed to them by law and not to be taken from them. On that day the convict could not be set to work and there were only three such days in the year.

And who knows what memories must have been stirred in the hearts of these outcasts at the coming of such a day! The great festivals of the Church make a vivid impression on the minds of peasants from childhood upwards. They are the days of rest from their hard toil, the days of family gatherings. In prison they must have been remembered with grief and heartache. Respect for the solemn day had passed indeed into a custom strictly observed among the convicts; very few caroused, all were serious and seemed preoccupied, though many of them had really nothing to do. But whether they drank or did nothing, they tried to keep up a certain dignity . . . It seemed as though laughter were prohibited. In fact they showed a tendency to be over-particular and irritably intolerant, and if anyone jarred on the prevailing mood, even by accident, the convicts set on him with outcries and abuse and were angry with him, as though he had shown disrespect to the holiday itself. This state of mind in the convicts was remarkable and positively touching. Apart from their innate reverence for the great day, the convicts felt unconsciously that by the observance of Christmas they were, as it were, in touch with the whole of the world, that they were not altogether outcasts and lost men, not altogether cut off; that it was the same in prison as amongst other people. They felt that; it was evident and easy to understand.

Akim Akimitch too made great preparations for the holiday. He had no home memories, for he had grown up an orphan among strangers, and had faced the hardships of military service before he was sixteen; he had nothing very joyful to remember in his life, for he had always lived regularly and monotonously, afraid of stepping one hair's-breadth out of the prescribed path; he was not particularly religious either, for propriety seemed to have swallowed up in him all other human qualities and attributes, all passions and desires, bad and good alike. And so he was preparing for the festival without anxiety or excitement, untroubled by painful and quite useless reminiscences, but with a quiet, methodical propriety which was just sufficient for the fulfilment of his duties and of the ritual that has been prescribed once and for all. As a rule he did not care for much reflection. The inner meaning of things never troubled his mind, but rules that had once been laid down for him he followed with religious exactitude. If it had been made the rule to do exactly the opposite, he would have done that tomorrow with the same docility and scrupulousness. Once only in his life he had tried to act on his own judgment, and that had brought him to prison. The lesson had not been thrown away on him. And though destiny withheld from him for ever all understanding of how he had been to blame, he had deduced a solitary principle from his misadventure – never to use his own judgment again under any circumstances, for sense 'was not his strong-point', as the convicts used to say. In his blind devotion to established ritual, he looked with a sort of anticipatory reverence even upon the festal sucking-pig, which he himself stuffed with kasha and roasted (for he knew how to cook), as though regarding it not as an ordinary pig which could be bought and roasted any day, but as a special, holiday pig. Perhaps he had been used from childhood to see a sucking-pig on the table at Christmas, and had deduced from it that a sucking-pig was indispensable on the occasion; and I am sure that if he had once missed tasting sucking-pig on Christmas Day he would for the rest of his life have felt a conscience-prick at having neglected his duty.

Until Christmas Day he remained in his old jacket and trousers, which were quite threadbare though neatly darned. It appeared now that he had been carefully keeping away in his box the new suit given to him four months ago and had refrained from touching it, with the delectable idea of putting it on for the first time on Christmas Day. And so he did. On Christmas Eve he got out his new suit, unfolded it, examined it, brushed it, blew on it and tried it on. The suit seemed a good fit; everything was as it should be, buttoning tightly to the collar; the high collar stood up as stiff as cardboard under his chin; at the waist it fitted closely, almost like a uniform. Akim Akimitch positively grinned with delight, and not without a certain swagger he turned before the tiny looking-glass, round which at some leisure moment he had pasted a border of gold paper. Only one hook on the collar seemed not quite in the right place. Noticing it Akim Akimitch made up his mind to alter it; he moved it, tried the coat on again and then it was perfectly right; then he folded it up as before and put it away in his box again, with his mind at rest. His head was satisfactorily shaven; but examining himself carefully in the looking-glass he noticed that his head did not seem perfectly smooth – there was a scarcely visible growth of hair and he went at once to 'the major' to be properly shaven according to regulation. And although Akim Akimitch was not to be inspected next day, he was shaven simply for conscience' sake, that he might leave no duty unperformed before Christmas. A reverence for epaulettes, buttons and details of uniform had from childhood been indelibly impressed upon his mind and upon his heart, as a duty that could not be questioned and as the highest form of the beautiful that could be attained by a decent man. After this, as the senior convict in the ward, he gave orders for hay to be brought in, and carefully superintended the laying of it on the floor. The same thing was done in the other wards. I don't know why, but hay was always laid on the floor at Christmas time. Then having finished his labours Akim Akimitch said his prayers, lay down on his bed and at once fell into a sweet sleep like a baby's, to wake up as early as possible next morning. All the convicts did the same, however. In all the wards they went to bed much earlier than usual. Their usual evening pursuits were laid aside, there was no thought of cards. All was expectation of the coming day.

At last it came. Quite early, before daybreak, as soon as the morning drum had sounded, the wards were unlocked and the sergeant on duty who came in to count over the prisoners gave them Christmas greetings, and was greeted by them in the same way, with warmth and cordiality. After hastily saying their prayers Akim Akimitch and many of the others who had geese or sucking-pigs in the kitchen hurried off to see what was being done with them, how the roasting was getting on, where they had been put and so on. From the little prison windows blocked up with snow and ice, we could see through the darkness in both kitchens bright fires that had been kindled before daybreak, glowing in all the six ovens. Convicts were already flitting across the court-yard with their sheepskins properly put on or flung across their shoulders, all rushing to the kitchen. Some, though very few, had already been to the 'publicans.' They were the most impatient. On the whole, all behaved decorously, peaceably, and with an exceptional seemliness. One heard nothing of the usual swearing and quarrelling. Everyone realised that it was a great day and a holy festival. Some went into other wards to greet special friends. One saw signs of something like friendship. I may mention in parenthesis that there was scarcely a trace of friendly feeling among the convicts – I don't mean general friendliness, that was quite out of the question, I mean the personal affection of one convict for another. There was scarcely a trace of such a feeling among us, and it is a remarkable fact: it is so different in the world at large. All of us, as a rule, with very rare exceptions, were rough and cold in our behaviour to one another, and this was, as it were, the accepted attitude adopted once for all.

I, too, went out of the ward. It was just beginning to get light. The stars were growing dim and a faint frosty haze was rising. The smoke was puffing in clouds from the kitchen chimneys. Some of the convicts I came upon in the yard met me with ready and friendly Christmas greetings. I thanked them, and greeted them in the same way. Some of them had never said a word to me till that day.

At the kitchen door I was overtaken by a convict from the military division with his sheepskin thrown over his shoulders. He had caught sight of me in the middle of the yard and shouted after me, 'Alexandr Petrovitch, Alexandr Petrovitch!' He was running towards the kitchen in a hurry. I stopped and waited for him. He was a young lad with a round face and a gentle expression; very taciturn with everyone; he had not spoken a word to me or taken any notice of me since I entered the prison; I did not even know his name. He ran up to me out of breath and stood facing me, gazing at me with a blank but at the same time blissful smile.

'What is it?' I asked wondering, seeing that he was standing and gazing at me with open eyes, was smiling but not saying a word.

'Why, it's Christmas,' he muttered, and realising that he could say nothing more, he left me and rushed into the kitchen.

I may mention here that we had never had anything to do with one another and scarcely spoke from that time till I left the prison.

In the kitchen round the glowing ovens there was great crowding and bustling, quite a crush. Everyone was looking after his property; the cooks were beginning to prepare the prison dinner, which was earlier that day. No one had yet begun eating, though some of them wanted to; but they had a regard for decorum in the presence of the others. They were waiting for the priest, and the fast was only to be broken after his visit. Meanwhile, before it was fully daylight, we heard the corporal at the prison gate calling the cooks. He shouted almost every minute and went on for nearly two hours. The cooks were wanted to receive the offerings, which were brought into the prison from all parts of the town. An immense quantity of provisions was brought, such as rolls, cheesecakes, pastries, scones, pancakes and similar good things. I believe there was not a housewife of the middle or lower class in the town who did not send something of her baking by way of Christmas greeting to the 'unfortunate' and captives. There were rich offerings – large quantities of fancy bread made of the finest flour. There were very humble offerings too – such as a farthing roll and a couple of rye cakes with a smear of sour cream on them: these were the gifts of the poor to the poor, and all they had to give. All were accepted with equal gratitude without distinction of gifts and givers. The convicts took off their caps as they received them, bowed, gave their Christmas greetings and took the offerings into the kitchen. When the offerings were piled up in heaps, the senior convicts were sent for, and they divided all equally among the wards. There was no scolding or quarrelling; it was honestly and equitably done. The share that was brought to our ward was divided among us by Akim Akimitch with the help of another convict. They divided it with their own hands, and with their own hands gave each convict his share. There was not the slightest protest, not the slightest jealousy; all were satisfied; there could be no suspicion of an offering being concealed or unfairly divided.

Having seen to his cooking, Akim Akimitch proceeded to array himself. He dressed himself with all due decorum and solemnity, not leaving one hook unfastened, and as soon as he was dressed he began saying his real prayers. He spent a good time over them. A good many of the convicts, chiefly the elder ones, were already standing saying their prayers. The younger ones did not pray much: the most they did even on a holiday was to cross themselves when they got up. When his prayers were over, Akim Akimitch came up to me and with a certain solemnity offered me his Christmas greeting. I at once invited him to join me at tea and he invited me to share his sucking-pig. Soon after, Petrov, too, ran up to greet me. He seemed to have been drinking already and, though he ran up out of breath, he did not say much; he only stood a little while before me as though expecting something, and soon went off into the kitchen again. Meanwhile in the military ward they were preparing for the priest. That ward was arranged differently from the others; the plank bed ran along the walls instead of being in the middle of the room as in all the other wards, so that it was the only room in the prison which had a clear space in the middle. It probably was so arranged in order that when necessary the convicts could be all gathered together there. In the middle of the room they put a table, covered it with a clean towel, and on it set the ikon and lighted the lamp before us. At last the priest came with the cross and the holy water. After repeating prayers and singing before the ikon, he stood facing the convicts and all of them with genuine reverence came forward to kiss the cross. Then the priest walked through all the wards and sprinkled them with holy water. In the kitchen he praised our prison bread, which was famous throughout the town, and the convicts at once wanted to send him two new freshly baked loaves; a veteran was at once dispatched to take them. They followed the cross out with the same reverence with which they had welcomed it and then almost immediately the governor and the major arrived. The governor was liked and even respected among us. He walked through all the wards, escorted by the major; he gave them all Christmas greetings, went into the kitchen and tried the prison soup. The soup was excellent: nearly a pound of beef for each prisoner had been put into it in honour of the occasion. There was boiled millet, too, and butter was liberally allowed. When he had seen the governor off, the major gave orders that they should begin dinner. The convicts tried to avoid his eye. We did not like the spiteful way in which he glanced to right and to left from behind his spectacles, trying even today to find something amiss, someone to blame.

We began dinner. Akim Akimitch's sucking-pig was superbly cooked. I don't know how to explain it, but immediately after the major had gone, within five minutes of his departure, an extraordinary number of people were drunk, and yet only five minutes before they had all been almost sober. One suddenly saw flushed and beaming faces and balalaikas were brought out. The little Pole with a fiddle was already at the heels of a reveller who had engaged him for the whole day; he was scraping away merry jig tunes. The talk began to grow louder and more drunken. But they got through dinner without much disturbance. Everyone had had enough. Many of the older and more sedate at once lay down to sleep. Akim Akimitch did the same, apparently feeling that on a great holiday one must sleep after dinner. The old dissenter from Starodubov had a brief nap and then clambered on the stove, opened his book and prayed almost uninterruptedly till the dead of night. It was painful to him to see the 'shamefulness', as he said, of the convicts' carousing. All the Circassians settled themselves on the steps and gazed at the drunken crowd with curiosity and a certain disgust. I came across Nurra: 'Bad, bad!' he said, shaking his head with pious indignation, 'Ough, it's bad! Allah will be angry!' Isay Fomitch lighted his candle with an obstinate and supercilious air and set to work, evidently wanting to show that the holiday meant nothing to him. Here and there, card parties were made up. The players were not afraid of the veterans, though they put men on the lookout for the sergeant, who for his part was anxious not to see anything. The officer on duty peeped into the prison three times during the day. But the drunken men were hidden and the cards were slipped away when he appeared, and he, too, seemed to have made up his mind not to notice minor offences. Drunkenness was looked on as a minor offence that day. Little by little, the convicts grew noisier. Quarrels began. Yet the majority were still sober and there were plenty to look after those who were not. But those who were drinking drank a vast amount. Gazin was triumphant. He swaggered up and down near his place on the bed, under which he had boldly stored away the vodka, hidden till that day under the snow behind the barracks, and he chuckled slyly as he looked at the customers coming to him. He was sober himself; he had not drunk a drop. He meant to carouse when the holidays were over, when he would have emptied the convicts' pockets. There was singing in all the wards. But drunkenness was passing into stupefaction and the singing was on the verge of tears. Many of the prisoners walked to and fro with their balalaikas, their sheepskins over their shoulders, twanging the strings with a jaunty air. In the special division they even got up a chorus of eight voices. They sang capitally to the accompaniment of balalaikas and guitars. Few of the songs were genuine peasant songs. I only remember one and it was sung with spirit.

> I, the young woman,
> Went at eve to the feast.

And I heard a variation of that song which I had never heard before. Several verses were added at the end.

> I, the young woman,
> Have tidied my house;
> The spoons are rubbed,
> The boards are scrubbed,
> The soup's in the pot,
> The peas are hot.

For the most part they sang what are called in Russia 'prison' songs, all well-known ones. One of them, 'In times gone by', was a comic song, describing how a man had enjoyed himself in the past and lived like a gentleman at large, but now was shut up in prison. It described how he had 'flavoured blancmange with champagne' in old days, and now

> Cabbage and water they give me to eat,
> And I gobble it up as though it were sweet.

A popular favourite was the hackneyed song:

> As a boy I lived in freedom,
> Had my capital as well.
> But the boy soon lost his money,
> Straightway into bondage fell.

and so on. There were mournful songs too. One was a purely convict song, a familiar one too, I believe:

> Now the dawn in heaven is gleaming,
> Heard is the awakening drum.
> Doors will open to the jailer,
> The recording clerk will come.
>
> We behind these walls are hidden,
> None can see us, none can hear.
> But the Lord of Heaven is with us,
> Even here we need not fear . . .

Another was even more depressing but sung to a fine tune and probably composed by a convict. The words were mawkish and somewhat illiterate. I remember a few lines of it.

Never more shall I behold
The country of my birth.
In suffering, guiltless, I'm condemned
To pass my life on earth.

The owl upon the roof will call
And grief my heart will tear,
His voice will echo in the woods,
And I shall not be there.

This song was often sung amongst us, not in chorus, but as a solo. Someone would go out on to the steps, sit down, ponder a little with his cheek on his hand and begin singing it in a high falsetto. It made one's heart ache to hear it. There were some good voices among us.

Meanwhile it was beginning to get dark. Sadness, despondency and stupefaction were painfully evident through the drunkenness and merrymaking. The man who had been laughing an hour before was sobbing, hopelessly drunk. Others had had a couple of fights by now. Others, pale and hardly able to stand, lounged about the wards picking quarrels with everyone. Men whose liquor never made them quarrelsome were vainly looking for friends to whom they could open their hearts and pour out their drunken sorrows. All these poor people wanted to enjoy themselves, wanted to spend the great holiday merrily, and, good God! how dreary, how miserable the day was for almost all of us. Everyone seemed disappointed. Petrov came to see me twice again. He had drunk very little all day and was almost sober. But up to the last hour he seemed to be still expecting that something must be going to happen, something extraordinary, festive and amusing. Though he said nothing about it, one could see this in his eyes. He kept flitting from ward to ward without wearying. But nothing special happened or was to be met with, except drunkenness, drunken, senseless oaths and men stupefied with drink. Sirotkin, too, wandered through the wards, well washed and looking pretty in a new red shirt; he, too, seemed quietly and naïvely expectant of something. By degrees it became unbearable and disgusting in the wards. No doubt there was a great deal that was laughable, but I felt sad and sorry for them all, I felt dreary and stifled among them.

Here were two convicts disputing which should treat the other. Evidently they had been wrangling for a long time and this was not their first quarrel. One in particular seemed to have an old grudge against the other. He was complaining and speaking thickly, was struggling to prove that the other had been unfair to him: some sheepskin coat had been sold, a sum of money had been made away with somehow, a year before at carnival. There was something else besides . . . He was a tall muscular fellow of peaceable disposition and by no means a fool. When he was drunk he was disposed to make friends with anyone and to open his heart to him. He even swore at his opponent and got up a grievance against him in order to be reconciled and more friendly afterwards. The other, a short, thick-set, stubby man, with a round face, was a sharp and wily fellow. He had drunk more than his companion, perhaps, but was only slightly drunk. He was a man of character and was reputed to be well off, but it was for some reason to his interest just now not to irritate his expansive friend, and he led him up to the vodka dealer; while the friend kept repeating that he should and must treat him 'if only you are an honest man'.

The 'publican', with a shade of respect for the short man and a shade of contempt for his expansive companion, because the latter was being treated and not drinking at his own expense, brought out some vodka and poured out a cupful.

'No, Styopka, you owe it me,' said the expansive friend, seeing he had gained his point, 'for it's what you owe me.'

'I am not going to waste my breath on you!' answered Styopka.

'No, Styopka, that's a lie,' protested the other, taking the cup from the 'publican,' 'for you owe me money, you've no conscience! Why, your very eyes are not your own but borrowed. You are a scoundrel, Styopka, that's what you are; that's the only word for you!'

'What are you whining about? – you've spilt your vodka. One stands you treat, so you might as well drink,' cried the publican to the expansive friend, 'You can't keep us standing here till tomorrow!'

'But I am going to drink it – what are you shouting about! A merry Christmas to you, Stepan Dorofeitch!' cup in hand he turned politely, and made a slight bow to Styopka whom half a minute before he had called a scoundrel. 'Good health to you for a hundred years, not reckoning what you've lived already!' He emptied his cup, cleared his throat and wiped his mouth. 'I could carry a lot of vodka in my day, lads,' he observed with grave dignity, addressing the world in general–)nd no one in particular, 'but now it seems age is coming upon me. Thank you, Stepan Dorofeitch.'

'Not at all.'

'But I shall always tell you of it, Styopka, and besides your behaving like a regular scoundrel to me, I tell you . . . '

'And I've something to tell you, you drunken lout,' Styopka broke in, losing all patience. 'Listen and mark my words. Look here: we'll halve the world between us – you take one half, and I'll take the other. You go your way and don't let me meet you again. I am sick of you.'

'Then you won't pay me the money?'

'What money, you drunken fool?'

'Ah, in the next world you'll be wanting to pay it, but I won't take it. We work hard for our money, with sweat on our brows and blisters on our hands. You'll suffer for my five kopecks in the other world.'

'Oh, go to the devil!'

'Don't drive me, I am not in harness yet.'

'Go on, go on!'

'Scoundrel!'

'You jail-bird!'

And abuse followed again, more violent than before.

Here two friends were sitting apart on the bed. One of them, a tall, thick-set, fleshy fellow with a red face, who looked like a regular butcher, was almost crying, for he was very much touched. The other was a frail-looking, thin, skinny little man, with a long nose which always looked moist and little piggy eyes which were fixed on the ground. He was a polished and cultivated individual; he had been a clerk and treated his friend a little superciliously, which the other secretly resented. They had been drinking together all day.

'He's taken a liberty!' cried the fleshy friend, shaking the clerk's head violently with his left arm, which he had round him. By 'taking a liberty' he meant that he had hit him. The stout one, who had been a sergeant, was secretly envious of his emaciated friend and so they were trying to outdo one another in the choiceness of their language.

'And I tell you that you are wrong too . . . ' the clerk began dogmatically, resolutely refusing to look at his opponent and staring at the floor with a dignified air.

'He's taken a liberty, do you hear!' the first man broke in, shaking his friend more violently than ever. 'You are the only friend I have in the world, do you hear? And that's why I tell you and no one else, he's taken a liberty!'

'And I tell you again, such a feeble justification, my friend, is only a discredit to you,' said the clerk in a high-pitched, bland voice. 'You'd better admit, my friend, that all this drunken business is due to your own incontinence.'

The stout convict staggered back a little, looked blankly with his drunken eyes at the self-satisfied clerk and suddenly and quite unexpectedly drove his huge fist with all his might into his friend's little face. That was the end of a whole day's friendship. His dear friend was sent flying senseless under the bed . . .

A friend of mine from the special division, a clever good-humoured fellow of boundless good-nature and extraordinarily simple appearance, who was fond of a joke but quite without malice, came into our ward. This was the man who on my first day in prison had been at dinner in the kitchen, asking where the rich peasant lived and declaring that he had pride, and who had drunk tea with me. He was a man of forty, with an extraordinarily thick lower lip and a large fleshy nose covered with pimples. He was holding a balalaika and carelessly twanging the strings. A diminutive convict with a very large head was following him about as though he were on a string. I had scarcely seen him before, and indeed no one ever noticed him. He was a queer fellow, mistrustful, always silent and serious; he used to work in the sewing-room, and evidently tried to live a life apart and to avoid having anything to do with the rest. Now, being drunk, he followed Varlamov about like a shadow. He followed him about in great excitement, waving his arms in the air, bringing his fist down on the wall and on the bed, and almost shedding tears. Varlamov seemed to be paying no attention to him, as though he were not beside him. It is worth remarking that these men had had scarcely anything to do with one another before; they had nothing in common in their pursuits or their characters. They belonged to different divisions and lived in different wards. The little convict's name was Bulkin.

Varlamov grinned on seeing me. I was sitting on my bed by the stove. He stood at a little distance facing me, pondered a moment, gave a lurch, and coming up to me with unsteady steps, he flung himself into a swaggering attitude and lightly touching the strings, chanted in measured tones with a faint tap of his boot:

Round face! fair face!
Like a tomtit in the meadow
  Hear my darling's voice!
When she wears a dress of satin
With some most becoming trimming,
  Oh, she does look nice!

This song seemed the last straw for Bulkin; he gesticulated, and addressing the company in general he shouted: 'He keeps telling lies, lads, he keeps telling lies! Not a word of truth in it, it is all a lie!'

'Respects to old Alexandr Petrovitch!' said Varlamov. He peeped into my face with a sly laugh, and was on the point of kissing me. He was very drunk. The expression 'old' So-and-so is used among the people all over Siberia even in addressing a lad of twenty. The word 'old' suggests respect, veneration, something flattering, in fact.

'Well, Varlamov, how are you getting on?'

'Oh, I am jogging along. If one's glad it's Christmas, one gets drunk early; you must excuse me!' Varlamov talked in rather a drawl.

'That's all lying, all lying again!' shouted Bulkin, thumping on the bed in a sort of despair. But Varlamov seemed determined to take no notice of him, and there was something very comic about it, because Bulkin had attached himself to Varlamov from early morning for no reason whatever, simply because Varlamov kept 'lying', as he somehow imagined. He followed him about like a shadow, found fault with every word he said, wrung his hands, banged them against the walls and the bed till they almost bled, and was distressed, evidently distressed, by the conviction that Varlamov 'was lying'. If he had had any hair on his head, I believe he would have pulled it out in his mortification. It was as though he felt responsible for Varlamov's conduct, as though all Varlamov's failings were on his conscience. But what made it comic was that Varlamov never even looked at him.

'He keeps lying, nothing but lying and lying! There's not a word of sense in all he says!' shouted Bulkin.

'But what's that to you?' responded the convicts laughing.

'I beg to inform you, Alexandr Petrovitch, that I was very handsome and that the wenches were awfully fond of me . . . ' Varlamov began suddenly, apropos of nothing.

'He's lying! He's lying again!' Bulkin broke in with a squeal. The convicts laughed.

'And didn't I swell it among them! I'd a red shirt and velveteen breeches; I lay at my ease like that Count Bottle, that is, as drunk as a Swede; anything I liked in fact!'

'That's a lie!' Bulkin protested stoutly.

'And in those days I had a stone house of two storeys that had been my father's. In two years I got through the two storeys, I'd nothing but the gate left and no gate-posts. Well, money is like pigeons that come and go.'

'That's a lie,' Bulkin repeated more stoutly than ever.

'So the other day I sent my parents a tearful letter; I thought maybe they'd send me something. For I've been told I went against my parents. I was disrespectful to them! It's seven years since I sent it to them.'

'And haven't you had an answer?' I asked laughing.

'No, I haven't,' he answered, suddenly laughing too, bringing his nose nearer and nearer to my face. 'And I've a sweetheart here, Alexandr Petrovitch . . . '

'Have you? A sweetheart?'

'Onufriev said the other day: "My girl may be pock-marked and plain, but look what a lot of clothes she's got; and yours may be pretty, but she is a beggar and goes about with a sack on her back." '

'And is it true?'

'It's true she is a beggar!' he answered, and he went off into a noiseless laugh; there was laughter among the other convicts too. Everyone knew indeed that he had picked up with a beggar girl and had only given her ten kopecks in the course of six months.

'Well, what of it?' I asked, wanting to get rid of him at last.

He paused, looked at me feelingly and pronounced tenderly: 'Why, things being so, won't you be kind enough to stand me a glass? I've been drinking tea all day, Alexandr Petrovitch,' he added with feeling, accepting the money I gave him, 'I've been swilling tea till I am short of breath, and it's gurgling in my belly like water in a bottle.'

When he was taking the money Bulkin's mental agitation reached its utmost limits. He gesticulated like a man in despair, almost crying.

'Good people!' he shouted, addressing the whole ward in his frenzy. 'Look at him! He keeps lying! Whatever he says, it's nothing but lies, lies and lies!'

'But what is it to you,' cried the convicts, wondering at his fury, 'you ridiculous fellow?'

'I won't let him tell lies!' cried Bulkin with flashing eyes, bringing his fist down on the bed with all his might. 'I don't want him to tell lies!'

Everyone laughed. Varlamov took the money, bowed to me and, grimacing, hurried out of the ward, to the publican, of course. And then he seemed for the first time to become aware of Bulkin.

'Well, come along!' he said to him, stopping in the doorway, as though he were of some use to him. 'You walking-stick!' he added as he contemptuously made way for the mortified Bulkin to pass out before him, and began twanging the balalaika again.

But why describe this Bedlam! The oppressive day came to an end at last. The convicts fell heavily asleep on the plank bed. They talked and muttered in their sleep that night even more than usual. Here and there they were still sitting over cards. The holiday, so long looked forward to, was over. Tomorrow the daily round, tomorrow work again.

CHAPTER ELEVEN

The Theatricals

On the third day in Christmas week we had the first performance of our theatricals. A great deal of trouble had no doubt been spent on getting them up, but the actors had undertaken it all so that the rest of us had no idea how things were going, what was being done. We did not even know for certain what was to be performed. The actors had done their best during those three days to get hold of costumes when they went out to work. When Baklushin met me he did nothing but snap his fingers with glee. Even the major seemed to be in a decent mood, though we really were not sure whether he knew of the theatricals. If he did know, would he give his formal sanction or only make up his mind to say nothing, winking at the convicts' project, insisting of course that everything should be as orderly as possible? I imagine he knew about the theatricals and could not but have known of them, but did not want to interfere, realising that he might make things worse by prohibiting them: the convicts would begin to be disorderly and drunken, so that it would really be much better for them to have something to occupy them. I assume that this was the major's line of argument, simply because it is most natural, sensible and correct. It may even be said if the convicts had not got up theatricals or some such entertainment for the holidays, the authorities ought to have thought of it themselves. But as our major's mind did not work like the minds of the rest of mankind but in quite the opposite way, it may very well be that I am quite in error in supposing that he knew of the theatricals and allowed them. A man like the major must always be oppressing someone, taking something away, depriving men of some right – making trouble somewhere, in fact. He was known all over the town for it. What did it matter to him if restrictions might lead to disturbances in prison? There were penalties for such disturbances (such is the reasoning of men like our major) and severity and strict adherence to the letter of the law is all that the scoundrelly convicts need. These obtuse ministers of the law absolutely fail to understand and are incapable of understanding that the strict adherence to the letter of it, without using their reason, without understanding the spirit of it, leads straight to disturbance, and has never led to anything else. 'It is the law, there's nothing more to be said,' they say, and they are genuinely astonished that they should be expected to show common sense and a clear head as well. This seems particularly unnecessary to many of them, a revolting superfluity, a restriction and a piece of intolerance.

But however that may have been, the senior sergeant did not oppose the convicts, and that was all they cared about. I can say with certainty that the theatricals and the gratitude felt for their being permitted were the reason why there was not one serious disturbance in the prison during the holidays: not one violent quarrel, not one case of theft. I myself witnessed the convicts themselves trying to repress the riotous or quarrelsome, simply on the ground that the theatricals might be prohibited. The sergeant exacted a promise from the convicts that everything should be orderly and that they would behave themselves. They agreed joyfully, and kept their promise faithfully; they were much flattered at their words being trusted. It must be added, however, that it cost the authorities nothing to allow the theatricals, they had not to contribute. No space had to be set apart for the theatre – the stage could be rigged up and taken to pieces again in a quarter of an hour. The performance lasted for an hour and a half, and if the order had suddenly come from headquarters to stop the performance, it could all have been put away in a trice. The costumes were hidden in the convicts' boxes. But before I describe how the theatricals were arranged and what the costumes were like, I must describe the programme, that is, what it was proposed to perform.

There was no written programme. But on the second and third performances a programme in the handwriting of Baklushin made its appearance for the benefit of the officers and of distinguished visitors generally who had honoured our theatricals by being present at the first performance. The officer of the guard usually came, and on one occasion the commanding officer of the guards came himself. The officer of the engineers came, too, on one evening, and it was for visitors like these the programme was prepared. It was assumed that the fame of the prison theatricals would spread far and wide in the fortress and would even reach the town, especially as there was no theatre in the town. There was a rumour that one performance had been got up by a society of amateurs, but that was all. The convicts were like children, delighted at the smallest success, vain over it indeed. 'Who knows,' they thought and said among themselves, 'perhaps even the highest authorities will hear about it, they'll come and have a look; then they'll see what the convicts are made of. It's not a simple soldiers' performance with dummy figures, floating boats, and dancing bears and goats. We have actors, real actors, they act high-class comedies, there's no theatre like it even in the town. General Abrosimov had a performance, they say, and is going to have another, but I dare say he'll only beat us in the dresses. As for the *conversations*, who knows whether they'll be as good! It will reach the governor's ears, maybe, and – you never can tell! – he may take it into his head to have a look at it himself. There's no theatre in the town . . . ' In fact the prisoners' imagination was so worked up during the holidays, especially after the first success, that they were ready to fancy they might receive rewards or have their term of imprisonment shortened, though at the same time they were almost at once ready to laugh very good-naturedly at their own expense. They were children, in fact, perfect children, though some of these children were over forty.

But though there was no regular programme I already knew in outline what the performance would consist of. The first piece was called *Filatka and Miroshka, or The Rivals*. Baklushin had boasted to me a week beforehand that the part of Filatka which he was undertaking would be acted in a style such as had never been seen even in the Petersburg theatres. He strolled about the wards bragging without shame or scruple, though with perfect good-nature; and now and then he would suddenly go through a bit of 'theatrical business', a bit of his part, that is, and they all would laugh, regardless of whether the performance was amusing; though even then, it must be admitted, the convicts knew how to restrain themselves and keep up their dignity. The only convicts who were enraptured by Baklushin's pranks and his stories of what was coming were either quite young people, greenhorns, deficient in reserve, or else the more important among the convicts whose prestige was firmly established, so that they had no reason to be afraid of giving vent to their feelings of any sort, however simple (that is, however unseemly, according to prison notions) they might be. The others listened to the gossip and rumours in silence; they did not, it is true, contradict or disapprove, but they did their utmost to take up an indifferent and even to some extent supercilious attitude to the theatricals. Only during the last days just before the performance everyone began to feel inquisitive. What was coming? How would our men do? What was the major saying? Would it be as successful as it was last year? and so on.

Baklushin assured me that the actors had been splendidly chosen, every one 'to fit his part'; that there would even be a curtain, that Filatka's betrothed was to be acted by Sirotkin 'and you will see what he is like in woman's dress,' he added, screwing up his eyes and clicking with his tongue. The benevolent lady was to wear a mantle and a dress with a flounce, and to carry a parasol in her hand. The benevolent gentleman was to come on in an officer's coat with epaulettes, and was to carry a cane in his hand. There was to be a second piece with a highly dramatic ending called *Kedril the Glutton*. The title aroused my curiosity, but in spite of all my enquiries I could learn nothing about this piece beforehand. I only learnt that they had not taken the play out of a book, but from a 'written copy'; that they got the play from a retired sergeant living in the town who had probably once taken part in a performance of it himself in some soldiers' entertainment. In our remote towns and provinces there are such plays which no one seems to know anything about, and which have perhaps never been printed, but seem to have appeared of themselves, and so have become an indispensable part of every 'people's theatre'. It would be a very, very good thing if some investigator would make a fresh and more careful study of the people's drama, which really does exist, and is perhaps by no means valueless. I refuse to believe that all I saw on our prison stage was invented by the convicts themselves. There must be a continuous tradition, established customs and conceptions handed down from generation to generation and consecrated by time. They must be looked for among soldiers, among factory hands, in factory towns, and even among the working classes in some poor obscure little towns. They are preserved, too, in villages and provincial towns among the servants of the richer country gentry. I imagine indeed that many old-fashioned plays have been circulated in written copies all over Russia by house-serfs. Many of the old-fashioned landowners and Moscow gentlemen had their own dramatic companies, made up of serf actors. And these theatres laid the foundations of the national dramatic art of which there are unmistakable signs. As for *Kedril the Glutton*, I was able to learn nothing about it beforehand, except that evil spirits appear on the stage and carry Kedril off to hell. But what does the name Kedril mean, why is it Kedril and not Kiril? Whether it is a Russian story or of foreign origin I could not find out. It was announced that finally there would be a 'pantomime to the accompaniment of music'. All this of course was very interesting. The actors were fifteen in number – all smart, spirited fellows. They bestirred themselves, rehearsed – sometimes behind the prison – held their tongues and kept things secret. In fact they meant to surprise us with something extraordinary and unexpected.

On working days the prison was locked up early, as soon as night came on. Christmas week was an exception: they did not lock up till the evening tattoo. This concession was made expressly for the sake of the theatre. Almost every afternoon during Christmas week they sent a messenger from the prison to the officer of the watch with a humble request 'to allow the theatricals and leave the wards unlocked a little longer', adding that this had been allowed the day before and there had been no disorder. The officer of the watch reasoned that 'there really had been no disorder the day before, and if they gave their word that there would be none today, it meant that they would see to that themselves and that made things safer than anything. Besides, if the theatricals were not allowed, maybe (there's no knowing with a lot of criminals!) they might get up some mischief through spite and get the watch into trouble.' Another point was that it was tedious to serve on the watch, and here was a play, not simply got up by the soldiers, but by the convicts, and convicts are an interesting lot; it would be amusing to see it. The officers of the watch always had the privilege of looking on.

If his superior officer came along he would ask, 'Where is the officer of the watch?' 'He is in the prison counting over the convicts and locking the wards' – a straightforward answer and a sufficient explanation. And so every evening through the Christmas holidays the officers of the watch allowed the performance, and did not lock the wards till the evening tattoo. The convicts knew beforehand that there would be no hindrance from the officers of the watch, and they had no anxiety on that ground.

About seven o'clock Petrov came to fetch me and we went to the performance together. Almost all the inmates of our ward went to the performance except the Old Believer and the Poles. It was only on the very last performance, on the fourth of January, that the Poles made up their minds to be present, and only then after many assurances that it was nice and amusing, and that there was no risk about it. The disdain of the Poles did not irritate the convicts in the very least, and they were welcomed on the fourth of January quite politely. They were even shown into the best places. As for the Circassians and still more Isay Fomitch, the performance was to them a real enjoyment. Isay Fomitch paid three kopecks every time, and on the last performance put ten kopecks in the plate and there was a look of bliss on his face. The actors decided to collect from the audience what they were willing to give for the expenses of the theatre and for their own 'fortifying'. Petrov assured me that I should be put into one of the best seats, however crowded the theatre might be, on the ground that being richer than most of them I should probably subscribe more liberally and also that I knew more about acting. And so it was. But I will first describe the room and the arrangement of the theatre.

The military ward in which our stage was arranged was fifteen paces long. From the yard one mounted some steps into the passage leading to the ward. This long ward, as I have mentioned already, was different from the others: the bed platform ran round the walls so that the middle of the room was free. The half of the room nearest to the steps was given up to the spectators and the other half which communicated with another ward was marked off for the stage. What struck me first of all was the curtain. It stretched for ten feet across the room. To have a curtain was such a luxury that it was certainly something to marvel at. What is more, it was painted in oil colours with a design of trees, arbours, lakes and stars. It was made of pieces of linen, old and new, such as they were able to collect among the convicts, old leg wrappers and shirts sewn together after a fashion into one large strip, and where the linen fell short the gap was filled simply with paper which had been begged, sheet by sheet, from various offices and departments. Our painters, amongst whom the 'Brüllov' of the prison, A., was conspicuous, had made it their work to decorate and paint it. The effect was surprising. Such a refinement delighted even the most morose and fastidious of the convicts, who, when it came to the performance, were without exception as childish in their admiration as the most enthusiastic and impatient. All were very much pleased and even boastful in their pleasure.

The stage was lighted by means of a few tallow candles which were cut into pieces. In front of the curtain stood two benches brought from the kitchen, and in front of the benches were three or four chairs from the sergeant's room. The chairs were intended for any officers that might come in, the benches for the sergeants and the engineering clerks, foremen and other persons in official positions, though not officers, in case any such looked in on the performance. And as a fact, spectators from outside were present at every performance; there were more on some evenings than on others, but at the last performance there was not a vacant seat on the benches. In the back of the room were the convicts themselves, standing, and in spite of the suffocating, steamy heat of the room wearing their coats or sheepskins and carrying their caps in their hands, out of respect for their visitors. Of course the space allotted to the convicts was too small. And not only were people literally sitting on others, especially in the back rows, but the beds too were filled up, as well as the spaces to right and left of the curtain, and there were even some ardent spectators who always went round behind the scenes, and looked at the performance from the other ward at the back. The crush in the first part of the ward was incredible, and might even be compared to the crush and crowding I had lately seen at the bath-house. The door into the passage was open and the passage, where the temperature was 20° below zero, was also thronged with people. Petrov and I were at once allowed to go to the front, almost up to the benches, where we could see much better than from the back. They looked upon me as to some extent a theatre-goer, a connoisseur, who had frequented performances very different from this; they had seen Baklushin consulting me all this time and treating me with respect;

so on this occasion I had the honour of a front place. The convicts were no doubt extremely vain and frivolous, but it was all on the surface. The convicts could laugh at me, seeing that I was a poor hand at their work. Almazov could look with contempt upon us 'gentlemen' and pride himself on knowing how to burn alabaster. But, mixed with their persecution and ridicule, there was another element: we had once been gentlemen; we belonged to the same class as their former masters, of whom they could have no pleasant memories. But now at the theatricals they made way for me. They recognised that in this I was a better critic, that I had seen and knew more than they. Even those who liked me least were (I know for a fact) anxious now for my approval of their theatricals, and without the slightest servility they let me have the best place. I see that now, recalling my impressions at the time. It seemed to me at the time – I remember – that in their correct estimate of themselves there was no servility, but a sense of their own dignity. The highest and most striking characteristic of our people is just their sense of justice and their eagerness for it. There is no trace in the common people of the desire to be cock of the walk on all occasions and at all costs, whether they deserve to be or not. One has but to take off the outer superimposed husk and to look at the kernel more closely, more attentively and without prejudice, and some of us will see things in the people that we should never have expected. There is not much our wise men could teach them. On the contrary, I think it is the wise men who ought to learn from the people.

Before we started, Petrov told me naïvely that I should have a front place partly because I should subscribe more. There was no fixed price of admission: everyone gave what he could or what he wished. When the plate was taken round almost everyone put something in it, even if it were only a halfpenny. But if I were given a front place partly on account of money, on the supposition that I should give more than others, what a sense of their own dignity there was in that again! 'You are richer than I am, so you can stand in front, and though we are all equal, you'll give more; and so a spectator like you is more pleasing to the actors. You must have the first place, for we are all here not thinking of the money, but showing our respect, so we ought to sort ourselves of our own accord.' How much fine and genuine pride there is in this! It is a respect not for money, but respect for oneself. As a rule there was not much respect for money, for wealth, in the prison, especially if one looks at convicts without distinction, as a gang, in the mass. I can't remember one of them seriously demeaning himself for the sake of money. There were men who were always begging, who begged even of me. But this was rather mischief, roguery, than the real thing; there was too much humour and naïveté in it. I don't know whether I express myself so as to be understood. But I am forgetting the theatricals. To return.

Till the curtain was raised, the whole room was a strange and animated picture. To begin with, masses of spectators crowded, squeezed tightly, packed on all sides, waiting with patient and blissful faces for the performance to begin. In the back rows men were clambering on one another. Many of them had brought blocks of wood from the kitchen; fixing the thick block of wood against the wall, a man would climb on to it, leaning with both hands on the shoulders of someone in front of him, and would stand like that without changing his attitude for the whole two hours, perfectly satisfied with himself and his position. Others got their feet on the lower step of the stove and stayed so all the time, leaning on men in front of them. This was quite in the hindmost rows, next to the wall. At the sides, too, men were standing on the bed in dense masses above the musicians. This was a good place. Five people had clambered on to the stove itself and, lying on it, looked down from it. They must have been blissful. The window-sills on the opposite wall were also crowded with people who had come in late or failed to get a good place. Everyone behaved quietly and decorously. Everyone wished to show himself in the best light before the gentry and the officers. All faces expressed a simple-hearted expectation. Every face was red and bathed in sweat from the closeness and heat. A strange light of childlike joy, of pure, sweet pleasure, was shining on these lined and branded brows and cheeks, on those faces usually so morose and gloomy, in those eyes which sometimes gleamed with such terrible fire. They were all bare-headed, and all the heads were shaven on the right side.

Suddenly sounds of bustle and hurrying were heard on the stage. In a minute the curtain would rise. Then the band struck up. This band deserves special mention. Eight musicians were installed on the bed on one side; two violins (one from the prison and one borrowed from someone in the fortress, but both the fiddlers were convicts), three balalaikas, all home-made, two guitars and a tambourine instead of a double-bass. The violins simply scraped and squealed, the guitars were wretched, but the balalaikas were wonderful. The speed with which they twanged the strings with their fingers was a positive feat of agility. They played dance tunes. At the liveliest part of the tunes, the balalaika-players would tap the case of the instruments with their knuckles; the tone, the taste, the execution, the handling of the instrument and the characteristic rendering of the tune, all was individual, original and typical of the convicts. One of the guitarists, too, played his instrument splendidly. This was the gentleman who had murdered his father. As for the tambourine, it was simply marvellous. The player whirled it round on his finger and drew his thumb across the surface; now we heard rapid, resonant, monotonous taps; then suddenly this loud distinct sound seemed to be broken into a shower of innumerable jangling and whispering notes. Two accordions also appeared on the scene. Upon my word I had had no idea till then what could be done with simple peasant instruments: the blending and harmony of sounds, above all, the spirit, the character of the conception and rendering of the tune in its very essence were simply amazing. For the first time I realised fully all the reckless dash and gaiety of the gay dashing Russian dance songs.

At last the curtain rose. There was a general stir, everyone shifted from one leg to the other, those at the back stood on tiptoe, someone fell off his block of wood, everyone without exception opened his mouth and stared, and absolute silence reigned . . . The performance began.

Near me was standing Aley in a group consisting of his brothers and all the other Circassians. They were all intensely delighted with the performance, and came every evening afterwards. All Mohammedans, Tatars and others, as I have noticed more than once, are passionately fond of spectacles of all sorts. Next to them Isay Fomitch had tucked himself in. From the moment the curtain rose, he seemed to be all ears and eyes, and simple-hearted, greedy expectations of delights and marvels. It would have been pitiful indeed if he had been disappointed. Aley's charming face beamed with such pure childlike joy that I must confess I felt very happy in looking at him, and I remember that at every amusing and clever sally on the part of the actors, when there was a general burst of laughter, I could not help turning to Aley and glancing at his face. He did not see me – he had no attention to spare for me! On the left side quite near me stood an old convict who was always scowling, discontented and grumbling. He, too, noticed Aley, and I saw him more than once turn with a half-smile towards him: he was so charming! 'Aley Semyonitch' he called him, I don't know why.

They began with *Filatka and Miroshka*. Filatka acted by Baklushin was really splendid. He played his part with amazing precision. One could see that he had thought out every phrase, every movement. Into the slightest word or gesture he knew how to put value and significance in perfect harmony with the character he was acting. And to this conscientious effort and study must be added an inimitable gaiety, simplicity and naturalness. If you had seen Baklushin, you would certainly have agreed that he was a born actor of real talent. I had seen *Filatka* more than once at theatres in Moscow and Petersburg, and I can say positively that the city actors were inferior to Baklushin in the part of Filatka. By comparison with him they were too much of *paysans*, and not real Russian peasants. They were too anxious to mimic the Russian peasant. Baklushin was stirred, too, by emulation. Everyone knew that in the second play the part of Kedril would be taken by the convict Potseykin, who was for some reason considered by all a more talented actor than Baklushin, and at this Baklushin was as chagrined as a child. How often he had come to me during those last few days to give vent to his feelings! Two hours before the performance he was in a perfect fever. When they laughed and shouted to him from the crowd: 'Bravo, Baklushin! First-rate!', his whole face beamed with pleasure, there was a light of real inspiration in his eyes. The scene of his kissing Miroshka, when Filatka shouts to him beforehand 'Wipe your nose!' and wipes his own, was killingly funny. Everyone was rocking with laughter. But what interested me more than all was the audience; they were all completely carried away. They gave themselves up to their pleasure without reserve. Shouts of approbation sounded more and more frequently. One would nudge his neighbour and hurriedly whisper his impressions, without caring or even noticing who was beside him. Another would turn ecstatically to the audience at an amusing passage, hurriedly look at everyone, wave his hand as though calling on everyone to laugh and immediately turn greedily round to the stage again. Another one simply clicked with his fingers and his tongue, and could not stand still, but being unable to move from his place, kept shifting from one leg to the other. By the end of the performance the general gaiety had reached its height. I am not exaggerating anything. Imagine prison, fetters, bondage, the vista of melancholy years ahead, the life of days as monotonous as the drip of water on a dull autumn day, and suddenly all these oppressed and outcast are allowed for one short hour to relax, to rejoice, to forget the weary dream, to create a complete theatre, and to create it to the pride and astonishment of the whole town – to show 'what fellows we convicts are!' Of course everything interested them, the dresses, for example; they were awfully curious for instance to see a fellow like Vanka Otpety or Netsvetaev or Baklushin in a different dress from that in which they had seen them every day for so many years. 'Why, he is a convict, a convict the same as ever, with the fetters jingling on him, and there he is in a frock-coat, with a round hat on, in a cloak – like an ordinary person! He's got on moustaches and a wig.! Here he's brought a red handkerchief out of his pocket, he is fanning himself with it, he is acting a gentleman – for all the world as though he were a gentleman!' And all were in raptures. 'The benevolent country gentleman' came on in an adjutant's uniform, a very old one, it's true, in epaulettes and a cap with a cockade, and made an extraordinary sensation. There were two competitors for the part, and, would you believe it, they quarrelled like little children as to which should play it: both were eager to appear in an adjutant's uniform with shoulder knots. The other actors parted them, and by a majority of votes gave the part to Netsvetaev, not because he was better-looking and more presentable than the other and so looked more like a gentleman, but because Netsvetaev assured them that he would come on with a cane and would wave it about and draw patterns on the ground with it like a real gentleman and tiptop swell, which Vanka Otpety could not do, for he had never seen any real gentlemen. And, indeed, when Netsvetaev came on the stage with his lady, he kept on rapidly drawing patterns on the floor with a thin reedy cane which he had picked up somewhere, no doubt considering this a sign of the highest breeding, foppishness and fashion. Probably at some time in his childhood, as a barefoot servant boy, he had happened to see a finely-dressed gentleman with a cane and been fascinated by his dexterity with it, and the impression had remained printed indelibly on his memory, so that now at thirty he remembered it exactly as it was, for the enchantment and delectation of the whole prison. Netsvetaev was so absorbed in his occupation that he looked at no one; he even spoke without raising his eyes, he simply watched the tip of his cane. 'The benevolent country lady', too, was a remarkable conception in its way: she came on in a shabby old muslin dress which looked no better than a rag, with her neck and arms bare, and her face horribly rouged and powdered, with a cotton nightcap tied under her chin, carrying a parasol in one hand and in the other a painted paper fan with which she continually fanned herself. A roar of laughter greeted this lady's appearance; the lady herself could not refrain from laughing several times. A convict called Ivanov took the part. Sirotkin dressed up as a girl looked very charming. The verses, too, went off very well. In fact, the play gave complete satisfaction to all. There was no criticism, and indeed there could not be.

The orchestra played the song, 'My porch, my new porch', by way of overture, and the curtain rose again. The second piece was *Kedril*, a play somewhat in the style of *Don Juan*; at least the master and servant are both carried off to hell by devils at the end. They acted all they had, but it was obviously a fragment, of which the beginning and the end were lost. There was no meaning or consistency in it. The action takes place in Russia, at an inn. The innkeeper brings a gentleman in an overcoat and a battered round hat into the room. He is followed by his servant Kedril carrying a trunk and a fowl wrapped up in a piece of blue paper. Kedril wears a sheepskin and a footman's cap. It is he who is the glutton. He was acted by Baklushin's rival, Potseykin. His master was acted by Ivanov, who had been the benevolent lady in the first piece. The innkeeper, Netsvetaev, warns them that the room is haunted by devils and then goes away. The gentleman, gloomy and pre-occupied, mutters that he knew that long ago and tells Kedril to unpack his things and prepare the supper. Kedril is a coward and a glutton. Hearing about the devils, he turns pale and trembles like a leaf. He would run away, but is afraid of his master. And, what's more, he is hungry. He is greedy, stupid, cunning in his own way, and cowardly; he deceives his master at every step and at the same time is afraid of him. He is a striking type, which obscurely and remotely suggests the character of Leporello. It was really remarkably rendered. Potseykin had unmistakable talent, and in my opinion was even a better actor than Baklushin. Of course, when I met Baklushin next day, I did not express my opinion quite frankly; I should have wounded him too much. The convict who acted the master acted pretty well, too. He talked the most fearful nonsense; but his delivery was good and spirited, and his gestures were appropriate. While Kedril was busy with the trunk, the master paced up and down the stage lost in thought, and announced aloud that that evening he had reached the end of his travels. Kedril listened inquisitively, made grimaces, spoke aside, and made the audience laugh at every word. He had no pity for his master, but he had heard of the devils; he wants to know what that meant and so he begins to talk and ask questions. His master at last informs him that in some difficulty in the past he had invoked the aid of hell; the devils had helped him and had extricated him; but that today the hour had come, and that perhaps that evening the devils would arrive according to their compact to carry off his soul. Kedril begins to be panic-stricken. But the gentleman keeps up his spirits and tells him to prepare the supper. Kedril brightens up, brings out the fowl, brings out some wine and now and then pulls a bit off the fowl and tastes it. The audience laughs. Then the door creaks, the wind rattles the shutters; Kedril shudders and hastily, almost unconsciously, stuffs into his mouth a piece of chicken too huge for him to swallow. Laughter again. 'Is it ready?' asks the gentleman striding about the room. 'Directly, sir . . . I am getting it ready,' says Kedril. He seats himself at the table and calmly proceeds to make away with his master's supper. The audience is evidently delighted at the smartness and cunning of the servant and at the master's being made a fool of. It must be admitted that Potseykin really deserved the applause he got. The words 'Directly, sir, I am getting it ready', he pronounced superbly. Sitting at the table, he began eating greedily, starting at every step his master took, for fear the latter should notice what he was about; as soon as the master turned round he hid under the table, pulling the chicken after him. At last he had taken off the edge of his appetite; the time came to think of his master. 'Kedril, how long will you be?' cries the master. 'Ready,' Kedril replies briskly, suddenly realising that there is hardly anything left for his master. There is nothing but one drumstick left on the plate. The gentleman, gloomy and preoccupied, sits down to the table noticing nothing, and Kedril stands behind his chair holding a napkin. Every word, every gesture, every grimace of Kedril's, when, turning to the audience, he winked at his simpleton of a master, was greeted by the spectators with irresistible peals of laughter. But as the master begins to eat, the devils appear. At this point the play became quite incomprehensible, and the devils' entrance was really too grotesque; a door opened in the wing and something in white appeared having a lantern with a candle in it instead of a head; another phantom, also with a lantern on his head, held a scythe. Why the lanterns, why the scythe, why the devils in white? No one could make out. Though, indeed, no one thought of it. It was evidently as it should be. The gentleman turns pretty pluckily to the devils and shouts to them that he is ready for them to take him. But Kedril is as frightened as a hare; he creeps under the table, but for all his fright does not forget to take the bottle with him. The devils vanish for a minute; Kedril creeps out from under the table. But as soon as the master attacks the chicken once more, three devils burst into the room again, seize the master from behind, and carry him off to the lower regions. 'Kedril, save me!' shouts his master, but Kedril has no attention to spare. This time he has carried off the bottle, a plate, and even the loaf under the table. Here he is now, alone; there are no devils, no master either. Kedril creeps out, looks about him and his face lights up with a smile. He winks slyly, sits down in his master's place, and nodding to the audience says in a half-whisper, 'Well, now I am alone . . . without a master!' Everyone roars at his being without a master, and then he adds in a half-whisper, turning confidentially to the audience and winking more and more merrily, 'The devils have got my master!'

The rapture of the audience was beyond all bounds! Apart from the master's being taken by the devils, this was said in such a way, with such slyness, such an ironically triumphant grimace, that it was impossible not to applaud. But Kedril's luck did not last long. He had hardly taken the bottle, filled his glass and raised it to his lips when the devils suddenly come back, steal up on tiptoe behind him, and seize him under the arms. Kedril screams at the top of his voice; he is so frightened he dare not look round. He cannot defend himself either; he has the bottle in one hand and the glass in the other, and cannot bring himself to part with either. For half a minute he sits, his mouth wide open with fright, staring at the audience with such a killing expression of cowardly terror that he might have sat for a picture. At last he is lifted up and carried away; still holding the bottle, he kicks and screams and screams. His screams are still heard from behind the scenes. But the curtain drops and everyone laughs, everyone is delighted . . . the orchestra strikes up the Kamarinsky.

They begin quietly, hardly audibly, but the melody grows stronger and stronger, the time more rapid; now and then comes the jaunty note of a flip on the case of the instrument. It is the Kamarinsky in all its glory, and indeed it would have been nice if Glinka could by chance have heard it in the prison. The pantomime begins to the music, which is kept up all through. The scene is the interior of a cottage. On the stage are a miller and his wife. The miller in one corner is mending some harness; in the other corner his wife is spinning flax. The wife was played by Sirotkin, the miller by Netsvetaev.

I may observe that our scenery was very poor. Both in this play and in the others we rather supplied the scene from our imagination than saw it in reality. By way of a background there was a rug or a horse-cloth of some sort; on one side a wretched sort of screen. On the left side there was nothing at all, so that we could see the bed, but the audience was not critical and was ready to supply all deficiences by their imagination, and indeed, convicts are very good at doing so. 'If you are told it's a garden, you've got to look on it as a garden, if it's a room it's a room, if it's a cottage it's a cottage – it doesn't matter, and there is no need to make a fuss about it.'

Sirotkin was very charming in the dress of a young woman. Several compliments were paid him in undertones among the audience. The miller finishes his work, takes up his hat, takes up his whip, goes up to his wife and explains to her by signs that he must go out, but that if his wife admits anyone in his absence then . . . and he indicates the whip. The wife listens and nods. Probably she is well acquainted with that whip: the hussy amuses herself when her husband is away. The husband goes off. As soon as he has gone, the wife shakes her fist after him. Then there is a knock: the door opens and another miller appears, a neighbour, a peasant with a beard, wearing a full coat. He has a present for her, a red kerchief. The woman laughs, but as soon as the neighbour tries to embrace her, there is another knock. Where can he hide? She hurriedly hides him under the table and sits down to her distaff again. Another admirer makes his appearance: an army clerk, in military dress. So far the pantomime had gone admirably, the gestures were perfectly appropriate. One could not help wondering as one looked at these impromptu actors; one could not help thinking how much power and talent in Russia are sometimes wasted in servitude and poverty. But the convict who acted the clerk had probably at some time been on some private or provincial stage, and he imagined that our performers, one and all, had no notion of acting and did not move on the stage as they ought to. And he paced the stage as we are told the classic heroes used to in the past: he would take one long stride, and before moving the other leg, stop short, throw his head and his whole body back, look haughtily around him and take another stride. If such deportment is absurd in the classical drama, in an army clerk in a comic scene it is even more ridiculous. But our audience thought that probably it was as it ought to be and took for granted the long strides of the lanky clerk without criticising them. The clerk had hardly reached the middle of the stage before another knock was heard: the woman was in a flutter again. Where was she to put the clerk? Into a chest which stood conveniently open. The clerk creeps into the chest and she shuts the lid on him. This time it is a different sort of visitor, a lover, too, but of a special kind. It is a Brahmin, and even dressed as one. There is an overwhelming burst of laughter from the audience. The Brahmin was acted by the convict Koshkin, and acted beautifully. He looked like a Brahmin. In pantomime he suggests the intensity of his feelings. He raises his hands to heaven, then lays them on his heart; but he has hardly begun to be sentimental when there is a loud knock at the door. From the sound one can tell it is the master of the house.

The frightened wife is beside herself, the Brahmin rushes about like one possessed and implores her to conceal him. She hurriedly puts him behind the cupboard and, forgetting to open the door, rushes back to her work and goes on spinning, heedless of her husband's knocking. In her alarm she twiddles in her fingers an imaginary thread and turns an imaginary distaff, while the real one lies on the floor. Sirotkin acted her terror very cleverly and successfully. But the husband breaks open the door with his foot, and whip in hand approaches his wife. He has been on the watch and has seen it all, and he plainly shows her on his fingers that she has three men hidden and then he looks for the stowaways. The one he finds first is the neighbour, and cuffing him he leads him out of the room. The terrified clerk wanting to escape puts his head out from under the lid and so betrays himself. The husband thrashes him with the whip, and this time the amorous clerk skips about in anything but a classic style. The Brahmin is left; the husband is a long while looking for him. He finds him in the corner behind the cupboard, bows to him politely and drags him by the beard into the middle of the stage. The Brahmin tries to defend himself, shouts 'Accursed man, accursed man!' (the only words uttered in the pantomime), but the husband takes no notice and deals with him after his own fashion. The wife, seeing that her turn is coming next, flings down the flax and the distaff and runs out of the room; the spinning-bench tips over on the floor, the convicts laugh. Aley tugs at my arm without looking at me, and shouts to me, 'Look! The Brahmin, the Brahmin!' laughing so that he can hardly stand. The curtain falls. A second scene follows.

But there is no need to describe them all. There were two or three more. They were all amusing and inimitably comic. If the convicts did not positively invent them, each of them put something of his own into them. Almost every one of the actors improvised something, so that the following evenings the same parts acted by the same actors were somewhat different. The last pantomime of a fantastic character concluded with a ballet. It was a funeral. The Brahmin with numerous attendants repeated various spells over the coffin, but nothing was of use. At last the strains of the 'Setting Sun' are heard, the corpse comes to life and all begin to dance with joy. The Brahmin dances with the resuscitated corpse and dances in a peculiar Brahminical fashion.

And so the theatricals were over till the next evening. The convicts dispersed merry and satisfied; they praised the actors, they thanked the sergeant. There were no sounds of quarrelling. Everyone was unusually contented, even as it were happy, and fell asleep not as on other nights, but almost with a tranquil spirit – and why, one wonders? And yet it is not a fancy of my imagination. It's the truth, the reality. These poor people were only allowed to do as they liked, ever so little, to be merry like human beings, to spend one short hour not as though in prison – and they were morally transformed, if only for a few minutes . . .

Now it is the middle of the night. I start and wake up. The old man is still praying on the stove, and will pray there till dawn. Aley is sleeping quietly beside me. I remember that he was still laughing and talking to his brothers about the theatricals as he fell asleep, and unconsciously I look closer into his peaceful childlike face. Little by little, I recall everything: the previous day, the holidays, the whole of that month . . . I lift up my head in terror and look round at my sleeping companions by the dim flickering light of the prison candle. I look at their poor faces, at their poor beds, at the hopeless poverty and destitution – I gaze at it – as though I wanted to convince myself that it is really true, and not the continuation of a hideous dream.

But it is true: I hear a moan, someone drops his arm heavily and there is the clank of chains. Another starts in his sleep and begins to speak, while the old man on the stove prays for all 'good Christians', and I hear the even cadence of his soft prolonged, 'Lord Jesus Christ, have mercy upon us.'

'After all, I am not here for ever, only for a few years,' I think, and I lay my head on the pillow again.

PART 2

CHAPTER ONE

The Hospital [1]

Soon after the holidays I was taken ill and went into our military hospital. It stood apart, half a mile from the fortress. It was a long one-storey building painted yellow. In the summer when the buildings were done up, an immense quantity of yellow ochre was spent on it. Round the huge courtyard of the hospital were grouped the offices, the doctors' houses and other buildings. The principal building consisted only of wards for the patients. There were a number of wards, but only two for the convicts, and these were always very crowded, especially in the summer, so that the beds had often to be moved close together. Our wards were full of all sorts of 'unfortunate people'. Our convicts, soldiers of all sorts awaiting trial, men who had been sentenced and men who were awaiting sentence, and men who were on their way to other prisons, all came here. There were some, too, from the disciplinary battalion – a strange institution to which soldiers who had been guilty of some offence or were not trustworthy were sent for reformation, and from which two or more years later they usually came out scoundrels such as are rarely to be met with. Convicts who were taken ill in our prison usually informed the sergeant of their condition in the morning. Their names were at once entered in the book, and with this book the invalid was sent to the battalion infirmary under escort. There the doctor made a preliminary examination of all the invalids from the various military divisions in the fortress, and any who were found to be really ill were admitted to the hospital. My name was entered in the book, and between one and two, when all the prisoners had gone out to work after dinner, I went to the hospital. The sick convict usually took with him all the money he could collect, some bread – for he could not expect to get rations at the hospital that day – a tiny pipe and a pouch of tobacco with a flint for lighting it. The latter articles he kept carefully hidden in his boots. I entered the precincts of the hospital, feeling some curiosity about this novel aspect of our prison life.

It was a warm, dull, depressing day, one of those days when an institution such as a hospital assumes a peculiarly callous, dejected and sour appearance. I went with the escort into the waiting-room, where there were two copper baths. There were two patients with their escort in the room already, not convicts, but men awaiting their trial. A hospital assistant came in, scanned us indolently with an air of authority, and still more indolently went to inform the doctor on duty. The latter soon made his appearance. He examined us, treated us very kindly, and gave each of us a medical chart with our name on it. The further description of the illness, the medicines and diet prescribed, were left for the doctor who was in charge of the convict wards. I had heard before that the convicts were never tired of praising the doctors. 'They are like fathers to us,' they said in answer to my enquiries when I was going to the hospital. Meanwhile, we had changed our clothes. The clothes we had come in were taken from us and we were dressed up in hospital underlinen and provided with long stockings, slippers, nightcaps and thick cloth dressing-gowns of dark brown colour, lined with something that might have been coarse linen or might have been sticking-plaster. In fact, the dressing-gown was filthy to the last degree, but I only fully realised this later. Then they took us to the convict wards, which were at the end of a very long, clean and lofty corridor. The appearance of cleanliness everywhere was very satisfactory; everything that caught the eye was shining – though perhaps this may have seemed so to me by contrast with the prison. The two prisoners awaiting trial went into the ward on the left, while I went to the right. At the door, which fastened with an iron bolt, stood a sentry with a gun; beside him stood a sub-sentry to relieve him. The junior sergeant (of the hospital guard) gave orders I should be admitted, and I found myself in a long, narrow room, along two walls of which were rows of beds, about twenty-two altogether, of which three or four were unoccupied. The bedsteads were wooden and painted green, of the kind only too familiar to all of us in Russia, the sort of bedstead which by some fatality is never free from bugs. I was put in the corner on the side where there were windows.

As I have said before, there were some convicts from our prison here. Some of these knew me already, or at least had seen me. But the majority were prisoners awaiting trial or from the disciplinary battalions. There were only a few who were too ill to get up. The others suffering from slight ailments, or convalescent, were either sitting on their beds or walking up and down the ward, where there was space enough for exercise between the two rows of beds. There was a suffocating hospital smell in the ward. The air was tainted with unpleasant effluvia of different sorts, as well as with the smell of drugs, although the fire was kept almost all day long in the stove in the corner. My bed had a striped quilt over it. I took it off. Under it was a cloth blanket lined with linen, and coarse sheets and pillow-cases of very doubtful cleanliness. Beside the bed stood a small table with a jug and a tin cup. All this was tidily covered with a little towel put ready for me. Underneath the table was a shelf on which patients kept a jug of kvas, or any such thing, and those who drank tea, a teapot; but very few of them did drink tea. The pipes and tobacco pouches which almost all the patients, even the consumptive ones, possessed were hidden under the mattresses. The doctor and the other attendants scarcely ever examined the beds, and even if they did find a man smoking, they pretended not to notice it. But the convicts were almost always on their guard, and went to the stove to smoke. It was only at night that they sometimes smoked in bed; but no one ever went through the wards at night, except perhaps the officer of the hospital guard.

I had never been a patient in a hospital till then, so everything surrounding me was perfectly new to me. I noticed that I excited some curiosity. They had already heard about me, and stared at me without ceremony, and even with a shade of superciliousness, as a new boy is looked at at school, or a petitioner is looked at in a government office. On the right of me lay a clerk awaiting his punishment, the illegitimate son of a captain. He was being tried for making counterfeit coin, and he had been for a year in the hospital apparently not ill in any way, though he assured the doctors that he had aneurism of the heart. He had attained his object and escaped penal servitude and corporal punishment. A year later he was sent to T—k to be kept at a hospital. He was a broad, sturdily built fellow of eight-and-twenty, a great rogue with a good knowledge of the law, very sharp, extremely self-confident, and free and easy in his behaviour. He was morbidly vain, had persuaded himself in earnest that he was the most truthful and honourable of men and, what is more, had done nothing wrong, and he clung to this conviction to the end. He spoke to me first; he began questioning me with curiosity, and described to me in some detail the external routine of the hospital. First of all, of course, he told me that he was the son of a captain. He was very anxious to make himself out a nobleman, or at least 'of good family'.

The next one who approached me was a patient from the disciplinary battalion, and he began to assure me that he knew many of the 'gentleman' exiles, mentioning them by their names. He was a grey-headed soldier; one could see from his face that he was romancing. His name was Chekunov. He was evidently trying to make up to me, probably suspecting I had money. Noticing that I had a parcel containing tea and sugar, he at once proffered his services in getting a teapot and making tea. M. had promised to send me a teapot next day from prison by one of the convicts who came to the hospital to work. But Chekunov managed all right. He got hold of an iron pot and even a cup, boiled the water, made the tea, in fact waited on me with extraordinary zeal, which at once called forth some malignant jeers at his expense from a patient lying opposite me. This was a man called Ustyantsev, a soldier under sentence, who from fear of corporal punishment had drunk a jug of vodka after steeping snuff in it, and had brought on consumption by so doing; I have mentioned him already. Till that moment he had been lying silent, breathing painfully, looking at me intently and earnestly and watching Chekunov with indignation. His extraordinarily bitter intensity gave a comic flavour to his indignation. At last he could stand it no longer:

'Ugh, the flunkey! He's found a master!' he said gasping, his voice broken with emotion. He was within a few days of his death.

Chekunov turned to him indignantly.

'Who's the flunkey?' he brought out, looking contemptuously at Ustyantsev.

'You are a flunkey!' the other replied in a self-confident tone, as though he had a full right to haul Chekunov over the coals, and in fact had been appointed to that duty.

'Me a flunkey?'

'That's what you are. Do you hear, good people, he doesn't believe it! He is surprised!'

'What is it to you? You see the gentleman is helpless. He is not used to being without a servant! Why shouldn't I wait on him, you shaggy-faced fool?'

'Who's shaggy-faced?'

'You are shaggy-faced.'

'Me shaggy-faced?'

'Yes, you are!'

'And are you a beauty? You've a face like a crow's egg . . . if I am shaggy-faced.'

'Shaggy-faced is what you are! Here God has stricken him, he might lie still and die quietly. No, he must poke his nose in! Why, what are you meddling for?'

'Why! Well, I'd rather bow down to a boot than to a dog. My father didn't knuckle under to anybody and he told me not to. I . . . I . . . '

He would have gone on but he had a terrible fit of coughing that lasted for some minutes, spitting blood. Soon the cold sweat of exhaustion came out on his narrow forehead. His cough interrupted him, or he would have gone on talking; one could see from his eyes how he was longing to go on scolding; but he simply waved his hand helplessly, so that in the end Chekunov forgot about him.

I felt that the consumptive's indignation was directed rather at me than at Chekunov. No one would have been angry with the latter, or have looked on him with particular contempt, for his eagerness to wait upon me and so earn a few pence. Everyone realised that he did this simply for gain. Peasants are by no means fastidious on that score, and very well understand the distinction. What Ustyantsev disliked was myself, he disliked my tea, and that even in fetters I was like 'a master', and seemed as though I could not get on without a servant, though I had not asked for a servant and did not desire one. I did, as a fact, always prefer to do everything for myself, and indeed I particularly wanted not even to look like a spoiled idle person, or to give myself the airs of a gentleman. I must admit while we are on the subject that my vanity was to some extent concerned in the matter. But – I really don't know how it always came to pass – I never could get away from all sorts of helpers and servants who fastened themselves upon me, and in the end took complete possession of me, so that it was really they who were my masters and I who was their servant, though it certainly did appear as though I were a regular 'gentleman', as though I gave myself airs, and could not get on without servants. This annoyed me very much, of course. But Ustyantsev was a consumptive and an irritable man. The other patients preserved an air of indifference, in which there was a shade of disdain. I remember they were all absorbed in something particular: from their conversation I learnt that a convict who was then being punished with the sticks was to be brought to us in the evening. The patients were expecting him with some interest. They said, however, that his punishment was a light one – only five hundred blows.

By degrees I took in my surroundings. As far as I could see, those who were really ill were suffering from scurvy and affections of the eye – diseases frequent in that region. There were several such in the ward. Of the others who were really ill, some had fever, skin diseases or consumption. This was not like other wards – here patients of all kinds were collected together, even those suffering from venereal diseases. I speak of 'those who were *really* ill', because there were some here who had come without any disease, 'to have a rest'. The doctors readily admitted such sham invalids from sympathy, especially when there were many beds empty. Detention in the guard-houses and prisons seemed so disagreeable, compared with the hospital, that many convicts were glad to come to the hospital in spite of the bad air and the locked ward. There were indeed some people, especially from the disciplinary battalion, who were fond of lying in bed and of hospital life in general. I looked at my new companions with interest, but I remember my curiosity was especially aroused by one from our prison, a man who was dying, also consumptive, and also at the last gasp. He was in the bed next but one beyond Ustyantsev, and so almost opposite me. His name was Mihailov; a fortnight before I had seen him in the prison. He had been ill a long while and ought to have been in the doctor's hands long before; but with obstinate and quite unnecessary patience he had controlled himself, and gone on, and only at Christmas he had come into the hospital to die three weeks later of galloping consumption; it was like a fire consuming him. I was struck this time by the awful change in his face, which was one of the first I noticed when I entered the prison; it somehow caught my eye then. Near him was a soldier of the disciplinary battalion, an old man of filthy and revolting habits . . . However, I cannot go over all the patients. I have mentioned this old man now simply because he made some impression on me at the time, and in the course of one minute gave me a full idea of some peculiarities of the convict ward. This old fellow, I remember, had a very heavy cold at the time. He was constantly sneezing, and went on sneezing for the whole of the following week, even in his sleep, in fits of five or six sneezes at a time, regularly repeating each time, 'Oh Lord, what an affliction.' At that minute he was sitting on the bed greedily stuffing his nose with snuff from a paper parcel, so that his sneezes might be more violent and complete. He sneezed into a checked cotton handkerchief of his own, that had been washed a hundred times and was faded to the last extreme; and as he sneezed he wrinkled up his nose in a peculiar way into tiny innumerable creases, and showed the relics of ancient blackened teeth between his red dribbling jaws. Then at once he opened his handkerchief, scrutinised the phlegm in it, and immediately smeared it on his brown hospital dressing-gown, so that the handkerchief remained comparatively clean. He did this the whole week. This persistent miserly care of his own handkerchief at the sacrifice of the hospital dressing-gown aroused no sort of protest from the other patients, though one of them would have to wear that dressing-gown after him. But our peasants are not squeamish and are strangely lacking in fastidiousness. I winced at that moment and I could not help at once beginning to examine with disgust and curiosity the dressing-gown I had just put on. Then I realised that it had been attracting my attention for a long time by its strong smell; by now it had become warm on me and smelt more and more strongly of medicines, plasters, and, as I thought, of something decomposing, which was not to be wondered at, since it had been for immemorial years on the backs of patients. Possibly the linen lining may have been washed sometimes; but I am not sure of that. At the present, anyway, it was saturated with all sorts of unpleasant discharges, lotions, matter from broken blisters, and so on. Moreover, convicts who had just received corporal punishment were constantly coming into the convict wards with wounded backs. Compresses were applied and then the dressing-gown being put on straight over the wet shirt could not possibly escape getting messed, and everything that dropped on it remained.

And the whole time I was in prison, that is, several years, I used to put on the dressing-gown with fear and mistrust whenever I had to be in hospital (and I was there pretty often). I particularly disliked the huge and remarkably fat lice I sometimes came across in those dressing-gowns. The convicts enjoyed killing them, so that when one was squashed under the convict's thick, clumsy nail, one could see from the hunter's face the satisfaction it gave him. We particularly disliked bugs, too, and sometimes the whole ward joined in their destruction on a long dreary winter evening. And though, apart from the bad smell, everything on the surface was as clean as possible in the ward, they were far from being fastidious over the cleanliness of the inside, so to speak. The patients were accustomed to it and even accepted it as natural. And indeed the very arrangements of the hospital were not conducive to cleanliness. But I will talk of these arrangements later.

As soon as Chekunov had made my tea (made, I may mention in parenthesis, with the water in the ward which was brought up only once in the twenty-four hours, and was quickly tainted in the foul atmosphere), the door was opened with some noise and the soldier who had just been punished was led in under a double escort. This was the first time I saw a man after corporal punishment. Afterwards they came in often, some so seriously injured that they had to be carried in, and this was always a source of great interest to the patients, who usually received them with an exaggeratedly severe expression and a sort of almost affected seriousness. However, their reception depended to some extent on the gravity of their crime, and consequently on the number of strokes they had received. Those who had been very badly beaten and were reputed to be great criminals enjoyed greater respect and greater consideration than a runaway recruit, like the one who was brought in now, for instance. But in neither case were there any remarks expressive of special compassion or irritation. In silence they helped the victim and waited upon him, especially if he could not do without assistance. The hospital attendants knew that they were leaving the patient in skilful and experienced hands. The necessary nursing usually took the form of constantly changing the sheet or shirt, which was soaked in cold water and applied to the torn flesh of the back, especially if the patient were too weak to look after himself. Another necessary operation was the skilful extraction of splinters, which were often left in the wounds from broken sticks, and this was usually very painful to the patient. But I was always struck by the extraordinary stoicism with which the victims bore their sufferings. I have seen many of them, sometimes terribly beaten, and hardly one of them uttered a groan! Only their faces changed and turned white, their eyes glowed, they looked preoccupied and uneasy, their lips quivered, so that the poor fellows often bit them till they almost bled.

The soldier who had come in was a strongly built, muscular lad of twenty-three, with a handsome face, tall, well-made and dark-skinned. His back had been rather badly beaten. The upper part of his body was stripped to below the waist; on his shoulders was laid a wet sheet, which made him shiver all over, as though he were in a fever, and for an hour and a half he walked up and down the ward. I looked into his face: it seemed to me he was thinking of nothing at that moment; he looked strangely and wildly around with wandering eyes, which it was evidently an effort for him to fix on anything. It seemed to me that he looked intently at my tea. The tea was hot and steaming; the poor fellow was chilled and his teeth were chattering. I offered him a drink. He turned to me mutely and abruptly, took the cup, drank it off standing and without putting in sugar, in great haste, seemingly purposely to avoid looking at me. When he had emptied it, he put back the cup without a word, and without even a nod to me began pacing up and down the ward again. He was beyond words or nods! As for the convicts, they all for some reason avoided speaking to him; on the contrary, though they helped him at first, they seemed to try expressly to take no further notice of him afterwards, perhaps feeling it best to leave him alone as much as possible, and not to bother him with questions or 'sympathy', and he seemed perfectly satisfied to be left alone.

Meanwhile it got dark and the night-lamp was lighted. Some, though very few, of the convicts had, it appeared, candlesticks of their own. At last, after the doctor's evening visit, the sergeant of the guard came in, counted over the patients and the ward was locked. A tub was first brought in, and I learnt with surprise that it was kept in the ward all night, for though there was accommodation only two steps away in the corridor, it was against the rules for the convicts to leave the ward on any pretext at night, and even during the day they were only allowed to be absent for a moment. The convict wards were not like the ordinary ones, and the convict had to bear his punishment even in illness. Who had first made this rule I do not know; I only know that there was no reason for it, and the utter uselessness of such formalism was nowhere more apparent than in this case. The doctors were certainly not responsible for the rule. I repeat, the convicts could not say enough in praise of their doctors, they looked on them as fathers and respected them. Everyone was treated with kindness and heard a friendly word from the doctor, and the convicts, cast off by all men, appreciated it, for they saw the genuineness and sincerity of these friendly words and this kindness. It might have been different: no one would have called the doctors to account if they had behaved differently, that is, more roughly and inhumanely; so they were kind from real humanity. And of course they knew that a sick man, even though he were a convict, needed fresh air as much as any other patient, even of the highest rank. Patients in the other wards, those who were convalescent, I mean, could walk freely about the corridors, take plenty of exercise, and breathe fresher air than that of the ward, which was always tainted and inevitably charged with stifling fumes. It is both terrible and disgusting to me now to realise how foul the tainted atmosphere of our ward must have been at night after the tub had been brought into the heated room, where there were patients suffering from dysentery and such complaints. When I said just now that the convict had to bear his punishment even though he were sick, I did not and I do not, of course, suppose that such a rule was made simply as a form of punishment. Of course, that would be senseless calumny on my part. It is useless to punish a sick man. And, since that is so, it follows that probably some stern, inevitable necessity had forced the authorities to a measure so pernicious in its effects. What necessity? But what is so vexatious is that it is impossible to find any explanation of this measure, and many others so incomprehensible that one cannot even conjecture an explanation of them. How explain such useless cruelty? On the theory that the convict will purposely sham illness to get into the hospital, will deceive the doctors, and if allowed to leave the ward at night will escape under cover of darkness? It is impossible to treat such a notion seriously. Where could he escape? How could he escape? In what clothes could he escape? By day they are allowed to leave the room one at a time, and it might be the same at night. At the door stands a sentinel with a loaded gun, and although the lavatory is only two steps from the door, the convict is always accompanied by a guard, and the one double window in it is covered by a grating. To get out of the window it would be necessary to break the grating and the double frame. Who would allow this? Even supposing anything so absurd as that he could first kill the guard without making a noise or letting him cry out, he would still have to break the window frame and the grating. Note that close beside the sentry sleep the ward attendants, and that ten paces away stands another armed sentinel at the door of another convict ward with another guard and other attendants beside him. And where can a man run in the winter in stockings and slippers, in a hospital dressing-gown and a nightcap? And since this is so, since there is so little danger (that is, really, none at all) why a rule so burdensome to the patients, perhaps in the last days of their lives, sick men who need fresh air even more than the healthy? What is it for? I could never understand it.

But since we have once begun asking why, I cannot pass over another point which for many years stood out as the most perplexing fact, for which I could never find a solution. I must say a few words about this before I go on with my description. I am thinking of the fetters, which are never removed from a convict, whatever illness he may be suffering from. Even consumptives have died before my eyes with their fetters on. Yet everyone was accustomed to it, everyone regarded it as an established fact that could not be altered. I doubt whether anybody even thought about it, since during the years I was there it never struck one of the doctors even to petition the authorities that a patient seriously ill, especially in consumption, might have his fetters removed. The fetters were in themselves not a very great weight. They weighed from eight to twelve pounds. It is not too great a burden for a healthy man to carry ten pounds. I was told, however, that after several years the convict's legs begin to waste from wearing fetters. I do not know whether it is true, though there is some probability of it. Even a small weight, a weight of no more than ten pounds, makes the limb abnormally heavy, and may have some injurious action after a length of time. But admitting that it is not too much for a healthy man, is it the same for a sick man? And even supposing it is not too much for an ordinary patient, is it not very different for the dangerously ill, for consumptives whose arms and legs waste away in any case, so that a straw's weight is too heavy for them? And, indeed, if the doctors succeeded in freeing only the consumptives, that would be in itself a really great and good action. Someone will say perhaps that the convict is a wicked man and does not deserve kindness; but surely there is no need to double the sufferings of one who is already stricken by the hand of God! And one cannot believe that this is done simply for the sake of punishment. Even by law the consumptive is exempt from corporal punishment. Consequently we must look upon the retention of fetters as a mysterious and important measure of precaution. But what the reason for it is I cannot imagine. There can really be no fear that the consumptive will escape. Who would dream of such a thing, especially in the advanced stages of the disease? To sham consumption and to deceive the doctors in order to escape is impossible. It is not a disease that can be simulated; it is unmistakable. And by the way, are convicts put into fetters merely to prevent them escaping, or to make it more difficult for them to do so? Certainly not. Fetters are simply a form of degradation, a disgrace, and a physical and moral burden. That at least is what they are meant to be. They could never hinder anyone from running away. The least skilful, the least expert convict can quickly and easily file them off or can smash the rivet with a stone. The fetters are no obstacle at all; and if that is so, if they are put on the condemned convict simply as a punishment, I ask again: is it right to punish a dying man in this way?

And now as I write this, I vividly recall the death of the consumptive patient, Mihailov, whose bed was nearly opposite mine, not far from Ustyantsev's. He died, I remember, four days after I came in. Possibly I have mentioned the case of the consumptives through unconsciously recalling the impressions and ideas which came into my mind at the sight of that death. I knew little of Mihailov himself, however. He was quite young, not more than five-and-twenty, tall, thin, and of extremely attractive appearance. He was in the 'special division', and was strangely silent, always gently and quietly melancholy, as though he were 'drying up' in prison, as the convicts said of him. He left a pleasant memory among them. I only remember that he had fine eyes, and I really do not know why he comes back to my mind so distinctly. He died at three o'clock in the afternoon on a bright frosty day. I remember the glowing slanting rays of the sun pierced through the green frozen panes of our windows. The sunshine was streaming full on the dying man. He was unconscious, and lay for several hours in the death agony. From early morning he had scarcely recognised those who went up to him. The patients would have liked to do something for him, seeing his distress; his breathing was deep, painful and raucous; his chest heaved as though he could not get air. He flung off his quilt and his clothes, and began at last to tear off his shirt; even that seemed a weight to him. The other patients went to his help and took off his shirt. It was terrible to see that long, long body, the arms and legs wasted to the bone, the sunken belly, the strained chest, the ribs standing out like a skeleton's. Nothing remained on his body but a wooden cross and a little bag with a relic in it, and his fetters which might, it seemed, have slipped off his wasted legs. Half an hour before his death the whole ward was hushed, we began to talk almost in whispers. Everyone moved about noiselessly. The patients did not talk much, and then of other things; they only looked now and then at the dying man, who was gasping more and more terribly. At last, with a straying and uncertain hand, he fumbled at the cross on his chest and began pulling it off, as though even that were a weight that worried and oppressed him. The patients removed the cross, too. Ten minutes later he died. They knocked at the door for the sentry and told him. An attendant came in, looked blankly at the dead man, and went to fetch a medical assistant. The medical assistant, a good-natured young fellow somewhat excessively occupied with his personal appearance, which was prepossessing however, soon came in, went up to the dead man with rapid steps that sounded noisy in the silent ward, and with a particularly unconcerned air, which he seemed to have assumed for the occasion, took his wrist, felt his pulse and went away with a wave of his hand. Word was sent to the sergeant in charge: the criminal was an important one and could not be certified as dead without special ceremony. While we were waiting for the sergeant, one of the convicts suggested in a low voice that it might be as well to close the dead man's eyes. Another man listened attentively, without a word went up to the dead man and closed his eyes. Seeing the cross lying on the pillow, he picked it up, looked at it, and put it round Mihailov's neck again; then he crossed himself. Meanwhile the dead face was growing rigid; the sunlight was flickering on it; the mouth was half open; two rows of white young teeth glistened between the thin parched lips.

At last the sergeant on duty came in, in a helmet and with a sabre, followed by two guards. He went up, moving more slowly as he got nearer, looking in perplexity at the hushed convicts who were gazing grimly at him from all sides. When he was a little way off, he stood stock-still, as though he were scared. The sight of the naked and wasted body with nothing on but the fetters impressed him, and he suddenly unbuckled his sword-belt, took off his helmet, which he was not required to do, and solemnly crossed himself. He was a grim-looking, grey-headed man who had seen many years of service. I remember that at that moment Chekunov, also a grey-headed man, was standing near. He stared the whole time mutely and intently into the sergeant's face, and with strange attention watched every movement he made. But their eyes met and something made Chekunov's lower lip quiver; he twisted it into a grin and, nodding rapidly, as it were involuntarily, towards the dead man, he said to the sergeant: 'He too had a mother!' and he walked away.

I remember those words stabbed me to the heart. What made him say them, what made him think of them? They began lifting the dead body: they lifted the bed as well; the straw rustled, the chains clanked loudly on the floor in the silent ward . . . they were picked up. The body was carried out. Suddenly everyone began talking aloud. We could hear the sergeant in the corridor sending someone for the smith. The fetters were to be removed from the dead man . . .

But I am digressing.

CHAPTER TWO

The Hospital [2]

The doctors went their rounds in the morning; between ten and eleven they made their appearance in our ward all together, with the chief doctor at their head, and an hour and a half before that our special ward doctor used to visit the ward. At that time our ward doctor was a friendly young man and a thoroughly good doctor. The convicts were very fond of him and only found one fault in him: that he was 'too soft'. He was in fact not very ready of speech and seemed ill at ease with us, he would almost blush and change the diet at the first request of the patient, and I believe he would even have prescribed the medicines to suit their fancy if they had asked him. But he was a splendid young man.

It may be said that many doctors in Russia enjoy the love and respect of the peasants, and, as far as I have observed, that is perfectly true. I know that my words will seem paradoxical when one considers the distrust of medicine and of foreign drugs universally felt by the common people in Russia. A peasant will, in fact, even in severe illness, go on for years consulting a wise woman, or taking his homemade remedies (which are by no means to be despised), rather than go to a doctor, or into a hospital. There is one important element in this feeling which has nothing to do with medicine, that is, the general distrust felt by the peasants for everything which is stamped with the hall-mark of government; moreover, the people are frightened and prejudiced against hospitals by all sorts of horrible tales and gossip, often absurd but sometimes not without a foundation of fact. But what they fear most is the German routine of the hospital, the presence of strangers about them all the time they are ill, the strict rules in regard to diet, the tales of the rigorous severity of the attendants and doctors and of the cutting open and dissection of the dead and so on. Besides, the people argue that they will be treated by 'the gentry', for doctors are after all 'gentlemen'. But all these terrors disappear very quickly when they come into closer contact with the doctors (generally speaking, not without exceptions, of course) which I think is greatly to the credit of our doctors, who are for the most part young men. The majority of them know how to gain the respect and even the love of the people. Anyway, I am writing of what I have myself seen and experienced many times and in many places, and I have no reason to think that things are different in other places. Here and there, of course, there are doctors who take bribes, make a great profit out of their hospitals and neglect their patients almost completely, till they forget all they have learnt. Such men are still to be found, but I am speaking of the majority or rather of the tendency, the spirit which animates the medical profession in our day. Whatever one may say in defence of these renegades, these wolves in the fold, however one may ascribe their shortcomings, for instance, to the 'environment' of which they too are the victims, they will always be greatly to blame, especially if they also show a lack of humanity. Humanity, kindness, brotherly sympathy are sometimes of more use to the patients than any medicines. It is high time we gave up apathetic complaints of being corrupted by our environment. It is true no doubt that it does destroy a great deal in us, but not everything, and often a crafty and knowing rogue, especially if he is an eloquent speaker or writer, will cover up not simply weakness but often real baseness, justifying it by the influence of his 'environment'.

But again I have wandered from my subject; I merely meant to say that the mistrust and hostility of the peasants are directed rather against medical administration than against the doctors themselves. When the peasant finds out what they are really like, he quickly loses many of his prejudices. The general arrangements of our hospitals are still in many respects out of harmony with the national spirit, their routine is still antagonistic to the people's habits, and not calculated to win their full confidence and respect. So at least it seems to me from some of my personal experiences.

Our ward doctor usually stopped before every patient, examined and questioned him gravely and with the greatest attention, and prescribed his medicine and his diet. Sometimes he noticed that there was nothing the matter with the patient, but as the convict had come for a rest from work, or to lie on a mattress instead of bare boards, and in a warm room instead of in the damp lock-up, where huge masses of pale and wasted prisoners were kept awaiting their trial (prisoners awaiting trial are almost always, all over Russia, pale and wasted – a sure sign that they are generally physically and spiritually worse off than convicted prisoners), our ward doctor calmly entered them as suffering from '*febris catarrhalis*' and sometimes let them stay even for a week. We all used to laugh over this '*febris catarrhalis*'. We knew very well that this was, by a tacit understanding between the doctor and the patient, accepted as the formula for malingering or 'handy shooting pains', which was the convicts' translation of 'febris catarrhalis'. Sometimes a patient abused the doctor's soft-heartedness and stayed on till he was forcibly turned out. Then you should have seen our ward doctor: he seemed shy, he seemed ashamed to say straight out to the patient that he must get well and make haste to ask for his discharge, though he had full right to discharge him by writing on his chart '*sanat est*' without any talk or cajoling. At first he gave him a hint, afterwards he tried as it were to persuade him: 'Isn't your time up? You are almost well, you know; the ward is crowded,' and so on and so on, till the patient himself began to feel ashamed, and at last asked for his discharge of his own accord. The chief doctor, though he was a humane and honest man (the convicts were very fond of him, too), was far sterner and more determined than the ward doctor; he could even show a grim severity on occasion, and he was particularly respected among us for it. He made his appearance followed by the whole staff, and also examined each patient separately, staying longer with those who were seriously ill, and he always managed to say a kind, encouraging word to them, often full of true feeling. Altogether he made a very good impression. Convicts who came in with a 'handy shooting pain' he never rejected nor turned out, but if the patient were too persistent, he simply discharged him: 'Well, brother, you've been here long enough, you've had a rest, you can go, you mustn't outstay your welcome.' Those who persisted in remaining were either lazy convicts who shirked work, especially in the summer when the hours were long, or prisoners who were awaiting corporal punishment. I remember special severity, even cruelty, being used in one such case to induce the convict to take his discharge. He came with an eye affection; his eyes were red and he complained of an acute shooting pain in them. He was treated with blisters, leeches, drops of some corrosive fluid, but the malady remained, the eyes were no better. Little by little, the doctors guessed that it was a sham: there was a continual slight inflammation which grew neither worse nor better, it was always in the same condition. The case was suspicious. The convicts had long known that he was shamming and deceiving people, though he did not confess it himself. He was a young fellow, rather good-looking, indeed, though he made an unpleasant impression on all of them: reserved, suspicious, frowning, he talked to no one, had a menacing look, held aloof from everyone as though he were suspicious. I remember it even occurred to some people that he might do something violent. He had been a soldier, had been found out in thieving on a large scale, and was sentenced to a thousand strokes and a convict battalion. To defer the moment of punishment, as I have mentioned before, convicts sometimes resorted to terrible expedients: by stabbing one of the officials or a fellow convict they would get a new trial, and their punishment would be deferred for some two months and their aim would be attained. It was nothing to them that the punishment when it did come, two months later, would be twice or three times as severe; all they cared about was deferring the awful moment if only for a few days at any cost – so extreme is sometimes the prostration of spirit of these poor creatures.

Some of the convicts whispered among themselves that we ought to be on our guard against this man – he might murder someone in the night. However, it was only talk, no special precautions were taken, even by those who slept next to him. It was seen, however, that he rubbed his eyes at night with plaster taken from the wall as well as with something else, that they might be red in the morning. At last the head doctor threatened him with a seton. In obstinate eye affections of long duration when every medical expedient has been tried, to preserve the sight, the doctors have recourse to a violent and painful remedy; they apply a seton to the patient as they would to a horse.

But even then the poor fellow would not consent to recover. He was too obstinate or perhaps too cowardly. A seton perhaps was not so bad as the punishment with sticks, but it was very painful too. The patient's skin, as much as one can grip in the hand, is pinched up behind the neck and all of it stabbed through with a knife which produces a long and wide wound all over the back of the neck. Through this wound they thrust a linen tape, rather wide – a finger's breadth. Then every day at a fixed hour they pull this tape in the wound so that it is opened again, that it may be continually separating and not healing. Yet for several days the poor fellow obstinately endured this torture, which was accompanied with horrible suffering, and only at last consented to take his discharge. His eyes became perfectly well in a single day, and as soon as his neck was healed he went to the lockup to receive next day the punishment of a thousand strokes with sticks.

Of course the minute before punishment is awful; so awful that I am wrong in calling the terror of it cowardice and weakness of spirit. It must be awful when men are ready to endure twice or thrice the punishment, if only they can avoid facing it at once. I have mentioned, however, that there were some who asked for their discharge before their backs were quite healed after the first beating, in order to endure the remainder of their punishment and have their sentence over; and detention in the lock-up awaiting punishment was without doubt incomparably worse for all than life in prison. But apart from the difference in temperaments, years of being accustomed to blows and punishments play a great part in the fortitude and fearlessness of some. Men who have been frequently flogged seem to harden their hearts and their backs; at last they look upon the punishment sceptically, almost as a trifling inconvenience and lose all fear of it. Speaking generally, this is true. One of our convicts in the special divisions, a Kalmuck, who had been christened Alexandr or 'Alexandra' as they used to call him in the prison, a queer fellow, sly, fearless and at the same time very good-natured, told me how he got through his four thousand 'sticks'. He told me about it, laughing and joking, but swore in earnest that if he had not from childhood – his earliest, tenderest childhood – always been under the lash, so that his back had literally never been free from scars all the while he lived with his horde, he never could have endured the punishment. He seemed to bless his education under the lash.

'I was beaten for everything, Alexandr Petrovitch!' he told me one evening, sitting on my bed, before the candles were lighted, 'for everything and nothing, whatever happened, I was beaten for fifteen years on end, as far back as I can remember, several times every day; anyone beat me who liked, so that in the end I got quite used to it.'

How he came to be a soldier I don't know; I don't remember, though perhaps he told me; he was an inveterate runaway and tramp. I only remember his account of how horribly frightened he was when he was condemned to four thousand 'sticks' for killing his superior officer.

'I knew I should be severely punished and that perhaps I shouldn't come out alive, and though I was used to the lash, four thousand strokes is no joke; besides, all the officers were furious with me! I knew, I knew for certain that I shouldn't get through it, that I couldn't stand it; I shouldn't come out alive. First I tried getting christened; I thought maybe they'd forgive me, and though the fellows told me it would be no use, I shouldn't be pardoned, I thought I'd try it. Anyway, they'd have more feeling for a Christian after all. Well, they christened me and at the holy christening called me Alexandr; but the sticks remained, they did not take one off; I thought it was too bad. I said to myself: "Wait a bit, I'll be a match for you all." And would you believe it, Alexandr Petrovitch, I was a match for them! I was awfully good at pretending to be dead, that is, not being quite dead, but just on the point of expiring. I was brought out for punishment; I was led through the ranks for the first thousand; it burnt me; I shouted. I was led back for the second thousand; well, thought I, my end is come, they've beaten all sense out of me; my legs were giving way, I fell on the ground; my eyes looked lifeless, my face was blue, I stopped breathing and there was foam on my mouth. The doctor came up. "He'll die directly," said he. They carried me to the hospital and I revived at once. Then they led me out twice again and they were angry with me too, awfully angry, and I cheated them twice again; the second time I looked like dead after one thousand; and when it came to the fourth thousand every blow was like a knife in my heart, every blow was as good as three, it hurt so! They were savage with me. That niggardly last thousand – damn it – was as bad as all the three thousand together and had I not died before the very end (there were only two hundred left) they would have beaten me to death. But I took my own part; I deceived them again and shammed death. Again they were taken in and how could they help being? The doctor believed I was dead. So they beat me for the last two hundred with all the fury they could, they beat me so that it was worse than two thousand, but yet they didn't kill me, no fear! And why didn't they kill me? Why, just because I've grown up from childhood under the lash. That's why I am alive to this day. Ach, I have been beaten in my day!' he added at the end of the story in a sort of mournful reverie, as though trying to recall and reckon how many times he had been beaten. 'But no,' he added, after a minute's silence. 'There's no counting the beatings I've had! How could I? They're beyond reckoning.' He glanced at me and laughed, but so good-naturedly that I could not help smiling in response. 'Do you know, Alexandr Petrovitch, that whenever I dream at night now, I always dream that I am being beaten? I never have any other dreams.' He certainly often cried out at night and so loudly that the other convicts waked him up at once by prodding him, and saying, 'What are you shouting for, you devil!' He was a short sturdy fellow of forty-five, good-humoured and restless; he got on well with everyone and though he was very fond of stealing, and often got a beating among us for that, after all everyone stole and every-one was beaten for it.

I will add one other point. I was always amazed at the extraordinary good-nature, the absence of vindictiveness, with which all these victims talked of how they had been beaten, and of the men who had beaten them. Often there was not the slightest trace of spite or hatred in their story, which gripped my heart at once, and made it throb violently. Yet they would tell the story and laugh like children.

M., for instance, described his punishment to me. He was not of the privileged class and received five hundred strokes. I heard of this from the others and asked him myself whether it were true, and how it happened. He answered with a certain brevity, as though with an inward pang; he seemed to avoid looking at me and his face flushed; half a minute later he did look at me; there was a gleam of hatred in his eyes, and his lips were quivering with indignation. I felt that he could never forget that page in his past.

But almost all our convicts (I will not guarantee that there were no exceptions) took quite a different view of it. It cannot be, I sometimes thought, that they consider themselves guilty and deserving of punishment, especially when they have committed an offence, not against one of their own class, but against someone in authority. The majority of them did not blame themselves at all. I have said already that I saw no signs of remorse even when the crime was against one of their class; as for crimes against officers in control of them, they did not count them at all. It sometimes seemed to me that for the latter class of crimes they had a peculiar, so to speak, practical, or rather matter-of-fact, point of view. They put it down to fate, to the inevitability of the act, and this was not done deliberately but was an unconscious attitude, a kind of creed. Though the convict is almost always disposed to consider himself justified in any crime against officers, so much so that there is no question about it in his mind, yet in practice he recognises that the authorities take a very different view of his crime, and that therefore he must be punished, and then they are quits. It is a mutual struggle. The criminal knows and never doubts that he will be acquitted by the verdict of his own class, who will never, he knows, entirely condemn him (and for the most part will fully acquit him), so long as his offence has not been against his equals, his brothers, his fellow peasants. His conscience is clear, and with that he is strong and not morally disturbed, and that is the chief thing. He feels, as it were, that he has something to rest upon, and so he feels no hatred, but takes what has happened to him as something inevitable which has not begun with him and will not end with him, but will go on for long ages as part of a passive but stubborn and old-established feud. No soldier hates the individual Turk he is fighting with; yet the Turk stabs him, hacks at him, shoots him.

Yet not all the stories I heard, however, showed the same coolness and indifference. They talked of Lieutenant Zherebyatnikov, for instance, with a certain shade of indignation, though even in this case the feeling was not very strong. I made the acquaintance of this Lieutenant Zherebyatnikov when I was first in hospital – from the convicts' stories about him, I mean. Afterwards I met him in the flesh when he was on duty at the prison. He was a tall man about thirty, big and fat, with red puffy cheeks, white teeth and with a loud laugh like Nozdryov's.* One could see from his face that he was a man who never thought about anything. He was particularly fond of flogging and punishing

* A character in Gogol's *Dead Souls – Translator's note.*

with 'sticks' when it was his duty to superintend. I hasten to add that I looked upon Lieutenant Zherebyatnikov at the time as a monster, and that was how he was regarded by the convicts themselves. There were, in the past, in that recent past, of course, of which 'the tradition is still fresh though it is hard to believe in it', other officers who were eager to do their duty conscientiously and zealously. But as a rule they did their work in all simplicity of heart without relishing it. Zherebyatnikov had something of the pleasure of an epicure in administering punishment. He was passionately fond of the art of punishing, and he loved it as an art. He enjoyed it and like the worn-out aristocratic debauchees of the Roman Empire, he invented all sorts of subtleties, all sorts of unnatural tricks to excite and agreeably thrill his crass soul.

The convict is led out for punishment; Zherebyatnikov is the officer in command; the mere sight of the long ranks of men drawn up with thick sticks in their hands inspires him. He walks round the ranks complacently, and repeats emphatically that every man is to do his duty thoroughly, conscientiously, or else . . . But the soldiers don't need to be told what that *or else* means. Then the criminal is brought out, and if he knows nothing of Zherebyatnikov, if he has not heard all about him, this would be the sort of trick the lieutenant would play on him – one of hundreds, of course; the lieutenant was inexhaustible in inventing them. At the moment when the convict is stripped and his hands are tied to the butt-ends of guns by which the sergeants afterwards drag him down the 'Green Street', it is the regular thing for him to beg in a plaintive, tearful voice, entreating the commanding officer to make his punishment easier and not to increase it by unnecessary severity. 'Your honour,' cries the poor wretch, 'have mercy on me, be a father to me; I'll pray for your honour all my life; don't destroy me, have pity on me!'

That was just what Zherebyatnikov wanted; he would pause, and would begin talking to the victim with a sentimental air.

'But what am I to do, my friend?' he would begin. 'It's not I am punishing you, it's the law!'

'Your honour, it's all in your hands, have pity on me!'

'Do you suppose I don't feel for you? Do you suppose it's a pleasure to me to see you beaten? I am a man too. Am I a man or not, do you suppose?'

'For sure, your honour, we all know you are our father, we are your children. Be a father to me!' cries the convict, beginning to hope.

'But judge for yourself, my friend – you've got sense; I know that as a fellow creature I ought to be merciful and indulgent even to a sinner like you.'

'It's the holy truth you are speaking, your honour.'

'Yes, to be merciful however sinful you may be. But it's not my doing, it's the law! Think of that! I have my duty to God and to my country; I shall be taking a great sin upon myself if I soften the law, think of that!'

'Your honour!'

'But there! So be it, for your sake! I know I am doing wrong, but so be it . . . I will have mercy on you this time. I'll let you off easy. But what if I am doing you harm? If I have mercy on you this once and let you off easily, and you'll reckon on it being the same next time and commit a crime again, what then? It will be on my conscience.'

'Your honour! I'd not let friend or foe! As before the throne of the Heavenly Father . . . '

'All right, all right! But do you swear to behave yourself for the future?'

'Strike me dead, may I never in the world to come . . . '

'Don't swear, it's a sin. I'll believe your word. Do you give me your word?'

'Your honour!!!'

'Well, I tell you, I'll spare you simply for your orphan's tears. You are an orphan, aren't you?'

'Yes, your honour, alone in the world, neither father nor mother . . . '

'Well, for the sake of your orphan's tears; but mind you, it's the last time . . . Take him,' he adds in such a soft-hearted way that the convict does not know how to pray devoutly enough for such a benefactor.

But the fearful procession begins; he is led along; the drum begins to boom; the sticks begin flying.

'Give it him!' Zherebyatnikov bawls at the top of his voice. 'Whack him! Flay him, flay him! Scorch him! Lay it on, lay it on! Hit him harder, the orphan, harder, the rascal! Touch him up, touch him up!'

And the soldiers hit as hard as they can, the poor wretch begins to scream and there are flashes before his eyes, while Zherebyatnikov runs after him along the line in peals of laughter, holding his sides, and hardly able to stand, so that one felt sorry for the dear man at last. He is delighted and amused and only from time to time there is a pause in his loud hearty roars of laughter, and one hears again: 'Flay him, flay him! Scorch him, the rascal, scorch him, the orphan! . . . '

Or he would invent another variation. The convict brought out to punishment begins to entreat him again. This time Zherebyatnikov does not grimace or play a part with him, but goes in for frankness: 'I tell you what, my good fellow,' he says, 'I shall punish you properly, for you deserve it. But I tell you what I'll do for you: I won't tie you to the guns. You shall go alone, but in a new way. Run as fast as you can along the line! Every stick will hit you just the same, but it will sooner be over; what do you think? Would you like to try?'

The convict listens with perplexity and mistrust and hesitates. 'Who knows,' he thinks to himself, 'maybe it will be easier. I'll run as hard as I can and the pain will not last a quarter so long and perhaps not all the sticks will hit me.'

'Very well, your honour, I agree.'

'Well, I agree too, then. Cut along! Mind now, look sharp!' he shouts to the soldiers, though he knows beforehand that not one stick will miss the guilty back; the soldier knows very well what would be in store for him if he missed.

The convict runs with all his might along the 'Green Street', but of course he doesn't get beyond the fifteenth soldier: the sticks fall upon his back like lightning, like the tattoo on a drum, and the poor wretch drops with a scream, as though he had been cut down or struck by a bullet.

'No, your honour, better the regular way,' he says, getting up slowly from the ground, pale and frightened.

And Zherebyatnikov, who knows the trick beforehand and how it ends, roars with laughter. But there is no describing all his diversions or all that was said about him.

Stories of somewhat different tone and spirit were told of Lieutenant Smekalov, who was commanding officer of our prison before our major was appointed. Though the convicts talked somewhat unconcernedly and without special anger of Zherebyatnikov, yet they did not admire his exploits, they did not speak well of him and were evidently disgusted by him. Indeed, they seemed to look down upon him with contempt. But Lieutenant Smekalov was remembered among us with enjoyment and delight. He had no particular liking for punishment. There was nothing of the Zherebyatnikov element in him. But he was by no means opposed to the lash; yet the fact is that even his floggings were remembered among the convicts with love and satisfaction – so successful was the man in pleasing them! And how? How did he gain such popularity? It is true that the convicts, like all the Russian people, perhaps, are ready to forget any tortures for the sake of a kind word; I mention it as a fact without qualifying it in one way or another. It was not difficult to please these people and to be popular among them. But Lieutenant Smekalov had won a peculiar popularity, so that even the way he used to administer punishment was remembered almost with tenderness. 'We had no need of a father,' the convicts would say, and they would sigh, comparing their recollections of their old commanding officer, Smekalov, with the present major. 'He was a jolly good fellow!'

He was a simple-hearted man, good-natured, perhaps, in his own way. But sometimes it happens that there is a man in authority who has not only good-nature but a generous spirit, and yet everyone dislikes him and sometimes they simply laugh at him. Smekalov knew how to behave so that they looked upon him as one of themselves, and this is a great art, or more accurately an innate faculty, which even those who possess it never think about. Strange to say, some men of this sort are not good-natured at all, yet they sometimes gain great popularity. They don't despise, they don't scorn the people under their control – in that, I think, lies the explanation. There is no sign of the fine gentleman, no trace of class superiority about them, there is a peculiar whiff of the peasant inborn in them; and, my word! what a keen scent the people have for it! What will they not give for it? They are ready to prefer the sternest man to the most merciful, if the former has a smack of their own homespun flavour. And what if the same man is really good-natured, too, even though in a peculiar way of his own? Then he is beyond all price.

Lieutenant Smekalov, as I have said already, sometimes punished severely, but he knew how to do it so that, far from being resented, his jokes on the occasion were, even in my day when it was all long past, remembered with enjoyment and laughter. He had not many such jokes, however: he was lacking in artistic fancy. In fact, he really had one solitary joke which was his mainstay for nearly a year; perhaps its charm lay in its uniqueness. There was much simplicity in it. The guilty convict would be brought in to be flogged. Smekalov comes in with a laugh and a joke, he asks the culprit some irrelevant questions about his personal life in the prison not with any sort of object, not to make up to him, but simply *because he really wants to know.* The birch-rods are brought and a chair for Smekalov. He sits down and even lights his pipe; he had a very long pipe. The convict begins to entreat him . . . 'No, brother, lie down . . . it's no use,' says Smekalov. The convict sighs and lies down. 'Come, my dear fellow, do you know this prayer by heart?'

'To be sure, your honour, we are Christians, we learnt it from childhood.'

'Well then, repeat it.'

And the convict knows what to say and knows beforehand what will happen when he says it, because this trick has been repeated thirty times already with others. And Smekalov himself knows that the convict knows it, knows that even the soldiers who stand with lifted rods over the prostrate victim have heard of this joke long ago and yet he repeats it again – it has taken such a hold on him once for all, perhaps from the vanity of an author, just because it is his own composition. The convict begins to repeat the prayer, the soldiers wait with their rods while Smekalov bends forward, raises his hand, leaves off smoking, and waits for the familiar word. After the first lines of the well-known prayer, the convict at last comes to the words, 'Thy Kingdom come'. That's all he is waiting for. 'Stay,' cries the inspired lieutenant and instantly turning with an ecstatic gesture to a soldier he cries, 'Now give him some.'

And he explodes with laughter. The soldiers standing round grin too, the man who thrashes grins, even the man who is being thrashed almost grins, although at the word of command, 'Now give him some', the rod whistles in the air to cut a minute later like a razor through his guilty flesh. And Smekalov is delighted,

delighted just because he has had such a happy thought, and has himself found the word to rhyme with 'come'.

And Smekalov goes away perfectly satisfied with himself and, indeed, the man who has been flogged goes away almost satisfied with himself and with Smekalov, and half an hour later he will be telling the story in the prison of how the joke that had been repeated thirty times before had now been repeated for the thirty-first time. 'He is a jolly good fellow! He loves a joke!'

There was even a flavour of maudlin sentimentality about some reminiscences of the good-natured lieutenant.

'Sometimes one would go by, brothers,' a convict would tell us, his face all smiles at the recollection, 'and he'd be sitting in the window in his dressing-gown, drinking his tea and smoking his pipe. I'd take off my cap. "Where are you off to, Aksyonov?" he'd say. "Why, to work, Mihail Vassilitch, first thing I must go to the work-room." He'd laugh to himself. He was a jolly good fellow! Jolly is the only word!'

'We shall never see his like again,' one of his listeners would add.

CHAPTER THREE

The Hospital [3] *

I have spoken about corporal punishment and the various officers who had to perform this interesting duty, because it was only when I went into the hospital that I formed an idea from actual acquaintance of these matters, of which, till then, I had only known by hearsay. From all the battalions, disciplinary and otherwise, stationed in our town and in the whole surrounding district, all who had received the punishment of the 'sticks' were brought into our two wards. In those early days when I still looked so eagerly at everything about me, all these strange proceedings, all these victims who had been punished or were preparing for punishment, naturally made a very strong impression on me. I was excited, overwhelmed and terrified. I remember that at the same time I began suddenly and impatiently going into all the details of these new facts, listening to the talk and tales of the other convicts on this subject. I asked them questions, tried to arrive at conclusions. I had a great desire to know among other things all about the various grades of sentences and punishments, the varying severity of the different forms of punishments, the attitude of the convicts themselves. I tried to picture to myself the psychological condition of men going to punishment. I have mentioned already that it is unusual for anyone to be unconcerned before punishment, even those who have been severely punished and on more than one occasion. The condemned are overcome by an acute purely physical terror, involuntary and irresistible, which masters the man's whole moral being. Even during my later years in prison, I could not help watching with interest the prisoners who, after being in hospital till the wounds left by the first half of their punishment were healed, were leaving to endure next

* All that I am writing here about corporal punishment was true in my time. Now I am told that all this is changed and still changing – *Author's note.*

day the second half of their sentence. This division of the punishment into two parts is always done by the decision of the doctor who is present at the punishment. If the number of strokes to be inflicted is too great for the prisoner to endure all at once, the sentence is inflicted in two or even three parts, according to the decision of the doctor at the actual time, as to whether the prisoner can safely go on walking through the ranks or whether doing so will endanger his life. As a rule five hundred, a thousand, or even fifteen hundred blows are endured at one time; but if the sentence is one of two or three thousand blows, the punishment has to be divided into two or even into three parts. Men leaving hospital for the second half of their punishment, after their wounded backs were healed, were usually gloomy, sullen and disinclined to talk on the day of their discharge and the day before. There was noticeable in them a certain dullness of intelligence, a sort of unnatural preoccupation. A man in this position does not readily enter into conversation, and is for the most part silent; what is interesting is that the convicts themselves never talk to him, and do not attempt to speak of what is in store for him. There is no unnecessary talk, nor attempt at consolation; they even try to pay no attention to him. Of course this is better for the victim.

There are exceptions: Orlov, for instance, whose story I have told already. After the first half of his punishment was over, the only thing that vexed him was that his back was so long healing, that he could not take his discharge sooner. He wanted to get the second half of his punishment over as soon as possible and to be sent off to his place of exile, hoping to escape on the road. But this man was kept up by the object he had in view, and God knows what was in his mind. His was a vital and passionate nature. He was much pleased and in a state of great excitement, though he controlled his feelings: for, before receiving the first part of his punishment, he had thought that they would not let him off alive, and that he would die under the sticks. Even while he was on his trial various rumours had reached him of what the authorities meant to do, and he prepared himself then to die. But, having got through the first half of the sentence, his spirits revived. He was brought into the hospital half dead: I had never seen such wounds; but he came in with joy in his heart, with the hope that he would outlive it, that the rumours were false. Having once come out alive from the sticks, he began now, after his long imprisonment, to dream of the open road, of escape, freedom, the plain and the forest. Two days after his discharge he died in the same hospital and in the same bed, after the second half of his punishment. But I have spoken of this already.

Yet the very prisoners whose days and nights were so gloomy beforehand endured the punishment itself with manly fortitude, even the most faint-hearted of them. I rarely heard a groan even on the first night of their arrival, and even from the most cruelly punished; the people as a rule know how to bear pain. I asked many questions about the pain. I wanted to find out definitely how bad the pain was, with what it might be compared. I really do not know what induced me to do this. I only remember one thing, that it was not from idle curiosity. I repeat that I was shaken and distressed. But I could not get a satisfactory answer from anyone I asked. It burns, scorches like fire – was all I could find out, and that was the one answer given by all. During those early days, as I got to know M. better, I asked him. 'It hurts dreadfully,' he said, 'and the sensation is burning like fire; as though your back were being roasted before the hottest fire.' In fact everyone said the same thing. But I remember that I made at the time one strange observation, for the accuracy of which I do not vouch, though the unanimous verdict of the prisoners on the subject strongly confirms it: that is that the birch, if many strokes are inflicted, is the worst of all punishments in use in Russia. At first sight it might seem that this was absurd and impossible. Yet five hundred, even four hundred, strokes may kill a man, and more than five hundred strokes are almost certain to. Even the man of the strongest endurance cannot survive a thousand. Yet five hundred blows with 'sticks' can be endured without the slightest danger to life. Even men of not very strong constitution can endure the punishment of a thousand 'sticks' without danger. Even two thousand will hardly kill a man of medium strength and healthy constitution. The convicts all said that the birch was worse than the 'sticks.' 'The birch smarts more,' they told me, 'it's more agony.' There is no doubt the birch is more agonising than the sticks. It is more irritating, it acts more acutely on the nerves, excites them violently, and strains them beyond endurance. I do not know how it is now, but in the recent past there were gentlemen who derived from the power of flogging their victims something that suggests the Marquis de Sade and the Marquise de Brinvilliers. I imagine there is something in this sensation which sends a thrill at once sweet and painful to the hearts of these gentlemen. There are people who are like tigers thirsting for blood. Anyone who has once experienced this power, this unlimited mastery of the body, blood and soul of a fellow man made of the same clay as himself, a brother in the law of Christ – anyone who has experienced the power and full licence to inflict the greatest humiliation upon another creature made in the image of God will unconsciously lose the mastery of his own sensations. Tyranny is a habit; it may develop, and it does develop at last, into a disease. I maintain that the very best of men may be coarsened and hardened into a brute by habit. Blood and power intoxicate; coarseness and depravity are developed; the mind and the heart are tolerant of the most abnormal things, till at last they come to relish them. The man and the citizen is lost for ever in the tyrant, and the return to human dignity, to repentance and regeneration becomes almost impossible. Moreover, the example, the possibility of such despotism, has a perverting influence on the whole of society: such power is a temptation. Society, which looks indifferently on such a phenomenon, is already contaminated to its very foundations. In short, the right of corporal punishment given to one man over another is one of the sores of social life, one of the strongest forces destructive of every germ, every effort in society towards civic feeling, and a sufficient cause for its inevitable dissolution.

The professional torturer is an object of disgust to society, but a gentleman torturer is far from being so. It is only lately that an opposite idea has been expressed, and that only in books and abstractly. Even those who express it have not all been able to extinguish in themselves the lust of power. Every manufacturer, every capitalist, must feel an agreeable thrill in the thought that his workman, with all his family, is sometimes entirely dependent on him. This is undoubtedly true: a generation does not so quickly get over what has come to it as a legacy from the past; a man does not so easily renounce what is in his blood, what he has, so to speak, sucked in with his mother's milk. Such rapid transformations do not occur. To acknowledge one's fault and the sins of one's fathers is little, very little; one must uproot the habit of them completely, and that is not so quickly done.

I have spoken of the torturer. The characteristics of the torturer exist in embryo in almost every man of today. But the brutal qualities do not develop equally. If they develop so as to overpower all the man's other qualities, he becomes, of course, a hideous and terrible figure. Torturers are of two kinds: some act of their own free will, others involuntarily, of necessity. The voluntary torturer is, of course, more degraded in every respect than the other, though the latter is so despised by the people, inspiring horror, loathing, an unaccountable, even mysterious, terror. Why this almost superstitious horror for one torturer and such an indifferent, almost approving, attitude to the other?

There are instances that are strange in the extreme. I have known people good-natured, even honest, and even respected by society who yet could not with equanimity let a man go until he screamed out under the lash, till he prayed and implored for mercy. It was the duty of men under punishment to cry out and pray for mercy. That was the accepted thing: it was looked upon as necessary and proper, and when, on one occasion, the victim would not scream, the officer, whom I knew personally and who might perhaps have been regarded in other relations as a good-natured man, took it as a personal insult. He had meant at first to let him off easily, but not hearing the usual 'your honour, father, have mercy, I'll pray to God for you all my life' and the rest of it, he was furious, and gave the man fifty lashes extra, trying to wring cries and supplications out of him – and he attained his end. 'It couldn't be helped, the man was rude,' he said to me quite seriously.

As for the actual executioner who is not a free agent but acts under compulsion, he is as everyone knows a condemned convict who escapes his sentence by turning executioner. At first he learns his calling from another executioner, and when he is expert, he is attached permanently to the prison, where he lives apart in a special room, keeping house for himself, though he is almost always guarded. Of course, a live man is not a machine; although the executioner beats as a duty, he sometimes grows keen on his work, but, though the beating may be some satisfaction to himself, he scarcely ever feels personal hatred for his victim. His dexterity, his knowledge of his art and his desire to show off before his fellow convicts and the public stimulate his vanity. He exerts himself for art's sake. Besides, he knows very well that he is an outcast, that he is met and followed everywhere by superstitious terror, and there is no saying that this may not have an influence on him, may not accentuate ferocity and brutal tendencies in him. Even children know that he 'has disowned father and mother'. Strange to say, though, of the executioners I have seen, all have been men of some education, men of sense and intelligence who had an extraordinary vanity, even pride. Whether this pride has been developed in them in reaction against the general contempt felt for them, or whether it has been increased by the consciousness of the terror they inspire in their victim and the feeling of mastery over him, I do not know. Possibly the very ceremony and theatrical surroundings with which they make their appearance on the scaffold before the public help to develop a certain haughtiness in them. I remember that I had once for some time opportunities of frequently meeting an executioner and closely observing him. He was a thin, muscular man of forty, of medium stature with a rather pleasant, intelligent face and a curly head. He was always extraordinarily calm and dignified, behaved like a gentleman, always answered briefly, sensibly and even affably; but there was a haughtiness in his affability, as though he felt superior to me. The officers on duty often addressed him before me, and they positively showed him a sort of respect. He was conscious of this and before the officers he redoubled his politeness, frigidity and sense of personal dignity. The more friendly the officer was to him, the more unbending he became, and though he never departed from his refined courtesy, I am sure that he felt himself at the moment infinitely superior to the officer who was addressing him. One could see this from his face. Sometimes on hot summer days he would be sent under guard with a long thin pole to kill dogs in the town. There were an immense number of these dogs, who belonged to no one and multiplied with extraordinary rapidity. In hot weather they became dangerous, and by order of the authorities the executioner was sent to destroy them. But even this degrading duty evidently did not in the least detract from his dignity. It was worth seeing the majesty with which he paced up and down the town, accompanied by the weary guard, scaring the women and children by his very appearance, and how calmly and even superciliously he looked at all who met him.

The executioners have a very good time of it, though. They have plenty of money, they are very well fed, and have vodka to drink. They get money from bribes. The civilian prisoner who is condemned to corporal punishment always makes the executioner a preliminary present of something, even if it is his last penny. But from some rich prisoners the executioner demands a sum suitable to the victim's supposed means; they will exact as much as thirty roubles, sometimes even more. They bargain dreadfully with very rich prisoners. But the executioner cannot punish a man very lightly; he would answer for it with his own back. For a certain sum, however, he will promise the victim not to chastise him very severely. The condemned men almost always agree to his terms, for if they don't he really will punish them savagely, and it lies almost entirely in his hands. It sometimes happens that he demands a considerable ransom from a very poor prisoner; the relations come, bargain and bow down to him, and woe betide them if they do not satisfy him. In such cases the superstitious terror he inspires is a great help to him. What wild stories are told of executioners! The convicts themselves assured me that an executioner can kill a man at one blow. But when has there been an instance of this? However, it may be so. Of this they spoke with absolute confidence. The executioner assured me himself that he could do so. They told me, too, that he could aim a swinging blow at the convict's back, yet so that not the slightest bruise would follow and the convict would feel no pain. But of all these tricks and subtleties too many stories have been told already.

But even if the executioner is bribed to let the victim off easily, he gives the first blow with all his might. That is the invariable habit. He softens the later blows, especially if he has received his payment. But whether he has been bought off or not, the first blow is his own affair. I really do not know why this is their custom – whether to prepare the victim for the later blows, on the theory that after a very bad one the slighter ones will seem less painful, or whether simply to show off his power to the victim, to strike terror into him, to crush him at once, that he may realise the sort of man he has to deal with, to display himself, in fact. In any case, the executioner is in a state of excitement before he begins his work; he feels his power, he is conscious of mastery; at that moment he is an actor; the public gazes at him with wonder and alarm, and there is no doubt that he enjoys shouting to his victim at the first stroke, 'Ready now, I'll scorch you' – the fatal and habitual phrase on these occasions. It is hard to imagine how far a man's nature may be distorted!

During those early days in the hospital, I listened with interest to all these convict stories. It was very dull for us all, lying in bed. One day was so much like another! In the morning we were entertained by the visit of the doctors, and soon after that, dinner. Eating, of course, was a great recreation in the monotony of our existence. The rations were various, as prescribed for the different patients. Some of them only had soup with some cereal in it, others only had porridge, others were restricted to semolina pudding, for which there were always many candidates. The convicts had grown nice from lying in bed so long and were fond of dainties. The convalescent received a slice of boiled beef, 'bull' as they called it. Those who had scurvy were the best fed of all – they got beef with onion, horseradish and such things, and sometimes a glass of vodka. The bread, too, differed according to the patient's complaint; some was black, while some was nearly white and was well baked. This formality and exactitude in prescribing their diet only served to amuse the patients. Of course some patients did not care to eat at all. But those who had an appetite ate whatever they liked. Some exchanged their rations, so that the diet appropriate for one complaint was eaten by a patient suffering from something quite different. Others who were prescribed a lowering diet bought the beef or the diet prescribed for the scurvy, drank kvas or the hospital beer, buying it from those to whom it was prescribed. Some individuals even consumed the rations of two. The plates of food were sold and resold for money. A helping of beef was priced rather high; it cost five farthings. If there was none to sell in our ward, we used to send the attendant to the other convict ward, and if we could not get it there, we would send to the soldiers' or 'free' ward, as it was called. Patients who wanted to sell it could always be found. They were left with nothing but bread, but they made money. Poverty, of course, was universal, but those who had money sent to market for rolls and even sweet things. Our attendants carried out all these commissions quite disinterestedly.

After dinner was the dreariest time; some of us, bored with nothing to do, fell asleep, while some were gossiping, others were quarrelling, others were telling stories. If no fresh patients were brought in, it was even duller. A new arrival almost always made some sensation, especially if no one knew him. The patients scrutinised him, tried to find out who and what he was, where he came from and what brought him there. They were particularly interested in those who were being forwarded to other prisons. These always had something to tell, though not as a rule about their personal life; if they did not speak of that of their own accord, they were never questioned about it, but were only asked where had they come from? With whom? What sort of a journey they had? Where they were going? and so on. Some were at once reminded by their account of something in their own past, and told of different journeys, parties and the officers in charge of them.

Prisoners who had suffered the punishment of the 'sticks' were brought in about that time also, towards evening, that is. Their arrival always made rather a sensation as I have mentioned already, but they did not come every day, and on the days when there were none of them we felt dreary; all the patients seemed fearfully bored with one another and they even began to quarrel. We were glad to see even the lunatics, who were brought in to be kept under observation. The trick of pretending to be mad to escape corporal punishment was frequently adopted by convicts. Some were quickly detected, or rather they changed their tactics, and the convict who had been playing antics for two or three days would suddenly, apropos of nothing, behave sensibly, calm down and begin gloomily asking to be discharged. Neither the convicts nor the doctors reproached such a man, or tried to put him to shame by reminding him of the farce he had been playing. They discharged him without a word and let him go. Two or three days' later he was brought back after punishment. Such cases were, however, rare on the whole.

But the real madmen who were brought for observation were a perfect curse for the whole ward. Some of the lunatics who were lively, in high spirits, who shouted, danced and sang were at first welcomed by the convicts almost with enthusiasm. 'Here's fun!'

they would say, watching the antics of some new arrival. But I found it horribly painful and depressing to see these luckless creatures. I could never look at madmen without feeling troubled.

But the continual capers and uneasy antics of the madman who was welcomed with laughter on his arrival soon sickened us all, and in a day or two exhausted our patience. One of them was kept in our ward for three weeks, till we all felt like running away. To make matters worse, another lunatic was brought in at that very time, who made a great impression upon me. This happened during my third year in the prison. During my first year, or rather my first months, in prison, in the spring I went to a brickyard a mile and a half away to carry bricks for a gang of convicts who worked as stove builders. They had to mend the kilns in readiness for making bricks in the summer. That morning M. and B. introduced me to the overseer of the brickyard, a sergeant called Ostrozhsky. He was a Pole, a tall thin old man of sixty, of extremely dignified and even stately appearance. He had been in the army for many years, and though he was a peasant by birth and had come to Siberia as a simple soldier after 1830,* yet M. and B. loved and respected him. He was always reading the Catholic Bible. I conversed with him and he talked with much friendliness and sense, described things interestingly, and looked good-natured and honest. I did not see him again for two years; I only heard that he had got into trouble about something; and suddenly he was brought into our ward as a lunatic. He came in shrieking and laughing, and began dancing about the ward with most unseemly and indecent actions. The convicts were in ecstasies, but I felt very sad. Three days later we did not know what to do with him; he quarrelled, fought, squealed, sang songs even at night, and was continually doing such disgusting things that all began to feel quite sick. He was afraid of no one. They put him in a strait waistcoat, but that only made things worse for us, though without it he had been picking quarrels and fighting with almost everyone. Sometimes during those three weeks the whole ward rose as one man and begged the senior doctor to transfer our precious visitor to the other convict ward. There a day or two later they begged that he should be transferred back. And, as there were two restless and quarrelsome lunatics in the hospital at once, the two convict wards had them turn and turn

* The year of the Polish rising – *Translator's note.*

about and they were one as bad as the other. We all breathed more freely when at last they were taken away.

I remember another strange madman. There was brought in one summer day a healthy and very clumsy-looking man of forty-five, with a face horridly disfigured by smallpox, with little red eyes buried in fat, and a very gloomy and sullen expression. They put him next to me. He turned out to be a very quiet fellow, he spoke to no one, but sat as though he were thinking about something. It began to get dark and suddenly he turned to me. He began telling me without the slightest preface, but as though he were telling me a great secret, that he was in a few days to have received two thousand 'sticks', but that now it would not come off because the daughter of Colonel G. had taken up his case. I looked at him in perplexity and answered that I should not have thought that the colonel's daughter could have done anything in such a case. I had no suspicions at the time; he had been brought in not as a lunatic but as an ordinary patient. I asked him what was the matter with him. He answered that he did not know, that he had been brought here for some reason, that he was quite well, but that the colonel's daughter was in love with him; that a fortnight ago she had happened to drive past the lock-up at the moment when he was looking out of the grated window. She had fallen in love with him as soon as she saw him. Since then, on various pretexts she had been three times in the lock-up; the first time she came with her father to see her brother, who was then an officer on duty there; another time she came with her mother to give them alms, and as she passed him she whispered that she loved him and would save him. It was amazing with what exact details he told me all this nonsense, which, of course, was all the creation of his poor sick brain. He believed devoutly that he would escape corporal punishment. He spoke calmly and confidently of this young lady's passionate love for him, and although the whole story was so absurd, it was uncanny to hear such a romantic tale of a love-sick maiden from a man nearly fifty of such a dejected, woebegone and hideous appearance. It is strange what the fear of punishment had done to that timid soul. Perhaps he had really seen someone from the window, and the insanity, begotten of terror and growing upon him every hour, had at once found its outlet and taken shape. This luckless soldier, who had very likely never given a thought to young ladies in his life before, suddenly imagined a whole romance, instinctively catching at this straw. I listened without answering and told the other convicts about it. But when the others showed their curiosity he preserved a chaste silence.

Next day the doctor questioned him at length, and as he said that he was not ill in any way, and as on examination this seemed to be true, he was discharged. But we only learnt that they had put *sanat* on his case-sheet after the doctors had left the ward, so that it was impossible to tell them what was the matter with him. And indeed we hardly realised ourselves at the time what was really the matter. It was all the fault of the officers who had sent him to the hospital without explaining why they had sent him. There must have been some oversight. And perhaps those responsible may not have been at all sure that he was mad, and had acted on vague rumours in sending him to the hospital to be watched. However that may have been, the poor fellow was taken out two days later to be punished. The unexpectedness of his fate seems to have been a great shock to him; he did not believe in it till the last minute, and when he was led between the ranks he screamed for help. When he was brought back to the hospital afterwards, he was taken to the other convict ward, as there was no bed empty in ours. But I enquired about him and learnt that for eight days he did not say a word to anyone, that he was crushed and terribly depressed. He was transferred elsewhere, I believe, when his back was healed. I never heard anything more of him, anyway.

As for the general treatment and the drugs, so far as I could see, the patients who were only slightly ill scarcely followed the prescriptions or took their medicines at all. But all who were seriously ill, all who were really ill, in fact, were very fond of being doctored, and took their mixtures and powders punctually, but what they liked best of all were external remedies. Cuppings, leeches, poultices and blood-letting – the remedies which our peasants are so fond of and put such faith in – were accepted by the patients readily, even with relish. I was interested by one strange circumstance. The very men who were so patient in enduring agonising pain from the sticks and the birch often complained, writhed and even groaned when they were cupped. Whether they had grown soft through illness or were simply showing off, I really do not know. It is true our cuppings were of a peculiar sort. The assistant had at some remote period lost, or spoilt, the instrument with which the skin was pierced, or perhaps it was worn out, so that he was obliged to make the necessary incisions with a lancet. About twelve such incisions are made for every cupping; with the proper instrument it does not hurt: twelve little pricks are made instantaneously and the pain is scarcely felt. But when the incisions are made by the lancet it is a very different matter: the lancet cuts comparatively slowly, the pain is felt, and as for ten cuppings, for example, a hundred and twenty of such cuts had to be made, the whole operation was rather unpleasant. I have tried it; but though it was painful and annoying, still it was not so bad that one couldn't help moaning over it. It was positively absurd sometimes to see a tall sturdy fellow wriggling and beginning to whine. Perhaps one may compare it with the way a man, who is firm and even self-possessed in a matter of importance, will sometimes be moody and fanciful at home when he has nothing to do, will refuse to eat what is given to him, scold and find fault, so that nothing is to his taste, everyone annoys him, everyone is rude to him, everyone worries him – will, in short, 'wax fat and wanton', as is sometimes said of such gentlemen, though they are met even among the peasantry, and, living altogether as we did, we saw too many of them in our prison. Such a weakling would often be chaffed by the other convicts in the ward, and sometimes even abused by them. Then he would subside, as though he had only been waiting for a scolding to be quiet. Ustyantsev particularly disliked this complaining and never lost an opportunity for abusing the grumbler. He seized every chance of finding fault with anyone, indeed. It was an enjoyment, a necessity for him, due partly to his illness no doubt, but partly also to the dullness of his mind. He would first stare at the offender intently and earnestly and then begin to lecture him in a voice of calm conviction. He meddled in everything, as though he had been appointed to watch over the discipline and the general morality of the ward.

'He has a finger in every pie,' the convicts would say, laughing. But they were not hard on him and avoided quarrelling with him; they only laughed at him sometimes.

'What a lot of talk!' they would say. 'More than three wagon loads.'

'A lot of talk? We don't take off our caps to a fool, we all know. Why does he cry out over a lancet prick? You must take the crust with the crumb, put up with it.'

'But what business is it of yours?'

'No, lads,' interrupted one of our convicts, 'the cupping is nothing, I've tried it; but there's no pain worse than having your ear pulled for too long.'

Everyone laughed.

'Why, have you had yours pulled?'

'Don't you believe it, then? Of course I have.'

'That's why your ears stick out so.'

The convict in question, whose name was Shapkin, actually had very long prominent ears. He had been a tramp, was still young, and was a quiet and sensible fellow who always spoke with a sort of serious concealed humour, which gave a very comical effect to some of his stories.

'But why should I suppose you'd had your ears pulled? And how was I to imagine it, you thickhead?' Ustyantsev put in his spoke again, addressing Shapkin with indignation, though the latter had not spoken to him but to the company in general. Shapkin did not even look at him.

'And who was it pulled your ear?' asked someone.

'Who? Why, the police captain, to be sure. That was in my tramping days, mates. We reached K. and there were two of us, me and another tramp, Efim, who had no surname. On the way we had picked up a little something at a peasant's at Tolmina. That's a village. Well, we got to the town and looked about to see if we could pick up something here and make off. In the country you are free to go north and south and west and east, but in the town you are never at ease, we know. Well, first of all we went to a tavern. We looked about us. A fellow came up to us, a regular beggar, with holes in his elbows, but not dressed like a peasant. We talked of one thing and another.

'"And allow me to ask, have you got papers* with you or not?"

'"No," we said, "we haven't."

'"Oh!" says he, "I haven't either. I have two other good friends here," says he, "who are in General Cuckoo's service too.† Here

* Passports are meant – *Author's note.*

† That is, living in the woods. He means that they too were tramps – *Author's note.*

we've been going it a little and meanwhile we've not earned a penny. So I make bold to ask you to stand us a pint."

'"With the greatest of pleasure," say we. So we drank. And they put us up to a job that is in our own line, housebreaking. There was a house at the end of the town and a rich man lived there, with lots of property; so we decided to call on him at night. But we were caught, all the five of us, that night in his house. We were taken to the police station and then straight to the police captain's. "I'll question them myself," says he. He came in with a pipe, a cup of tea was brought in after him. He was a hearty-looking fellow, with whiskers. He sat down. Three others were brought in besides ourselves, tramps too. A tramp's a funny chap, you know, brothers: he never remembers anything; you might break a post on his head, you won't make him remember; he knows nothing. The police captain turned straight to me. "Who are you?" he growled out at me with a voice that came out of his boots. Well, of course, I said what we all do: "I don't remember anything, your honour, I've forgotten."

'"Wait a bit, I shall have something more to say to you, I know your face," says he, staring, all eyes, at me. But I had never seen him before. Then to the next: "Who are you?"

'"Cut-and-run, your honour."

'"Is that your name?"

'"Yes, your honour."

'"All right, you're Cut-and-run; and you?" he turns to the third.

'"And I follow him, your honour."

'"But what's your name?"

'"That's my name, your honour: I follow him."

'"But who has given you that name, you rascal?"

'"Good people, your honour. There are good people in the world, your honour, we all know."

'"And who are these good people?"

'"I've rather forgotten, your honour, you must graciously forgive me."

'"You've forgotten them all?"

'"Yes, all, your honour."

'"But you must have had a father and mother? You must remember them, anyway?"

'"It must be supposed I had them, your honour, but I've rather forgotten them too; perhaps I did have them, your honour."

'"But where have you lived till now?"

'"In the woods, your honour."

'"Always in the woods?"

'"Always."

'"And what about the winter?"

'"I haven't seen the winter, your honour."

'"And you, what's your name?"

'"Hatchet, your honour."

'"And you?"

'"Quick-sharpener, your honour."

'"And you?"

'"Sharpener – for sure, your honour."

'"You none of you remember anything?"

'"None of us, your honour."

'He stands and laughs and they look at him and laugh. But another time he might give you one in the jaw, it's all luck. And they were such a fat sturdy lot. "Take them to prison," says he, "I'll talk to them later, but you stay here," says he to me. "Come this way, sit down." I look – there's a table, paper and pen. What is he up to now? thinks I. "Sit down on the chair," says he, "take the pen, write," and he took hold of my ear and pulled it. I looked at him as the devil looked at the priest: "I can't, your honour," says I. "Write!" says he. "Have mercy, your honour!" "Write," says he, "write as best you can." And he kept pulling and pulling my ear and suddenly gave it a twist. Well, I tell you, lads, I'd rather have had three hundred lashes. There were stars before my eyes! "You write, and that's all about it."'

'Why, was he crazy or what?'

'No, he wasn't crazy. But not long before a clerk at. T. had played a fine prank: he nabbed the government money and made off with it, and he had ears that stuck out too. Well, they sent word of it in all directions and I seemed like the description. So he was trying whether I knew how to write and how I wrote.'

'What a position, lad! And did it hurt?'

'I tell you it did.'

There was a general burst of laughter.

'Well, and did you write?'

'Why, how could I write? I began moving the pen and I moved it about over the paper; he gave it up. He gave me a dozen swipes in the face and then let me go, to prison too, of course.'

'And do you know how to write?'

'I did once, but since folks began writing with pens I lost the art.'

Well, it was in tales like these or rather in chatter like this that our weary hours were spent. Good God, how wearisome it was! The days were long, stifling, exactly like one another. If one had only a book! And yet I was constantly going to the hospital, especially at first, sometimes because I was ill and sometimes simply for a rest, to get away from the prison. It was unbearable there, more unbearable than here, morally more unbearable. The hatred, enmity, quarrelling, envy, the continual attacks on us 'the gentlemen', the spiteful, menacing faces! Here in the hospital all were more on an equal footing and lived more amicably. The saddest time of the whole day was the beginning of the evening when the candles were lit and night was coming on. They settled down to sleep early. The dim night-lamp gleamed, a spot of brightness in the distance near the door, while at our end it was half dark. The air grew close and fetid. Some patient unable to sleep would get up and sit for a couple of hours on his bed, his head bent forward in his nightcap, as though pondering something. One looks at him for an hour to pass the time and wonders what he is thinking about, or one begins to dream and think of the past, while fancy draws pictures in vivid colours with wide horizons. One recalls details which one would not remember at another time, and which one would not feel as one does then. And one speculates on the future, how one will get out of prison. Where will one go? When will that be? Whether one will return to one's native place? One muses and muses, and hope begins to stir in one's heart . . . At other times one simply begins counting one, two, three, and so on, to put oneself to sleep. I have sometimes counted to three thousand and not slept. Someone would stir. Ustyantsev would cough his sickly consumptive cough and then groan feebly, and every time would add, 'Lord, I have sinned!' And it is strange to hear this sick, broken, moaning voice in the complete stillness. In another corner there are others awake, talking together from their beds. One begins to tell something of his past, some event long gone by, of his tramping, of his children, of his wife, of the old days. You feel from the very sound of the far-away whisper that all he is telling is long over and can never return, and that he, the speaker, has cut off all connection with it. The other listens. One can hear nothing but a soft measured whisper, like water trickling far away. I remember one long winter night I heard a story. It seemed to me at first like a nightmare, as though I had been lying in fever and had dreamed it all in delirium.

CHAPTER FOUR

Akulka's Husband

[*a story*]

It was rather late at night, about twelve o'clock. I had fallen asleep but soon woke up. The tiny dim light of the night-lamp glimmered faintly in the ward . . . Almost all were asleep. Even Ustyantsev was asleep, and in the stillness one could hear how painfully he breathed and the husky wheezing in his throat at every gasp. Far away in the passage there suddenly sounded the heavy footsteps of the sentry coming to relieve the watch. There was a clang of a gun against the floor. The ward door was opened: the corporal, stepping in cautiously, counted over the patients. A minute later the ward was shut up, a new sentry was put on duty, the watchman moved away, and again the same stillness. Only then I noticed that on the left at a little distance from me there were two patients awake, who seemed to be whispering together. It used to happen in the ward sometimes that two men would lie side by side for days and months without speaking, and suddenly would begin talking, excited by the stillness of the night, and one would reveal his whole past to the other.

They had evidently been talking for a long time already. I missed the beginning and even now I could not make it all out; but by degrees I grew used to it and began to understand it all. I could not get to sleep; what could I do but listen? One was speaking with heat, half reclining on the bed, with his head raised, and craning his neck towards his companion. He was obviously roused and excited; he wanted to tell his story. His listener was sitting sullen and quite unconcerned in his bed, occasionally growling in answer or in token of sympathy with the speaker, more as it seemed out of politeness than from real feeling, and at every moment stuffing his nose with snuff. He was a soldier called Cherevin from the disciplinary battalion, a man of fifty, a sullen pedant, a cold formalist and a conceited fool. The speaker, whose name was Shishkov, was a young fellow under thirty, a convict in the civil division in our prison, who worked in the tailor's workshop. So far, I had taken very little notice of him, and I was not drawn to see more of him during the remainder of my time in prison. He was a shallow, whimsical fellow; sometimes he would be silent, sullen and rude and not say a word for weeks together. Sometimes he would suddenly get mixed up in some affair, would begin talking scandal, would get excited over trifles and flit from one ward to another repeating gossip, talking endlessly, frantic with excitement. He would be beaten and relapse into silence again. He was a cowardly, mawkish youth. Everyone seemed to treat him with contempt. He was short and thin, his eyes were restless and sometimes had a blank dreamy look. At times he would tell a story; he would begin hotly, with excitement, gesticulating with his hands, and suddenly he would break off or pass to another subject, carried away by fresh ideas and forgetting what he had begun about. He was often quarrelling, and whenever he quarrelled would reproach his opponent for some wrong he had done him, would speak with feeling and almost with tears . . . He played fairly well on the balalaika and was fond of playing it. On holidays he even danced, and danced well when they made him. He could very easily be made to do anything. It was not that he was specially docile but he was fond of making friends and was ready to do anything to please.

For a long time I could not grasp what he was talking about. I fancy, too, that at first he was constantly straying away from his subject into other things. He noticed perhaps that Cherevin took scarcely any interest in his story, but he seemed anxious to convince himself that his listener was all attention, and perhaps it would have hurt him very much if he had been convinced of the contrary.

'. . . He would go out into the market,' he went on. 'Everyone would bow to him. They felt he was a rich man; that's the only word for it.'

'He had some trade, you say?'

'Yes, he had. They were poor folks there, regular beggars. The women used to carry water from the river ever so far up the steep bank to water their vegetables; they wore themselves out and did not get cabbage enough for soup in the autumn. It was poverty. Well, he rented a big piece of land, kept three labourers to work it; besides he had his own beehives and sold honey, and cattle too in our parts, you know; he was highly respected. He was pretty old, seventy if he was a day, his old bones were heavy, his hair was grey, he was a great big fellow. He would go into the market-place in a fox-skin coat and all did him honour. They felt what he was, you see! "Good morning, Ankudim Trofimitch, sir." "Good day to you," he'd say. He wasn't too proud to speak to anyone, you know. "Long life to you, Ankudim Trofimitch!" "And how's your luck?" he'd ask. "Our luck's as right as soot is white; how are you doing, sir?" "I am doing as well as my sins will let me, I am jogging along." "Good health to you, Ankudim Trofimitch!" He wasn't too proud for anyone, but if he spoke, every word he said was worth a rouble. He was a Bible reader, an educated man, always reading something religious. He'd set his old woman before him: "Now wife, listen and mark!" and he'd begin expounding to her. And the old woman was not so very old, she was his second wife, he married her for the sake of children, you know, he had none from the first. But by the second, Marya Stepanovna, he had two sons not grown up. He was sixty when the youngest, Vasya, was born, and his daughter, Akulka, the eldest of the lot, was eighteen.'

'Was that your wife?'

'Wait a bit. First there was the upset with Filka Morozov. "You give me my share," says Filka to Ankudim. "Give me my four hundred roubles – am I your servant? I won't be in business with you and I don't want your Akulka. I am going to have my fling. Now my father and mother are dead, so I shall drink up my money and then hire myself out, that is, go for a soldier, and in ten years I'll come back here as a field-marshal." Ankudim gave him the money and settled up with him for good – for his father and the old man had set up business together. "You are a lost man," says he, "Whether I am a lost man or not, you, grey-beard, you'd teach one to sup milk with an awl. You'd save off every penny, you'd rake over rubbish to make porridge. I'd like to spit on it all. Save every pin and the devil you win. I've a will of my own," says he. "And I am not taking your Akulka, anyway. I've slept with her as it is," says he. "What!" says Ankudim, "do you dare shame the honest daughter of an honest father? When have you slept with her, you adder's fat? You pike's blood!" And he was all of a tremble, so Filka told me.

' "I'll take good care," says he, "that your Akulka won't get any husband now, let alone me; no one will have her, even Mikita Grigoritch won't take her, for now she is disgraced. I've been carrying on with her ever since autumn. I wouldn't consent for a hundred crabs now. You can try giving me a hundred crabs, I won't consent . . ."

'And didn't he run a fine rig among us, the lad! He kept the country in an uproar and the town was ringing with his noise. He got together a crew of companions, heaps of money; he was carousing for three months, he spent everything. "When I've got through all the money," he used to say, "I'll sell the house, sell everything, and then I'll either sell myself for a soldier or go on the tramp." He'd be drunk from morning till night, he drove about with bells and a pair of horses. And the way the wenches ran after him was tremendous. He used to play the *torba* finely.'

'Then he'd been carrying on with Akulka before?'

'Stop, wait a bit. I'd buried my father just then too, and my mother used to make cakes, she worked for Ankudim, and that was how we lived. We had a hard time of it. We used to rent a bit of ground beyond the wood and we sowed it with corn, but we lost everything after father died, for I went on the spree too, my lad. I used to get money out of my mother by beating her.'

'That's not the right thing, to beat your mother. It's a great sin.'

'I used to be drunk from morning till night, my lad. Our house was all right, though it was tumbledown, it was our own, but it was empty as a drum. We used to sit hungry, we had hardly a morsel from one week's end to another. My mother used to keep on nagging at me; but what did I care? I was always with Filka Morozov in those days. I never left him from morning till night. "Play on the guitar and dance," he'd say to me, "and I'll lie down and fling money at you, for I'm an extremely wealthy man!" And what wouldn't he do! But he wouldn't take stolen goods. "I'm not a thief," he says, "I'm an honest man. But let's go and smear Akulka's gate with pitch, for I don't want Akulka to marry Mikita Grigoritch. I care more for that than for jelly." The old man had been meaning to marry Akulka to Mikita Grigoritch for some time past. Mikita, too, was an old fellow in spectacles and a widower with a business. When he heard the stories about Akulka he drew back: "That would be a great disgrace to me, Ankudim Trofimitch," says he, "and I don't want to get married in my old age." So we smeared Akulka's gate. And they thrashed her, thrashed her for it at home . . . Marya Stepanovna cried, "I'll wipe her off the face of the earth!" "In ancient years," says the old man, "in the time of the worthy patriarchs, I should have chopped her to pieces at the stake, but nowadays it's all darkness and rottenness." Sometimes the neighbours all along the street would hear Akulka howling – they beat her from morning till night. Filka would shout for the whole market-place to hear: "Akulka's a fine wench to drink with," says he, "You walk in fine array, who's your lover, pray! I've made them feel it," says he, "they won't forget it."

'About that time I met Akulka one day carrying the pails and I shouted at her, "Good morning, Akulina Kudimovna. Greetings to your grace! You walk in the fine array. Where do you get it, pray? Come, who's your lover, say!" That was all I said. But how she did look at me. She had such big eyes and she had grown as thin as a stick. And as she looked at me her mother thought she was laughing with me and shouted from the gateway, "What are you gaping at, shameless hussy?" and she gave her another beating that day. Sometimes she'd beat her for an hour together. "I'll do for her," says she, "for she is no daughter of mine now." '

'Then she was a loose wench?'

'You listen, old man. While I was always drinking with Filka, my mother comes up to me one day – I was lying down. "Why are you lying there, you rascal?" says she. "You are a blackguard," says she. She swore at me in fact. "You get married," says she. "You marry Akulka. They'll be glad to marry her now even to you, they'd give you three hundred roubles in money alone." "But she is disgraced in the eyes of all the world," says I. "You are a fool," says she, "the wedding ring covers all, it will be all the better for you if she feels her guilt all her life. And their money will set us on our feet again. I've talked it over with Marya Stepanovna already. She is very ready to listen." "Twenty roubles down on the table and I'll marry her," says I. And would you believe it, right up to the day of the wedding I was drunk. And Filka Morozov was threatening me, too: "I'll break all your ribs, Akulka's husband," says he, "and I'll sleep with your wife every night if I please." "You lie, you dog's flesh," says I. And then he put me to shame before all the street. I ran home: "I won't be married," says I, "if they don't lay down another fifty roubles on the spot." '

'But did they agree to her marrying you?'

'Me? Why not? We were respectable people. My father was only ruined at the end by a fire; till then we'd been better off than they. Ankudim says, "You are as poor as a rat," says he. "There's been a lot of pitch smeared on your gate," I answered. "There's no need for you to cry us down," says he. "You don't know that she has disgraced herself, but there's no stopping people's mouths. Here's the ikon and here's the door," says he. "You needn't take her. Only pay back the money you've had." Then I talked it over with Filka and I sent Mitri Bikov to tell him I'd dishonour him now over all the world; and right up to the wedding, lad, I was dead drunk. I was only just sober for the wedding. When we were driven home from the wedding and sat down, Mitrofan Stepanovitch, my uncle, said, "Though it's done in dishonour, it's just as binding," says he, "the thing's done and finished." Old Ankudim was drunk too and he cried, he sat there and the tears ran down his beard. And I tell you what I did, my lad: I'd put a whip in my pocket, I got it ready before the wedding. I'd made up my mind to have a bit of fun with Akulka, to teach her what it meant to get married by a dirty trick and that folks might know I wasn't being fooled over the marriage.

'Quite right too! To make her feel it for the future . . . '

'No, old chap, you hold your tongue. In our part of the country they take us straight after the wedding to a room apart while the others drink outside. So they left Akulka and me inside. She sits there so white, not a drop of blood in her face. She was scared, to be sure. Her hair, too, was as white as flax, her eyes were large and she was always quiet, you heard nothing of her, she was like a dumb thing in the house. A strange girl altogether. And can you believe it, brother, I got that whip ready and laid it beside me by the bed, but it turned out she had not wronged me at all, my lad!'

'You don't say so!'

'Not at all. She was quite innocent. And what had she had to go through all that torment for? Why had Filka Morozov put her to shame before all the world?'

'Yes . . . '

'I knelt down before her then, on the spot, and clasped my hands. "Akulina Kudimovna," says I, "forgive me, fool as I am, for thinking ill of you too. Forgive a scoundrel like me," says I. She sat before me on the bed looking at me, put both hands on my shoulders while her tears were flowing. She was crying and laughing . . . Then I went out to all of them. "Well," says I, "if I meet Filka Morozov now he is a dead man!" As for the old people, they did not know which saint to pray to. The mother almost fell at her feet, howling. And the old fellow said, "Had we known this, we wouldn't have found a husband like this for you, our beloved daughter."

'When we went to church the first Sunday, I in my astrakhan cap, coat of fine cloth and velveteen breeches, and she in her new hareskin coat with a silk kerchief on her head, we looked a well matched pair: didn't we walk along! People were admiring us. I needn't speak for myself, and though I can't praise Akulina up above the rest, I can't say she was worse: and she'd have held her own with any dozen.'

'That's all right, then.'

'Come, listen. The day after the wedding, though I was drunk, I got away from my visitors and I escaped and ran away. "Bring me that wretch Filka Morozov," says I, "bring him here, the scoundrel!" I shouted all over the market. Well, I was drunk too: I was beyond the Vlasovs' when they caught me, and three men brought me home by force. And the talk was all over the town. The wenches in the market-place were talking to each other: "Girls, darlings, have you heard? Akulka is proved innocent."

'Not long after, Filka says to me before folks, "Sell your wife and you can drink. Yashka the soldier got married just for that," says he. "He didn't sleep with his wife, but he was drunk for three years." I said to him, "You are a scoundrel." "And you," says he, "a fool. Why, you weren't sober when you were married," says he, "how could you tell about it when you were drunk?" I came home and shouted, "You married me when I was drunk," said I. My mother began scolding me. "Your ears are stopped with gold, mother. Give me Akulka." Well, I began beating her. I beat her, my lad, beat her for two hours, till I couldn't stand up. She didn't get up from her bed for three weeks.'

'To be sure,' observed Cherevin phlegmatically, 'if you don't beat them, they'll . . . But did you catch her with a lover?'

'Catch her? No, I didn't,' Shishkov observed, after a pause, and, as it were, with an effort. 'But I felt awfully insulted. People teased me so and Filka led the way. "You've a wife for show," says he, "for folks to look at." Filka invited us with others, and this was the greeting he gave me: "His wife is a tender-hearted soul," says he, "honourable and polite, who knows how to behave, nice in every way – that's what he thinks now. But you've forgotten, lad, how you smeared her gate with pitch yourself!" I sat drunk and then he seized me by the hair suddenly and holding me by the hair he shoved me down. "Dance," says he, "Akulka's husband! I'll hold you by your hair and you dance to amuse me!" "You are a scoundrel,' I shouted. And he says to me, "I shall come to you with companions and thrash Akulka, your wife, before you, as much as I like." Then I, would you believe it, was afraid to go out of the house for a whole month. I was afraid he'd come and disgrace me. And just for that I began beating her . . .'

'But what did you beat her for? You can tie a man's hands but you can't stop his tongue. You shouldn't beat your wife too much. Show her, give her a lesson, and then be kind to her. That's what she is for.'

Shishkov was silent for some time.

'It was insulting,' he began again. 'Besides, I got into the habit of it: some days I'd beat her from morning till night; everything she did was wrong. If I didn't beat her, I felt bored. She would sit without saying a word, looking out of the window and crying . . . She was always crying, I'd feel sorry for her, but I'd beat her. My mother was always swearing at me about her: "You are a scoundrel," she'd say, "you're a jailbird!" "I'll kill her," I cried, "and don't let anyone dare to speak to me; for they married me by a trick." At first old Ankudim stood up for her; he'd come himself: "You are no one of much account," says he, "I'll find a law for you." But he gave it up. Marya Stepanovna humbled herself completely. One day she came and prayed me tearfully, "I've come to entreat you, Ivan Semyonovitch, it's a small matter, but a great favour. Bid me hope again," she bowed down, "soften your heart, forgive her. Evil folk slandered our daughter. You know yourself she was innocent when you married her." And she bowed down to my feet and cried. But I lorded it over her. "I won't hear you now! I shall do just what I like to you all now, for I am no longer master of myself. Filka Morozov is my mate and my best friend . . . "

'So you were drinking together again then?'

'Nothing like it! There was no approaching him. He was quite mad with drink. He'd spent all he had and hired himself out to a storekeeper to replace his eldest son, and in our part of the country when a man sells himself for a soldier, up to the very day he is taken away everything in the house has to give way to him, and he is master over all. He gets the sum in full when he goes and till that time he lives in the house; he sometimes stays there for six months and the way he'll go on, it's a disgrace to a decent house. "I am going for a soldier in place of your son," the fellow would say, "so I am your benefactor, so you must all respect me, or I'll refuse." So Filka was having a rare time at the shopkeeper's, sleeping with the daughter, pulling the father's beard every day after dinner, and doing just as he liked. He had a bath every day and insisted on using vodka for water, and the women carrying him to the bath-house in their arms. When he came back from a walk he would stand in the middle of the street and say, "I won't go in at the gate, pull down the fence," so they had to pull down the fence in another place beside the gate for him to go through. At last his time was up, they got him sober and took him off. The people came out in crowds into the street saying, "Filka Morozov's being taken for a soldier!" He bowed in all directions. Just then Akulka came out of the kitchen garden. When Filka saw her just at our gate, "Stop," he cried, and leapt out of the cart and bowed down before her. "You are my soul," he said, "my darling, I've loved you for two years, and now they are taking me for a soldier with music. Forgive me," said he, "honest daughter of an honest father, for I've been a scoundrel to you and it's all been my fault!" And he bowed down to the ground again. Akulka stood, seeming scared at first, then she made him a low bow and said, "You forgive me too, good youth, I have no thought of any evil you have done." I followed her into the hut. "What did you say to him, dog's flesh?"

And you may not believe me but she looked at me: "Why, I love him now more than all the world," said she.'

'You don't say so!'

'I did not say one word to her all that day . . . only in the evening. "Akulka, I shall kill you now," says I. All night I could not sleep; I went into the passage to get some kvas to drink, and the sun was beginning to rise. I went back into the room. "Akulka," said I, "get ready to go out to the field." I had been meaning to go before and mother knew we were going. "That's right," said she. "It's harvest-time now and I hear the labourer's been laid up with his stomach for the last three days." I got the cart out without saying a word. As you go out of our town there's a pine forest that stretches for ten miles, and beyond the forest was the land we rented. When we had gone two miles I stopped the horse. "Get out, Akulina," said I, "your end has come." She looked at me, she was scared; she stood up before me, she did not speak. "I am sick of you," says I, "say your prayers!" ' And then I snatched her by the hair; she had two thick long plaits. I twisted them round my hand and held her tight from behind between my knees. I drew out my knife, I pulled her head back and I slid the knife along her throat. She screamed, the blood spurted out, I threw down the knife, flung my arms round her, lay down on the ground, embraced her and screamed over her, yelling; she screamed and I screamed; she was fluttering all over, struggling to get out of my arms, and the blood was simply streaming, simply streaming on to my face and on to my hands. I left her, a panic came over me, and I left the horse and set off running, and ran home along the backs of the houses and straight to the bath-house. We had an old bath-house we didn't use: I squeezed myself into a corner under the steps and there I sat. And there I sat till nightfall.'

'And Akulka?'

'She must have got up, too, after I had gone and walked homewards too. They found her a hundred paces from the place.'

'Then you hadn't killed her?'

'Yes . . . ' Shishkov paused for a moment.

'There's a vein, you know,' observed Cherevin, 'if you don't cut through that vein straightaway a man will go on struggling and won't die, however much blood is lost.'

'But she did die. They found her dead in the evening. They informed the police, began searching for me, and found me at nightfall in the bath-house! . . . And here I've been close upon four years,' he added, after a pause.

'H'm . . . to be sure, if you don't beat them there will be trouble,' Cherevin observed coolly and methodically, pulling out his tobacco-pouch again. He began taking long sniffs at intervals. 'Then again you seem to have been a regular fool, young fellow, too. I caught my wife with a lover once. So I called her into the barn; I folded the bridle in two. "To whom do you swear to be true? To whom do you swear to be true?" says I. And I did give her a beating with that bridle, I beat her for an hour and a half. "I'll wash your feet and drink the water," she cried at last. Ovdotya was her name.'

CHAPTER FIVE

Summer Time

But now it is the beginning of April, and Easter is drawing near. Little by little the summer work begins. Every day the sun is warmer and more brilliant; the air is fragrant with spring and has a disquieting influence on the nerves. The coming of spring agitates even the man in fetters, arouses even in him vague desires, cravings and a yearning melancholy. I think one pines for liberty more in the bright sunshine than in dull winter or autumn days, and that may be noticed in all prisoners. Although they seem glad of the fine days, yet at the same time their impatience and restlessness is intensified. In fact I have noticed that quarrels in prison become more frequent in the spring. Noise, shouting and uproar are heard more often, rows are more common; yet sometimes at work one suddenly notices dreamy eyes fixed on the blue distance, where far away beyond the Irtish stretch the free Kirghiz steppes, a boundless plain for a thousand miles. One hears a man heave a deep sigh from a full heart, as though he yearned to breathe that far-away free air and to ease with it his stifled and fettered soul. 'Ech-ma!' the convict exclaims at last, and suddenly, as though shaking off dreams and brooding, he sullenly and impatiently snatches up the spade or the bricks he has to move from place to place. A minute later he has forgotten his sudden feeling and begun laughing or swearing according to his disposition. Or he suddenly sets to his task, if he has one, with extraordinary and quite superfluous zeal, and begins working with all his might, as though trying to stifle in himself something which is cramping and oppressing him within. They are all vigorous, men for the most part in the flower of their age and their strength . . . Fetters are hard to bear at this season! I am not poetising and am convinced of the truth of what I say. Apart from the fact that in the warmth, in the brilliant sunshine, when, in all your soul, in all your being, you feel nature with infinite force springing into life again around you, prison doors, guards and bondage are harder to bear than ever – apart from that, with the coming of spring and the return of the lark, tramping begins all over Siberia and Russia; God's people escape from prison and take refuge in the forests. After stifling dungeons, law courts, fetters and beatings, they wander at their own free will wherever they please, wherever it seems fair and free to them; they eat and drink what they find, what God sends them, and at night they fall asleep peacefully under God's eye in the forest, or the fields, troubling little for the future, and free from the sadness of prison, like the birds of the forest, with none to say goodnight to but the stars. There is no denying that one may have to face hardship, hunger and exhaustion 'in the service of General Cuckoo'. One may have to go for days together without bread; one must keep in hiding, out of sight of everyone; one may be driven to steal, to rob and sometimes even to murder. 'A convict free is like a baby, what he wants he takes,' is what they say in Siberia of the convict settlers. This saying applies in full force and even with some additions to the tramp. It is rare for a tramp not to be a robber and he is always a thief, more from necessity than from vocation, of course.

There are inveterate tramps. Some, after their imprisonment is over, run away from settlements. One would have thought that a man would be satisfied in the settlement and free from anxiety, but no, something lures him, beckons him away. Life in the forest, a life poor and terrible, but free and adventurous, has a fascination, a mysterious charm for those who have once known it, and one may sometimes see a sedate precise man, who was promising to become a capable farmer and a good settled inhabitant, run away to the forest. Sometimes a man will marry and have children, live for five years in one place, and suddenly one fine day disappear somewhere, leaving his wife, his children and the whole parish in amazement. A wanderer of this kind was pointed out to me in prison. He had never committed any special crime, at least I never heard anything of the kind spoken of, but he was always running away, he had been running away all his life. He had been on the southern frontier of Russia beyond the Danube, and in the Kirghiz steppes, and in Eastern Siberia and in the Caucasus – he had been everywhere. Who knows, perhaps in other circumstances, with his passion for travelling he might have been another Robinson Crusoe. But I was told all this about him by other people; he spoke very little in prison himself and then only of necessity. He was a little peasant of fifty, extremely meek, with an extremely calm and even vacant face, calm to the point of idiocy. In the summer he was fond of sitting in the sun, always humming some song to himself, but so quietly that five steps away he was inaudible. His features were somehow wooden; he ate little and chiefly bread; he never bought a roll or a glass of vodka and I doubt whether he ever had any money or knew how to count. He was perfectly unconcerned about everything. He sometimes fed the prison dogs with his own hands and no one else ever did. Indeed, Russians in general are not given to feeding dogs. They said he had been married, twice indeed; it was said that he had children somewhere . . . How he got into prison I have no idea. The convicts all expected him to give us the slip too, but either the time had not come or he was too old for it, for he went on living amongst us, calmly contemplating the strange environment in which he found himself. However, there was no reckoning on him, though one would have thought that he had nothing to run away for, that he would gain nothing by it.

Yet, on the whole, the life of a tramp in the forest is paradise compared with prison. That is easy to understand and indeed there can be no comparison. Though it's a hard life, it is freedom. That is why every convict in Russia, whatever prison he may be in, grows restless in the spring with the first kindly rays of sunshine. Though by no means everyone intends to run away; one may say with certainty, indeed, that owing to the difficulty of escape and the penalties attaching to it, not more than one in a hundred ventures upon it; yet the other ninety-nine dream at least of how they might escape and where they would escape to and comfort their hearts with the very desire, with the very imagination of its being possible. Some recall how they have run away in the past . . . I am speaking now only of those who are serving their sentence. But of course those who are awaiting sentence take the risks of flight far more frequently than other prisoners. Convicts condemned for a term run away only at the beginning of their imprisonment, if at all. When a convict has been two or three years in prison, those years begin to have a value in his mind and by degrees he makes up his mind that he would rather finish his term in the legal way and become a settler than run such risks, and take the chances of ruin if he fails. And failure is so possible. Scarcely one in ten succeeds in *changing his luck*. Another class of convicts, who more frequently take the hazards of flight, consists of those who are condemned to very long terms. Fifteen or twenty years seem an eternity, and a man condemned for such lengthy periods is always ready to dream of changing his luck, even if he has passed ten years in prison.

The branding does something to prevent prisoners attempting flight.

To *change one's luck* is a technical expression, so much so that even in cross-examination a prisoner caught trying to escape will answer that he wanted to change his luck. This rather bookish expression is exactly what is meant. Every fugitive looks forward, not exactly to complete freedom – he knows that is almost impossible – but either to getting into another institution or being sent as a settler, or being tried again for a fresh offence committed when he was tramping; in fact he does not care what becomes of him, so long as he is not sent back to the old place he is sick of, his former prison. If these fugitives do not, in the course of the summer, succeed in finding some exceptional place in which to spend the winter, if for instance they do not chance upon someone willing for interested motives to shelter a fugitive, if they do not, sometimes by means of murder, obtain a passport of some sort with which they can live anywhere they like, they are all either caught by the police or go in autumn of their own accord in crowds into the towns and the prisons and remain there for the winter, not, of course without hopes of escaping again in the summer.

Spring had an influence on me too. I remember how eagerly I sometimes peeped through the chinks in the fence and how long I used to stand with my head against the fence looking obstinately and insatiably at the greenness of the grass on our prison rampart and the deeper and deeper blue of the sky in the distance. My restlessness and depression grew stronger every day, and the prison became more and more hateful to me. The dislike with which as a 'gentleman' I was continually regarded by the convicts during my first few years became intolerable, poisoning my whole life.

During those first few years I often used to go into the hospital, though I had no illness, simply to avoid being in prison, simply to escape from this obstinate, irreconcilable hatred. 'You have beaks of iron, you've pecked us to death,' the convicts used to say to us, and how I used to envy the peasants who were brought to the prison! They were looked upon as comrades by everyone at once. And so the spring, the phantom of freedom, the general rejoicing of nature affected me with melancholy and nervous restlessness. At the end of Lent, I think in the sixth week, I took the sacrament. All the prisoners had been at the beginning of Lent divided by the senior sergeant into seven relays, one to take the sacrament during each week of the fast. Each of the relays consisted of about thirty men. I very much liked the week of the preparation for the sacrament. We were relieved of work. We went to the church, which was not far from the prison, twice or three times a day. It was long since I had been to church. The Lenten service so familiar to me from far-away days of childhood in my father's house, the solemn prayers, the prostrations – all this stirred in my heart the far, far-away past, bringing back the days of my childhood, and I remember how pleasant it was walking over the frozen ground in the early morning to the house of God, escorted by guards with loaded guns. The guards did not, however, go into the church. We stood all together in a group close to the church door, so far back that we could only hear the loud-voiced deacon and from time to time catch a glimpse of the black cope and the bald head of the priest through the crowd. I remembered how sometimes standing in church as a child I looked at the peasants crowding near the entrance and slavishly parting to make way for a thickly epauletted officer, a stout gentleman, or an over-dressed but pious lady, who invariably made for the best places and were ready to quarrel over them. I used to fancy then that at the church door they did not pray as we did, that they prayed humbly, zealously, abasing themselves and fully conscious of their humble state.

Now I, too, had to stand in the background, and not only in the background; we were fettered and branded as felons; everyone avoided us, everyone seemed to be even afraid of us, alms were always given to us, and I remember that this was positively pleasing to me in a way; there was a special subtlety in this strange pleasure.

'So be it,' I thought. The convicts prayed very earnestly and every one of them brought his poor farthing to the church every time to buy a candle, or to put in the collection. 'I, too, am a man,' he thought, and felt perhaps as he gave it, 'in God's eyes we are all equal . . . ' We took the sacrament at the early mass. When with the chalice in his hands the priest read the words, ' . . . accept me, O Lord, even as the thief,' almost all of them bowed down to the ground with a clanking of chains, apparently applying the words literally to themselves.

And now Easter had come. We received from the authorities an egg each and a piece of white bread made with milk and eggs. Loads of offerings for the prisoners were brought from the town again. Again there was a visit from the priest with a cross, again a visit of the authorities, again a cabbage soup with plenty of meat in it, again drinking and desultory idleness – exactly as at Christmas, except that now one could walk about the prison yard and warm oneself in the sun. There was more light, more space than in the winter, but yet it was more melancholy. The long endless summer day seemed particularly unbearable in the holidays. On ordinary days, at least, it was shortened by work.

The summer tasks turned out to be far harder than our work in winter. All were chiefly employed upon building. The convicts dug out the earth, laid the bricks; some were employed as carpenters, locksmiths or painters in doing up the government buildings. Others went to the brickyard to make bricks. This was considered the hardest work of all. The brickyard was two or three miles from the fortress. At six o'clock, every summer morning, a whole party of convicts, some fifty in number, set off for the brickyard. For this work they chose unskilled labourers, that is, men who had no special craft or trade. They took bread with them, for, as the place was so far off, it was waste of time going six miles home to dinner and back, so they had dinner on their return in the evening. The tasks were set for the whole day and we could only just get through them by working all day long. To begin with, one had to dig and carry the clay, to fetch water, to pound the clay in a pit, and finally to make a great number of bricks out of it – I believe it was two hundred, or perhaps even two hundred and fifty, a day. I only went twice to the brickyard. The brickyard men returned in the evening, worn out and exhausted, and all the summer they were continually throwing it up against the others, declaring that they were doing the hardest work. That seemed to be their consolation. Yet some of them were very ready to go to the brickyard: in the first place, it was outside the town, it was a free open space on the banks of the Irtish. It was a relief to look about one, anyway – to see something not the regulation prison surroundings! One could smoke freely and even lie down for half an hour with great satisfaction.

I used to go as before to pound alabaster, or to the workshop, or I was employed to carry bricks on the building. I once had to carry bricks a distance of about a hundred and sixty yards, from the bank of the Irtish to the barracks that were being built on the other side of the fortress rampart, and I had to go on doing this every day for two months. I positively liked the work, though the cord in which I had to carry the bricks always cut my shoulder. But I liked to feel that I was obviously gaining muscular strength through the work. At first I could only carry eight bricks and each brick weighed nearly eleven pounds. But I got up to twelve and even fifteen bricks later on, and that was a great joy to me. In prison physical strength is no less necessary than moral strength to enable one to endure the hardships of that accursed manner of life.

And I wanted to go on living when I got out of prison.

I liked carrying bricks not only because it strengthened my muscles but also because the work took me to the bank of the Irtish. I speak of the river-bank so often because it was only from there one had a view of God's world, of the pure clear distance, of the free solitary steppes, the emptiness of which made a strange impression on me. It was only on the bank of the Irtish that one could stand with one's back to the fortress and not see it. All our other tasks were done either in the fortress or close by it. From the very first days I hated that fortress, some of the buildings particularly. The major's house seemed to me a damnable, loathsome place, and I always looked at it with hatred every time I passed by. On the river-bank one might forget oneself: one would look at that boundless solitary vista as a prisoner looks out to freedom from his window. Everything there was sweet and precious in my eyes, the hot brilliant sun in the fathomless blue sky and the faraway song of the Kirghiz floating from the further bank. One gazes into the distance and makes out at last the poor smoke-blackened tent of some Kirghiz. One discerns the smoke rising from the tent, the Kirghiz woman busy with her two sheep. It is all poor and barbarous, but it is free. One descries a bird in the limpid blue air and for a long time one watches its flight: now it darts over the water, now it vanishes in the blue depths, now it reappears again, a speck flitting in the distance . . . Even the poor sickly flower which I found early in spring in a crevice of the rocky bank drew my attention almost painfully.

The misery of all that first year in prison was intolerable, and it had an irritating, bitter effect on me. During that first year I failed to notice many things in my misery. I shut my eyes and did not want to look. Among my spiteful and hostile companions in prison, I did not observe the good ones – the men who were capable of thought and feeling in spite of their repellent outer husk. In the midst of ill-natured sayings, I sometimes failed to notice kind and friendly words, which were the more precious because they were uttered with no interested motives, and often came straight from a heart which had suffered and endured more than mine. But why enlarge on this? I was very glad to get thoroughly tired: I might go to sleep when I got home. For the nights were an agony in the summer, almost worse than in the winter. The evenings, it is true, were sometimes very nice. The sun, which had been on the prison yard all day, set at last. Then followed the cool freshness of evening and then the comparatively cold night of the steppes. The convicts wandered in groups about the yard, waiting to be locked in. The chief mass, it is true, were crowding into the kitchen. There some burning question of the hour was always being agitated; they argued about this and that, sometimes discussed some rumour, often absurd, though it aroused extraordinary interest in these men cut off from the outer world; a report came for instance that our major was being turned out. Convicts are as credulous as children; they know themselves that the story is ridiculous, that it has been brought by a notorious gossip, an 'absurd person' – the convict Kvasov whom it had long been an accepted rule not to believe, and who could never open his mouth without telling a lie; yet everyone pounced on his story, talked it over and discussed it, amusing themselves and ending by being angry with themselves and ashamed of themselves for having believed Kvasov.

'Why, who's going to send him away?' shouted one. 'No fear, his neck is thick, he can hold his own.'

'But there are others over him, surely!' protested another, an eager and intelligent fellow who had seen something of life, but was the most argumentative man in the world.

'One raven won't pick out another's eyes!' a third, a grey-headed old man who was finishing his soup in the corner in solitude, muttered sullenly as though to himself.

'I suppose his superior officers will come to ask you whether they're to sack him?' a fourth added casually, strumming lightly on the balalaika.

'And why not?' answered the second furiously. 'All the poor people could petition for it, you must all come forward if they begin questioning. To be sure, with us it's all outcry, but when it comes to deeds we back out.'

'What would you have?' said the balalaika player. 'That's what prison's for!'

'The other day,' the excited speaker went on, not heeding him, 'there was some flour left. We scraped together what little there was and were sending it to be sold. But no, he heard of it; our foreman let him know; it was taken away; he wanted to make something out of it, to be sure. Was that fair now?'

'But who is it you want to complain to?'

'Who? Why, the inspector that's coming.'

'What inspector?'

'That's true, lads, that an inspector's coming,' said a lively young fellow of some education who had been a clerk and was reading *The Duchess la Vallière*, or something of the kind. He was always merry and amusing, but he was was respected for having a certain knowledge of life and of the world. Taking no notice of the general interest aroused by the news that an inspector was coming, he went straight up to one of the cooks and asked for some liver. Our cooks often used to sell such things. They would, for instance, buy a large piece of liver at their own expense, cook it, and sell it in small pieces to the convicts.

'One ha'p'orth or two ha'p'orths?' asked the cook.

'Cut me two ha'p'orths; let folks envy me,' answered the convict. 'There's a general, lads – a general coming from Petersburg; he'll inspect all Siberia. That's true. They said so at the commander's.'

This news produced an extraordinary sensation. For a quarter of an hour there was a stream of questions: who was it, what general, what was his rank, was he superior to the generals here? Convicts are awfully fond of discussing rank, officials, which of them takes precedence, which can lord it over the other, and which has to give way; they even quarrel and dispute and almost fight over the generals. One wonders what difference it can make to them. But a minute knowledge of generals and the authorities altogether is the criterion of a man's knowledge, discrimination and previous importance in the world. Talk about the higher authorities is generally considered the most refined and important conversation in prison.

'Then it turns out to be true, lads, that they are coming to sack the major,' observes Kvasov, a little red-faced man, excitable and remarkably muddle-headed. He had been the first to bring the news about the major.

'He'll bribe them,' the grim, grey-headed convict, who had by now finished his soup, brought out jerkily.

'To be sure he will,' said another. 'He's grabbed money enough! He had a battalion before he came to us. The other day he was wanting to marry the head priest's daughter.'

'But he didn't – they showed him the door, he was too poor. He's not much of a match! When he gets up from a chair he takes all he's got with him. He lost all his money gambling at Easter. Fedka said so.'

'Yes; the lad's not one to spend, but he gets through cash no end.'

'Ah, brother, I was married, too. It's no use for a man to be married; when you are married the night's too short,' remarked Skuratov, putting his word in.

'Oh, indeed! It was you we were talking about, of course,' observed the free-and-easy youth who had been a clerk. 'But you are a silly fool, Kvasov, let me tell you. Do you suppose the major could bribe a general like that, and that such a general would come all the way from Petersburg to inspect the major? You are a fool, my lad, let me tell you.'

'Why, because he's a general won't he take it?' someone in the crowd observed sceptically.

'Of course he won't; if he does, he'll take a jolly big one.'

'To be sure, he will; to match his rank.'

'A general will always take bribes,' Kvasov observed with decision.

'You've tried it on, I suppose?' said Baklushin, suddenly coming in and speaking contemptuously. 'I don't believe you've ever seen a general.'

'I have, though!'

'You are lying!'

'Liar yourself!'

'Lads, if he has seen one, let him tell us all directly what general he knows. Come, speak away – for I know all the generals.'

'I've seen General Ziebert,' Kvasov answered with strange hesitation.

'Ziebert? There isn't such a general. He looked at your back, I suppose, your Ziebert, when he was a lieutenant-colonel maybe, and you fancied in your fright he was a general!'

'No, listen to me!' cried Skuratov, 'for I am a married man. There really was such a general at Moscow, Ziebert, of German family though he was a Russian. He used to confess to a Russian priest every year, at the fast of the Assumption, and he was always drinking water, lads, like a duck. Every day he'd drink forty glasses of Moscow river water. They said that he took it for some disease, his valet told me so himself.'

'He bred carp in his belly, I bet, with all that water,' observed the convict with the balalaika.

'Come, do shut up! We are talking business and they . . . What is this inspector, brothers?' a fussy old convict called Martinov, who had been a hussar, anxiously enquired.

'What nonsense people talk!' observed a sceptic. 'Where do they get it from and how do they fit it in? And it's all nonsense!'

'No, it's not nonsense,' Kulikov, who had hitherto been majestically silent, observed dogmatically. He was a man of some consequence, about fifty, with an exceptionally prepossessing countenance and disdainfully dignified manners. He was aware of the fact, and was proud of it. He was a veterinary surgeon, partly of gypsy descent, who used to earn money by doctoring horses in the town, and sold vodka in prison. He was a clever fellow and had seen a good deal. He dropped his words as though he were bestowing roubles.

'That's the truth, lads,' he went on calmly. 'I heard it last week. There's a general coming, a very important one; he'll inspect the whole of Siberia. We all know he will be bribed, too, but not by our old Eight-eyes; he wouldn't dare to come near him. There are generals and generals, brothers. There are some of all sorts. Only I tell you, our major will stay where he is, anyway. That's a sure thing. We can't speak, and none of the officers will speak against one of their own lot. The inspector will look into the prison and then he'll go away and report that he found everything all right . . . '

'That's right, lads, but the major's in a funk: he's drunk from morning till night.'

'But in the evening he drives a different sort of cart. Fedka was saying so.'

'You'll never wash a black dog white. It's not the first time he's been drunk, is it?'

'I say, what if the general really does nothing? It is high time they took notice of their goings on!' the convicts said to each other in excitement.

The news about the inspector was all over the prison in a moment; men wandered about the yard impatiently, repeating the news to one another, though some were purposely silent and maintained an indifferent air, evidently trying to increase their importance by so doing. Others remained genuinely unconcerned. Convicts with balalaikas were sitting on the barrack steps. Some went on gossiping. Others struck up songs, but all were in a state of great excitement that evening.

Between nine and ten we were all counted over, driven into the barracks and locked up for the night. The nights were short, we were waked between four and five, and we were never all asleep before eleven. There was always noise and talking till that hour and sometimes, as in winter, there were card parties. It became insufferably hot and stifling in the night. Though there were wafts of the cool night air from the open window, the convicts tossed about on their beds all night as though in delirium. The fleas swarmed in myriads. There were fleas in the winter, too, and in considerable numbers, but from the beginning of spring they swarmed in multitudes. Though I had been told of it before, I could not believe in the reality till I experienced it. And as the summer advanced, they grew more and more ferocious. It is true that one can get used to fleas – I have learnt this by experience; but still one has a bad time of it. They torment one so much that one lies at last as though in a fever, feeling that one is not asleep but in delirium. When at last, towards morning, the fleas desist, and as it were subside, and when one really drops into a sweet sleep in the cool of dawn, the pitiless tattoo of the drum booms out at the prison gate and the morning watch begins. Rolled up in your sheepskin you hear with a curse the loud, distinct sounds, as it were counting them, while through your sleep there creeps into your mind the insufferable thought that it will be the same tomorrow and the day after tomorrow, and for years together, right on to the day of freedom. But when, one wonders, will that freedom be, and where is it? Meanwhile, one must wake up; the daily movement and bustle begins . . . men dress and hurry out to work. It is true one can sleep for an hour at midday.

The story of the inspector was true. The rumour received more and more confirmation each day, and at last we all knew for a fact that an important general was coming from Petersburg to inspect the whole of Siberia, that he had already arrived, that he was by now at Tobolsk. Every day fresh reports reached the prison. News came, too, from the town. We heard that everyone was frightened and fluttered, and trying to show things the best side up. It was said that the higher officers were preparing receptions, balls, festivities. The convicts were sent out in parties to level the road to the fortress, to remove hillocks, to paint the fences and posts, to repair the stucco, to whitewash; in fact, they tried all in a minute to set right everything that had to be shown.

The convicts understood all this very well, and talked with more and more heat and defiance among themselves. Their fancy took immense flights. They even prepared to make a *complaint* when the general should enquire whether they were satisfied. Meanwhile they quarrelled and abused each other.

The major was in great excitement. He used to visit the prison more frequently, he shouted at people, and fell upon them, sent prisoners to the guard-house more frequently and was more zealous about cleanliness and decency. It was just at that time, as luck would have it, that a little incident took place which did not, however, as might have been expected, disturb the major at all, but on the contrary gave him positive satisfaction. A convict stuck an awl into another's chest, just over the heart.

The convict who committed this crime was called Lomov; the man who was wounded was called Gavrilka among us; he was an inveterate tramp. I don't know if he had any other name; among us he was called Gavrilka.

Lomov had been a prosperous peasant from the K. district of T. province. All the Lomovs lived together in one family, the old father with his brother and three sons. They were well-to-do peasants. It was rumoured all over the province that they were worth as much as a hundred thousand roubles. They tilled the land, tanned skins, traded, but did more in the way of moneylending, sheltering tramps, receiving stolen goods, and such pursuits. Half the peasants in the district were in their debt and in bondage to them. They were reputed to be shrewd and crafty peasants, but at last they became puffed up with pride, especially when one important person in the district took to putting up at their house when he travelled, saw the old father and took to him for his quick-wittedness and practical ability. They began to think they could do what they liked, and ran greater and greater risks in illegal undertakings of all sorts. Everyone was complaining of them, everyone was wishing the earth would swallow them up; but they held their heads higher and higher. They cared nothing for police captains and excise officials. At last they came to grief and were ruined, but not for any wrongdoing, not for their secret crimes, but for something of which they were not guilty. They had a big outlying farm some seven miles from the village. Once they had living there in the autumn six Kirghiz, who had worked for them as bondsmen under a contract for many years. One night all these Kirghiz labourers were murdered. An inquiry was made. It lasted a long while. Many other misdeeds were discovered in the course of the inquiry. The Lomovs were accused of murdering their labourers. They told the tale themselves, and everyone in the prison knew about it; it was suspected that they owed a great deal to their labourers, and as they were greedy and miserly in spite of their wealth, they had murdered the Kirghiz to escape paying them the arrears of their wages. During the trial and legal proceedings they lost all their property. The old father died. The sons were scattered. One of the sons and his uncle were sent to our prison for twelve years. And after all they were completely innocent as far as the death of the Kirghiz was concerned. There afterwards turned up in our prison a notorious rogue and tramp called Gavrilka, a brisk and lively fellow, who was responsible for the crime. I did not hear, however, whether he admitted it himself, but the whole prison was convinced that he had a share in the murder. Gavrilka had had dealings with the Lomovs when he had been a tramp. He had come to the prison for a short term as a deserter from the army and a tramp. He had murdered the Kirghiz with the help of three other tramps; they had hoped to plunder the farm and carry off a lot of booty.

The Lomovs were not liked among us; why, I don't know. One of them, the nephew, was a fine fellow, clever and easy to get on with; but his uncle, who stuck the awl into Gavrilka, was a stupid and quarrelsome man. He had quarrelled with many of the prisoners before and had been often soundly beaten. Gavrilka everyone liked for his cheerful and easy temper. Though the Lomovs knew that he was the criminal and that they were suffering for his crime, they did not quarrel with him, although they were never friendly with him; and he took no notice of them either. And suddenly a quarrel broke out between Gavrilka and the uncle Lomov over a most disgusting girl. Gavrilka began boasting of her favours; Lomov was jealous, and one fine day he stabbed him with the awl.

Though the Lomovs had been ruined by their trial, yet they lived in comfort in prison. They evidently had money. They had a samovar, drank tea. Our major knew of it and hated the two Lomovs intensely. Everyone could see that he was always finding fault with them and trying to get them into trouble. The Lomovs put this down to the major's desire to get a bribe out of them. But they never offered him a bribe.

Of course, if Lomov had driven the awl a very little further in, he would have killed Gavrilka. But the assault ended in nothing worse than a scratch. It was reported to the major. I remember how he pranced in, out of breath, and obviously delighted. He treated Gavrilka with wonderful gentleness, quite as if he had been his own son.

'Well, my boy, can you walk to the hospital or not? No, you'd better drive. Get the horse out at once!' he shouted in excited haste to the sergeant.

'But I don't feel anything, your honour. He only gave me a little prick, your honour.'

'You don't know, you don't know, my dear boy; we shall see . . . It's a dangerous place; it all depends on the place; he struck you just over the heart, the ruffian! And you, you,' he roared, addressing Lomov, 'now I'll make you smart! . . . To the guard-house!'

And he certainly did make him smart. Lomov was tried and, though the wound turned out to be the slightest of pricks, the intent was unmistakable. The criminal's term of imprisonment was increased and he was given a thousand strokes. The major was thoroughly satisfied.

At last the inspector arrived. The day after he arrived in the town he visited our prison. It was on a holiday. For some days before everything in the prison had been scrubbed, polished, cleaned. The prisoners were freshly shaven. Their clothes were white and clean. In the summer the regulation dress for the prisoners was white linen jacket and trousers. Every one of them had a black circle about four inches in diameter sewn on the back of his jacket. A whole hour was spent in drilling the convicts to answer properly if the great man should greet them. There were rehearsals. The major bustled about like one possessed. An hour before the general's appearance the convicts were all standing in their places like posts with their arms held stiffly to their sides. At last, at one o'clock, the general arrived. He was a general of great consequence, of such consequence that I believe all official hearts must have throbbed all over Western Siberia at his arrival. He walked in sternly and majestically, followed by a great suite of the local authorities in attendance on him, several generals and colonels among them. There was one civilian, a tall and handsome gentleman in a swallow-tail coat and low shoes, who had come from Petersburg, too, and who behaved with extreme freedom and independence. The general frequently turned to him and with marked courtesy. This interested the convicts immensely – a civilian and treated with such esteem and by such a general, too! Later on they found out his surname and who he was, but there were numbers of theories. Our major, wearing a tight uniform with an orange-coloured collar, with his bloodshot eyes and crimson pimply face, did not, I fancy, make a particularly agreeable impression on the general. As a sign of special respect to the distinguished visitor, he had taken off his spectacles. He stood at a little distance, stiffly erect, and his whole figure seemed feverishly anticipating the moment when he might be wanted to fly to carry out his excellency's wishes. But he was not wanted. The general walked through the prison-ward in silence, he glanced into the kitchen; I believe he tried the soup. I was pointed out to him, they told him my story, and that I was of the educated class.

'Ah!' answered the general. 'And how is he behaving himself now?'

'So far, satisfactorily, your excellency,' they answered him.

The general nodded, and two minutes later he went out of the prison. The convicts were, of course, dazzled and bewildered, but yet they remained in some perplexity. Complaints against the major were of course, out of the question. And the major was perfectly certain of that beforehand.

CHAPTER SIX

Prison Animals

The purchase of Sorrel, an event which took place shortly afterwards in the prison, occupied and entertained the prisoners far more agreeably than the grand visit. We kept a horse in the prison for bringing water, carrying away refuse and such things. A convict was told off to look after it. He used to drive it, too, accompanied, of course, by a guard. There was a great deal of work for our horse, both in the morning and in the evening. The former Sorrel had been in our service for a long time. It was a good horse, but worn out. One fine morning, just before St Peter's Day, this old Sorrel fell down after bringing in the barrel of water for the evening, and died within a few minutes. They were sorry for him; they all collected around him, discussing and disputing. The old cavalrymen, the gypsies, and the veterinary surgeons among us showered great erudition as regards horses on the occasion and even came to abusing one another, but they did not get old Sorrel on to his legs again. He lay dead with distended belly, which they all seemed to feel bound to poke at with their fingers. The major was informed of this act of God, and he at once decided that a new horse should be bought. On the morning of St Peter's Day after mass, when we were all assembled together, horses for sale were led in. It was a matter of course that the convicts themselves should make the selection. There were some genuine connoisseurs in horse-flesh amongst us, and to deceive two hundred and fifty men who were specialists on the subject would be difficult. Kirghiz nomads, horse-dealers, gypsies, and townspeople turned up with horses. The convicts awaited with impatience the arrival of each fresh horse. They were as happy as children. What flattered them most of all was that they were buying a horse as though for themselves, as though they were really paying for it out of their own money, and had a full right to buy it like free men. Three horses were led in and taken away before they settled upon the fourth. The dealers who came in looked about them with some astonishment and even timidity and glanced round from time to time at the guards who led them in. A rabble of two hundred of these fellows, shaven, branded and fettered, at home in their own prison nest, the threshold of which no one ever crosses, inspired a certain sort of respect. Our fellows invented all sorts of subtleties by way of testing each horse that was brought; they looked it over and felt it in every part, and what is more, with an air as businesslike, as serious and important as though the welfare of the prison depended upon it. The Circassians even took a gallop on the horse. Their eyes glowed and they gabbled in their incomprehensible dialect, showing their white teeth and nodding with their swarthy, hook-nosed faces. Some of the Russians kept their whole attention riveted upon the Circassians' discussion, gazing into their eyes as though they would jump into them. Not understanding their language, they tried to guess from the expression of their eyes whether they had decided that the horse would do or not, and such strained attention might well seem strange to a spectator. One wonders why a convict should be so deeply concerned in the matter – and a convict so insignificant, humble and downtrodden that he would not have dared to lift up his voice before some of his own comrades – as though he had been buying a horse for himself, as though it made any difference to him what sort of horse were bought. Besides the Circassians, the former horse-dealers and gypsies were the most conspicuous; they were allowed the first word, there was even something like a chivalrous duel between two convicts in particular – Kulikov, who had been a gypsy horse-stealer and horse-dealer, and a self-taught vet, a shrewd Siberian peasant who had lately come to the prison and had already succeeded in carrying off all Kulikov's practice in the town. Our prison vets were greatly esteemed in the town, and not only the shopkeepers and merchants, but even the higher gentry applied to the prison when their horses fell ill, in spite of the fact that there were several regular veterinary surgeons in the town. Kulikov had had no rival until Yolkin, the Siberian peasant, had appeared upon the scene; he had a large practice and was, of course, paid for his services. He was a terrible gypsy and charlatan, and knew much less than he pretended. As far as money went he was an aristocrat among us and by his experience, intelligence, audacity and determination he had long won the involuntary respect of all the convicts in the prison. He was listened to and obeyed among us. But he talked little; he spoke as though he were making one a present of his words, and only opened his lips on the most important occasions. He was a regular fop, but he had a great deal of genuine energy. He was no longer young, but very handsome and very clever. He behaved to us convicts of the upper class with a sort of refined courtesy, and at the same time with extraordinary dignity. I believe that if he had been dressed-up and introduced into some club in Moscow or Petersburg as a count he would have been quite at home even there, would have played whist, would have talked well, speaking little but with weight, and that perhaps it would not have been detected all the evening that he was not a count but a tramp. I am speaking seriously; he was so clever, resourceful and quick-witted, moreover he had excellent manners and a good deal of style. He must have had many experiences of different kinds in his life. But his past was wrapped in the mists of obscurity. He was in the special division. But after the arrival of Yolkin, who, though he was a peasant, was a very crafty man of fifty, a dissenter, Kulikov's fame as a vet began to decline. In two months' time Yolkin had carried off almost the whole of his practice in the town; he cured, and it seemed quite easily, horses that Kulikov had given up as hopeless. Yolkin even cured some that the town veterinary surgeons had looked upon as incurable.

This peasant had been brought to prison with some others for false coining. What had induced him at his age to mix himself up in such doings! He used to tell us, laughing at himself, that by melting down three real gold coins they could only turn out one counterfeit one. Kulikov was rather mortified at Yolkin's veterinary successes and indeed his glory began to wane among the convicts. He kept a mistress in the town, wore a velveteen coat, had a silver ring on his finger, wore an earring, and boots of his own with decorated tops. Now, from want of money, he was forced to begin trading in vodka. Therefore everyone expected that the enemies would be sure to have a fight over the purchase of the new Sorrel; the convicts awaited it with curiosity. Each of them had his followers; the leading spirits on both sides were already getting excited and were gradually beginning to fall foul of one another. Yolkin had already pursed up his crafty face in a most sarcastic smile. But it turned out that they were mistaken. Kulikov did not attempt to be abusive, but he behaved in a masterly way. He began by giving way and even listening with attention to his rival's criticism, but, catching up one of his sayings, he observed modestly and emphatically that he was mistaken, and before Yolkin could recover and correct himself, he proved to him that he was in error on this point and on that. In fact Yolkin was routed quite unexpectedly and skilfully, and though he still carried the day, Kulikov's followers were satisfied.

'No, lads, you don't beat him easily; he can take his own part, rather!' said some.

'Yolkin knows more!' observed others, but they observed it rather deprecatingly. Both parties spoke suddenly in very conciliatory tones.

'It's not that he knows more, simply he has a lighter hand. And as for treating cattle, Kulikov is equal to anything there!'

'That he is, lad!'

'That he is.'

Our new Sorrel was at last chosen and bought. It was a capital horse, young, strong and good-looking, with an extremely pleasant, good-humoured expression. It was, of course, irreproachable in all other respects. The convicts began haggling. The dealers asked thirty roubles, our fellows offered twenty-five. The bargaining was hot and lengthy. They kept adding and subtracting. At last they were amused at it themselves.

'Are you going to take the money out of your own purse? What are you bargaining about?' said some.

'Do you want to spare the government?' cried others.

'But, after all, lads, after all, it's sort of common money.'

'Common money! Well, to be sure, there's no need to sow fools like us, we spring up of ourselves.'

At last the bargain was clinched for twenty-eight roubles. The major was informed and the purchase was completed. Of course they brought out bread and salt and led the new Sorrel into the prison with all due ceremony. I don't think there was a convict who did not, on this occasion, pat the horse on the neck or stroke its nose. On the same day Sorrel was harnessed to bring in the water, and everyone looked with curiosity to see the new Sorrel drawing his barrel. Our water-carrier, Roman, looked at the new horse with extraordinary self-satisfaction. He was a peasant of fifty, of a silent and stolid character. And all Russian coachmen are of a very sedate and even taciturn character, as though it were really the case that constant association with horses gave a man a special sedateness and even dignity. Roman was quiet, friendly to everyone, not talkative; he used to take pinches from a horn of tobacco and had always from time immemorial looked after the prison Sorrels. The one that had just been bought was the third of that name. The convicts were all convinced that a horse of sorrel colour was suited to the prison, that it would be, so to speak, better for the house. Roman, too, maintained this idea. Nothing would have induced them to buy a piebald horse, for instance. The task of water-carrier was, by some special privilege, always reserved for Roman, and none of us would ever have dreamt of disputing his right. When the last Sorrel died, it never occurred to anyone, even the major, to blame Roman; it was God's will, that was all about it, and Roman was a good driver.

Soon the new Sorrel became the favourite of the prison. Though the convicts are a rough set of men, they often went up to stroke him. It sometimes happened that Roman, returning from the river with the water, got down to close the gate which the sergeant had opened for him, and Sorrel would stand still in the yard with the barrel, waiting for him, and looking towards him out of the corner of his eyes. 'Go on alone,' Roman would shout to him, and Sorrel would immediately go on alone, right up to the kitchen door, where he would stop, waiting for the cooks and the slop-pail men to come with their buckets for the water. 'Clever Sorrel,' the prisoners shouted to him; 'he's brought the water alone! He does as he is told!'

'There, upon my word! Only a beast, but he understands!' 'He is a capital fellow, Sorrel!'

Sorrel snorts and shakes his head as though he really did understand and is pleased at the praise. And someone is sure to bring him bread and salt at this point. Sorrel eats it and nods his head again as though to say: 'I know you, I know you! I am a nice horse and you are a good man.'

I used to like taking bread to Sorrel. It was pleasant to look into his handsome face and to feel on the palm of one's hand his soft warm lips quickly picking up the offering.

Our prisoners in general would readily have been fond of animals, and if they had been allowed, they would gladly have reared all sorts of domestic birds and animals in prison. And could anything be more calculated to soften and elevate the harsh and savage character of the convicts than such occupation? But this was not allowed. It was forbidden by the regulations, and there was no place suitable for it.

Yet it happened that there were several animals in prison during my time there. Besides Sorrel, we had dogs, geese, the goat Vaska and, for some time, there was an eagle.

We had as a permanent prison dog, as I mentioned already, Sharik, a clever, good-natured animal with whom I was always on friendly terms. But as among the peasants everywhere the dog is always looked upon as an unclean animal whom one should scarcely notice, hardly anyone paid any attention to Sharik. The dog was simply there, slept in the yard, lived on the scraps from the kitchen, and no one took any particular interest in him; it knew everyone, however, and looked upon everyone in prison as its master. When the prisoners came in from work, as soon as the shout 'Corporals!' was heard at the guard-house, the dog ran to the gates with a friendly greeting for every group, wagging his tail and looking affectionately in the face of every convict as he came in, hoping for some sort of caress. But for many years he did not succeed in winning a caress from anyone except me, and so he loved me more than all.

I don't remember how it was that another dog, Byelka, came among us. The third, Kultyapka, I introduced myself, bringing him in as a puppy from where we were working. Byelka was a strange creature. He had once been run over by a cart and his spine was curved inwards, so that when he ran it looked like two white animals running, grown together. He was mangy too, and had discharging eyes; his tail, which was always between his legs, was mangy and patchy, almost without hair. A victim of destiny, he had evidently made up his mind to accept his lot without repining. He never barked or growled at anyone, as though he had not courage to. He lived for the most part behind the prison barracks in the hope of picking up food; if he saw any of us he would immediately, while we were some paces away, turn over on his back as a sign of humility, as much as to say, 'Do with me what you will, you see I have no thought of resistance.' And every convict before whom he rolled over would give him a kick with his boot, as though he felt it incumbent on him to do so. 'Ah, the nasty brute,' the convicts would say. But Byelka did not even dare to squeal, and if the pain was too much for him would give a muffled plaintive whine. He would roll over in the same way before Sharik or any other dog when anything called him outside the prison walls. He used to turn over and lie humbly on his back when some big long-eared dog rushed at him growling and barking. But dogs like humility and submissiveness in their fellows. The savage dog was at once softened and stood with some hesitation over the submissive creature lying before him with his legs in the air, and slowly, with great curiosity, he would begin sniffing him all over. What could the trembling Byelka have been thinking all this time? What if he bites me, the ruffian? was probably what was in his mind. But after sniffing him over attentively, the dog would leave him at last, finding nothing particularly interesting about him. Byelka would at once leap up and again hobble after the long string of dogs who were following some charming bitch, and though he knew for a certainty that he would never be on speaking terms with the charmer, still he hobbled after in the distance and it was a comfort to him in his trouble. He had apparently ceased to consider the point of honour; having lost all hope of a career in the future, he lived only for daily bread, and was fully aware of the fact. I once tried to caress him; it was something so new and unexpected for him that he suddenly collapsed on all fours on the ground trembling all over and beginning to whine aloud with emotion. I often patted him from compassion. After that he could not meet me without whining. As soon as he saw me in the distance, he would begin whining tearfully and hysterically. He ended by being killed by dogs on the rampart outside the prison.

Kultyapka was a dog of quite a different character. Why I brought him from the workshop into the prison when he was still a blind puppy, I don't know. I liked feeding him and bringing him up. Sharik at once took Kultyapka under his wing and used to sleep with him. When Kultyapka began to grow up, Sharik would let him bite his ears, pull his coat and play with him, as grown-up dogs usually play with puppies. Strange to say, Kultyapka hardly grew at all in height, but only in length and breadth. His coat was shaggy and of a light mouse colour; one ear hung down and one stood up. He was of a fervent and enthusiastic disposition like every puppy, who will as a rule squeal and bark with delight at seeing his master, dart up to lick his face and be ready to give the rein to all his other emotions, feeling that the proprieties are not to be considered and that all that matters is to show his enthusiasm. Wherever I might be, if I called 'Kultyapka!' he would appear at once round some corner as though he had sprung out of the earth, and would fly to me with squealing rapture, turning somersaults and rolling over like a ball as he came. I was awfully fond of this little monster. It seemed as though fate had nothing in store for him but joy and prosperity. But one fine day a convict called Neustroev, who made women's shoes and tanned skins, happened to take special notice of him. An idea seemed to strike him. He called Kultyapka to him, felt his coat and rolled him on his back in a friendly way. Kultyapka, suspecting nothing, squealed with delight. But next morning he disappeared. I looked for him for a long time; he had utterly vanished. And only a fortnight later all was explained. Neustroev had taken a particular fancy to Kultyapka's coat. He skinned him, tanned the skin and lined with it the warm velvet boots which had been bespoken by the auditor's wife. He showed me the boots when they were finished. The dog-skin lining looked wonderfully well. Poor Kultyapka!

Many prisoners tanned skins, and they often brought into the prison dogs with good coats, who instantly disappeared. Some of these dogs were stolen, some even bought. I remember once seeing two convicts behind the kitchen consulting together and very busy about something. One of them held by a string a magnificent big black dog evidently of an expensive breed. Some rascal of a servant had brought it from his master's and sold it for about sixpence to our shoemakers. The convicts were just going to hang it. This was a thing very easily done; they would strip off the skin and flung the dead body into the big deep cesspool in the furthest corner of the prison yard, which stank horribly in the hottest days of summer. It was rarely cleaned out. The poor dog seemed to understand the fate in store for it. It glanced at each of the three of us in turn with searching and uneasy eyes and from time to time ventured to wag its drooping bushy tail, as though trying to soften us by this sign of its trust. I made haste to move away, and they no doubt finished the job to their satisfaction.

It was by chance that we came to keep geese. Who first introduced them and to whom they really belonged I don't know, but for some time they were a source of great diversion to the convicts and even became familiar objects in the town. They were hatched in the prison and were kept in the kitchen. When all the goslings were full grown, they all used to follow the convicts to work in a flock. As soon as the drum sounded and the prisoners began to move towards the gates, our geese would run after us, cackling, fluttering their wings, one after another leaping over the high sill of the gate, and would unhesitatingly turn towards the right wing and there draw up and wait till the convicts were ready to start. They always attached themselves to the largest party, and while the convicts were at work they would graze close by. As soon as the party began to move off again towards the prison, the geese started too. It was reported in the fortress how the geese followed the convicts to work. 'Hullo, here are the convicts with their geese,' people would say when they met them. 'How did you train them?' 'Here's something for the geese,' another would add and give us alms. But in spite of their devotion they were all killed for some feast day.

On the other hand nothing would have induced the convicts to kill our goat, Vaska, if it had not been for a special circumstance. I don't know where he came from either, or who brought him into the prison, but one day a very charming little white kid made his appearance. In a few days we all grew fond of him and began to find entertainment and even consolation in him. They even found an excuse for keeping him by saying, 'If we have a stable in the prison, we must have a goat.' He did not, however, live in the stable, but at first in the kitchen and afterwards all over the prison. He was a very graceful, very mischievous creature. He ran up when he was called, jumped on benches and tables, butted at the convicts, and was always merry and amusing. One evening when his horns had grown fairly big, a Lezghian called Babay, who was sitting on the steps with a group of other convicts, took it into his head to butt at the goat; they were knocking their foreheads together for a long time – to play like this with the goat was a favourite pastime of the convicts – when suddenly Vaska skipped on to the topmost step, and as soon as Babay turned aside, the goat instantly reared on its hind legs and, bending his fore-legs inward, he butted with all his might at the back of Babay's head so that the man flew head over heels off the steps, to the intense glee of all present, especially Babay himself. Everyone was awfully fond of Vaska, in fact.

When he began to be full grown it was decided after a long and earnest deliberation to perform a certain operation on him which our veterinary specialists were very skilful in, 'or he will smell so goaty,' said the convicts. After that Vaska grew fearfully fat. The convicts used to feed him, too, as though they were fattening him up. He grew at last into a fine and handsome goat of extraordinary size with very long horns. He waddled as he walked. He, too, used to follow us to work, to the diversion of the convicts and of everyone we met. Everyone knew the prison goat, Vaska. Sometimes if they were working on the bank of the river, for instance, the convicts would gather tender willow shoots and other leaves and pick flowers on the rampart to decorate Vaska with them; they would wreathe flowers and green shoots round his horns and hang garlands all over his body. Vaska would return to the prison always in front of the convicts, decked out, and they would follow him, and seem proud of him when they met anyone. This admiration for the goat reached such a pitch that some of our men, like children, suggested that they might gild Vaska's horns. But they only talked of doing this, it was never actually done. I remember, however, asking Akim Akimitch, who, after Isay Fomitch, was our best gilder, whether one could really gild goats' horns. At first he looked attentively at the goat and after serious consideration he replied that it was perhaps possible, but that it would not be lasting and would besides be utterly useless. With that the matter dropped. And Vaska might have lived for years in the prison and would perhaps have died of shortness of breath. But one day as he was returning home decked out with flowers at the head of the convicts, he was met by the major in his droshki. 'Stop!' he roared;

'whose goat is it?' It was explained to him. 'What! a goat in the prison and without my permission! Sergeant!' The sergeant came forward and the order was promptly given that the goat should be immediately killed, that the skin should be sold in the market, and the money for it be put into the prison purse, and that the meat should be served out to the convicts in the soup. There was a great deal of talk and lamentation in the prison, but they did not dare to disobey. Vaska was slaughtered over the cesspool in the yard. One of the convicts bought the whole of the meat, paying a rouble and a half for it into the prison purse. With this money they bought rolls and the convict sold the meat in portions to the prisoners to be roasted. The meat turned out really to be exceptionally good.

We had for some time in the prison an eagle, one of the small eagles of the steppes. Someone brought him into the prison wounded and exhausted. All the prisoners crowded round him; he could not fly; his right wing hung down on the ground, one leg was dislocated. I remember how fiercely he glared at us, looking about him at the inquisitive crowd, and opened his crooked beak, prepared to sell his life dearly. When they had looked at him long enough and were beginning to disperse, he hopped limping on one leg and fluttering his uninjured wing to the furthest end of the prison yard, where he took refuge in a corner right under the fence. He remained with us for three months, and all that time would not come out of his corner. At first the convicts often went to look at him and used to set the dog at him. Sharik would fly at him furiously, but was evidently afraid to get too near. This greatly diverted the convicts. 'Savage creature! He'll never give in!' they used to say. Later Sharik began cruelly ill-treating him. He got over his fear, and when they set him on the eagle he learnt to catch him by his injured wing. The eagle vigorously defended himself with his beak and, huddled in his corner, he looked fiercely and proudly like a wounded king at the inquisitive crowd who came to stare at him.

At last everyone was tired of him; everyone forgot him, abandoned him, yet every day there were pieces of fresh meat and a broken pot of water near him. So someone was looking after him. At first he would not eat, and ate nothing for several days; at last he began taking food, but he would never take it from anyone's hand or in the presence of people. It happened that I watched him more than once. Seeing no one and thinking that he was alone, he sometimes ventured to come a little way out of his corner and limped a distance of twelve paces along the fence, then he went back and then went out again, as though he were taking exercise. Seeing me he hastened back to his corner, limping and hopping, and throwing back his head, opening his beak, with his feathers ruffled, at once prepared for battle. None of my caresses could soften him; he pecked and struggled, would not take meat from me, and all the time I was near him he used to stare intently in my face with his savage, piercing eyes. Fierce and solitary he awaited death, mistrustful and hostile to all. At last the convicts seemed to remember him, and though no one had mentioned him, or done anything for him for two months, everyone seemed suddenly to feel sympathy for him. They said that they must take the eagle out. 'Let him die if he must, but not in prison,' they said.

'To be sure, he is a free, fierce bird; you can't get him used to prison,' others agreed.

'It's not like us, it seems,' added someone.

'That's a silly thing to say. He's a bird and we are men, aren't we?'

'The eagle is the king of the forests, brothers,' began Skuratov, but this time they did not listen to him.

One day, after dinner, when the drum had just sounded for us to go to work, they took the eagle, holding his beak, for he began fighting savagely, and carried him out of the prison. We got to the rampart. The twelve men of the party were eagerly curious to see where the eagle would go. Strange to say, they all seemed pleased, as though they too had won a share of freedom.

'See, the cur, one does something for his good, and he keeps biting one,' said the convict who was carrying him, looking at the fierce bird almost with affection.

'Let him go, Mikitka!'

'It's no use rigging up a jack-in-the-box for him, it seems. Give him freedom, freedom full and free!'

He threw the eagle from the rampart into the plain. It was a cold, gloomy day in late autumn, the wind was whistling over the bare plain and rustling in the yellow, withered, tussocky grass of the steppes. The eagle went off in a straight line, fluttering his injured wing, as though in haste to get away from us anywhere. With curiosity the convicts watched his head flitting through the grass.

'Look at him!' said one dreamily. 'He doesn't look round!' added another. 'He hasn't looked round once, lads, he just runs off!'

'Did you expect him to come back to say thank you?' observed a third.

'Ah, to be sure it's freedom. It's freedom he sniffs.'

'You can't see him now, mates . . . '

'What are you standing for? March!' shouted the guards, and we all trudged on to work in silence.

CHAPTER SEVEN

The Complaint

In beginning this chapter the editor of the late Alexandr Petrovitch Goryanchikov's notes feels it his duty to make the following statement to the reader –

In the first chapter of *Notes from a Dead House* some words were said about a parricide belonging to the upper class. Among other things he was quoted as an instance of the callousness with which the convicts will sometimes speak of their crimes. It was stated, too, that the murderer did not admit his guilt at his trial, but that judging by accounts given by people who knew all the details of his story, the facts were so clear that it was impossible to have any doubt of his guilt. These people told the author of the notes that the criminal was a man of reckless behaviour, that he had got into debt, and had killed his father because he coveted the fortune he would inherit from him. But all the people in the town where this parricide had lived told the story in the same way. Of this last fact the editor of these notes has fairly trustworthy information. Finally, it was stated in these notes that the criminal was always in the best of spirits in prison; that he was a whimsical, frivolous fellow, extremely lacking in common sense, though by no means a fool, that the author had never noticed in him any sign of cruelty. And the words are added: 'Of course I did not believe in that crime.'

The other day the editor of the notes from 'the Dead House' received information from Siberia that the criminal really was innocent and had suffered ten years in penal servitude for nothing; that his innocence had been established before a court, officially, that the real criminals had been found and had confessed, and that the luckless fellow had been already released from prison. The editor can feel no doubt of the truth of this news. There is nothing more to add. There is no need to enlarge on all the tragic significance of this fact, and to speak of the young life crushed under this terrible charge. The fact is too impressive, it speaks for itself.

We believe, too, that if such a fact can be possible, this possibility adds a fresh and striking feature to the description of the 'Dead House', and puts a finishing touch to the picture.

Now we will continue.

I have already said that I did at last become accustomed to my position in prison. But this came to pass painfully and with difficulty and far too gradually. It took me almost a year, in fact, to reach this stage, and that was the hardest year of my life. And that is why the whole of it is imprinted on my memory for ever. I believe I remember every successive hour of that year. I said, also, that other convicts, too, could not get used to that life. I remember how in that first year I often wondered to myself what they were feeling, could they be contented? And I was much occupied with these questions. I have mentioned already that all the convicts lived in prison not as though they were at home there, but as though they were at a hotel, on a journey, at some temporary halt. Even men sentenced for their whole life were restless or miserable, and no doubt every one of them was dreaming of something almost impossible. This everlasting uneasiness, which showed itself unmistakably, though not in words, this strange impatient and intense hope, which sometimes found involuntary utterance, at times so wild as to be almost like delirium, and what was most striking of all, often persisted in men of apparently the greatest common sense – gave a special aspect and character to the place, so much so that it constituted perhaps its most typical characteristic. It made one feel, almost from the first moment, that there was nothing like this outside the prison walls. Here all were dreamers, and this was apparent at once. What gave poignancy to this feeling was the fact that this dreaminess gave the greater number of the prisoners a gloomy and sullen, almost abnormal, expression. The vast majority were taciturn and morose to the point of vindictiveness; they did not like displaying their hopes. Candour, simplicity were looked on with contempt. The more fantastical his hopes, and the more conscious the dreamer himself was of their fantastical character, the more obstinately and shyly he concealed them in his heart, but he could not renounce them. Who knows, some perhaps were inwardly ashamed of them. There is so much sober-mindedness and grasp of reality in the Russian character, and with it such inner mockery of self. Perhaps it was this continual hidden self-dissatisfaction which made these men so impatient with one another in the daily affairs of life, so irritable and sneering with one another, and if, for instance, some one of them rather simpler and more impatient than the rest were to make himself conspicuous by uttering aloud what was in the secret mind of all, and were to launch out into dreams and hopes, the others roughly put him down at once, suppressed him and ridiculed him; but I fancy that the harshest of his assailants were just those who perhaps out-stripped him in their own hopes and dreams. Candid and simple people were, as I have said already, looked upon generally as the vulgarest fools, and they were treated with contempt. Every man was so ill-humoured and vain that he despised anyone good-natured and free from vanity. All but these naïve and simple chatterers, all the taciturn, that is, may be sharply divided into the ill-natured and the good-natured, the sullen and the serene. There were far more of the ill-natured and the sullen, and those of them who were naturally talkative were infallibly uneasy backbiters and slanderers. They meddled in everyone's affairs, though of their own hearts, their own private affairs, they showed no one a glimpse. That was not the thing, not correct. The good-natured – a very small group – were quiet, hid their imaginings in their hearts, and were of course more prone than the ill-natured to put faith and hope in them. Yet I fancy that there was another group of prisoners who had lost all hope. Such was the old dissenter from the Starodubovsky settlements; there were very few of these. The old man was externally calm (I have described him already), but from certain symptoms I judge that his inner misery was terrible. But he had his means of escape, his salvation – prayer, and the idea of martyrdom. The convict whom I have described already, who used to read the Bible, and who went out of his mind and threw a brick at the major, was probably one of the desperate class too, one of those who have lost their last hope, and as life is impossible without hope he found a means of escape in a voluntary and almost artificial martyrdom. He declared that he attacked the major without malice, simply to 'accept suffering'. And who knows what psychological process was taking place in his heart then! Without some goal and some effort to reach it no man can live. When he has lost all hope, all object in life, man often becomes a monster in his misery. The one object of the prisoners was freedom and to get out of prison.

But here I have been trying to classify all the prisoners, and that is hardly possible. Real life is infinite in its variety in comparison with even the cleverest abstract generalisation, and it does not admit of sharp and sweeping distinctions. The tendency of real life is always towards greater and greater differentiation. We, too, had a life of our own of a sort, and it was not a mere official existence but a real inner life of our own.

But, as I have mentioned already, I did not, and indeed could not, penetrate to the inner depths of this life at the beginning of my time in prison, and so all its external incidents were a source of unutterable misery to me then. I sometimes was simply beginning to hate those men who were sufferers like myself. I even envied them for being, anyway, among their equals, their comrades, understanding one another; though in reality they were all as sick and weary as I was of this companionship enforced by stick and lash, of this compulsory association, and everyone was secretly looking towards something far away from all the rest. I repeat again, there were legitimate grounds for the envy which came upon me in moments of ill-humour. Those who declare that it is no harder for a gentleman, an educated man and all the rest of it, in our prisons and in Siberia than it is for any peasant are really quite wrong. I know I have heard of theories on the subject of late, I have read of them. There is something true and humane at the back of this idea – all are men, all are human beings. But the idea is too abstract. It overlooks too many practical aspects of the question, which cannot be grasped except by experience. I don't say this on the grounds that the gentleman, the man of education, may be supposed to be more refined and delicate in his feelings, that he is more developed. There is no standard by which to measure the soul and its development. Even education itself is no test. I am ready to be the first to testify that, in the midst of these utterly uneducated and downtrodden sufferers, I came across instances of the greatest spiritual refinement. Sometimes one would know a man for years in prison and despise him and think that he was not a human being but a brute. And suddenly a moment will come by chance when his soul will suddenly reveal itself in an involuntary outburst, and you see in it such wealth, such feeling, such heart, such a vivid understanding of its own suffering, and of the suffering of others, that your eyes are open and for the first moment you can't believe what you have seen and heard yourself. The contrary happens too; education is sometimes found side by side with such barbarity, such cynicism, that it revolts you, and in spite of the utmost good-nature and all previous theories on the subject, you can find no justification or apology.

I am not speaking of the change of habits, of manner of life, of diet, etc., though that is harder of course for a man of the wealthier class than for a peasant, who has often been hungry when free, and in prison at least has enough to eat. I am not going to argue about that. Let us assume that for a man of any strength of will all this is of little consequence compared with other discomforts, though in reality a change of habits is not a trifling matter nor of little consequence. But there are discomforts beside which all this is so trivial that one ceases to notice the filth of one's surroundings, the fetters, the close confinement, the insufficient and unclean food. The sleekest fine gentleman, the softest weakling will be able to eat black bread and soup with beetles in it, after working in the sweat of his brow, as he has never worked in freedom. To this one can get accustomed, as described in the humorous prison song which tells of a fine gentleman in prison.

> Cabbage and water they give me to eat,
> And I gobble it up as though it were sweet.

No; what is much more important than all this is that while two hours after his arrival an ordinary prisoner is on the same footing as all the rest, is *at home*, has the same rights in the community as the rest, is understood by everyone, understands everyone, knows everyone, and is looked on by everyone as a comrade, it is very different with the *gentleman*, the man of a different class. However straightforward, good-natured and clever he is, he will for years be hated and despised by all; he will not be understood, and what is more he will not be trusted. He is not a friend, and not a comrade, and though he may at last in the course of years attain such a position among them that they will no longer insult him, yet he will never be one of them, and will for ever be painfully conscious that he is solitary and remote from all. This remoteness sometimes comes to pass of itself unconsciously through no ill-natured feeling on the part of the convicts. He is not one of themselves, and that's all. Nothing is more terrible than living out of one's natural surroundings. A peasant transported from Taganrog to the port of Petropavlovsk at once finds the Russian peasants there exactly like himself, at once understands them, and gets on with them, and in a couple of hours they may settle down peaceably to live in the same hut or shanty. It is very different with gentlemen. They are divided from the peasants by an impassable gulf, and this only becomes fully apparent when the *gentleman* is by force of external circumstances completely deprived of his former privileges, and is transformed into a peasant. You may have to do with the peasants all your life, you may associate with them every day for forty years, officially for instance, in the regulation administrative forms, or even simply in a friendly way, as a benefactor or, in a certain sense, a father – you will never know them really. It will all be an optical illusion and nothing more. I know that all who read what I say will think that I am exaggerating. But I am convinced of its truth. I have reached the conviction, not from books, not from abstract theory, but from experience, and I have had plenty of time to verify it. Perhaps in time everyone will realise the truth of this.

Events, as ill-luck would have it, confirmed my observations from the first and had a morbid and unhingeing influence on me. That first summer I wandered about the prison in almost complete loneliness, without a friend. As I have mentioned already, I was in such a state of mind that I could not even distinguish and appreciate those of the prisoners who were later on able to grow fond of me, though they never treated me as an equal. I had comrades too of my own class, but their comradeship did not ease my heart of its oppression. I hated the sight of everything and I had no means of escape from it. And here, for instance, is one of the incidents which from the beginning made me understand how completely I was an outsider, and how peculiar my position was in the prison.

One day that summer, early in July, on a bright hot working day at one o'clock, when usually we rested before our afternoon work, the prisoners all got up like one man and began forming in the yard. I had heard nothing about it till that minute. At that time I used to be so absorbed in myself that I scarcely noticed what was going on about me. Yet the prisoners had for the last three days been in a state of suppressed excitement. Perhaps this excitement had begun much earlier, as I reflected afterwards when I recalled snatches of talk, and at the same time the increased quarrelsomeness of the convicts and the moroseness and peculiar irritability that had been conspicuous in them of late. I had put it down to the hard work, the long wearisome summer days, the unconscious dreams of the forest and of freedom, and the brief nights, in which it was difficult to get enough sleep. Perhaps all this was working together now into one outbreak, but the pretext for this outbreak was the prison food. For some days past there had been loud complaints and indignation in the prison, and especially when we were gathered together in the kitchen at dinner or supper; they were discontented with the cooks and even tried to get a new one, but quickly dismissed him and went back to the old. In fact all were in an unsettled state of mind.

'They work us hard and they feed us on tripe,' someone would growl in the kitchen.

'If you don't like it, order a blancmange,' another would reply.

'I like soup made of tripe, lads,' a third would put in, 'it's nice.'

'But if you never get anything else but tripe, is it nice?'

'Now, to be sure, it's time for meat,' said a fourth; 'we toil and toil at the brickyard; when one's work's done, one wants something to eat. And what is tripe?'

'And if it is not tripe, it's heart.'

'Yes, there's that heart too. Tripe and heart, that's all they give us. Fine fare that is! Is that justice or is it not?'

'Yes, the food's bad.'

'He's filling his pockets, I warrant.'

'It's not your business.'

'Whose then? It's my belly. If everybody would make a complaint we should get something done.'

'A complaint?'

'Yes.'

'It seems you didn't get flogged enough for that complaint. You image!'

'That's true,' another who had hitherto been silent said grumpily. 'It's easy talking. What are you going to say in your complaint? You'd better tell us that first, you blockhead!'

'All right, I'll tell you. If all would come, I'd speak with all. It's being poor, it is! Some of us eat their own food, and some never sit down but to prison fare.'

'Ah, the sharp-eyed, envious fellow! His eyes smart to see others well off.'

'Don't covet another man's pelf, but up and earn it for yourself!'

'I'll dispute that with you till my hair is grey. So you are a rich man, since you want to sit with your arms folded?'

'Eroshka is fat with a dog and a cat!'

'But truly, lads, why sit still? We've had enough of putting up with their fooling. They are skinning us. Why not go to them?'

'Why not? You want your food chewed, and put into your mouth, that's what you are used to. Because it's prison, that's why!'

'When simple folk fall out, the governor grows fat.'

'Just so. Eight-eyes has grown fat. He's bought a pair of greys.'

'Yes, and he is not fond of drinking, eh?'

'He was fighting the other day with the veterinary over cards. They were at it all night. Our friend was two hours at fisticuffs with him. Fedka said so.'

'That's why we have stewed heart.'

'Ah, you fools! It's not for us to put ourselves forward.'

'But if we all go, then we shall see what defence he will make. We must insist on that.'

'Defence! He'll give you a punch in the face and that will be all.'

'And then court-martial us afterwards.'

In short everyone was excited. At that time our food really was poor. And besides, all sorts of things came simultaneously – above all, the general mood of depression, the continual hidden misery. The convict is from his very nature fault-finding, mutinous; but the mutiny of all or even of a large number is rare, owing to the continual dissensions among them. Every one of them is aware of it; that's why they are much more given to violent language than to deeds. But this time the excitement did not pass off without action. They began collecting in groups about the prison wards, arguing; they recalled with oaths the whole of the major's term of office, ferreted out every detail. Some were particularly excited. Agitators and ringleaders always turn up at such times. The ringleaders on these occasions – that is, on the occasion of a complaint being made – are always remarkable men, and not only in prison, but in gangs of workmen, companies of soldiers and so on. They are of a special type and everywhere have something in common. They are spirited men, eager for justice, and in perfect simplicity and honesty persuaded of its inevitable, direct and, above all, immediate possibility. These men are no stupider than their fellows, in fact there are some very clever ones among them, but they are too ardent to be shrewd and calculating. If there are men who are capable of skilfully leading the masses and winning their cause, they belong to a different class of popular heroes and natural leaders of the people, a type extremely rare among us. But those agitators and ringleaders of whom I am speaking now almost always fail, and are sent to prison and penal servitude in consequence. Through their zeal they fail, but it is their zeal that gives them their influence over the masses. Men follow them readily. Their warmth and honest indignation have an effect on everyone and in the end the most hesitating give their adherence to them. Their blind confidence in success seduces even the most inveterate sceptics, although sometimes this confidence has such feeble, such childish foundations that one wonders, looking on, how they can have gained a following. The great thing is that they march in the front and go forward fearing nothing. They rush straight before them like bulls, with their heads down, often with no knowledge of the affair, no caution, none of that practical casuistry by means of which the most vulgar and degraded man will sometimes succeed, attain his object and save his skin. They inevitably come to grief themselves. In ordinary life these people are choleric, contemptuous, irritable and intolerant. Most often they are of very limited intelligence and that, indeed, partly makes their strength. What is most annoying in them is that, instead of going straight for their object, they often go off on a side-issue into trifles, and it is this that is their ruin. But the people can understand them and therein lies their strength. I must, however, say a few words to explain what is meant by a *complaint*.

There were some men in our prison who had been sent there for making a complaint. They were the men who were most excited now. Especially one called Martinov, who had been in the hussars, a hot-headed, restless and suspicious man, but honest and truthful. Another was Vassily Antonov, a man as it were coldly irritated, with an insolent expression and a haughty, sarcastic smile, extremely intelligent, however. He too was honest and truthful. But I cannot describe all of them, there were a great many. Petrov among others was continually flitting backwards and forwards listening to all the groups, saying little, but evidently excited, and he was the first to run out when they began to assemble in the yard.

The sergeant whose duty it was to keep order among us at once came out in a panic. The convicts, drawn up in the yard, asked him politely to tell the major that the prisoners wanted to speak to him in person and to ask him about one or two points. All the veterans followed the sergeant and drew themselves up on the other side facing the prisoners. The message given to the sergeant was an extraordinary one and filled him with horror. But he dared not refuse to take it at once to the major. To begin with, since the prisoners had already come to this, something worse might happen – all the prison officials were extraordinarily cowardly with regard to the convicts. In the second place, even if there were nothing wrong and they should all think better of it and disperse at once, even then it was the duty of the sergeant to report everything that happened to the major at once. Pale and trembling with fear, he hastily went without attempting to question the convicts or reason with them himself. He saw that they would not even talk to him now.

Knowing nothing about it, I, too, went out to stand with the others. I only learnt the details of the affair later. I thought that some inspection was going on, but not seeing the soldiers whose duty it was to carry out the inspection, I wondered and began looking about me. The men's faces were excited and irritated. Some were even pale. All looked anxious and silent, in anticipation of speaking to the major. I noticed that several looked at me with extraordinary amazement, but turned away in silence. It obviously seemed strange to them that I should have joined them. They evidently did not believe that I had come out to take part in the complaint, but soon afterwards all who were around me turned to me again. All looked at me enquiringly.

'What are you here for?' Vassily Antonov, who stood further off than the rest, asked me in a loud, rude voice. Till then he had always addressed me formally and treated me with politeness.

I looked at him in perplexity, still trying to understand what it all meant, and beginning to guess that something extraordinary was happening.

'Yes, what need have you to stand here? Go indoors,' said a young convict of the military division, a quiet, good-natured fellow whom I knew nothing of. 'It's nothing to do with you.'

'But they are all forming up, I thought there was an inspection,' I said.

'I say, so he has crawled out, too!' shouted another.

'Iron beak!' said another. 'Fly-crushers!' said a third with ineffable contempt. This new nickname evoked general laughter.

'He sits with us in the kitchen as a favour,' answered someone.

'They're in clover everywhere. This is prison, but they have rolls to eat and buy sucking-pig. You eat your own provisions, why are you poking in here?'

'This is not the place for you, Alexandr Petrovitch,' said Kulikov, approaching me in a nonchalant way; he took me by the arm and led me out of the ranks.

He was pale, his black eyes were gleaming, and he was biting his lower lip. He was not awaiting the major with indifference. I particularly liked looking at Kulikov, by the way, on all such occasions, that is, on all occasions when he had to show what he was. He posed fearfully, but he did what had to be done. I believe he would have gone to the scaffold with a certain style and gallantry. At this moment, when everyone was being rude and familiar to me, he with evident intention redoubled his courtesy to me, and at the same time his words were peculiarly, as it were disdainfully, emphatic and admitted of no protest.

'This is our affair, Alexandr Petrovitch, and you've nothing to do with it. You go away and wait. All your friends are in the kitchen; you go there.'

'Under the ninth beam, where Antipka nimble-heels lives!' someone put in.

Through the open window of the kitchen I did, in fact, see our Poles. I fancied, however, that there were a good many people there besides. Disconcerted, I went into the kitchen. I was pursued by laughter, oaths and cries of tyu-tyu-tyu (the sound which took the place of whistling in prison).

'He didn't like it! Tyu-tyu-tyu! At him!' I had never before been so insulted in the prison, and this time I felt it very bitterly. But I had turned up at the wrong moment. In the entry to the kitchen I met T., a young man of strong will and generous heart, of no great education, though he was a man of good birth. He was a great friend of B's. The other convicts marked him out from the rest of us 'gentlemen' and had some affection for him. He was brave, manly and strong, and this was somehow apparent in every gesture.

'What are you doing, Goryanchikov?' he shouted to me; 'come here!'

'But what's the matter?'

'They are presenting a complaint, don't you know? It won't do them any good; who'll believe convicts? They'll try to find out the instigators, and if we are there they'll be sure to pitch on us first as responsible for the mutiny. Remember what we came here for. They will simply be flogged and we shall be tried. The major hates us all, and will be glad to ruin us. And by means of us he'll save himself.'

'And the convicts would be glad to betray us,' added M., as we went into the kitchen.

'You may be sure they wouldn't spare us,' T. assented.

There were a great many other people, some thirty, besides us 'gentlemen' in the kitchen. They had all remained behind, not wishing to take part in the complaint – some from cowardice, others from a full conviction of the uselessness of any sort of complaint. Among them was Akim Akimitch, who had a natural and inveterate hostility to all such complaints, as destructive of morality and official routine. He said nothing, but waited in perfect tranquillity for the end of the affair, not troubling himself as to its result, and thoroughly convinced of the inevitable triumph of discipline and the will of the authorities. Isay Fomitch was there, too, looking much perplexed, and with drooping nose listening greedily and apprehensively to our conversation. He was in great anxiety. All the Poles of the peasant class were here, too, with their compatriots of the privileged class. There were some other timid souls, people who were always silent and dejected.

They had not dared to join the others, and were mournfully waiting to see how it would end. There were also some morose and always sullen convicts who were not of a timid character. They stayed behind from obstinacy and a contemptuous conviction that it was all foolishness, and that nothing but harm would come of it. But yet I fancy they felt somewhat awkward now; they did not look perfectly at their ease. Though they knew they were perfectly right about the complaint, as they were proved to be in the sequel, yet they felt rather as though they had cut themselves off from their mates, as though they had betrayed their comrades to the major. Another man who was in the kitchen was Yolkin, the Siberian peasant condemned for false coinage who had carried off Kulikov's practice as a vet in the town. The Starodubovsky Old Believer was there, too. The cooks to a man had remained in the kitchen, probably convinced that they constituted part of the prison management, and consequently that it was not seemly for them to act in opposition to it.

'Almost all have gone out except these, though,' I observed hesitatingly to M.

'What, is it true?' muttered B.

'We should have run a hundred times more risk than they do if we went out, and why should we? *Je haïs ces brigands*. And can you imagine for a moment that their complaint will have any effect? Why should we meddle in this foolishness?'

'Nothing will come of it,' put in another convict, a stubborn and exasperated old man. Almazov, who was present, made haste to agree with him, saying: 'Except that fifty of them will get a flogging, nothing will come of it.'

'The major has come!' shouted someone, and all rushed eagerly to the windows.

The major flew up, spiteful and infuriated, flushed and wearing spectacles. Mutely but resolutely he went up to the front row. On such occasions he was really bold and never lost his presence of mind. Besides, he was almost always half drunk. Even his greasy forage cap with the orange band on it and his dirty silver epaulettes had a sinister aspect at this moment. He was followed by Dyatlov, the clerk, a very important person, who in reality governed everyone in the prison, and even had an influence over the major; he was a sly man, very cunning, but not a bad fellow. The convicts liked him. He was followed by our sergeant, who had evidently just come in for a fearful wigging, and was expecting something ten times worse later on. Behind him were three or four guards, not more. The convicts, who had been standing with their caps off ever since they had sent the sergeant to fetch the major, now all drew themselves up and pulled themselves together; every man of them shifted from one leg to the other, and then they all stood mute and rigid, waiting for the first word or rather for the first shout of the major.

It followed promptly; at his second word the major bawled at the top of his voice, almost squealed, in fact; he was in a violent fury. From the windows we could see him running along the front rank, rushing up to the men, questioning them. But it was too far off for us to hear his questions or the convicts' replies. We could only hear him shouting shrilly: 'Mutineers! . . . Beating! . . . Ringleaders! You are a ringleader? You are a ringleader?' he shouted, pouncing on somebody.

No answer was audible. But a minute later we saw a convict leave the general body and walk towards the guard-house. A minute later another followed him in the same direction, then a third.

'All under arrest! I'll teach you! Whom have you got there in the kitchen?' he squealed, seeing us at the open windows. 'All come here! Drive them here at once!'

The clerk Dyatlov came to us in the kitchen. In the kitchen he was told that we had no complaint to make. He returned at once and reported to the major.

'Ah, they haven't!' he repeated two notes lower, obviously relieved. 'No matter, send them all here!'

We went out. I felt rather ashamed of coming out. And indeed, we all walked with hanging heads.

'Ah, Prokofyev! Yolkin too. Is that you, Almazov? Stand here – stand here all together,' the major said to us in a soft but hurried voice, looking at us amicably. 'M., you are here, too . . . Make a list of them, Dyatlov! Dyatlov, make a list at once of those who are satisfied and those who are dissatisfied; every one of them, and bring the list to me. I'll put you all . . . under arrest. I'll teach you, you rascals!'

The list had an effect.

'We are satisfied!' a grating voice said suddenly from the crowd of the dissatisfied, but he spoke rather hesitatingly.

'Ah, you are satisfied! Who's satisfied? Those who are satisfied come forward.'

'We are satisfied, we are satisfied,' several voices chimed in.

'Satisfied? Men, you've been led astray. So there have been agitators working upon you. So much the worse for them!'

'Good God, what's happening!' said a voice in the crowd.

'Who's that who shouted?' roared the major, rushing in the direction from which the voice came. 'Is that you, Rastorguyev? You shouted? To the guard-house!'

Rastorguyev, a tall, puffy-faced young fellow, stepped out and walked at once towards the guard-house. It was not he who had spoken, but as he had been pitched upon he went.

'You don't know when you are well off!' the major howled after him. 'Ah, you fat-face! I'll find you all out! Those who are satisfied, step forward!'

'We are satisfied, your honour!' murmured some dozens of gloomy voices; the rest remained stubbornly silent. But that was enough for the major. It was evidently to his advantage to end the scene as quickly as possible, and to end it somehow pacifically.

'Ah, now all are satisfied!' he said hurriedly. 'I saw that . . . I knew it. It's the work of agitators! There must be agitators among them!' he went on, addressing Dyatlov. 'We must go into that more carefully. But now . . . now it's time for work. Beat the drum!'

He was present himself at the telling off of convicts to their different tasks. The convicts dispersed in mournful silence to their work, glad at any rate to be out of his sight as soon as possible. But after they had gone, the major at once went to the guard-house and punished the 'ringleaders', not very cruelly, however. He hurried over it, in fact. One of them, we were told afterwards, begged his pardon, and was at once let off. It was evident that the major was not perfectly at his ease, and was perhaps even a little scared. A complaint is always a ticklish matter, and though the convicts' protest could hardly be called a complaint, because it was presented not to a higher authority, but to the major himself, yet it was awkward, it was not the right thing. What disconcerted him most was that almost all the prisoners had taken part in the protest. He must suppress it at all costs. They soon released the ringleaders.

Next day the food was better, but the improvement did not last long. For some days afterwards the major visited the prison more frequently and found fault more frequently. Our sergeant went about looking anxious and perplexed, as though he could not get over his amazement. As for the convicts, they could not settle down for a long time afterwards, but they were not so much excited as before, they were in a state of dumb perplexity and bewilderment. Some of them were deeply despondent. Others expressed their discontent, but sparingly. Many in their exasperation jeered at themselves aloud, as though to punish themselves for having got up the protest.

'Put it in your pipe and smoke it,' someone would say.

'We had our joke and now we must pay for it!' another would add.

'What mouse can bell the cat?' observed a third.

'There's no teaching us without the stick, we all know. It's a good thing he didn't flog us all.'

'For the future think more and talk less and you'll do better!' someone would observe malignantly.

'Why, are you setting up to teach?'

'To be sure I am.'

'And who are you to put yourself forward?'

'Why, I am a man so far, and who are you?'

'You are a dog's bone, that's what you are.'

'That's what you are.'

'There, there, shut up! What's the shindy about!' the others shouted at the disputants from all sides.

The same evening, that is, on the day of the complaint, on my return from work, I met Petrov behind the barracks. He was looking for me. Coming up to me he muttered something, two or three vague exclamations, but soon relapsed into absent-minded silence and walked mechanically beside me. All this affair was still painfully weighing on my heart, and I fancied that Petrov could explain something to me.

'Tell me, Petrov,' said I, 'are they angry with us?'

'Who angry?' he asked, as though waking up.

'The convicts angry with us – the gentlemen.'

'Why should they be angry with you?'

'Because we did not take part in the complaint.'

'But why should you make a complaint?' he asked, as though trying to understand me. 'You buy your own food.'

'Good heavens! But some of you who joined in it buy your own food, too. We ought to have done the same – as comrades.'

'But . . . but how can you be our comrades?' he asked in perplexity.

I looked at him quickly; he did not understand me in the least, he did not know what I was driving at. But I understood him thoroughly at that instant. A thought that had been stirring vaguely within me and haunting me for a long time had at last become clear to me, and I suddenly understood what I had only imperfectly realised. I understood that they would never accept me as a comrade, however much I might be a convict, not if I were in for life, not if I were in the special division. But I remember most clearly Petrov's face at that minute. His question, 'how can you be our comrade?' was full of such genuine simplicity, such simple-hearted perplexity. I wondered if there were any irony, any malicious mockery in the question. There was nothing of the sort: simply we were not their comrades and that was all. You go your way, and we go ours; you have your affairs, and we have ours.

And, indeed, I had expected that after the complaint they would simply torment us to death without mercy, and that life would be impossible for us. Nothing of the sort, we did not hear one word of reproach, not a hint of reproach; there was no increase of ill-feeling against us. They simply gibed at us a little on occasions, as they had done before – nothing else. They were not in the least angry either with the other convicts who had remained in the kitchen and not joined in the complaint; nor with those who had first shouted that they were satisfied. No one even referred to it. This last fact puzzled me especially.

CHAPTER EIGHT

Comrades

I was, of course, most attracted to the men of my own sort, the 'gentlemen' that is, especially at first. But of the three Russian convicts of that class who were in our prison (Akim Akimitch, the spy A., and the man who was believed to have killed his father) the only one I knew and talked to was Akim Akimitch. I must confess that I resorted to Akim Akimitch only, so to say, in despair, at moments of the most intense boredom and when there was no prospect of speaking to anyone else. In the last chapter I have tried to arrange all the convicts in classes, but now I recall Akim Akimitch, I think that one might add another class. It is true that he would be the only representative of it – that is, the class of the absolutely indifferent convicts. Absolutely indifferent convicts, those, that is, to whom it was a matter of indifference whether they lived in prison or in freedom, one would have supposed did not and could not exist, but I think Akim Akimitch was an example of one. He had established himself in prison, indeed, as though he meant to spend his life there; everything about him, his mattress, his pillows, his pots and pans, all were on a solid and permanent footing. There was nothing of a temporary, bivouacking character about him. He had many years still to be in prison, but I doubt whether he ever thought of leaving it. But if he were reconciled to his position, it was not from inclination, but from subordination, though, indeed, in his case it amounted to the same thing. He was a good-natured man, and he helped me, indeed, at first with advice and kind offices; but I confess, sometimes, especially at first, he produced in me an intense depression which still further increased my misery. Yet it was my misery drove me to talk to him. I longed sometimes for a living word, however bitter or impatient or spiteful; we might at least have railed at our destiny together. But he was silent, gumming his paper lamps, or he would tell me of the review in which he had taken part in such a year, and who was the commanding officer of the division and what his Christian name was, and whether he had been satisfied with the review, and how the signals for the gunners had been changed, and all in the same even, decorous voice like the dripping of water. He scarcely showed the slightest animation when he told me that he had been deemed worthy to receive the ribbon of St Anne on his sword for the part he had taken in some action in the Caucasus. Only at that moment his voice became extraordinarily dignified and solemn; it dropped to a mysterious undertone when he pronounced the words 'St Anne,' and for three minutes afterwards he became particularly silent and sedate . . . During that first year I had stupid moments when I (and always quite suddenly) began, I don't know why, almost to hate Akim Akimitch, and I cursed the fate which had put me with my head next his on the common bed. Usually an hour later I reproached myself for the feeling. But this was only during my first year; later on I became quite reconciled to Akim Akimitch in my heart, and was ashamed of my foolishness. Outwardly, as far as I remember, we were always on good terms.

Besides these three Russians there were eight others, Polish prisoners, of the upper class in the prison while I was there. Some of them I got to know pretty well, and was glad of their friendship, but not all. The best of them were morbid, exceptional and intolerant to the last degree. With two of them I gave up talking altogether in the end. Only three of them were well educated: B., M., and Z., who had been a professor of mathematics, a nice, good-natured old man, very eccentric and not at all clever, I think, in spite of his education. M. and B. were men of a quite different type. I got on well with M. from the first; I respected him and never quarrelled with him, but I never could get fond of him or feel any affection for him. He was a profoundly mistrustful and embittered man with a wonderful power of self-control. But this very excess of self-control was what I did not like; one somehow felt that he would never open his heart to anyone. But perhaps I am mistaken. He was a man of strong and very noble character. His extreme and almost Jesuitical skill and circumspection in dealing with people betrayed his profound inner scepticism. Yet his was a soul tormented just by this duality – scepticism and a deep steadfast faith in some of his own hopes and convictions. But for all his skill in getting on with people, he was an irreconcilable enemy of B. and of the latter's friend T. B. was a man in ill-health, of consumptive tendency, nervous and irritable, but at bottom a very kind-hearted and even great-hearted man. His irritability sometimes reached the pitch of extreme intolerance and caprice. I could not put up with his temper, and in the end I gave up having anything to do with B., but I never ceased to love him; with M. I never quarrelled, but I never was fond of him. It happened that, through cutting off my relations with B., I had also to give up T., the young man of whom I have spoken in the last chapter when I described our 'complaint'. I was very sorry for that. Though T. was not an educated man, he was kind-hearted and manly, a splendid young fellow, in fact. He was so fond of B., had such a respect and reverence for him that if anyone were ever so little at variance with B. he at once looked upon him almost as an enemy. I believe in the end he was estranged even from M. on B.'s account, though he held out for a long time. But they were all morally sick, embittered, irritable and mistrustful. It was easy to understand; it was very hard for them, much worse than for us. They were far from their own country. Some of them were exiled for long periods, ten or twelve years, and what was worse they regarded everyone around them with intense prejudice, saw in the convicts nothing but their brutality, could not discern any good quality, anything human in them, and had indeed no wish to do so. And, as was very easy to understand also, they were led to this unfortunate point of view by the force of circumstance, by fate. There is no doubt that they were very miserable in prison. To the Circassians, to the Tatars and to Isay Fomitch they were cordial and friendly, but shunned the other convicts with abhorrence. Only the Starodubovsky Old Believer won their entire respect. It is remarkable, however, that all the while I was in prison none of the convicts ever taunted them with their nationality and their religion, or their ideas, as Russian peasants sometimes, though very rarely, do with foreigners, especially Germans. Though perhaps they do no more than laugh at the Germans; a German is always an extremely comic figure in the eyes of the Russian peasant. The convicts treated our foreign prisoners respectfully in prison, far more so than the Russian 'gentlemen' prisoners indeed, and they never *touched* them. But the latter seemed unwilling to notice and consider this fact. I have spoken of T. It was he who, when they were walking from their first place of exile to our prison, carried B. in his arms almost the whole journey, when the latter, weak in health and constitution, broke down before half the day's march was over. They had at first been exiled to U. There, so they said, they were well off, that is, much better off than in our prison. But they got up a correspondence, of a perfectly harmless character however, with some other exiles in another town, and for this reason it was considered necessary to exile these three to our fortress, where they would be under the eye of a higher official. Their third comrade was Z. Till they came, M. was the only Pole in the prison. How miserable he must have been in his first year there!

This Z. was the old man who was always saying his prayers, as I have mentioned before. All our political prisoners were young, some mere boys; only Z. was a man of over fifty. He was a man of unquestionable honesty, but rather strange. His comrades B. and T. disliked him very much; they did not even speak to him; they used to say of him that he was quarrelsome, obstinate and fussy. I don't know how far they were right. In prison, as in all places where people are kept together in a crowd against their will, I think people quarrel and even hate one another more easily than in freedom. Many circumstances combine to bring this about. But Z. certainly was a rather stupid and perhaps disagreeable man. None of his other comrades were on good terms with him. Though I never quarrelled with him, I did not get on with him particularly well. I believe he knew his own subject, mathematics. I remember that he was always trying to explain to me in his broken Russian some special astronomical system he had invented. I was told that he had once published an account of it, but the learned world had only laughed at him. I think he was a little cracked. For whole days together he was on his knees saying his prayers, for which all the convicts respected him to the day of his death. He died before my eyes in our hospital after a severe illness. He won the convicts' respect, however, from the first moment in prison after the incident with our major. On the journey from U. to our prison they had not been shaved and they had grown beards, so when they were led straight to the major he was furiously indignant at such a breach of discipline, though they were in no way to blame for it.

'What do they look like!' he roared; 'they are tramps, brigands!'

Z., who at that time knew very little Russian and thought they were being asked who they were – tramps or brigands? – answered: 'We are not tramps, we are political prisoners.'

'Wha – aat? You are insolent! Insolent!' roared the major. 'To the guard-house! A hundred lashes, at once, this instant!'

The old man was flogged. He lay down under the lashes without a protest, bit his hand and endured the punishment without a cry, a moan, or a movement. Meanwhile B. and T. went into the prison, where M., already waiting for them at the gate, fell on their necks, though he had never seen them before. Agitated by the way the major had received them, they told M. all about Z. I remember how M. told me about it.

'I was beside myself,' he said. 'I did not know what was happening to me and shivered as though I were in a fever. I waited for Z. at the gate. He would have to come straight from the guard-house where the flogging took place. Suddenly the gate opened: Z. came out with a pale face and trembling white lips, and without looking at anyone passed through the convicts who were assembled in the yard and already knew that a "gentleman" was being flogged; he went into the prison ward, straight to his place, and without saying a word knelt down and began to pray. The convicts were impressed and even touched. When I saw that old grey-headed man,' said M., 'who had left a wife and children in his own country – when I saw him on his knees praying, after a shameful punishment, I rushed behind the prison, and for two hours I did not know what I was doing; I was frantic . . . '

The convicts had a great respect for Z. from that time forward and they always treated him respectfully. What they particularly liked was that he had not cried out under punishment.

One must be fair, however: one cannot judge of the behaviour of the authorities in Siberia to prisoners of the educated class, whoever they may be, Poles or Russians, from this instance. This instance only shows that one may come across a bad man, and, of course, if that bad man is an independent senior officer somewhere, the fate of an exile whom that bad man particularly disliked would be very insecure. But one must admit that the highest authorities in Siberia, upon whom the tone and disposition of all the other commanding officers depend, are very scrupulous in regard to exiles of the upper class, and are even in some cases disposed to favour them in comparison with the other convicts of the peasant class. The reasons for this are clear: these higher authorities, to begin with, belong to the privileged class themselves; secondly, it has happened in the past that some of the exiles of this class have refused to lie down to be flogged and have attacked the officers, which has led to terrible consequences; and, thirdly, I believe the chief explanation is that thirty-five years ago a great mass of exiles of the upper class were sent to Siberia all at once, and these exiles had succeeded in the course of thirty years in establishing their character throughout Siberia, so that from an old traditional habit the government in my day could not help looking upon political prisoners as very different from ordinary convicts. The subordinate officers were accustomed to look upon them in the same way, taking their tone and attitude from the higher authorities, of course, and following their lead. But many of these commanding officers of inferior rank were stupid and secretly critical of the instructions given them, and they would have been very glad if they could have made their own arrangements without being checked. But this was not altogether permitted. I have good reason for this belief and I will give it. The second class of penal servitude in which I was serving – imprisonment in the fortress under military command – was incomparably more severe than the other two divisions, that is, servitude in the mines and in government works. It was not only harder for prisoners of the privileged class but for all the convicts, simply because the government and organisation of this division was all military and not unlike that of the disciplinary battalions in Russia. Military government is harsher, the regulations are stricter, one is always in chains, always under guard, always behind bars and bolts; and this is not so much the case in the other two divisions. So at least all our convicts said, and there were some amongst them who knew what they were talking about. They would all gladly have passed into the first division, which is reckoned by the law to be the hardest, and often dreamed of the change. Of the disciplinary battalions in Russia, all who had been in them spoke with horror, declaring that in all Russia nothing was harder than the disciplinary battalions in the fortresses, and that Siberia was paradise compared with the life in them. So if, in such harsh conditions as in our prison under military rule, before the eyes of the Governor-General himself, and in spite of the possibility (such things sometimes occurred) of officious outsiders through spite or jealousy secretly reporting that certain political prisoners were favoured by officers of doubtful loyalty – if in such circumstances, I repeat, the political prisoners were looked upon somewhat differently from the other convicts, they must have been treated even more leniently in the first and third divisions. So I believe I can judge in this respect of all Siberia by the place where I was. All the tales and rumours that reached me on this subject from exiles of the first and third divisions confirmed my conclusion. In reality all of us, prisoners of the upper class, were treated by the authorities with more attention and circumspection in our prison. We certainly had no favour shown us in regard to work or other external conditions: we had the same work, the same fetters, the same bolts and bars – in fact, we had everything exactly like the other convicts. And indeed it was impossible to mitigate our lot. I know that in that town in *the recent but so remote past* there were so many spies, so many intrigues, so many people laying traps for one another, that it was natural that the governing authorities should be afraid of being denounced. And what could be more terrible at that period than to be accused of showing favour to political prisoners? And so all were afraid, and we lived on an equal footing with all the convicts; but as regards corporal punishment there was a certain difference. It is true they would readily have flogged us if we had deserved it, that is, had committed a misdemeanour. That much was dictated by official duty and equality as regards corporal punishment. But they would not have flogged us at random on the impulse of the moment; and, of course, cases of such wanton treatment of the common convicts did occur, especially with some commanding officers of lower rank, who enjoyed domineering and intimidation. We knew that the governor of the prison was very indignant with the major when he knew the story of old Z., and impressed upon him the necessity of restraining himself in the future. So I was told by everyone. It was known also in prison that the Governor-General, too, though he trusted and to some extent liked our major as a man of some ability who did his duty, reprimanded him about that affair. And the major had made a note of it. He would dearly have liked, for example, to lay hands upon

M., whom he hated from the tales A. told him, but he was never able to flog him, though he persecuted him and was on the lookout for a pretext and ready to pounce upon him. The whole town soon heard of the Z. affair, and public opinion condemned the major; many people reproved him, and some made themselves very unpleasant.

I remember at this moment my first encounter with the major. When we were at Tobolsk, the other political prisoner with whom I entered the prison and myself, they frightened us by telling us of this man's ferocious character. Some old political exiles, who had been in Siberia for twenty-five years and who met us at Tobolsk with great sympathy and kept up relations with us all the time we were in the forwarding prison, warned us against our future commanding officer and promised to do what they could, through certain prominent persons, to protect us from his persecution. Three daughters of the Governor-General, who had come from Russia and were staying with their father, did, in fact, receive letters from them and spoke about us to their father. But what could he do? He merely told the major to be more careful. About three o'clock in the afternoon my comrade and I arrived in the town, and the guards took us at once to the major. We stood in the entry waiting for him. Meanwhile they sent for the prison sergeant. As soon as he appeared, the major, too, came out. His spiteful, purple, pimply face made a very depressing impression: it was as though a malicious spider had run out to pounce on some poor fly that had fallen into its web.

'What's your name?' he asked my comrade. He spoke rapidly, sharply, abruptly; he evidently wished to make an impression on us.

'So-and-so.'

'You?' he went on, addressing me and glaring at me through his spectacles.

'So-and-so.'

'Sergeant! To prison with them at once, shave them in the guard-house – half the head, as civilian prisoners; change their fetters tomorrow. What coats are those? Where did you get them?' he answered suddenly, his attention being caught by the grey overcoats with yellow circles on the back which had been given us at Tobolsk and which we were wearing in his illustrious presence. 'That's a new uniform! It must be a new uniform . . .

A new pattern . . . from Petersburg,' he added, making us turn round one after the other. 'They've nothing with them?' he asked the escort.

'They've got their own clothes, your honour,' said the gendarme, drawing himself up suddenly with a positive start. Everyone knew of the major, everyone had heard of him, everyone was frightened of him.

'Take away everything! Only give them back their underlinen, the white things; if there are any coloured things take them away; and sell all the rest by auction. The money for the prison funds. The convict has no property,' he added, looking at us sternly. 'Mind you behave yourselves! Don't let me hear of you! Or . . . cor–po–ral pu–nishment. For the least misdemeanour – the lash!'

This reception, which was unlike anything I was used to, made me almost ill the whole evening. And the impression was increased by what I saw in the prison; but I have already described my first hours in prison.

I have mentioned already that the authorities did not, and dared not, show us any favour or make our tasks lighter than those of the other convicts. But on one occasion they did try to do so: for three whole months B. and T. used to go to the engineer's office to do clerical work there. But this was done in strict secrecy, and was the engineering officer's doing. That is to say, all the other officials concerned knew of it, but they pretended not to. That happened when G. was commanding officer. Lieutenant-Colonel G. was a perfect godsend for the short time he was with us – not more than six months, if I mistake not, rather less perhaps. He made an extraordinary impression on the convicts before he left them to return to Russia. It was not simply that the convicts loved him; they adored him, if such a word may be used in this connection. How he did it I don't know, but he gained their hearts from the first moment. 'He is a father to us, a father! We've no need of a father!' the convicts were continually saying all the time he was at the head of the engineering department. I believe he was a terribly dissipated character. He was a little man with a bold, self-confident expression. But at the same time he was kind, almost tender, with the convicts, and he really did love them like a father. Why he was so fond of the convicts I can't say, but he could not see a convict without saying something kindly and good-humoured to him, without making a joke or laughing with him, and the best of it was there was no trace of the authoritative manner in it, nothing suggestive of condescending or purely official kindness. He was their comrade and completely one of themselves. But although he was instinctively democratic in manner and feeling, the convicts were never once guilty of disrespect or familiarity with him. On the contrary. But the convict's whole face lighted up when he met the lieutenant-colonel and, taking off his cap, he was all smiles when the latter came up to him. And if the officer spoke the convict felt as though he had received a present. There are popular people like this. He looked a manly fellow, he walked with an erect and gallant carriage. 'He is an eagle,' the convicts used to say of him. He could, of course, do nothing to mitigate their lot; he was only at the head of the engineering work, which, having been settled and laid down by law once for all, went on unchanged, whoever was in command. At most, if he chanced to come across a gang of convicts whose work was finished, he would let them go home before the drum sounded, instead of keeping them hanging about for nothing. But the convicts liked his confidence in them, the absence of petty fault-finding and irritability, the utter lack of anything insulting in speech or manner in his official relations with them. If he had lost a thousand roubles, and a convict had picked the money up, I do believe, if it were the worst thief in prison, he would have restored it. Yes, I am sure of that. With intense sympathy the convicts learnt that their 'eagle' had a deadly quarrel with our hated major. It happened during the first month G. was there. Our major had at some time served with him in the past. After years of separation they met as friends and used to drink together. But their relations were suddenly cut short. They quarrelled and G. became his mortal enemy. There was a rumour that they had even fought on the occasion, which was by no means out of the question with our major: he often did fight. When the convicts heard of this their delight knew no bounds. 'As though old Eight-eyes could get on with a man like him! He is an eagle, but the major a . . . ' and here usually followed a word quite unfit for print. The prisoners were fearfully interested to know which had given the other a beating. If the rumours of the fight had turned out to be false (which was perhaps the case) I believe our convicts would have been very much annoyed. 'You may be sure the colonel got the best of it,' they used to say; 'he's a plucky one, though he is small, and the major crawled under the bed to get away from him, they say.'

But G. soon left us and the convicts sank into despondency again. Our engineering commanders were all good, however; three or four succeeded one another in my time. 'But we shall never have another like him,' the convicts used to say; 'he was an eagle, an eagle and our champion.' This G. was very fond of us political prisoners, and towards the end he used to make B. and me come to work in his office sometimes. After he went away this was put on a more regular footing. Some in the engineering department (especially one of them) were very sympathetic with us. We used to go there and copy papers, our handwriting began to improve even, when suddenly there came a peremptory order from the higher authorities that we were to be sent back to our former tasks: someone had already played the spy. It was a good thing, however; we had both begun to be fearfully sick of the office! Afterwards for two years B. and I went almost inseparably to the same tasks, most frequently to the workshops. We used to chat together, talk of our hopes and convictions. He was a splendid fellow; but his ideas were sometimes very strange and exceptional. There is a certain class of people, very intelligent indeed, who sometimes have utterly paradoxical ideas. But they have suffered so much for them in their lives, they have paid such a heavy price for them, that it would be too painful, almost impossible, to give them up. B. listened to every criticism with pain and answered with bitterness. I daresay he was more right than I was in many things – I don't know; but at last we parted, and I was very sad about it: we had shared so many things together.

Meanwhile M. seemed to become more melancholy and gloomy every year. He was overwhelmed by depression. During my early days in prison he used to be more communicative, his feelings found a fuller and more frequent utterance. He had been two years in prison when I first came. At first he took interest in a great deal of what had happened in the world during those two years, of which he had no idea in prison; he questioned me, listened, was excited. But towards the end, as the years went on, he seemed to be more concentrated within and shut up in his own mind. The glowing embers were being covered up by ash. His exasperation grew more and more marked. '*Je haïs ces brigands,*' he often repeated to me, looking with hatred at the convicts, whom I had by then come to know better, and nothing I could say in their favour had any influence. He did not understand what I said, though he sometimes gave an absentminded assent; but next day he would say again: '*Je haïs ces brigands.*' We used often to talk in French, by the way; and on this account a soldier in the engineers, called Dranishnikov, nicknamed us the 'medicals' – I don't know from what connection of ideas. M. only showed warmth when he spoke of his mother. 'She is old, she is ill,' he said to me; 'she loves me more than anything in the world, and here I don't know whether she is alive or dead. To know that I had to run the gauntlet was enough for her . . . ' M. did not come of the privileged class, and before being sent to exile had received corporal punishment. He used to clench his teeth and look away when he recalled it. Towards the end he used more and more frequently to walk alone.

One morning, about midday, he was summoned by the governor. Our governor came out to him with a good-humoured smile.

'Well, M., what did you dream about last night?' he asked.

'I trembled,' M. told us afterwards, 'I felt as though I had been stabbed to the heart.'

'I dreamt I had a letter from my mother,' he answered.

'Better than that, better than that!' replied the governor. 'You are free! Your mother has petitioned in your favour, and her petition has been granted. Here is her letter and here is the order relating to you. You will leave the prison at once.'

He came back to us pale, unable to recover from the shock. We congratulated him. He pressed our hands with his cold and trembling hands. Many of the common convicts, too, congratulated him and were delighted at his good luck.

He was released and remained in our town as a 'settler'. Soon he was given a post. At first he often came to our prison, and when he could, told us all sorts of news. Politics was what interested him most.

Besides M., T., B. and Z., there were two quite young men who had been sent for brief terms, boys of little education, but honest, simple, and straightforward. A third, A—chukovsky, was quite a simpleton, and there was nothing special about him. But a fourth, B—m, a middle-aged man, made a very disagreeable impression upon all of us. I don't know how he came to be one of the political prisoners, and, indeed, he denied all connection with them himself. He had the coarse soul of a petty huckster, and the habits and principles of a shopkeeper who had grown rich by cheating over halfpence. He was entirely without education, and took no interest in anything but his trade. He was a painter, and a first-rate one – magnificent. Soon the authorities heard of his talent, and all the town began wanting B—m to paint their walls and ceilings. Within two years he had painted almost all the officials' houses. Their owners paid him out of their own pockets, and so he was not at all badly off. But the best of it was that his comrades, too, began to be sent to work with him. Two who went out with him continually learnt the trade, too, and one of them, T—zhevsky, became as good a painter as he was himself. Our major, who lived in a government house himself, sent for B—m in his turn, and told him to paint all the walls and ceilings. Then B—m did his utmost: even the Governor-General's house was not so well painted. It was a tumbledown, very mangy-looking, one-storey wooden house; but the interior was painted as though it were a palace, and the major was highly delighted . . . He rubbed his hands, and declared that now he really must get married: 'with such a house one must have a wife,' he added quite seriously. He was more and more pleased with B—m, and through him with the others who worked with him. The work lasted a whole month. In the course of that month the major quite altered his views of the political prisoners, and began to patronise them. It ended by his summoning Z. one day from the prison.

'Z.,' said he, 'I wronged you. I gave you a flogging for nothing. I know it. I regret it. Do you understand that? *I, I, I* – regret it!'

Z. replied that he did understand it.

'Do you understand that *I, I,* your commanding officer, have sent for you, to ask you your forgiveness; Do you feel that? What are *you* beside me? A worm! Less than a worm: you are a convict. And I, by the grace of God,* am a major. A major! Do you understand that?'

Z. answered that he understood that, too.

* This expression was literally used in my time, not only by the major, but by many petty officers, especially those who had risen from the lower ranks – *Author's note.*

'Well, now I am making peace with you. But do you feel it, do you feel it fully, in all its fullness? Are you capable of understanding it? Only think: *I*, *I*, the major . . . ' and so on.

Z. told me of the whole scene himself. So even this drunken, quarrelsome, and vicious man had some humane feeling. When one takes into consideration his ideas and lack of culture, such an action may almost be called magnanimous. But probably his drunken condition had a good deal to do with it.

His dreams were not realised; he did not get married, though he had fully made up his mind to do so by the time the decoration of his house was finished. Instead of being married he was arrested, and he was ordered to send in his resignation. At the trial all his old sins were brought up against him. He had previously been a provost of the town . . . The blow fell on him unexpectedly. There was immense rejoicing in the prison at the news. It was a festive day, a day of triumph! They said that the major howled like an old woman and was dissolved in tears. But there was nothing to be done. He retired, sold his pair of greys, and then his whole property, and even sank into poverty. We came across him afterwards, a civilian wearing a shabby coat and a cap with a cockade in it. He looked viciously at the convicts. But all his prestige went with his uniform. In a uniform he was terrible, a deity. In civil dress he became absolutely a nonentity, and looked like a lackey. It's wonderful what the uniform does for men like that.

CHAPTER NINE

An Escape

Soon after our major was removed, there were fundamental changes in our prison. They gave up using the place as a prison for penal servitude convicts and founded instead a convict battalion, on the pattern of the Russian disciplinary battalions. This meant that no more convicts of the second class were brought to our prison. It began to be filled at this time only with convicts of the military division, men therefore not deprived of civil rights, soldiers like all other soldiers except that they were undergoing punishment in the prison for brief terms, six years at the utmost. At the expiration of their sentence they would go back to their battalions as privates, just as before. Those, however, who came back to the prison after a second offence were punished as before by a sentence of twenty years. There had been, indeed, even before this change a division of convicts of the military class, but they lived with us because there was no other place for them. Now the whole prison became a prison for this military section. The old convicts, genuine civil convicts, who had been deprived of all rights, had been branded, and shaved on one side of the head, remained, of course, in the prison till their full terms were completed. No new ones came, and those who remained gradually worked out their terms of servitude and went away, so that ten years later there could not have been a convict left in our prison. The special division was left, however, and to it from time to time were sent convicts of the military class who had committed serious crimes, and they were kept there till certain penal works were established in Siberia. So in reality life went on for us as before, the same conditions, the same food, and almost the same regulations; but the officers in command were different and more numerous. A staff officer was appointed, a commander of the battalion and four superior officers who were on duty in the prison in turns. The veterans, too, were abolished and twelve sergeants and a quartermaster were appointed. The prisoners were divided into tens and corporals were appointed from the convicts themselves, nominally, of course, and Akim Akimitch at once became a corporal. All these new institutions and the whole prison, with its officials and convicts, were as before left under the control of the governor of the prison as the highest authority. That was all that happened.

The convicts were, of course, very much excited at first; they talked, guessed and tried to read the characters of their commanders, but when they saw that in reality everything went on as before, they calmed down and our life went on in its old way. But the great thing was that we were all saved from the old major; everyone seemed to breathe freely and to be more confident. They lost their panic-stricken air; all knew now that in case of need one could have things out with the authorities and that the innocent would not be punished for the guilty except by mistake. Vodka was sold just as before and on the same system, although instead of the veterans we had sergeants. These sergeants turned out to be for the most part a good sort of sensible men who understood their position. Some of them, however, at first showed an inclination to domineer, and, of course, in their inexperience thought they could treat the convicts like soldiers, but soon even these realised the position. Those who were too slow in understanding had it pointed out to them by the convicts. There were some sharp encounters; for instance, they would tempt a sergeant and make him drunk, and afterwards point out to him, in their own fashion, of course, that he had drunk with them, and consequently . . . It ended in the sergeants looking on unconcerned, or rather trying not to see, when vodka was brought in in bladders and sold. What is more, they went to the market as the veterans had done before and brought the convicts rolls, beef, and all the rest of it; that is, anything that was not too outrageous. Why all these changes were made, why convict battalions were formed, I don't know. It happened during my last years in prison. But I had two years to spend under these new regulations.

Shall I describe all that life, all my years in prison? I don't think so. If I were to describe in order, in succession, all that happened and all that I saw and experienced in those years, I might have written three times, four times as many chapters as I have. But such a description would necessarily become too monotonous. All the incidents would be too much in the same key, especially if, from the chapters already written, the reader has succeeded in forming a fairly satisfactory conception of prison life in the second division. I wanted to give a vivid and concrete picture of our prison and of all that I lived through in those years. Whether I have attained my object I don't know. And, indeed, it is not quite for me to judge of it. But I am convinced that I can end my story here. Besides, I am sometimes depressed by these memories myself. And I can hardly recollect everything. The later years have somehow been effaced from my memory. Many circumstances, I am quite sure, I have entirely forgotten. I remember that all those years, which were so much alike, passed drearily, miserably. I remember that those long wearisome days were monotonous, as drops of water trickling from the roof after rain. I remember that nothing but the passionate desire to rise up again, to be renewed, to begin a new life, gave me the strength to wait and to hope. And at last I mastered myself; I looked forward, and I reckoned off every day, and although a thousand remained, I took pleasure in ticking them off one by one. I saw the day off; I buried it, and I rejoiced at the coming of another day, because there were not a thousand left but nine hundred and ninety-nine days. I remember that all that time, though I had hundreds of companions, I was fearfully lonely, and at last I grew fond of that loneliness. In my spiritual solitude I reviewed all my past life, went over it all to the smallest detail, brooded over my past, judged myself sternly and relentlessly, and even sometimes blessed fate for sending me this solitude, without which I could not have judged myself like this, nor have reviewed my past life so sternly. And what hopes set my heart throbbing in those days! I believed, I resolved, I swore to myself that in my future life there should be none of the mistakes and lapses there had been in the past. I sketched out a programme for myself for the whole future, and I firmly resolved to keep to it. The blind faith that I should and could keep these resolutions rose up in my heart again. I looked forward eagerly to freedom, I prayed for it to come quickly; I longed to test myself again in fresh strife. At times I was overcome by nervous impatience. But it hurts me to recall now my spiritual condition at that time. Of course, all that concerns no one but me. But I have written all this because I think everyone will understand it, for the same thing must happen to everyone if he is sent to prison for a term of years in the flower of his youth and strength.

But why talk of it? I had better describe something else, that I may not end too abruptly.

It occurs to me that someone may ask, was it really impossible for anyone to escape from prison, and did no one escape in all those years? As I have said already, a prisoner who has spent two or three years in prison begins to attach a value to those years and cannot help coming to the conclusion that it is better to serve the rest of his time without trouble and risk and leave the prison finally in the legal way as a 'settler'. But this conclusion can only occur to a convict who has been sentenced to a brief term. The man with many years before him might well be ready to risk anything. But somehow this did not often happen in our prison. I don't know whether it was that they were very cowardly, whether the supervision was particularly strict and military, whether the situation of our town in the open steppes was in many ways unfavourable; it is hard to say. I imagine all these considerations had their influence. Certainly it was rather difficult to escape from us. And yet one such case did happen in my time; two convicts ventured on the attempt and those two were among the most important criminals.

After the major had gone, A. (the convict who had played the spy for him in the prison) was left quite friendless and unprotected. He was still young, but his character had grown stronger and steadier as he grew older. He was altogether a bold, resolute and even very intelligent man. Though he would have gone on spying and making his living in all sorts of underhand ways if he had been given his freedom, he would not have been caught so stupidly and imprudently as before and have paid so dearly for his folly. While he was in prison, he practised making false passports a little. I cannot speak with certainty about this, however. But I was told so by the convicts. It was said that he used to work in that line at the time when he frequented the major's kitchen and of course he picked up all he could there. In short he was capable of anything 'to change his luck'. I had an opportunity of reading his character and seeing to some extent into his mind; cynicism in him reached a pitch of revolting impudence and cold mockery, and it excited an invincible repugnance. I believe that, if he had had a great desire for a glass of vodka and if he could not have got it except by murdering someone, he would certainly have committed the murder, if he could only have done it in secret so that no one could discover it. In prison he learnt prudence. And this man caught the attention of Kulikov, a convict in the special division.

I have already spoken of Kulikov. He was a man no longer young, but passionate, vital, vigorous, with great and varied abilities. There was strength in him and he still had a longing for life. Such men feel the same thirst for life up to extreme old age. And if I had wondered why none of the convicts escaped from the prison, the first I should have thought of would have been Kulikov. But Kulikov made up his mind at last. Which of them had the most influence on the other – A. on Kulikov or Kulikov on A. – I do not know, but they were a match for one another and well suited for such an enterprise. They became friends. I fancy Kulikov reckoned on A.'s preparing the passports. A. was a 'gentleman', had belonged to good society; that promised something different from the usual adventures, if only they could get to Russia. Who can tell how they came to an agreement and what hopes they had? But it is certain that they were hoping for something very different from the usual routine of tramping in Siberia. Kulikov was an actor by nature; he could play many and varied parts in life; he might hope for many things, at least for a great variety of things. Prison must weigh heavily on such men. They agreed to escape.

But it was impossible to escape without the help of a guard. They had to persuade a guard to join them. In one of the battalions stationed in the fortress there was a Pole, a man of energy, deserving perhaps of a better fate; he was middle-aged and serious, but he was a fine, spirited fellow. In his youth, soon after he had come as a soldier to Siberia, he had deserted from intense home-sickness. He was caught, punished and kept for two years in a disciplinary battalion. When he was sent back to serve as an ordinary soldier again, he thought better of it and began to be zealous and to do his best in his work. For distinguished service he was made a corporal. He was an ambitious, self-reliant man who knew his own value. He spoke and looked like a man who knows his own value. I met him several times during those years among our guards. The Poles too, had spoken of him to me. It seemed to me that his home-sickness had turned to a hidden, dumb, unchanging hatred. This man was capable of doing anything and Kulikov was right in choosing him as a comrade. His name was Koller.

They agreed and fixed on a day. It was in the hot days of June. The climate was fairly equable in our town; in the summer there was hot settled weather, and that just suited tramps. Of course they could not set off straight from the fortress; the whole town stands on rising ground open on all sides. There was no forest for a long distance round. They had to change into ordinary dress, and to do this they had first to get to the edge of the town, where there was a house that Kulikov had long frequented. I do not know whether his friends there were fully in the secret. One must suppose that they were, though the point was not fully established when the case was tried afterwards. That year in a secluded nook at the edge of the town a very prepossessing young woman, nicknamed Vanka-Tanka, who showed great promise and to some extent fulfilled it later on, was just beginning her career. Another nickname for her was Fire. I believe she, too, had some share in the escape. Kulikov had been spending lavishly upon her for a whole year.

Our heroes went out as usual into the prison yard in the morning and cleverly succeeded in being sent with Shilkin, a convict who made stoves and did plastering, to plaster the empty barracks, which the soldiers had left some time before to go into camp. A. and Kulikov went with Shilkin to act as porters. Koller turned up as one of the guards, and as two guards were required for three convicts, Koller, as an old soldier and a corporal, was readily entrusted with a young recruit that he might train him and teach him his duties. Our fugitives must have had great influence on Koller and he must have had great confidence in them, since after his lengthy and in latter years successful service, clever, prudent, sensible man as he was, he made up his mind to follow them.

They came to the barracks. It was six o'clock in the morning. There was no one there except them. After working for an hour, Kulikov and A. said to Shilkin that they were going to the workshop to see someone and to get some tool, which it seemed they had come without. They had to manage cleverly, that is, as naturally as possible, with Shilkin. He was a Moscow stove-maker, shrewd, clever, full of dodges, and sparing of his words. He was frail and wasted-looking. He ought to have been always wearing a waistcoat and a dressing-gown in the Moscow fashion, but fate had decreed otherwise, and after long wanderings he was settled for good in our prison in the special division, that is, in the class of the most dangerous military criminals. How he had deserved such a fate I don't know, but I never noticed any sign of special dissatisfaction in him; he behaved peaceably and equably, only sometimes got as drunk as a cobbler, but even then he behaved decently. He was certainly not in the secret and his eyes were sharp. Kulikov, of course, winked to him signifying that they were going to get vodka, of which a store had been got ready in the workshop the day before. That touched Shilkin; he parted from them without any suspicion and remained alone with the recruit, while A., Kulikov and Koller set off for the edge of the town.

Half an hour passed; the absent men did not return and at last, on reflection, Shilkin began to have his doubts. He had seen a good deal in his day. He began to remember things. Kulikov had been in a peculiar humour, A. had seemed to whisper to him twice, anyway Kulikov had twice winked to him, he had seen that; now he remembered it all. There was something odd about Koller, too, as he went away with them; he had begun lecturing the recruit as to how he was to behave in his absence, and that was somehow not quite natural, in Koller, at least. In fact the more Shilkin thought about it, the more suspicious he became. Meanwhile time was getting on, they did not come back, and his uneasiness became extreme. He realised thoroughly his position and his own danger; the authorities might turn their suspicions upon him. They might think that he let his comrades go knowingly and had an understanding with them, and if he delayed to give notice of the disappearance of A. and Kulikov, there would seem to be more grounds for suspicion. There was no time to lose. At that point he recollected that Kulikov and A. had been particularly thick of late, had often been whispering, and had often been walking together behind the prison out of sight of everyone. He remembered that even at the time he had thought something about them. He looked searchingly at his guard; the latter was leaning on his gun, yawning and very innocently picking his nose. So Shilkin did not deign to communicate his suspicions to him, but simply told him that he must follow him to the engineer's workshop. He had to ask whether they had been there. But it appeared that no one had seen them there. Shilkin's last doubts were dissipated. 'They might have simply gone to drink and have a spree at the edge of the town, as Kulikov sometimes did,' thought Shilkin, 'but no, that could hardly be it. They would have told him, they would not have thought it worth while to conceal that from him.' Shilkin left his work and, without returning to the barracks, he went straight off to the prison.

It was almost nine o'clock when he presented himself before the chief sergeant and informed him of what had happened. The sergeant was aghast and at first was unwilling to believe it. Shilkin, of course, told him all this simply as a guess, a suspicion. The sergeant rushed off to the commanding officer, and the latter at once informed the governor of the prison. Within a quarter of an hour all the necessary steps had been taken. The Governor-General was informed. The criminals were important ones, and there might be serious trouble from Petersburg on their account. Correctly or not, A. was reckoned a political prisoner; Kulikov was in the special division, that is, a criminal of the first magnitude and a military one, too. There had never been an instance of a prisoner's escaping from the special division before. It was incidentally recalled that every convict of the special division should be escorted to work by two guards, or, at the least, have one each. This rule had not been observed. So it looked an unpleasant business. Messengers were sent to all the villages through all the surrounding country to announce the escape of the fugitives and to leave their description everywhere. Cossacks were sent out to overtake and catch them; neighbouring districts and provinces were written to. The authorities were in a great panic, in fact.

Meanwhile there was excitement of a different sort in prison. As the convicts came in from work, they learnt at once what had happened. The news flew round to all. Everyone received it with extraordinary secret joy. It set every heart throbbing. Besides breaking the monotony of prison life and upsetting the ant-hill, an escape, and such an escape, appealed to something akin in every heart and touched on long-forgotten chords; something like hope, daring, the possibility of 'changing their luck' stirred in every soul. 'Men have escaped, it seems, why then . . . ?' And at this thought everyone plucked up his spirit and looked defiantly at his mates. At any rate, they all seemed suddenly proud and began looking condescendingly at the sergeants. Of course the authorities swooped down on the prison at once. The governor of the prison came himself. Our convicts were in high spirits, and they looked bold, even rather contemptuous, and had a sort of silent stern dignity, as though to say, 'We know how to manage things.' Of course they had foreseen at once that all the authorities would visit the prison. They foresaw, too, that there would be a search and got everything hidden in readiness for it. They knew that the authorities on such occasions are always wise after the event. And so it turned out; there was a great fuss, everything was turned upside down, everything was searched and nothing was found, of course. The convicts were sent out to their afternoon work and escorted by a larger number of guards. Towards evening the sentries looked into the prison every minute; the men were called over an extra time and mistakes in the counting were made twice as often as usual. This led to further confusion; all the men were sent out into the yard and counted over again. Then there was another counting over in the prison wards. There was a great deal of fuss.

But the convicts were not in the least disturbed. They all looked extremely independent and, as is always the case on such occasions, behaved with extraordinary decorum all that evening, as though to say, 'There's nothing you can find fault with.' The authorities, of course, wondered whether the fugitives had not left accomplices in prison and gave orders that the convicts should be watched and spied upon. But the convicts only laughed. 'As though one would leave accomplices behind one in a job of that sort!' 'A thing of that sort is done on the quiet and nohow else!' 'And as though a man like Kulikov, a man like A., would leave traces in an affair like that! They've managed in a masterly way, every sign hidden; they're men who've seen a thing or two; they'd get through locked doors!'

In fact the glory of Kulikov and A. was vastly increased; everyone was proud of them. The convicts felt that their exploit would be handed down to the remotest generation of convicts, would outlive the prison.

'They're master-hands!' some would say.

'You see, it was thought there was no escaping from here. They've escaped, though,' others added.

'Escaped!' a third would pronounce, looking round with an air of some authority. 'But who is it has escaped? The likes of you, do you suppose?'

Another time the convict to whom this question referred would certainly have taken up the challenge and defended his honour, but now he was modestly silent, reflecting: 'Yes, really, we are not all like Kulikov and A.; we must show what we can do before we talk.'

'And why do we go on living here, after all, brother?' said a fourth, breaking the silence. He was sitting modestly at the kitchen window with his cheek propped on his hand. He spoke in a rather sing-song voice, full of sentimental but secretly complacent feeling. 'What are we here for? We are not alive though we are living and we are not in our graves though we are dead. E-e-ch!'

'It's not a shoe, you can't cast it off. What's the use of saying "e-e-ch"?'

'But you see, Kulikov . . . ' a green youth, one of the impulsive sort, tried to interpose.

'Kulikov!' Another cut him short at once, cocking his eye contemptuously at the green youth. 'Kulikov!'

This was as much as to say, 'Are there many Kulikovs here?'

'And A. too, lads, he is a cute one, oh, he is a cute one!'

'Rather! He could turn even Kulikov round his finger! You won't catch him!'

'I wonder whether they've got far by now, lads? I should like to know.'

At once there followed a discussion of whether they had gone far, and in what direction they had gone, and where it would have been best for them to go, and which district was nearer. There were people who knew the surrounding country; they were listened to with interest. They talked of the inhabitants of the neighbouring villages and decided that they were not people to reply upon. They were too near a town to be simple. They wouldn't help a convict, they'd catch him and hand him over.

'The peasants hereabouts are a spiteful set, mates, that they are!'

'There's no depending on them!'

'They're Siberians, the beggars. If they come across you, they'll kill you.'

'Well, but our fellows . . . '

'To be sure, there's no saying which will get the best of it. Our men are not easy customers either.'

'Well, we shall hear, if we live long enough.'

'Why, do you think they'll catch them?'

'I don't believe they'll ever catch them!' another of the enthusiasts pronounces, banging the table with his fist.

'H'm! That's all a matter of luck.'

'And I tell you what I think, lads,' Skuratov breaks in: 'if I were a tramp, they'd never catch me.'

'You!'

There is laughter, though some pretend not to want to listen. But there is no stopping Skuratov.

'Not if I know it!' he goes on vigorously. 'I often think about it and wonder at myself, lads. I believe I'd creep through any chink before they catch me.'

'No fear! You'd get hungry and go to a peasant for bread.'

General laughter.

'For bread? Nonsense!'

'But why are you wagging your tongue? Uncle Vasya and you killed the cow plague.* That's why you came here.'

The laughter was louder than ever. The serious ones looked on with even greater indignation.

'That's nonsense!' shouted Skuratov. 'That's a fib of Mikita's, and it's not about me, but Vaska, and they've mixed me up in it. I'm a Moscow man and I was brought up to tramping from a child. When the deacon was teaching me to read, he used to pull me by the ear and make me repeat, "Lead me not into temptation in Thy infinite mercy," and soon I used to repeat, "lead me to the police-station in Thy infinite mercy," and so on. So that's how I used to go on from my childhood up.'

Everyone burst out laughing again. But that was all Skuratov wanted. He could not resist playing the fool. Soon the convicts left him and fell to serious conversation again. It was mainly the old men, authorities on such affairs, who gave their opinions. The younger and humbler prisoners looked on in silent enjoyment and craned their heads forward to listen. A great crowd gathered in the

* That is, killed a man or woman, suspecting that he or she had put a spell on the cattle, causing their death. We had one such murderer amongst us – *Author's note.*

kitchen; there were, of course, no sergeants present. They would not have spoken freely before them.

Among those who were particularly delighted, I noticed a Tatar, called Mametka, a short man with high cheek-bones, an extremely comic figure. He could hardly speak Russian at all and could hardly understand anything of what was said, but he, too, was craning his head forward out of the crowd and listening, listening with relish.

'Well, Mametka, *yakshee*?'* Skuratov, abandoned by all and not knowing what to do with himself, fastened upon him.

'*Yakshee,* oh, *yakshee*!' Mametka muttered in great animation, nodding his ridiculous head to Skuratov. '*Yakshee*!'

'They won't catch them, *yok*?'

'*Yok, yok*!' and Mametka began babbling, gesticulating as well.

'So you lie, me not understand, eh?'

'Yes, yes, *yakshee*,' Mametka assented, nodding.

'*Yakshee* to be sure!' and Skuratov, giving the Tatar's cap a tweak that sent it over his eyes, went out of the kitchen in the best of spirits, leaving Mametka somewhat perplexed.

For a whole week there was strict discipline in the prison, and search and pursuit were kept up vigorously in the neighbourhood. I don't know how, but the convicts got immediate and accurate information of the manoeuvres of the police outside the prison. The first few days the news was all favourable to the fugitives; there was no sight or sound of them, every trace was lost. The convicts only laughed. All anxiety as to the fate of the runaways was over. 'They won't find anything, they won't catch anyone,' was repeated in prison with complacency.

'Nothing. They've gone like a shot.'

'Goodbye, don't cry, back by-and-by.' It was known in prison that all the peasants in the neighbourhood had been roused. All suspicious places, all the woods and ravines were being watched.

'Foolishness!' said the convicts, laughing. 'They must have some friend they are staying with now.'

'No doubt they have,' said the others. 'They are not fools; they would have got everything ready beforehand.'

They went further than this in their suppositions; they began to say that the runaways were still perhaps in the outskirts of the town, living somewhere in a cellar till the excitement was over and

* Tatar word.

their hair had grown, that they would stay there six months or a year and then go on.

Everyone, in fact, was inclined to romance. But, suddenly, eight days after the escape there was a rumour that a clue had been found. This absurd rumour was, of course, rejected at once with contempt. But the same evening the rumour was confirmed. The convicts began to be uneasy. The next morning it was said in the town that they had been caught and were being brought back. In the afternoon further details were learnt; they had been caught about fifty miles away, at a certain village. At last a definite piece of news was received. A corporal, returning from the major, stated positively that they would be brought that evening straight to the guard-house. There was no possibility of doubt. It is hard to describe the effect this news had on the convicts. At first they all seemed angry, then they were depressed. Then attempts at irony were apparent. There were jeers, not now at the pursuers, but at the captives, at first from a few, then from almost all, except some earnest and resolute men who thought for themselves and who could not be turned by taunts. They looked with contempt at the shallowness of the majority and said nothing.

In fact, they now ran Kulikov and A. down, enjoyed running them down as much as they had crying them up before. It was as though the runaways had done them all some injury. The convicts, with a contemptuous air, repeated that the fugitives had been very hungry, that they had not been able to stand, and had gone to a village to ask for bread from the peasants. This is the lowest depth of ignominy for a tramp. These stories were not true, however. The fugitives had been tracked; they had hidden in the forest; the forest had been surrounded by a cordon. Seeing that they had no hope of escape, they had surrendered. There was nothing else left for them to do.

But when in the evening they really were brought back by the gendarmes, their arms and legs tied, all the convicts trooped out to the fence to see what would be done with them. They saw nothing, of course, except the carriages of the major and the governor outside the guard-house. The runaways were put in a cell apart, fettered, and next day brought up for trial. The contempt and the jeers of the convicts soon passed off. They learnt more fully the circumstances, they found out that there was nothing for them to do but surrender, and all began following the course of the proceedings sympathetically.

'They'll give them a thousand,' said some of them.

'A thousand, indeed!' said the others. 'They'll do for them. A. a thousand, perhaps, but Kulikov will be beaten to death, because he is in the special division.'

They were mistaken, however. A. got off with five hundred blows; his previous good behaviour and the fact that it was his first offence were taken into account. Kulikov, I believe, received fifteen hundred, but the punishment was administered rather mercifully. Like sensible men, the fugitives implicated no one else at the trial, gave clear and exact answers; they said they had run straight away from the fortress without staying anywhere in the town. I felt sorriest of all for Koller; he had lost everything, his last hopes; his sentence was the worst of all, I believe two thousand 'sticks', and he was sent away to another prison as a convict. Thanks to the doctors, A.'s punishment was light and humane, but he gave himself airs and talked loudly in the hospital of his being ready for anything, of his sticking at nothing now, and of doing something much more striking. Kulikov behaved as usual, that is, with dignity and decorum, and when he returned to prison after the punishment, he looked as though he had never left it. But the convicts looked at him differently; though Kulikov always and everywhere knew how to stand up for himself, the convicts had somehow inwardly ceased to respect him and began to treat him with more familiarity. In fact, from this time Kulikov's glory greatly declined. Success means so much to men.

CHAPTER TEN

How I Left Prison

All this happened during my last year in prison. The last year was almost as memorable as the first one, especially the last days in prison. But why go into detail! I only remember that that year, in spite of my impatience for the end of my time, I found life easier than during all my previous years in prison. In the first place I had by then in the prison a number of friends and well-wishers, who had quite made up their minds that I was a good man. Many of them were devoted to me and loved me sincerely. The 'pioneer' almost shed tears when he saw me and my comrade off on the day we left the prison, and when, after leaving, we spent a month in the town, he came almost every day to see us, with no object except to have a look at us. There were some of the convicts, however, who remained morose and churlish to the end and seemed, God knows why, to grudge having to speak to me. It seemed as though there existed a kind of barrier between us.

I enjoyed more privileges towards the last than in the early years of my life in prison. I discovered among the officers serving in the town some acquaintances and even old schoolfellows of mine. I renewed my acquaintance with them. Through their good offices I was able to obtain larger supplies of money, was able to write home and even to have books. It was some years since I had read a book, and it is difficult to describe the strange and agitating impression of the first book I read in the prison. I remember I began reading in the evening when the ward was locked up and I read all night long, till daybreak. It was a magazine. It was as though news had come to me from another world; my former life rose up before me full of light and colour, and I tried from what I read to conjecture how far I had dropped behind. Had a great deal happened while I had been away, what emotions were agitating people now, what questions were occupying their minds? I pored over every word, tried to read between the lines and to find secret meanings and allusions to the past; I looked for traces of what had agitated us in my time. And how sad it was for me to realise how remote I was from this new life, how cut off I was from it all. I should have to get used to everything afresh, to make acquaintance with the new generation again. I pounced with special eagerness on articles signed by men I had known and been intimate with. But there were new names too; there were new leaders, and I was in eager haste to make their acquaintance, and I was vexed that I had the prospect of so few books to read, and that it was so difficult to get hold of them. In old days, under our old major, it was positively dangerous to smuggle a book into prison. If there had been a search, there would immediately have been questions where the book had come from, where one had got it from. It would be surmised that one had acquaintances in the town. And what could I have answered to such enquiries? And therefore, living without books I had unconsciously become absorbed in myself, set myself problems, tried to solve them, worried over them sometimes. But there's no describing all that!

I had entered the prison in the winter and therefore I was to leave it and be free in the winter too, on the anniversary of my arrival. With what impatience I looked forward to the winter, with what enjoyment at the end of the summer I watched the leaves withering and the grass fading in the steppes. And now the summer had passed, the autumn wind was howling; at last the first flakes of snow fluttered down. At last the winter I had so long looked forward to had come! At times my heart began throbbing dumbly at the great thought of freedom. But, strange to say, as time went on and the end came nearer, the more and more patient I became. In the last few days I was really surprised and reproached myself. It seemed to me that I had become quite unconcerned and indifferent. Many of the convicts who met me in the yard in our leisure time would speak to me and congratulate me.

'You'll soon be going out to freedom, Alexandr Petrovitch, soon, soon. You'll leave us all alone, poor devils.'

'And you, Martynov, will your time soon be up?' I would respond.

'Me! Oh, well, I have another seven years to pine away.'

And he would sigh to himself, stand still and look lost in thought, as though staring into the future . . . Yes, many joyfully and sincerely congratulated me. It seemed to me as though all of them began to be more cordial to me. They had evidently begun to think of me as no longer one of themselves; they were already taking leave of me. K—chinksky, one of the educated Poles, a quiet and gentle young man, was, like me, fond of walking about the yard in his leisure time. He hoped by exercise and fresh air to preserve his health and to counteract the evil effect of the stifling nights in the prison ward.

'I am impatiently looking forward to your release,' he said with a smile, meeting me one day as we walked. 'When you leave the prison, I shall know that I have exactly a year before I leave.'

I may mention here parenthetically that our dreams and our long divorce from the reality made us think of freedom as somehow freer than real freedom, that is, than it actually is. The convicts had an exaggerated idea of real freedom, and that is so natural, so characteristic of every convict. Any officer's servant was looked on by us almost as in his way a king, almost as the ideal of a free man compared with the convicts, simply because he was not shaven and went about unfettered and unguarded.

On the evening before the last day I walked in the dusk *for the last time* all round our prison by the fence. How many thousands of times I had walked along that fence during those years! Here behind the barracks during my first year in prison I used to pace up and down, alone, forlorn and dejected. I remember how I used to reckon then how many thousand days were before me. Good God, how long ago it was! Here in this corner our eagle had lived in captivity; here Petrov often used to meet me. Even now he was constantly at my side. He would run up and, as though guessing my thoughts, would walk in silence beside me, seeming as though he were secretly wondering. Mentally, I took leave of the blackened rough timbered walls of our prison. How unfriendly they had seemed to me *then*, in those first days! They, too, must have grown older by now, but I saw no difference in them. And how much youth lay uselessly buried within those walls, what mighty powers were wasted here in vain! After all, one must tell the whole truth; those men were exceptional men. Perhaps they were the most gifted, the strongest of our people. But their mighty energies were vainly wasted, wasted abnormally, unjustly, hopelessly. And who was to blame, whose fault was it?

That's just it, who was to blame?

Early next morning as soon as it began to get light, before the convicts went out to work, I walked through the prison wards to say goodbye to all the convicts. Many strong, horny hands were held out to me cordially. Some, but they were not many, shook hands quite like comrades. Others realised thoroughly that I should at once become quite a different sort of man from them. They knew that I had friends in the town, that I was going straight from the prison to 'the gentry', and that I should sit down with them as their equal. They understood that and, although they said goodbye to me in a friendly and cordial way, they did not speak to me as to a comrade, but as to a gentleman. Some turned away from me and sullenly refused to respond to my greeting. Some even looked at me with a sort of hatred.

The drum beat and all went out to work, and I remained at home. Sushilov had got up almost before anyone that morning and was doing his utmost to get tea ready for me before he went. Poor Sushilov! He cried when I gave him my convict clothes, my shirts, my fetter-wrappers and some money. 'It's not that that I want, not that,' he said, with difficulty controlling his trembling lips. 'It's dreadful losing you, Alexandr Petrovitch! What shall I do here without you!'

I said goodbye for the last time to Akim Akimitch, too.

'You'll be going soon, too,' I said to him.

'I've long, very long to be here still,' he muttered as he pressed my hand. I threw myself on his neck and we kissed.

Ten minutes after the convicts had gone out, we, too, left the prison, never to return. My comrade had entered prison with me and we left together. We had to go straight to the blacksmith's to have our fetters knocked off. But no guard followed us with a gun; we went accompanied only by a sergeant. Our fetters were removed by our convicts in the engineer's workshop. While they were doing my comrade, I waited and then I, too, went up to the anvil. The blacksmiths turned me round so that my back was towards them, lifted my leg up and laid it on the anvil. They bestirred themselves, tried to do their best, their most skilful.

'The rivet, the rivet, turn that first of all!' the senior commanded, 'hold it, that's it, that's right. Hit it with the hammer now.'

The fetters fell off. I picked them up. I wanted to hold them in my hand, to look at them for the last time. I seemed already to be wondering that they could have been on my legs a minute before.

'Well, with God's blessing, with God's blessing!' said the convicts in coarse, abrupt voices, in which, however, there was a note of pleasure.

Yes, with God's blessing! Freedom, new life, resurrection from the dead . . . What a glorious moment!

THE GAMBLER

from the diary of a young man

CHAPTER ONE

At last I have come back from my fortnight's absence. Our friends have already been two days in Roulettenburg. I imagined that they were expecting me with the greatest eagerness; I was mistaken, however. The General had an extremely independent air, he talked to me condescendingly and sent me away to his sister. I even fancied that the General was a little ashamed to look at me. Marya Filippovna was tremendously busy and scarcely spoke to me; she took the money, however, counted it, and listened to my whole report. They were expecting Mezentsov, the little Frenchman, and some Englishman; as usual, as soon as there was money there was a dinner-party, in the Moscow style. Polina Alexandrovna, seeing me, asked why I had been away so long, and without waiting for an answer went off somewhere. Of course, she did that on purpose. We must have an explanation, though. Things have accumulated.

They had assigned me a little room on the fourth storey of the hotel. They know here that I belong to the *General's suite*. It all looks as though they had managed to impress the people. The General is looked upon by everyone here as a very rich Russian grandee. Even before dinner he commissioned me, among other things, to change two notes for a thousand francs each. I changed them at the office of the hotel. Now we shall be looked upon as millionaires for a whole week, at least. I wanted to take Misha and Nadya out for a walk, but on the stairs I was summoned back to the General; he had graciously bethought him to enquire where I was taking them. The man is absolutely unable to look me straight in the face; he would like to very much, but every time I meet his eyes with an intent, that is, disrespectful air, he seems overcome with embarrassment. In very bombastic language, piling one sentence on another, and at last losing his thread altogether, he gave me to understand that I was to take the children for a walk in the park, as far as possible from the Casino. At last he lost his temper completely, and added sharply: 'Or else maybe you'll be taking them into the gambling saloon. You must excuse me,' he added, 'but I know you are still rather thoughtless and capable, perhaps, of gambling. In any case, though, I am not your mentor and have no desire to be, yet I have the right, at any rate, to desire that you will not compromise me, so to speak . . .'

'But I have no money,' I said calmly; 'one must have it before one can lose it.'

'You shall have it at once,' answered the General, flushing a little; he rummaged in his bureau, looked up in an account book, and it turned out that he had a hundred and twenty roubles owing me.

'How are we to settle up?' he said. 'We must change it into thalers. Come, take a hundred thalers – the rest, of course, won't be lost.'

I took the money without a word.

'Please don't be offended by my words, you are so ready to take offence . . . If I did make an observation, it was only, so to speak, by way of warning, and, of course, I have some right to do so . . .'

On my way home before dinner, with the children, I met a perfect cavalcade. Our party had driven out to look at some ruin. Two magnificent carriages, superb horses! In one carriage was Mlle Blanche with Marya Filippovna and Polina; the Frenchman, the Englishman and our General were on horseback. The passers-by stopped and stared; a sensation was created; but the General will have a bad time, all the same. I calculated that with the four thousand francs I had brought, added to what they had evidently managed to get hold of, they had now seven or eight thousand francs; but that is not enough for Mlle Blanche.

Mlle Blanche, too, is staying at the hotel with her mother; our Frenchman is somewhere in the house, too. The footman calls him 'Monsieur le Comte'. Mlle Blanche's mother is called 'Madame la Comtesse'; well, who knows, they may be Comte and Comtesse.

I felt sure that M. le Comte would not recognise me when we assembled at dinner. The General, of course, would not have thought of introducing us or even saying a word to him on my behalf; and M. le Comte has been in Russia himself, and knows what is called an *uchitel* is very small fry. He knows me very well, however. But I must confess I made my appearance at dinner unbidden; I fancy the General forgot to give orders, or else he would certainly have sent me to dine at the *table d'hôte*. I came of my own accord, so that the General looked at me with astonishment. Kind-hearted Marya Filippovna immediately made a place for me; but my meeting with Mr Astley saved the situation, and I could not help seeming to belong to the party.

I met this strange Englishman for the first time in the train in Prussia, where we sat opposite to one another, when I was travelling to join the family; then I came across him as I was going into France, and then again in Switzerland: in the course of that fortnight twice – and now I suddenly met him in Roulettenburg. I never met a man so shy in my life. He is stupidly shy and, of course, is aware of it himself, for he is by no means stupid. He is very sweet and gentle, however. I drew him into talk at our first meeting in Prussia. He told me that he had been that summer at North Cape, and that he was very anxious to visit the fair at Nizhni Novgorod. I don't know how he made acquaintance with the General; I believe that he is hopelessly in love with Polina. When she came in he glowed like a sunset. He was very glad that I was sitting beside him at the table and seemed already to look upon me as his bosom friend.

At dinner the Frenchman gave himself airs in an extraordinary way; he was nonchalant and majestic with everyone. In Moscow, I remember, he used to blow soap bubbles. He talked a great deal about finance and Russian politics. The General sometimes ventured to contradict, but discreetly, and only so far as he could without too great loss of dignity.

I was in a strange mood; of course, before we were half through dinner I had asked myself my usual invariable question: 'Why I went on dancing attendance on this General, and had not left them long ago?' From time to time I glanced at Polina Alexandrovna. She took no notice of me whatever. It ended by my flying into a rage and making up my mind to be rude.

I began by suddenly, apropos of nothing, breaking in on the conversation in a loud voice. What I longed to do above all things was to be abusive to the Frenchman. I turned round to the General and very loudly and distinctly, I believe, interrupted him. I observed that this summer it was utterly impossible for a

Russian to dine at *table d'hôte*. The General turned upon me an astonished stare.

'If you are a self-respecting man,' I went on, 'you will certainly be inviting abuse and must put up with affronts to your dignity. In Paris, on the Rhine, even in Switzerland, there are so many little Poles, and French people who sympathise with them, that there's no chance for a Russian to utter a word.'

I spoke in French. The General looked at me in amazement. I don't know whether he was angry or simply astonished at my so forgetting myself.

'It seems someone gave you a lesson,' said the Frenchman carelessly and contemptuously.

'I had a row for the first time with a Pole in Paris,' I answered; 'then with a French officer who took the Pole's part. And then some of the French came over to my side when I told them how I tried to spit in Monseigneur's coffee.'

'Spit?' asked the General, with dignified perplexity, and he even looked about him aghast.

The Frenchman scanned me mistrustfully.

'Just so,' I answered. 'After feeling convinced for two whole days that I might have to pay a brief visit to Rome about our business, I went to the office of the Papal Embassy to get my passport *viséed*. There I was met by a little abbé, a dried-up little man of about fifty, with a frost-bitten expression. After listening to me politely, but extremely dryly, he asked me to wait a little. Though I was in a hurry, of course I sat down to wait, and took up *L'Opinion Nationale* and began reading a horribly abusive attack on Russia. Meanwhile, I heard someone in the next room ask to see Monseigneur; I saw my abbé bow to him. I addressed the same request to him again; he asked me to wait – more dryly than ever. A little later someone else entered, a stranger, but on business, some Austrian; he was listened to and at once conducted upstairs. Then I felt very much vexed; I got up, went to the abbé and said resolutely that as Monseigneur was receiving, he might settle my business, too. At once the abbé drew back in great surprise. It was beyond his comprehension that an insignificant Russian should dare to put himself on a level with Monseigneur's guests. As though delighted to have an opportunity of insulting me, he looked me up and down, and shouted in the most insolent tone:

"Can you really suppose that Monseigneur is going to leave his coffee on your account?" Then I shouted, too, but more loudly than he: "Let me tell you I'm ready to spit in your Monseigneur's coffee! If you don't finish with my passport this minute, I'll go to him in person."

' "What! When the Cardinal is sitting with him!" cried the abbé, recoiling from me with horror, and, flinging wide his arms, he stood like a cross, with an air of being ready to die rather than let me pass.

'Then I answered him that "I was a heretic and a barbarian, *que je suis hérétique et barbare*", and that I cared nothing for all these Archbishops, Cardinals, Monseigneurs and all of them. In short, I showed I was not going to give way. The abbé looked at me with uneasy ill-humour, then snatched my passport and carried it upstairs. A minute later it had been *viséed*. Here, wouldn't you like to see it?' I took out the passport and showed the Roman *visé*.

'Well, I must say . . . ' the General began.

'What saved you was saying that you were a heretic and barbarian,' the Frenchman observed, with a smile. '*Celà n'était pas si bête.*'

'Why, am I to model myself upon our Russians here? They sit, not daring to open their lips, and almost ready to deny they are Russians. In Paris, anyway in my hotel, they began to treat me much more attentively when I told everyone about my passage-at-arms with the abbé. The fat Polish *pan*, the person most antagonistic to me at *table d'hôte*, sank into the background. The Frenchmen did not even resent it when I told them that I had, two years previously, seen a man at whom, in 1812, a French *chasseur* had shot simply in order to discharge his gun. The man was at that time a child of ten, and his family had not succeeded in leaving Moscow.

'That's impossible,' the Frenchman boiled up; 'a French soldier would not fire at a child!'

'Yet it happened,' I answered. 'I was told it by a most respectable captain on the retired list, and I saw the scar on his cheek from the bullet myself.'

The Frenchman began talking rapidly and at great length. The General began to support him, but I recommended him to read, for instance, passages in the *Notes* of General Perovsky, who was a prisoner in the hands of the French in 1812. At last Marya Filippovna began talking of something else to change the conversation.

The General was very much displeased with me, for the Frenchman and I had almost begun shouting at one another. But I fancy my dispute with the Frenchman pleased Mr Astley very much. Getting up from the table, he asked me to have a glass of wine with him.

In the evening I duly succeeded in getting a quarter of an hour's talk with Polina Alexandrovna. Our conversation took place when we were all out for a walk. We all went into the park by the Casino. Polina sat down on a seat facing the fountain, and let Nadenka play with some children not far from her. I, too, let Misha run off to the fountain, and we were at last left alone.

We began, of course, at first with business. Polina simply flew into a rage when I gave her only seven hundred guldens. She had reckoned positively on my pawning her diamonds in Paris for two thousand guldens, if not more.

'I must have money, come what may,' she said. 'I must get it or I am lost.'

I began asking her what had happened during my absence.

'Nothing, but the arrival of two pieces of news from Petersburg: first that Granny was very ill, and then, two days later, that she seemed to be dying. The news came from Timofey Petrovitch,' added Polina, 'and he's a trustworthy man. We are expecting every day to hear news of the end.'

'So you are all in suspense here?' I asked.

'Of course, all of us, and all the time; we've been hoping for nothing else for the last six months.'

'And are *you* hoping for it?' I asked.

'Why, I'm no relation. I am only the General's step-daughter. But I am sure she will remember me in her will.'

'I fancy you'll get a great deal,' I said emphatically.

'Yes, she was fond of me; but what makes *you* think so?'

'Tell me,' I answered with a question, 'our *marquis* is initiated into all our secrets, it seems?'

'But why are you interested in that?' asked Polina, looking at me dryly and austerely.

'I should think so; if I'm not mistaken, the General has already succeeded in borrowing from him.'

'You guess very correctly.'

'Well, would he have lent the money if he had not known about your "granny"? Did you notice at dinner, three times speaking of her, he called her "granny". What intimate and friendly relations!'

'Yes, you are right. As soon as he knows that I have come into something by the will, he will pay his addresses to me at once. That is what you wanted to know, was it?'

'He will only begin to pay you his addresses? I thought he had been doing that for a long time.'

'You know perfectly well that he hasn't!' Polina said, with anger. 'Where did you meet the Englishman?' she added, after a minute's silence.

'I knew you would ask about him directly.'

I told her of my previous meetings with Mr Astley on my journey.

'He is shy and given to falling in love, and, of course, he's fallen in love with you already.'

'Yes, he's in love with me,' answered Polina.

'And, of course, he's ten times as rich as the Frenchman. Why, is it certain that the Frenchman has anything? Isn't that open to doubt?'

'No, it is not. He has a château of some sort. The General has spoken of that positively. Well, are you satisfied?'

'If I were in your place I should certainly marry the Englishman.'

'Why?' asked Polina.

'The Frenchman is better looking, but he is nastier; and the Englishman, besides being honest, is ten times as rich,' I snapped out.

'Yes, but on the other hand, the Frenchman is a *marquis* and clever,' she answered, in the most composed manner.

'But is it true?' I went on, in the same way.

'It certainly is.'

Polina greatly disliked my questions, and I saw that she was trying to make me angry by her tone and the strangeness of her answers. I said as much to her at once.

'Well, it really amuses me to see you in such a rage. You must pay for the very fact of my allowing you to ask such questions and make such suppositions.'

'I certainly consider myself entitled to ask you any sort of question,' I answered calmly, 'just because I am prepared to pay any price you like for it, and I set no value at all on my life now.'

Polina laughed.

'You told me last time at the Schlangenberg that you were prepared, at a word from me, to throw yourself head foremost from the rock, and it is a thousand feet high, I believe. Some day I shall utter that word, solely in order to see how you will pay the price, and, trust me, I won't give way. You are hateful to me, just because I've allowed you to take such liberties, and even more hateful because you are so necessary to me. But so long as you are necessary to me, I must take care of you.'

She began getting up. She spoke with irritation. Of late she had always ended every conversation with me in anger and irritation, real anger.

'Allow me to ask you, what about Mlle Blanche?' I asked, not liking to let her go without explanation.

'You know all about Mlle Blanche. Nothing more has happened since. Mlle Blanche will, no doubt, be Madame la Générale, that is, if the rumour of Granny's death is confirmed, of course, for Mlle Blanche and her mother and her cousin twice removed – the Marquis – all know very well that we are ruined.'

'And is the General hopelessly in love?'

'That's not the point now. Listen and remember: take these seven hundred florins and go and play. Win me as much as you can at roulette; I must have money now, come what may.'

Saying this, she called Nadenka and went into the Casino, where she joined the rest of the party. I turned into the first path to the left, wondering and reflecting. I felt as though I had had a blow on the head after the command to go and play roulette. Strange to say, I had plenty to think about, but I was completely absorbed in analysing the essential nature of my feeling towards Polina. It was true I had been more at ease during that fortnight's absence than I was now on the day of my return, though on the journey I had been as melancholy and restless as a madman, and at moments had even seen her in my dreams. Once, waking up in the train (in Switzerland), I began talking aloud, I believe, with Polina, which amused all the passengers in the carriage with me. And once more now I asked myself the question: 'Do I love her?' and again I could not answer it, or, rather, I answered for the hundredth time that I hated her. Yes, she was hateful to me. There were moments (on every occasion at the end of our talks) when I would have given my life to strangle her! I swear if it had been possible on the spot to plunge a sharp knife in her bosom, I believe I should have snatched it up with relish. And yet I swear by all that's sacred that if at the Schlangenberg, at the fashionable peak, she really had said to me, 'Throw yourself down', I should have thrown myself down at once, also with positive relish. I knew that. In one way or another it must be settled. All this she understood wonderfully well, and the idea that I knew, positively and distinctly, how utterly beyond my reach she was, how utterly impossible my mad dreams were of fulfilment – that thought, I am convinced, afforded her extraordinary satisfaction; if not, how could she, cautious and intelligent as she was, have been on such intimate and open terms with me? I believe she had hitherto looked on me as that empress of ancient times looked on the slave before whom she did not mind undressing because she did not regard him as a human being. Yes, often she did not regard me as a human being!

I had her commission, however, to win at roulette, at all costs. I had no time to consider why must I play, and why such haste, and what new scheme was hatching in that ever-calculating brain. Moreover, it was evident that during that fortnight new facts had arisen of which I had no idea yet. I must discover all that and get to the bottom of it and as quickly as possible. But there was no time now; I must go to roulette.

CHAPTER TWO

I confess it was disagreeable to me. Though I had made up my mind that I would play, I had not proposed to play for other people. It rather threw me out of my reckoning, and I went into the gambling saloon with very disagreeable feelings. From the first glance I disliked everything in it. I cannot endure the flunkeyishness of the newspapers of the whole world, and especially our Russian papers, in which, almost every spring, the journalists write articles upon two things: first, on the extraordinary magnificence and luxury of the gambling saloons on the Rhine, and secondly, on the heaps of gold which are said to lie on the tables. They are not paid for it; it is simply done from disinterested obsequiousness. There was no sort of magnificence in these trashy rooms, and not only were there no piles of gold lying on the table, but there was hardly any gold at all. No doubt some time, in the course of the season, some eccentric person, either an Englishman or an Asiatic of some sort, a Turk, perhaps (as it was that summer), would suddenly turn up and lose or win immense sums; all the others play for paltry guldens, and on an average there is very little money lying on the tables.

As soon as I went into the gambling saloon (for the first time in my life), I could not for some time make up my mind to play. There was a crush besides. If I had been alone, even then, I believe, I should soon have gone away and not have begun playing. I confess my heart was beating and I was not cool. I knew for certain, and had made up my mind long before, that I should not leave Roulettenburg unchanged, that some radical and fundamental change would take place in my destiny; so it must be and so it would be. Ridiculous as it may be that I should expect so much for myself from roulette, yet I consider even more ridiculous the conventional opinion accepted by all that it is stupid and absurd to expect anything from gambling. And why should gambling be worse than any other means of making money – for instance, commerce? It is true that only one out of a hundred wins, but what is that to me?

In any case I determined to look about me first and not to begin anything in earnest that evening. If anything did happen that evening it would happen by chance and be something slight, and I staked my money accordingly. Besides, I had to study the game; for, in spite of the thousand descriptions of roulette which I had read so eagerly, I understood absolutely nothing of its working, until I saw it myself.

In the first place it all struck me as so dirty, somehow, morally horrid and dirty. I am not speaking at all of the greedy, uneasy faces which by dozens, even by hundreds, crowd round the gambling tables. I see absolutely nothing dirty in the wish to win as quickly and as much as possible. I always thought very stupid the answer of that fat and prosperous moralist, who replied to someone's excuse 'that he played for a very small stake', 'So much the worse, it is such petty covetousness.' As though covetousness were not exactly the same, whether on a big scale or a petty one. It is a matter of proportion. What is paltry to Rothschild is wealth to me, and as for profits and winnings, people, not only at roulette, but everywhere, do nothing but try to gain or squeeze something out of one another. Whether profits or gains are nasty is a different question. But I am not solving that question here. Since I was myself possessed by an intense desire of winning, I felt as I went into the hall all this covetousness, and all this covetous filth if you like, in a sense congenial and convenient. It is most charming when people do not stand on ceremony with one another, but act openly and above-board. And, indeed, why deceive oneself? Gambling is a most foolish and imprudent pursuit! What was particularly ugly at first sight, in all the rabble round the roulette table, was the respect they paid to that pursuit, the solemnity and even reverence with which they all crowded round the tables. That is why a sharp distinction is drawn here between the kind of game that is *mauvais genre* and the kind that is permissible to well-bred people. There are two sorts of gambling: one the gentlemanly sort: the other the plebeian, mercenary sort, the game played by all sorts of riff-raff. The distinction is sternly observed here, and how contemptible this distinction really is! A gentleman may stake, for instance, five or ten louis d'or, rarely more; he may, however, stake as much as a thousand francs if he is very rich; but only for the sake of the play, simply for amusement, that is, simply to look on at the process of winning or of losing, but must on no account display an interest in winning. If he wins, he may laugh aloud, for instance; may make a remark to one of the bystanders; he may even put down another stake, and may even double it, but solely from curiosity, for the sake of watching and calculating the chances, and not from the plebeian desire to win. In fact, he must look on all gambling, roulette, *trente et quarante*, as nothing else than a pastime got up entirely for his amusement. He must not even suspect the greed for gain and the shifty dodges on which the bank depends. It would be extremely good form, too, if he should imagine that all the other gamblers, all the rabble, trembling over a gulden, were rich men and gentlemen like himself and were playing simply for their diversion and amusement. This complete ignorance of reality and innocent view of people would be, of course, extremely aristocratic. I have seen many mammas push forward their daughters, innocent and elegant Misses of fifteen and sixteen, and, giving them some gold coins, teach them how to play. The young lady wins or loses, invariably smiles and walks away, very well satisfied. Our General went up to the table with solid dignity; a flunkey rushed to hand him a chair, but he ignored the flunkey; he, very slowly and deliberately, took out his purse, very slowly and deliberately took three hundred francs in gold from his purse, staked them on the black, and won. He did not pick up his winnings, but left them on the table. Black turned up again; he didn't pick up his winnings that time either; and when, the third time, red turned up, he lost at once twelve hundred francs. He walked away with a smile and kept up his dignity. I am positive he was raging inwardly, and if the stake had been two or three times as much he would not have kept up his dignity but would have betrayed his feelings. A Frenchman did, however, before my eyes, win and lose as much as thirty thousand francs with perfect gaiety and no sign of emotion. A real gentleman should not show excitement even if he loses his whole fortune. Money ought to be so much below his gentlemanly dignity as to be scarcely worth noticing. Of course, it would have been extremely aristocratic not to notice the sordidness of all the rabble and all the surroundings. Sometimes, however, the opposite pose is no less aristocratic – to notice – that is, to look about one, even, perhaps, to stare through a lorgnette at the rabble; though always taking the rabble and the sordidness as nothing else but a diversion of a sort, as though it were a performance got up for the amusement of gentlemen. One may be jostled in that crowd, but one must look about one with complete conviction that one is oneself a spectator and that one is in no sense part of it. Though, again, to look very attentively is not quite the thing; that, again, would not be gentlemanly because, in any case, the spectacle does not deserve much, or close, attention. And, in fact, few spectacles do deserve a gentleman's close attention. And yet it seemed to me that all this was deserving of very close attention, especially for one who had come not only to observe it, but sincerely and genuinely reckoned himself as one of the rabble. As for my hidden moral convictions, there is no place for them, of course, in my present reasonings. Let that be enough for the present. I speak to relieve my conscience. But I notice one thing: that of late it has become horribly repugnant to me to test my thoughts and actions by any moral standard whatever. I was guided by something different . . .

The rabble certainly did play very sordidly. I am ready to believe, indeed, that a great deal of the most ordinary thieving goes on at the gaming table. The croupiers who sit at each end of the table look at the stakes and reckon the winnings; they have a great deal to do. They are rabble, too! For the most part they are French. However, I was watching and observing, not with the object of describing roulette. I kept a sharp look out for my own sake, so that I might know how to behave in the future. I noticed, for instance, that nothing was more common than for someone to stretch out his hand and snatch what one had won. A dispute would begin, often an uproar, and a nice job one would have to find witnesses and to prove that it was one's stake!

At first it was all an inexplicable puzzle to me. All I could guess and distinguish was that the stakes were on the numbers, on odd and even, and on the colours. I made up my mind to risk a hundred guldens of Polina Alexandrovna's money. The thought that I was not playing for myself seemed to throw me out of my reckoning. It was an extremely unpleasant feeling, and I wanted to be rid of it as soon as possible. I kept feeling that by beginning for Polina I should break my own luck. Is it impossible to approach the gambling table without becoming infected with superstition? I began by taking out five friedrichs d'or (fifty gulden) and putting them on the even. The wheel went round and thirteen turned up – I had lost. With a sickly feeling I staked another five friedrich d'or on red, simply in order to settle the matter and go away. Red turned up. I staked all the ten friedrichs d'or – red turned up again. I staked all the money again on the same, and again red turned up. On receiving forty friedrichs d'or I staked twenty upon the twelve middle figures, not knowing what would come of it. I was paid three times my stake. In this way from ten friedrichs d'or I had all at once eighty. I was overcome by a strange, unusual feeling which was so unbearable that I made up my mind to go away. It seemed to me that I should not have been playing at all like that if I had been playing for myself. I staked the whole eighty friedrichs d'or, however, on even. This time four turned up; another eighty friedrichs d'or was poured out to me, and, gathering up the whole heap of a hundred and sixty friedrichs d'or, I set off to find Polina Alexandrovna.

They were all walking somewhere in the park and I only succeeded in seeing her after supper. This time the Frenchman was not of the party, and the General unbosomed himself. Among other things he thought fit to observe to me that he would not wish to see me at the gambling tables. It seemed to him that it would compromise him if I were to lose too much: 'But even if you were to win a very large sum I should be compromised, too,' he added significantly. 'Of course, I have no right to dictate your actions, but you must admit yourself . . . ' At this point he broke off, as his habit was. I answered, dryly, that I had very little money, and so I could not lose very conspicuously, even if I did play. Going upstairs to my room I succeeded in handing Polina her winnings, and told her that I would not play for her another time.

'Why not?' she asked, in a tremor.

'Because I want to play on my own account,' I answered, looking at her with surprise; 'and it hinders me.'

'Then you will continue in your conviction that roulette is your only escape and salvation?' she asked ironically.

I answered very earnestly, that I did; that as for my confidence that I should win, it might be absurd; I was ready to admit it, but that I wanted to be let alone.

Polina Alexandrovna began insisting I should go halves with her in today's winnings, and was giving me eighty friedrichs d'or, suggesting that I should go on playing on those terms. I refused the half, positively and finally, and told her that I could not play for other people, not because I didn't want to, but because I should certainly lose.

'Yet I, too,' she said, pondering, 'stupid as it seems, am building all my hopes on roulette. And so you must go on playing, sharing with me, and – of course – you will.'

At this point she walked away, without listening to further objections.

CHAPTER THREE

Yet all yesterday she did not say a single word to me about playing, and avoided speaking to me altogether. Her manner to me remained unchanged: the same absolute carelessness on meeting me; there was even a shade of contempt and dislike. Altogether she did not care to conceal her aversion; I noticed that. In spite of that she did not conceal from me, either, that I was in some way necessary to her and that she was keeping me for some purpose. A strange relation had grown up between us, incomprehensible to me in many ways when I considered her pride and haughtiness with everyone. She knew, for instance, that I loved her madly, even allowed me to speak of my passion; and, of course, she could not have shown greater contempt for me than by allowing me to speak of my passion without hindrance or restriction. It was as much as to say that she thought so little of my feelings that she did not care in the least what I talked about to her and what I felt for her. She had talked a great deal about her own affairs before, but had never been completely open. What is more, there was this peculiar refinement in her contempt for me: she would know, for instance, that I was aware of some circumstance in her life, or knew of some matter that greatly concerned her, or she would tell me herself something of her circumstances, if to forward her objects she had to make use of me in some way, as a slave or an errand-boy; but she would always tell me only so much as a man employed on her errands need know, and if I did not know the whole chain of events, if she saw herself how worried and anxious I was over her worries and anxieties, she never deigned to comfort me by giving me her full confidence as a friend; though she often made use of me for commissions that were not only troublesome, but dangerous, so that to my thinking she was bound to be open with me. Was it worth her while, indeed, to trouble herself about my feelings, about my being worried, and perhaps three times as much worried and tormented by her anxieties and failures as she was herself?

I knew of her intention to play roulette three weeks before. She had even warned me that I should have to play for her, and it would be improper for her to play herself. From the tone of her words, I noticed even then that she had serious anxieties, and was not actuated simply by a desire for money. What is money to her for its own sake? She must have some object, there must be some circumstance at which I can only guess, but of which so far I have no knowledge. Of course, the humiliation and the slavery in which she held me might have made it possible for me (it often does) to question her coarsely and bluntly. Seeing that in her eyes I was a slave and utterly insignificant, there was nothing for her to be offended at in my coarse curiosity. But the fact is that though she allowed me to ask questions, she did not answer them, and sometimes did not notice them at all. That was the position between us.

A great deal was said yesterday about a telegram which had been sent off four days before, and to which no answer had been received. The General was evidently upset and preoccupied. It had, of course, something to do with Granny. The Frenchman was troubled, too. Yesterday, for instance, after dinner, they had a long, serious talk. The Frenchman's tone to all of us was unusually high and mighty, quite in the spirit of the saying: 'Seat a pig at table and it will put its feet on it.' Even with Polina he was casual to the point of rudeness; at the same time he gladly took part in the walks in the public gardens and in the rides and drives into the country. I had long known some of the circumstances that bound the Frenchman to the General: they had made plans for establishing a factory together in Russia; I don't know whether their project had fallen through, or whether it was being discussed. Moreover, I had by chance come to know part of a family secret. The Frenchman had actually, in the previous year, come to the General's rescue, and had given him thirty thousand roubles to make up a deficit of Government monies missing when he resigned his duties. And, of course, the General is in his grip; but now the principal person in the whole business is Mlle Blanche; about that I am sure I'm not mistaken.

What is Mlle Blanche? Here among us it is said that she is a distinguished Frenchwoman, with a colossal fortune and a mother accompanying her. It is known, too, that she is some sort of relation of our Marquis, but a very distant one: a cousin, or something of the sort. I am told that before I went to Paris, the Frenchman and Mlle Blanche were on much more ceremonious, were, so to speak, on a more delicate and refined footing; now their acquaintance, their friendship and relationship, was of a rather coarse and more intimate character. Perhaps our prospects seemed to them so poor that they did not think it very necessary to stand on ceremony and keep up appearances with us. I noticed even the day before yesterday how Mr Astley looked at Mlle Blanche and her mother. It seemed to me that he knew them. It even seemed to me that our Frenchman had met Mr Astley before. Mr Astley, however, is so shy, so reserved and silent, that one can be almost certain of him – he won't wash dirty linen in public. Anyway, the Frenchman barely bows to him and scarcely looks at him, so he is not afraid of him. One can understand that, perhaps, but why does Mlle Blanche not look at him either? Especially when the Marquis let slip yesterday in the course of conversation – I don't remember in what connection – that Mr Astley had a colossal fortune and that he – the Marquis – knew this for a fact; at that point Mlle Blanche might well have looked at Mr Astley. Altogether the General was uneasy. One can understand what a telegram announcing his aunt's death would mean!

Though I felt sure Polina was, apparently for some object, avoiding a conversation with me, I assumed a cold and indifferent air: I kept thinking that before long she would come to me of herself. But both today and yesterday I concentrated my attention principally on Mlle Blanche. Poor General! He is completely done for! To fall in love at fifty-five with such a violent passion is a calamity, of course! When one takes into consideration the fact that he is a widower, his children, the ruin of his estate, his debts, and, finally, the woman it is his lot to fall in love with. Mlle Blanche is handsome. But I don't know if I shall be understood if I say that she has a face of the type of which one might feel frightened. I, anyway, have always been afraid of women of that sort. She is probably five-and-twenty. She is well grown and broad, with sloping shoulders; she has a magnificent throat and bosom; her complexion is swarthy yellow. Her hair is as black as Indian ink, and she has a tremendous lot of it, enough to make two ordinary coiffures. Her eyes are black with yellowish whites; she has an insolent look in her eyes; her teeth are very white; her lips are always painted; she smells of musk. She dresses effectively, richly and with *chic*, but with much taste. Her hands and feet are exquisite. Her voice is a husky contralto. Sometimes she laughs, showing all her teeth, but her usual expression is a silent and impudent stare – before Polina and Marya Filippovna, anyway (there is a strange rumour that Marya Filippovna is going back to Russia). I fancy that Mlle Blanche has had no sort of education. Possibly she is not even intelligent; but, on the other hand, she is striking and she is artful. I fancy her life has not passed without adventures. If one is to tell the whole truth, it is quite possible that the Marquis is no relation of hers at all, and that her mother is not her mother. But there is evidence that in Berlin, where we went with them, her mother and she had some decent acquaintances. As for the Marquis himself, though I still doubt his being a marquis, yet the fact that he is received in decent society – among Russians, for instance, in Moscow, and in some places in Germany – is not open to doubt. I don't know what he is in France. They say he has a château.

I thought that a great deal would have happened during this fortnight, and yet I don't know if anything decisive has been said between Mlle Blanche and the General. Everything depends on our fortune, however; that is, whether the General can show them plenty of money. If, for instance, news were to come that Granny were not dead, I am convinced that Mlle Blanche would vanish at once. It surprises and amuses me to see what a gossip I've become. Oh! how I loathe it all! How delighted I should be to drop it all, and them all! But can I leave Polina, can I give up spying round her? Spying, of course, is low, but what do I care about that?

I was interested in Mr Astley, too, today and yesterday. Yes, I am convinced he's in love with Polina. It is curious and absurd how much may be expressed by the eyes of a modest and painfully chaste man, moved by love, at the very time when the man would gladly sink into the earth rather than express or betray anything by word or glance. Mr Astley very often meets us on our walks. He takes off his hat and passes by, though, of course, he is dying to join us. If he is invited to do so, he immediately refuses. At places where we rest – at the Casino, by the bandstand, or before the fountain – he always stands somewhere not far from our seat; and wherever we may be – in the park, in the wood, or on the Schlangenberg – one has only to glance round, to look about one, and somewhere, either in the nearest path or behind the bushes, Mr Astley's head appears. I fancy he is looking for an opportunity to have a conversation with me apart. This morning we met and exchanged a couple of words. He sometimes speaks very abruptly. Without saying 'good-morning', he began by blurting out: 'Oh, Mlle Blanche! . . . I have seen a great many women like Mlle Blanche!'

He paused, looking at me significantly. What he meant to say by that I don't know. For on my asking what he meant, he shook his head with a sly smile, and added, 'Oh, well, that's how it is. Is Mlle Pauline very fond of flowers?'

'I don't know; I don't know at all,' I answered.

'What? You don't even know that!' he cried, with the utmost amazement.

'I don't know; I haven't noticed at all,' I repeated, laughing.

'H'm! That gives me a queer idea.'

Then he shook his head and walked away. He looked pleased, though. We talked the most awful French together.

CHAPTER FOUR

Today has been an absurd, grotesque, ridiculous day. Now it is eleven o'clock at night. I am sitting in my little cupboard of a room, recalling it. It began with my having to go to roulette to play for Polina Alexandrovna. I took the hundred and sixty friedrichs d'or, but on two conditions: first, that I would not go halves – that is, if I won I would take nothing for myself; and secondly, that in the evening Polina should explain to me why she needed to win, and how much money. I can't, in any case, suppose that it is simply for the sake of money. Evidently the money is needed, and as quickly as possible, for some particular object. She promised to explain, and I set off. In the gambling hall the crowd was awful. How insolent and how greedy they all were! I forced my way into the middle and stood near the croupier; then I began timidly experimenting, staking two or three coins at a time. Meanwhile, I kept quiet and looked on; it seemed to me that calculation meant very little, and had by no means the importance attributed to it by some players. They sit with papers before them scrawled over in pencil, note the strokes, reckon, deduce the chances, calculate, finally stake and – lose exactly as we simple mortals who play without calculations. On the other hand, I drew one conclusion which I believe to be correct: that is, though there is no system, there really is a sort of order in the sequence of casual chances – and that, of course, is very strange. For instance, it happens that after the twelve middle numbers come the twelve later numbers; twice, for instance, it turns up on the twelve last numbers and passes to the twelve first numbers. After falling on the twelve first numbers, it passes again to numbers in the middle third, turns up three or four times in succession on numbers between thirteen and twenty-four, and again passes to numbers in the last third; then, after turning up two numbers between twenty-five and thirty-six, it passes to a number among the first twelve, turns up once again on a number among the first third, and again passes for three strokes in succession to the middle numbers, and in that way goes on for an hour and a half or two hours. One, three and two – one, three and two. It's very amusing. One day or one morning, for instance, red will be followed by black and back again almost without any order, shifting every minute, so that it never turns up red or black for more than two or three strokes in succession. Another day, or another evening, there will be nothing but red over and over again, turning up, for instance, more than twenty-two times in succession, and so for a whole day. A great deal of this was explained to me by Mr Astley, who spent the whole morning at the tables, but did not once put down a stake.

As for me, I lost every farthing very quickly. I staked straight off twenty friedrichs d'or on even and won, staked again and again won, and went on like that two or three times. I imagine I must have had about four hundred friedrichs d'or in my hands in about five minutes. At that point I ought to have gone away, but a strange sensation rose up in me, a sort of defiance of fate, a desire to challenge it, to put out my tongue at it. I laid down the largest stake allowed – four thousand gulden – and lost it. Then, getting hot, I pulled out all I had left, staked it on the same number, and lost again, after which I walked away from the table as though I were stunned. I could not even grasp what had happened to me, and did not tell Polina Alexandrovna of my losing till just before dinner. I spent the rest of the day sauntering in the park.

At dinner I was again in an excited state, just as I had been three days before. The Frenchman and Mlle Blanche were dining with us again. It appeared that Mlle Blanche had been in the gambling hall that morning and had witnessed my exploits. This time she addressed me, it seemed, somewhat attentively. The Frenchman set to work more directly, and asked me: was it my own money I had lost? I fancy he suspects Polina. In fact, there is something behind it. I lied at once and said it was.

The General was extremely surprised. Where had I got such a sum? I explained that I had begun with ten friedrichs d'or, that after six or seven times staking successfully on equal chances I had five or six hundred gulden, and that afterwards I had lost it all on two turns.

All that, of course, sounded probable. As I explained this I looked at Polina, but I could distinguish nothing from her face. She let me lie, however, and did not set it right; from this I concluded that I had to lie and conceal that I was in collaboration with her. In any case, I thought to myself, she is bound to give me an explanation, and promised me this morning to reveal something.

I expected the General would have made some remark to me, but he remained mute; I noticed, however, signs of disturbance and uneasiness in his face. Possibly in his straitened circumstances it was simply painful to him to hear that such a pile of gold had come into, and within a quarter of an hour had passed out of, the hands of such a reckless fool as me.

I suspect that he had a rather hot encounter with the Frenchman yesterday. They were shut up together talking for a long time. The Frenchman went away seeming irritated, and came to see the General again early this morning – probably to continue the conversation of the previous day.

Hearing what I had lost, the Frenchman observed bitingly, even spitefully, that one ought to have more sense. He added – I don't know why – that though a great many Russians gamble, Russians were not, in his opinion, well qualified even for gambling.

'To my mind,' said I, 'roulette is simply made for Russians.'

And when at my challenge the Frenchman laughed contemptuously, I observed that I was, of course, right, for to speak of the Russians as gamblers was abusing them far more than praising them, and so I might be believed.

'On what do you base your opinion?' asked the Frenchman.

'On the fact that the faculty of amassing capital has, with the progress of history, taken a place – and almost the foremost place – among the virtues and merits of the civilised man of the West. The Russian is not only incapable of amassing capital, but dissipates it in a reckless and unseemly way. Nevertheless we Russians need money, too,' I added, 'and consequently we are very glad and very eager to make use of such means as roulette, for instance, in which one can grow rich all at once, in two hours, without work. That's very fascinating to us; and since we play badly, recklessly, without taking trouble, we usually lose!'

'That's partly true,' observed the Frenchman complacently.

'No, it is not true, and you ought to be ashamed to speak like that of your country,' observed the General, sternly and impressively.

'Excuse me,' I answered. 'I really don't know which is more disgusting: Russian unseemliness or the German faculty of accumulation by honest toil.'

'What an unseemly idea!' exclaimed the General.

'What a Russian idea!' exclaimed the Frenchman.

I laughed; I had an intense desire to provoke them.

'Well, I should prefer to dwell all my life in a Kirgiz tent,' I cried, 'than bow down to the German idol.'

'What idol?' cried the General, beginning to be angry in earnest.

'The German faculty for accumulating wealth. I've not been here long, but yet all I have been able to observe and verify revolts my Tatar blood. My God! I don't want any such virtue! I succeeded yesterday in making a round of eight miles, and it's all exactly as in the edifying German picture-books: there is here in every house a *vater* horribly virtuous and extraordinarily honest – so honest that you are afraid to go near him. I can't endure honest people whom one is afraid to go near. Every such German *vater* has a family, and in the evening they read improving books aloud. Elms and chestnut trees rustle over the house. The sun is setting; there is a stork on the roof, and everything is extraordinarily practical and touching . . . Don't be angry, General; let me tell it in a touching style. I remember how my father used to read similar books to my mother and me under the lime trees in the garden . . . So I am in a position to judge. And in what complete bondage and submission every such family is here. They all work like oxen and all save money like Jews. Suppose the *vater* has saved up so many gulden and is reckoning on giving his son a trade or a bit of land; to do so, he gives his daughter no dowry, and she becomes an old maid. To do so, the youngest son is sold into bondage or into the army, and the money is added to the family capital. This is actually done here; I've been making enquiries. All this is done from nothing but honesty, from such intense honesty that the younger son who is sold believes that he is sold from nothing but honesty: and that is the ideal when the victim himself rejoices at being led to the sacrifice. What more? Why, the elder son is no better off: he has an Amalia and their hearts are united, but they can't be married because the pile of gulden is not large enough. They, too, wait with perfect morality and good faith, and go to the sacrifice with a smile. Amalia's cheeks grow thin and hollow. At last, in twenty years, their prosperity is increased; the gulden have been honestly and virtuously accumulating. The *vater* gives his blessing to the forty-year-old son and his Amalia of thirty-five, whose chest has grown hollow and whose nose has turned red . . . With that he weeps, reads them a moral sermon, and dies. The eldest son becomes himself a virtuous *vater* and begins the same story over again. In that way, in fifty or seventy years, the grandson of the first *vater* really has a considerable capital, and he leaves it to his son, and he to his, and he to his, till in five or six generations one of them is a Baron Rothschild or goodness knows who. Come, isn't that a majestic spectacle? A hundred or two hundred years of continuous toil, patience, intelligence, honesty, character, determination, prudence, the stork on the roof! What more do you want? Why, there's nothing loftier than that; and from that standpoint they are beginning to judge the whole world and to punish the guilty; that is, any who are ever so little unlike them. Well, so that's the point: I would rather waste my substance in the Russian style or grow rich at roulette. I don't care to be Goppe and Co. in five generations. I want money for myself, and I don't look upon myself as something subordinate to capital and necessary to it. I know that I have been talking awful nonsense, but, never mind, such are my convictions.'

'I don't know whether there is much truth in what you have been saying,' said the General thoughtfully, 'but I do know you begin to give yourself insufferable airs as soon as you are permitted to forget yourself in the least . . . '

As his habit was, he broke off without finishing. If our General began to speak of anything in the slightest degree more important than his ordinary everyday conversation, he never finished his sentences. The Frenchman listened carelessly with rather wide-open eyes; he had scarcely understood anything of what I had said. Polina gazed with haughty indifference. She seemed not to hear my words, or anything else that was said that day at table.

CHAPTER FIVE

She was unusually thoughtful, but directly we got up from table she bade me escort her for a walk. We took the children and went into the park towards the fountain.

As I felt particularly excited, I blurted out the crude and stupid question: why the Marquis des Grieux, our Frenchman, no longer escorted her when she went out anywhere, and did not even speak to her for days together.

'Because he is a rascal,' she answered me strangely.

I had never heard her speak like that of des Grieux, and I received it in silence, afraid to interpret her irritability.

'Have you noticed that he is not on good terms with the General today?'

'You want to know what is the matter?' she answered dryly and irritably. 'You know that the General is completely mortgaged to him; all his property is his, and if Granny doesn't die, the Frenchman will come into possession of everything that is mortgaged to him.'

'And is it true that everything is mortgaged? I had heard it, but I did not know that everything was.'

'To be sure it is.'

'Then farewell to Mlle Blanche,' said I. 'She won't be the General's wife, then! Do you know, it strikes me the General is so much in love that he may shoot himself if Mlle Blanche throws him over. It is dangerous to be so much in love at his age.'

'I fancy that something will happen to him, too,' Polina Alexandrovna observed musingly.

'And how splendid that would be!' I cried. 'They couldn't have shown more coarsely that she was only marrying him for his money! There's no regard for decency, even; there's no ceremony about it whatever. That's wonderful! And about Granny – could there be anything more comic and sordid than to be continually sending telegram after telegram: "Is she dead, is she dead?"? How do you like it, Polina Alexandrovna?'

'That's all nonsense,' she said, interrupting me with an air of disgust. 'I wonder at your being in such good spirits. What are you so pleased about? Surely not at having lost my money?'

'Why did you give it to me to lose? I told you I could not play for other people – especially for you! I obey you, whatever you order me to do, but I can't answer for the result. I warned you that nothing would come of it. Are you very much upset at losing so much money? What do you want so much for?'

'Why these questions?'

'Why, you promised to explain to me . . . Listen: I am absolutely convinced that when I begin playing for myself (and I've got twelve friedrichs d'or) I shall win. Then you can borrow as much from me as you like.'

She made a contemptuous grimace.

'Don't be angry with me for such a suggestion,' I went on. 'I am so deeply conscious that I am nothing beside you – that is, in your eyes – that you may even borrow money from me. Presents from me cannot insult you. Besides, I lost yours.'

She looked at me quickly, and seeing that I was speaking irritably and sarcastically, interrupted the conversation again.

'There's nothing of interest to you in my circumstances. If you want to know, I'm simply in debt. I've borrowed money and I wanted to repay it. I had the strange and mad idea that I should be sure to win here at the gambling table. Why I had the idea I can't understand, but I believed in it. Who knows, perhaps I believed it because no other alternative was left me.'

'Or because it was quite *necessary* you should win. It's exactly like a drowning man clutching at a straw. You will admit that if he were not drowning he would not look at a straw as a branch of a tree.'

Polina was surprised.

'Why,' she said, 'you were reckoning on the same thing yourself! A fortnight ago you said a great deal to me about your being absolutely convinced that you could win here at roulette, and tried to persuade me not to look upon you as mad; or were you joking then? But I remember you spoke so seriously that it was impossible to take it as a joke.'

'That's true,' I answered thoughtfully. 'I am convinced to this moment that I shall win. I confess you have led me now to wonder why my senseless and unseemly failure today has not left the slightest doubt in me. I am still fully convinced that as soon as I begin playing for myself I shall be certain to win.'

'Why are you so positive?'

'If you will have it – I don't know. I only know that I *must* win, that it is the only resource left me. Well, that's why, perhaps, I fancy I am bound to win.'

'Then you, too, absolutely *must* have it, since you are so fanatically certain?'

'I bet you think I'm not capable of feeling that I *must* have anything?'

'That's nothing to me,' Polina answered quietly and indifferently. 'Yes, if you like. I doubt whether anything troubles you in earnest. You may be troubled, but not in earnest. You are an unstable person, not to be relied on. What do you want money for? I could see nothing serious in the reasons you brought forward the other day.'

'By the way,' I interrupted, 'you said that you had to repay a debt. A fine debt it must be! To the Frenchman, I suppose?'

'What questions! You're particularly impertinent today. Are you drunk, perhaps?'

'You know that I consider myself at liberty to say anything to you, and sometimes ask you very candid questions. I repeat, I'm your slave, and one does not mind what one says to a slave, and cannot take offence at anything he says.'

'And I can't endure that "slave" theory of yours.'

'Observe that I don't speak of my slavery because I want to be your slave. I simply speak of it as a fact which doesn't depend on me in the least.'

'Tell me plainly, what do you want money for?'

'What do you want to know that for?'

'As you please,' she replied, with a proud movement of her head.

'You can't endure the "slave" theory, but insist on slavishness: "Answer and don't argue." So be it. Why do I want money? you ask. How can you ask? Money is everything!'

'I understand that, but not falling into such madness from wanting it! You, too, are growing frenzied, fatalistic. There must be something behind it, some special object. Speak without beating about the bush; I wish it.'

She seemed beginning to get angry, and I was awfully pleased at her questioning me with such heat.

'Of course there is an object,' I answered, 'but I don't know how to explain what it is. Nothing else but that with money I should become to you a different man, not a slave.'

'What? How will you manage that?'

'How shall I manage it? What, you don't even understand how I could manage to make you look at me as anything but a slave? Well, that's just what I don't care for, such surprise and incredulity!'

'You said this slavery was a pleasure to you. I thought it was myself.'

'You thought so!' I cried, with a strange enjoyment. 'Oh, how delightful such *naïveté* is from you! Oh, yes, yes, slavery to you is a pleasure. There is – there is a pleasure in the utmost limit of humiliation and insignificance!' I went on maundering. 'Goodness knows, perhaps there is in the knout when the knout lies on the back and tears the flesh . . . But I should perhaps like to enjoy another kind of enjoyment. Yesterday, in your presence, the General thought fit to read me a lecture for the seven hundred roubles a year which perhaps I may not receive from him after all. The Marquis des Grieux raises his eyebrows and stares at me without noticing me. And I, perhaps, have a passionate desire to pull the Marquis des Grieux by the nose in your presence!'

'That's the speech of a milksop. One can behave with dignity in any position. If there is a struggle, it is elevating, not humiliating.'

'That's straight out of a copybook! You simply take for granted that I don't know how to behave with dignity; that is, that perhaps I am a man of moral dignity, but that I don't know how to behave with dignity. You understand that that perhaps may be so. Yes, all Russians are like that; and do you know why? Because Russians are too richly endowed and many-sided to be able readily to evolve a code of manners. It is a question of good form. For the most part we Russians are so richly endowed that we need genius to evolve our code of manners. And genius is most often absent, for, indeed, it is a rarity at all times. It's only among the French, and perhaps some other Europeans, that the code of manners is so well defined that one may have an air of the utmost dignity and yet be a man of no moral dignity whatever. That's why good form means so much with them. A Frenchman will put up with an insult, a real, moral insult, without blinking, but he wouldn't endure a flip on the nose for anything, because that is a breach of the received code, sanctified for ages. That's why our Russian young ladies have such a weakness for Frenchmen, that their manners are so good. Though, to my thinking, they have no manners at all; it's simply the cock in them; *le coq gaulois*. I can't understand it, though; I'm not a woman. Perhaps cocks are nice. And, in fact, I've been talking nonsense, and you don't stop me. You must stop me more often. When I talk to you I long to tell you everything, everything, everything. I am oblivious of all good manners. I'll even admit that I have no manners, no moral qualities either. I tell you that. I don't even worry my head about moral qualities of any sort; everything has come to a standstill in me now; you know why. I have not one human idea in my head. For a long time past I've known nothing that has gone on in the world, either in Russia or here. Here I've been through Dresden, and I don't remember what Dresden was like. You know what has swallowed me up. As I have no hope whatever and am nothing in your eyes, I speak openly: I see nothing but you everywhere, and all the rest is naught to me. Why and how I love you I don't know. Perhaps you are not at all nice really, you know. Fancy! I don't know whether you are good or not, even to look at. You certainly have not a good heart; your mind may very well be ignoble.'

'Perhaps that's how it is you reckon on buying me with money,' she said, 'because you don't believe in my sense of honour.'

'When did I reckon on buying you with money?' I cried.

'You have been talking till you don't know what you are saying. If you don't think of buying me, you think of buying my respect with your money.'

'Oh no, that's not it at all. I told you it was difficult for me to explain. You are overwhelming me. Don't be angry with my chatter. You know why you can't be angry with me: I'm simply mad. Though I really don't care, even if you are angry. When I am upstairs in my little garret I have only to remember and imagine the rustle of your dress, and I am ready to bite off my hands. And what are you angry with me for? For calling myself your slave? Make use of my being your slave, make use of it, make use of it!

Do you know that I shall kill you one day? I shall kill you not because I shall cease to love you or be jealous, I shall simply kill you because I have an impulse to devour you. You laugh . . . '

'I'm not laughing,' she answered wrathfully. 'I order you to be silent.'

She stood still, almost breathless with anger. Upon my word, I don't know whether she was handsome, but I always liked to look at her when she stood facing me like that, and so I often liked to provoke her anger. Perhaps she had noticed this and was angry on purpose. I said as much to her.

'How disgusting!' she said, with an air of repulsion.

'I don't care,' I went on. 'Do you know, too, that it is dangerous for us to walk together? I often have an irresistible longing to beat you, to disfigure you, to strangle you. And what do you think – won't it come to that? You are driving me into brain fever. Do you suppose I am afraid of a scandal? Your anger – why, what is your anger to me? I love you without hope, and I know that after this I shall love you a thousand times more than ever. If ever I do kill you I shall have to kill myself, too. Oh, well, I shall put off killing myself as long as possible, so as to go on feeling this insufferable pain of being without you. Do you know something incredible? I love you *more* every day, and yet that is almost impossible. And how can I help being a fatalist? Do you remember the day before yesterday, on the Schlangenberg, I whispered at your provocation, "Say the word, and I will leap into that abyss"? If you had said that word I should have jumped in then. Don't you believe that I would have leapt down?'

'What stupid talk!' she cried.

'I don't care whether it is stupid or clever!' I cried. 'I know that in your presence I must talk, and talk, and talk – and I do talk. I lose all self-respect in your presence, and I don't care.'

'What use would it be for me to order you to jump off the Schlangenberg?' she said in a dry and peculiarly insulting manner. 'It would be absolutely useless to me.'

'Splendid,' I cried; 'you said that splendid "useless" on purpose to overwhelm me. I see through you. Useless, you say? But pleasure is always of use, and savage, unbounded power – if only over a fly – is a pleasure in its way, too. Man is a despot by nature, and loves to be a torturer. You like it awfully.'

I remember she looked at me with peculiar fixed attention. My face must have expressed my incoherent and absurd sensations. I remember to this moment that our conversation actually was almost word for word exactly as I have described it here. My eyes were bloodshot. There were flecks of foam on my lips. And as for the Schlangenberg, I swear on my word of honour even now, if she had told me to fling myself down I should have flung myself down! If only for a joke she had said it, with contempt, if with a jeer at me she had said it, I should even then have leapt down!

'No, why? I believe you,' she pronounced, as only she knows how to speak, with such contempt and venom, with such scorn that, by God, I could have killed her at the moment.

She risked it. I was not lying about that, too, in what I said to her.

'You are not a coward?' she asked me suddenly.

'Perhaps I am a coward. I don't know . . . I have not thought about it for a long time.'

'If I were to say to you, "Kill this man", would you kill him?'

'Whom?'

'Whom I choose.'

'The Frenchman?'

'Don't ask questions, but answer. Whom I tell you. I want to know whether you spoke seriously just now?'

She waited for my answer so gravely and impatiently that it struck me as strange.

'Come, do tell me, what has been happening here?' I cried. 'What are you afraid of – me, or what? I see all the muddle here for myself. You are the stepdaughter of a mad and ruined man possessed by a passion for that devil – Blanche. Then there is this Frenchman, with his mysterious influence over you, and – here you ask me now so gravely . . . such a question. At any rate let me know, or I shall go mad on the spot and do something. Are you ashamed to deign to be open with me? Surely you can't care what I think of you?'

'I am not speaking to you of that at all. I asked you a question and I'm waiting for an answer.'

'Of course I will kill anyone you tell me to,' I cried. 'But can you possibly . . . could you tell me to do it?'

'Do you suppose I should spare you? I shall tell you to, and stand aside and look on. Can you endure that? Why, no, as though you could! You would kill him, perhaps, if you were told, and then you would come and kill me for having dared to send you.'

I felt as though I were stunned at these words. Of course, even then I looked upon her question as half a joke, a challenge; yet she had spoken very earnestly. I was struck, nevertheless, at her speaking out so frankly, at her maintaining such rights over me, at her accepting such power over me and saying so bluntly: 'Go to ruin, and I'll stand aside and look on.' In those words there was something so open and cynical that to my mind it was going too far. That, then, was how she looked at me. This was something more than slavery or insignificance. If one looks at a man like that, one exalts him to one's own level, and absurd and incredible as all our conversation was, yet there was a throb at my heart.

Suddenly she laughed. We were sitting on a bench, before the playing children, facing the place where the carriages used to stop and people used to get out in the avenue before the Casino.

'Do you see that stout baroness?' she cried. 'That is Baroness Burmerhelm. She has only been here three days. Do you see her husband – a tall, lean Prussian with a stick? Do you remember how he looked at us the day before yesterday? Go up to the Baroness at once, take off your hat, and say something to her in French.'

'Why?'

'You swore that you would jump down the Schlangenberg; you swear you are ready to kill anyone if I tell you. Instead of these murders and tragedies I only want to laugh. Go without discussing it. I want to see the Baron thrash you with his stick.'

'You challenge me; you think I won't do it?'

'Yes, I do challenge you. Go; I want you to!'

'By all means, I am going, though it's a wild freak. Only, I say, I hope it won't be unpleasant for the General, and through him for you. Upon my honour, I am not thinking of myself, but of you and the General. And what a mad idea to insult a woman!'

'Yes, you are only a chatterer, as I see,' she said contemptuously. 'Your eyes were fierce and bloodshot, but perhaps that was only because you had too much wine at dinner. Do you suppose that I don't understand that it is stupid and vulgar, and that the General would be angry? I simply want to laugh; I want to, and that's all about it! And what should you insult a woman for? Why, just to be thrashed.'

I turned and went in silence to carry out her commission. Of course it was stupid, and of course I did not know how to get out of it, but as I began to get closer to the Baroness I remember, as it were, something within myself urging me on; it was an impulse of schoolboyish mischief. Besides, I was horribly overwrought, and felt just as though I were drunk.

CHAPTER SIX

Now two days have passed since that stupid day. And what a noise and fuss and talk and uproar there was! And how unseemly and disgraceful, how stupid and vulgar, it was! And I was the cause of it all. Yet at times it's laughable – to me, at any rate. I can't make up my mind what happened to me, whether I really was in a state of frenzy, or whether it was a momentary aberration and I behaved disgracefully till I was pulled up. At times it seemed to me that my mind was giving way. And at times it seems to me that I have not outgrown childhood and schoolboyishness, and that it was simply a crude schoolboy's prank.

It was Polina, it was all Polina! Perhaps I shouldn't have behaved like a schoolboy if it hadn't been for her. Who knows? perhaps I did it out of despair (stupid as it seems, though, to reason like that). And I don't understand, I don't understand what there is fine in her! She is fine, though; she is; I believe she's fine. She drives other men off their heads, too. She's tall and graceful, only very slender. It seems to me you could tie her in a knot or bend her double. Her foot is long and narrow – tormenting. Tormenting is just what it is. Her hair has a reddish tint. Her eyes are regular cat's eyes, but how proudly and disdainfully she can look with them. Four months ago, when I had only just come, she was talking hotly for a long while one evening with des Grieux in the drawing-room, and looked at him in such a way . . . that afterwards, when I went up to my room to go to bed, I imagined that she must have just given him a slap in the face. She stood facing him and looked at him. It was from that evening that I loved her.

To come to the point, however.

I stepped off the path into the avenue, and stood waiting for the Baron and the Baroness. When they were five paces from me I took off my hat and bowed.

I remember the Baroness was wearing a light grey dress of immense circumference, with flounces, a crinoline, and a train. She was short and exceptionally stout, with such a fearful double chin that she seemed to have no neck. Her face was crimson. Her eyes were small, spiteful and insolent. She walked as though she were doing an honour to all beholders. The Baron was lean and tall. Like most Germans, he had a wry face covered with thousands of fine wrinkles, and wore spectacles; he was about forty-five. His legs seemed to start from his chest: that's a sign of race. He was as proud as a peacock. He was rather clumsy. There was something like a sheep in the expression of his face that would pass with them for profundity.

All this flashed upon my sight in three seconds.

My bow and the hat in my hand gradually arrested their attention. The Baron slightly knitted his brows. The Baroness simply sailed straight at me.

'*Madame la baronne,*' I articulated distinctly, emphasising each word, '*j'ai l'honneur d'être votre esclave.*'

Then I bowed, replaced my hat, and walked past the Baron, turning my face towards him with a polite smile.

She had told me to take off my hat, but I had bowed and behaved like an impudent schoolboy on my own account. Goodness knows what impelled me to! I felt as though I were plunging into space.

'*Hein*!' cried, or rather croaked, the Baron, turning towards me with angry surprise.

I turned and remained in respectful expectation, still gazing at him with a smile. He was evidently perplexed, and raised his eyebrows as high as they would go. His face grew darker and darker. The Baroness, too, turned towards me, and she, too, stared in wrathful surprise. The passers-by began to look on. Some even stopped.

'*Hein*!' the Baron croaked again, with redoubled gutturalness and redoubled anger.

'*Ja wohl*!' I drawled, still looking him straight in the face.

'*Sind sie rasend*?' he cried, waving his stick and beginning, I think, to be a little nervous. He was perhaps perplexed by my appearance. I was very well, even foppishly, dressed, like a man belonging to the best society.

'*Ja wo-o-ohl*!' I shouted suddenly at the top of my voice, drawling the *o* like the Berliners, who use the expression '*ja wohl*' in every sentence, and drawl the letter *o* more or less according to the shade of their thought or feeling.

The Baron and Baroness turned away quickly and almost ran away from me in terror. Of the spectators, some were talking, others were gazing at me in amazement. I don't remember very clearly, though.

I turned and walked at my ordinary pace to Polina Alexandrovna.

But when I was within a hundred paces of her seat, I saw her get up and walk with the children towards the hotel.

I overtook her at the door.

'I have performed . . . the foolery,' I said, when I reached her.

'Well, what of it? Now you can get out of the scrape,' she answered. She walked upstairs without even glancing at me.

I spent the whole evening walking about the park. I crossed the park and then the wood beyond and walked into another state. In a cottage I had an omelette and some wine; for that idyllic repast they extorted a whole thaler and a half.

It was eleven o'clock before I returned home. I was at once summoned before the General.

Our party occupied two suites in the hotel; they have four rooms. The first is a big room – a drawing-room with a piano in it. The next, also a large room, is the General's study. Here he was awaiting me, standing in the middle of the room in a majestic pose. Des Grieux sat lolling on the sofa.

'Allow me to ask you, sir, what have you been about?' began the General, addressing me.

'I should be glad if you would go straight to the point, General,' said I. 'You probably mean to refer to my encounter with a German this morning?'

'A German? That German was Baron Burmerhelm, a very important personage! You insulted him and the Baroness.'

'Not in the least.'

'You alarmed them, sir!' cried the General.

'Not a bit of it. When I was in Berlin the sound was for ever in my ears of that *ja wohl*, continually repeated at every word and disgustingly drawled out by them. When I met them in the avenue that *ja wohl* suddenly came into my mind, I don't know why, and – well, it had an irritating effect on me . . . Besides, the Baroness, who has met me three times, has the habit of walking straight at me as though I were a worm who might be trampled underfoot. You must admit that I, too, may have my proper pride. I took off my hat and said politely (I assure you I said it politely): "*Madame, j'ai l'honneur d'être votre esclave.*" When the Baron turned round and said, "*Hein*!" I felt an impulse to shout, "*Ja wohl*!" I shouted it twice: the first time in an ordinary tone, and the second – I drawled it as much as I could. That was all.'

I must own I was intensely delighted at this extremely schoolboyish explanation. I had a strange desire to make the story as absurd as possible in the telling.

And as I went on, I got more and more to relish it.

'Are you laughing at me?' cried the General. He turned to the Frenchman and explained to him in French that I was positively going out of my way to provoke a scandal! Des Grieux laughed contemptuously and shrugged his shoulders.

'Oh, don't imagine that; it was not so at all!' I cried. 'My conduct was wrong, of course, I confess that with the utmost candour. My behaviour may even be called a stupid and improper schoolboy prank, but – nothing more. And do you know, General, I heartily regret it. But there is one circumstance which, to my mind at least, almost saves me from repentance. Lately, for the last fortnight, indeed, I've not been feeling well: I have felt ill, nervous, irritable, moody, and on some occasions I lose all control of myself. Really, I've sometimes had an intense impulse to attack the Marquis des Grieux and . . . However, there's no need to say, he might be offended. In short, it's the sign of illness. I don't know whether the Baroness Burmerhelm will take this fact into consideration when I beg her pardon (for I intend to apologise). I imagine she will not consider it, especially as that line of excuse has been somewhat abused in legal circles of late. Lawyers have taken to arguing in criminal cases that their clients were not responsible at the moment of their crime, and that it was a form of disease. "He killed him," they say, "and has no memory of it." And only imagine, General, the medical authorities support them – and actually maintain that there are illnesses, temporary aberrations in which a man scarcely remembers anything, or has only a half or a quarter of his memory. But the Baron and Baroness are people of the older generation; besides, they are Prussian *junkers* and landowners, and so are probably unaware of this advance in the world of medical jurisprudence, and will not accept my explanation. What do you think, General?'

'Enough, sir,' the General pronounced sharply, with surprised indignation; 'enough! I will try once for all to rid myself of your mischievous pranks. You are not going to apologise to the Baron and Baroness. Any communication with you, even though it were to consist solely of your request for forgiveness, would be beneath their dignity. The Baron has learnt that you are a member of my household; he has already had an explanation with me at the Casino, and I assure you that he was within an ace of asking me to give him satisfaction. Do you understand what you have exposed me to – me, sir? I – I was forced to ask the Baron's pardon, and gave him my word that immediately, this very day, you would cease to be a member of my household.'

'Excuse me, excuse me; General – did he insist on that himself, that I should cease to belong to your household, as you were pleased to express it?'

'No, but I considered myself bound to give him that satisfaction, and, of course, the Baron was satisfied. We must part, sir. There is what is owing to you, four friedrichs d'or and three florins, according to the reckoning here. Here is the money, and here is the note of the account; you can verify it. Goodbye. From this time forth we are strangers. I've had nothing but trouble and unpleasantness from you. I will call the *kellner* and inform him from this day forth that I am not responsible for your hotel expenses. I have the honour to remain your obedient servant.'

I took the money and the paper upon which the account was written in pencil, bowed to the General, and said to him very seriously –

'General, the matter cannot end like this. I am very sorry that you were put into an unpleasant position with the Baron, but, excuse me, you were to blame for it yourself. Why did you take it upon yourself to be responsible for me to the Baron? What is the meaning of the expression that I am a member of your household? I am simply a teacher in your house, that is all. I am neither your son nor your ward, and you cannot be responsible for my actions. I am a legally responsible person, I am twenty-five, I am a graduate of the university, I am a nobleman, I am not connected with you in any way. Nothing but my unbounded respect for your dignity prevents me now from demanding from you the fullest explanation and satisfaction for taking upon yourself the right to answer for me.'

The General was so much amazed that he flung up his hands, then turned suddenly to the Frenchman and hurriedly informed him that I had just all but challenged him to a duel.

The Frenchman laughed aloud.

'But I am not going to let the Baron off,' I said, with complete composure, not in the least embarrassed by M. des Grieux's laughter; 'and as, General, you consented to listen to the Baron's complaint today and have taken up his cause, and have made yourself, as it were, a party in the whole affair, I have the honour to inform you that no later than tomorrow morning I shall ask the Baron on my own account for a formal explanation of the reasons which led him to apply to other persons – as though I were unable or unfit to answer for myself.'

What I foresaw happened. The General, hearing of this new absurdity, became horribly nervous.

'What, do you mean to keep up this damnable business?' he shouted. 'What a position you are putting me in – good heavens! Don't dare, don't dare, sir, or, I swear! . . . There are police here, too, and I . . . I . . . in fact, by my rank . . . and the Baron's, too . . . in fact, you shall be arrested and turned out of the state by the police, to teach you not to make a disturbance. Do you understand that, sir?' And although he was breathless with anger, he was also horribly frightened.

'General,' I answered, with a composure that was insufferable to him, 'you can't arrest anyone for making a disturbance before they have made a disturbance. I have not yet begun to make my explanations to the Baron, and you don't know in the least in what form or on what grounds I intend to proceed. I only wish to have an explanation of a position insulting to me, *i.e.* that I am under the control of a person who has authority over my freedom of action. There is no need for you to be so anxious and uneasy.'

'For goodness' sake, for goodness' sake, Alexey Ivanovitch, drop this insane intention!' muttered the General, suddenly changing his wrathful tone for one of entreaty, and even clutching me by the hand. 'Fancy what it will lead to! Fresh unpleasantness! You must see for yourself that I must be particular here . . . particularly now! particularly now! . . . Oh, you don't know, you don't know all my circumstances! . . . When we leave this place I shall be willing to take you back again; I was only speaking of now, in fact – of course, you understand there are reasons!' he cried in despair. 'Alexey Ivanovitch, Alexey Ivanovitch . . . '

Retreating to the door, I begged him more earnestly not to worry himself, promised him that everything should go off well and with propriety, and hastily withdrew.

The Russian abroad is sometimes too easily cowed, and is horribly afraid of what people will say, how they will look at him, and whether this or that will be the proper thing. In short, they behave as though they were in corsets, especially those who have pretensions to consequence. The thing that pleases them most is a certain established traditional etiquette, which they follow slavishly in hotels, on their walks, in assemblies, on a journey . . . But the General had let slip that, apart from this, there was a particular circumstance, that he must be 'particular'. That was why he so weakly showed the white feather and changed his tone with me. I took this as evidence and made a note of it; and, of course, he might have brought my folly to the notice of the authorities, so that I really had to be careful.

I did not particularly want to anger the General, however; but I did want to anger Polina. Polina had treated me so badly, and had thrust me into such a stupid position, that I could not help wanting to force her to beg me to stop. My schoolboyish prank might compromise her, too. Moreover, another feeling and desire was taking shape in me: though I might be reduced to a nonentity in her presence, that did not prove that I could not hold my own before other people, or that the Baron could thrash me. I longed to have the laugh against them all, and to come off with flying colours. Let them see! She would be frightened by the scandal and call me back again, or, even if she didn't, at least she would see that I could hold my own.

* * *

(A wonderful piece of news! I have just heard from the nurse, whom I met on the stairs, that Marya Filippovna set off today, entirely alone, by the evening train to Karlsbad to see her cousin.

What's the meaning of that? Nurse says that she has long been meaning to go; but how was it no one knew of it? Though perhaps I was the only one who did not know it. The nurse let slip that Marya Filippovna had words with the General the day before yesterday. I understand. No doubt that is Mlle Blanche. Yes, something decisive is coming.)

CHAPTER SEVEN

In the morning I called for the *kellner* and told him to make out a separate bill for me. My room was not such an expensive one as to make me feel alarmed and anxious to leave the hotel. I had sixteen friedrichs d'or, and there . . . there perhaps was wealth! Strange to say, I have not won yet, but I behave, I feel and think like a rich man, and cannot imagine anything else.

In spite of the early hour I intended to go at once to see Mr Astley at the Hôtel d'Angleterre, which was quite close by, when suddenly des Grieux came in to me. That had never happened before, and, what is more, that gentleman and I had for some time past been on very queer and strained terms. He openly displayed his contempt for me, even tried not to conceal it; and I – I had my own reasons for disliking him. In short, I hated him. His visit greatly surprised me. I at once detected that something special was brewing.

He came in very politely and complimented me on my room. Seeing that I had my hat in my hand, he enquired whether I could be going out for a walk so early. When he heard that I was going to see Mr Astley on business, he pondered, he reflected, and his face assumed an exceedingly careworn expression.

Des Grieux was like all Frenchmen; that is, gay and polite when necessary and profitable to be so, and insufferably tedious when the necessity to be gay and polite was over. A Frenchman is not often naturally polite. He is always polite, as it were, to order, with a motive. If he sees the necessity for being fantastic, original, a little out of the ordinary, then his freakishness is most stupid and unnatural, and is made up of accepted and long-vulgarised traditions. The natural Frenchman is composed of the most plebeian, petty, ordinary practical sense – in fact, he is one of the most wearisome creatures in the world. In my opinion, only the innocent and inexperienced – especially Russian young ladies – are fascinated by

Frenchmen. To every decent person the conventionalism of the established traditions of drawing-room politeness, ease and gaiety are at once evident and intolerable.

'I have come to see you on business,' he began, with marked directness, though with courtesy, 'and I will not disguise that I have come as an ambassador, or rather as a mediator, from the General. As I know Russian very imperfectly I understood very little of what passed yesterday, but the General explained it to me in detail, and I confess . . . '

'But, listen, M. des Grieux,' I interrupted; 'here you have undertaken to be a mediator in this affair. I am, of course, an *uchitel*, and have never laid claim to the honour of being a great friend of this family, nor of being on particularly intimate terms with it, and so I don't know all the circumstances; but explain: are you now entirely a member of the family? You take such an interest in everything and are certain at once to be a mediator . . . '

This question did not please him. It was too transparent for him, and he did not want to speak out.

'I am connected with the General partly by business, partly by *certain special* circumstances,' he said dryly. 'The General has sent me to ask you to abandon the intentions you expressed yesterday. All you thought of doing was no doubt very clever; but he begged me to represent to you that you would be utterly unsuccessful; what's more, the Baron will not receive you, and in any case is in a position to rid himself of any further unpleasantness on your part. You must see that yourself. Tell me, what is the object of going on with it? The General promises to take you back into his home at the first convenient opportunity, and until that time will continue your salary, *vos appointements*. That will be fairly profitable, won't it?'

I retorted very calmly that he was rather mistaken; that perhaps I shouldn't be kicked out at the Baron's, but, on the contrary, should be listened to; and I asked him to admit that he had probably come to find out what steps I was going to take in the matter.

'Oh, heavens! Since the General is so interested, he will, of course, be glad to know how you are going to behave, and what you are going to do.'

I proceeded to explain, and he began listening, stretching himself at his ease, and inclining his head on one side towards me, with an obvious, undisguised expression of irony on his face. Altogether he behaved very loftily. I tried with all my might to pretend that I took a very serious view of the matter. I explained that since the Baron had addressed a complaint of me to the General as though I were the latter's servant, he had, in the first place, deprived me thereby of my position; and secondly, had treated me as a person who was incapable of answering for himself and who was not worth speaking to. Of course, I said, I felt with justice that I had been insulted; however, considering the difference of age, position in society, and so on, and so on (I could scarcely restrain my laughter at this point), I did not want to rush into fresh indiscretion by directly insisting on satisfaction from the Baron, or even proposing a duel to him; nevertheless, I considered myself fully entitled to offer the Baron, and still more the Baroness, my apologies, especially since of late I had really felt ill, overwrought, and, so to say, fanciful, and so on, and so on. However, the Baron had, by his applying to the General, which was a slight to me, and by his insisting that the General should deprive me of my post, put me in such a position that now I could not offer him and the Baroness my apologies, because he and the Baroness and all the world would certainly suppose that I came to apologise because I was frightened and in order to be reinstated in my post. From all this it followed that I found myself now compelled to beg the Baron first of all to apologise to me in the most formal terms; for instance, to say that he had no desire to insult me. And when the Baron said this I should feel that my hands were set free, and with perfect candour and sincerity I should offer him my apologies. In brief, I concluded, I could only beg the Baron to untie my hands.

'Fie! how petty and how far-fetched! And why do you want to apologise? Come, admit, *monsieur . . . monsieur* . . . that you are doing all this on purpose to vex the General . . . and perhaps you have some special object . . . *mon cher monsieur . . . pardon, j'ai oublié votre nom, M. Alexis*? . . . *N'est-ce pas*?'

'But excuse me, *mon cher marquis*, what has it to do with you?'

'*Mais le général* . . . '

'But what about the General? He said something last night, that he had to be particularly careful . . . and was so upset . . . but I did not understand it.'

'There is, there certainly is a particular circumstance,' des Grieux caught me up in an insistent voice, in which a note of vexation was more and more marked. 'You know Mlle de Cominges . . . ?'

'That is, Mlle Blanche?'

'Why, yes, Mlle Blanche de Cominges . . . *et madame sa mère*. You see for yourself, the General . . . in short, the General is in love; in fact . . . in fact, the marriage may be celebrated here. And fancy, scandal, gossip . . . '

'I see no scandal or gossip connected with the marriage in this.'

'But *le baron est si irascible un caractère Prussien, vous savez, enfin il fera une querelle d'Allemand.*'

'With me, then, and not with you, for I no longer belong to the household . . . ' (I tried to be as irrational as possible on purpose.) 'But, excuse me, is it settled, then, that Mlle Blanche is to marry the General? What are they waiting for? I mean, why conceal this from us, at any rate, from the members of the household?'

'I cannot . . . however, it is not quite . . . besides . . . you know, they are expecting news from Russia; the General has to make arrangements . . . '

'*A*! *a*! *La baboulinka*!'

Des Grieux looked at me with hatred.

'In short,' he interrupted, 'I fully rely on your innate courtesy, on your intelligence, on your tact . . . You will certainly do this for the family in which you have been received like one of themselves, in which you have been liked and respected . . . '

'Excuse me, I've been dismissed! You maintain now that that is only in appearance; but you must admit, if you were told: "I won't send you packing, but, for the look of the thing, kindly take yourself off." . . . You see, it comes almost to the same thing.'

'Well, if that's how it is, if no request will have any influence on you,' he began sternly and haughtily, 'allow me to assure you that steps will be taken. There are authorities here; you'll be turned out today – *que diable*! *un blanc-bec comme vous* wants to challenge a personage like the Baron! And do you think that you will not be interfered with? And, let me assure you, nobody is afraid of you here! I have approached you on my own account, because you have been worrying the General. And do you imagine that the Baron will not order his flunkeys to turn you out of the house?'

'But, you see, I'm not going myself,' I answered, with the utmost composure. 'You are mistaken, M. des Grieux; all this will be done much more decorously than you imagine. I am just setting off to Mr Astley, and I am going to ask him to be my intermediary; in fact, to be my second. The man likes me, and certainly will not refuse. He will go to the Baron, and the Baron will receive him. Even if I am an *uchitel* and seem to be something subordinate and, well, defenceless, Mr Astley is a nephew of a lord, of a real lord; everyone knows that – Lord Pibroch – and that lord is here. Believe me, the Baron will be courteous to Mr Astley and will listen to him. And if he won't listen, Mr Astley will look upon it as a personal affront (you know how persistent Englishmen are), and will send a friend to call on the Baron; he has powerful friends. You may reckon, now, upon things not turning out quite as you expect.

The Frenchman was certainly scared; all this was really very much like the truth, and so it seemed that I really might be able to get up a scandal.

'Come, I beg you,' he said in a voice of actual entreaty, 'do drop the whole business! It seems to please you that it will cause a scandal! It is not satisfaction you want, but a scandal! As I have told you, it is very amusing and even witty – which is perhaps what you are aiming at. But, in short,' he concluded, seeing that I had got up and was taking my hat, 'I've come to give you these few lines from a certain person; read them; I was charged to wait for an answer.'

Saying this, he took out of his pocket a little note, folded and sealed with a wafer, and handed it to me.

It was in Polina's handwriting.

I fancy that you intend to go on with this affair, but there are special circumstances which I will explain to you perhaps later; please leave off and give way. It is all such silliness! I need you, and you promised yourself to obey me. Remember the Schlangenberg; I beg you to be obedient, and, if necessary, I command you. – Your P.

P.S. – If you are angry with me for what happened yesterday, forgive me.

Everything seemed to be heaving before my eyes when I read these lines. My lips turned white and I began to tremble. The accursed Frenchman watched me with an exaggerated air of discretion, with his eyes turned away as though to avoid noticing my confusion. He had better have laughed at me outright.

'Very good,' I answered; 'tell Mademoiselle that she may set her mind at rest. Allow me to ask you,' I added sharply, 'why you have been so long giving me this letter. Instead of chattering about all sorts of nonsense, I think you ought to have begun with that . . . if you came expressly with that object.'

'Oh, I wanted . . . all this is so strange that you must excuse my natural impatience. I was in haste to learn from you in person what you intended to do. Besides, I don't know what is in that note, and I thought there was no hurry for me to give it you.'

'I understand: the long and the short of it is you were told only to give me the letter in case of the utmost necessity, and if you could settle it by word of mouth you were not to give it me. Is that right? Tell me plainly, M. des Grieux.'

'*Peut-être*,' he said, assuming an air of peculiar reserve, and looking at me with a peculiar glance.

I took off my hat; he took off his hat and went out. It seemed to me that there was an ironical smile on his lips. And, indeed, what else could one expect?

'We'll be quits yet, Frenchy; we'll settle our accounts,' I muttered as I went down the stairs. I could not think clearly; I felt as though I had had a blow on my head. The air revived me a little.

Two minutes later, as soon as ever I was able to reflect clearly, two thoughts stood out vividly before me: the *first* was that such trivial incidents, that a few mischievous and far-fetched threats from a mere boy, had caused such *universal* consternation! The *second* thought was: what sort of influence had this Frenchman over Polina? A mere word from him and she does anything he wants – writes a note and even *begs* me. Of course, their relations have always been a mystery to me from the very beginning, ever since I began to know them; but of late I have noticed in her a positive aversion and even contempt for him, while he did not even look at her, was absolutely rude to her. I had noticed it. Polina herself had spoken of him to me with aversion; she had dropped some extremely significant admissions . . . so he simply had her in his power. She was in some sort of bondage to him.

CHAPTER EIGHT

On the promenade, as it is called here, that is, in the chestnut avenue, I met my Englishman.

'Oh, oh!' he began, as soon as he saw me. 'I was coming to see you, and you are on your way to me. So you have parted from your people?'

'Tell me, first, how it is that you know all this?' I asked in amazement. 'Is it possible that everybody knows of it?'

'Oh, no, everyone doesn't; and, indeed, it's not worth their knowing. No one is talking about it.'

'Then how do you know it?'

'I know, that is, I chanced to learn it. Now, where are you going when you leave here? I like you and that is why I was coming to see you.'

'You are a splendid man, Mr Astley,' said I (I was very much interested, however, to know where he could have learnt it), 'and since I have not yet had my coffee, and most likely you have not had a good cup, come to the café in the Casino. Let us sit down and have a smoke there, and I will tell you all about it, and . . . you tell me, too . . . '

The café was a hundred steps away. They brought us some coffee. We sat down and I lighted a cigarette. Mr Astley did not light one and, gazing at me, prepared to listen.

'I am not going anywhere. I am staying here,' I began.

'And I was sure you would,' observed Mr Astley approvingly.

On my way to Mr Astley I had not meant to tell him anything of my love for Polina, and, in fact, I expressly intended to say nothing to him about it. He was, besides, very reserved. From the first I noticed that Polina had made a great impression upon him, but he never uttered her name. But, strange to say, now no sooner had he sat down and turned upon me his fixed, pewtery eyes than I felt, I don't know why, a desire to tell him everything, that is, all about my love in all its aspects. I was talking to him for half an hour and it was very pleasant to me; it was the first time I had talked of it! Noticing that at certain ardent sentences he was embarrassed, I purposely exaggerated my ardour. Only one thing I regret: I said, perhaps, more than I should about the Frenchman . . .

Mr Astley listened, sitting facing me without moving, looking straight into my eyes, not uttering a word, a sound; but when I spoke of the Frenchman, he suddenly pulled me up and asked me, severely, whether I had the right to refer to this circumstance which did not concern me. Mr Astley always asked questions very strangely.

'You are right. I am afraid not,' I answered.

'You can say nothing definite, nothing that is not supposition about that Marquis and Miss Polina?'

I was surprised again at such a point-blank question from a man so reserved as Mr Astley.

'No, nothing definite,' I answered; 'of course not.'

'If so, you have done wrong, not only in speaking of it to me, but even in thinking of it yourself.'

'Very good, very good; I admit it, but that is not the point now,' I interrupted, wondering at myself. At this point I told him the whole of yesterday's story in full detail: Polina's prank, my adventure with the Baron, my dismissal, the General's extraordinary dismay, and, finally, I described in detail des Grieux's visit that morning. Finally I showed him the note.

'What do you deduce from all this?' I asked. 'I came on purpose to find out what you think. For my part, I could kill that Frenchman, and perhaps I shall.'

'So could I,' said Mr Astley. 'As regards Miss Polina, you know . . . we may enter into relations even with people who are detestable to us if we are compelled by necessity. There may be relations of which you know nothing, dependent upon outside circumstances. I think you may set your mind at rest – to some extent, of course. As for her action yesterday, it was strange, of course; not that she wanted to get rid of you and expose you to the Baron's walking-stick (I don't understand why he did not use it, since he had it in his hands), but because such a prank is improper . . . for such an . . . exquisite young lady. Of course, she couldn't have expected that you would carry out her jesting wish so literally . . . '

'Do you know what?' I cried suddenly, looking intently at Mr Astley. 'It strikes me that you have heard about this already – do you know from whom? From Miss Polina herself!'

Mr Astley looked at me with surprise.

'Your eyes are sparkling and I can read your suspicion in them,' he said, regaining his former composure; 'but you have no right whatever to express your suspicions. I cannot recognise the right, and I absolutely refuse to answer your question.'

'Enough! There's no need,' I cried, strangely perturbed, and not knowing why it had come into my head. And when, where and how could Mr Astley have been chosen by Polina to confide in? Though of late, indeed, I had to some extent lost sight of Mr Astley, and Polina was always an enigma to me, such an enigma that now, for instance, after launching into an account of my passion to Mr Astley, I was suddenly struck while I was speaking by the fact that there was scarcely anything positive and definite I could say about our relations. Everything was, on the contrary, strange, unstable, and, in fact, quite unique.

'Oh, very well, very well. I am utterly perplexed and there is a great deal I can't understand at present,' I answered, gasping as though I were breathless. 'You are a good man, though. And now, another matter, and I ask not your advice, but your opinion.'

After a brief pause I began.

'What do you think? why was the General so scared? Why did he make such a to-do over my stupid practical joke? Such a fuss that even des Grieux thought it necessary to interfere (and he interferes only in the most important matters); visited me (think of that!), begged and besought me – he, des Grieux – begged and besought me! Note, finally, he came at nine o'clock, and by that time Miss Polina's letter was in his hands. One wonders when it was written. Perhaps they waked Miss Polina up on purpose! Apart from what I see clearly from this, that Miss Polina is his slave (for she even begs my forgiveness!) – apart from that, how is she concerned in all this, she personally, why is she so much interested? Why are they frightened of some Baron? And what if the General is marrying Mlle Blanche Cominges? They say that, owing to that circumstance, they must be *particular*, but you must admit that this is somewhat too particular! What do you think? I am sure from your eyes you know more about it than I do!'

Mr Astley laughed and nodded.

'Certainly. I believe I know much more about it than you,' he said. 'Mlle Blanche is the only person concerned, and I am sure that is the absolute truth.'

'Well, what about Mlle Blanche?' I cried impatiently. (I suddenly had a hope that something would be disclosed about Mlle Polina.)

'I fancy that Mlle Blanche has at the moment special reasons for avoiding a meeting with the Baron and Baroness, even more an unpleasant meeting, worse still, a scandalous one.'

'Well, well . . . '

'Two years ago Mlle Blanche was here at Roulettenburg in the season. I was here, too. Mlle Blanche was not called Mlle de Cominges then, and her mother, Madame la maman Cominges, was non-existent then. Anyway, she was never mentioned. Des Grieux – des Grieux was not here either. I cherish the conviction that, far from being relations, they have only very recently become acquainted. He – des Grieux – has only become a marquis very recently, too – I am sure of that from one circumstance. One may assume, in fact, that his name has not been des Grieux very long either. I know a man here who has met him passing under another name.'

'But he really has a very respectable circle of acquaintances.'

'That may be. Even Mlle Blanche may have. But two years ago, at the request of that very Baroness, Mlle Blanche was invited by the police to leave the town, and she did leave it.'

'How was that?'

'She made her appearance here first with an Italian, a prince of some sort, with an historical name – Barberini, or something like it – a man covered with rings and diamonds, not false ones either. They used to drive about in a magnificent carriage. Mlle Blanche used to play *trente et quarante*, at first winning, though her luck changed later on, as far as I remember. I remember one evening she lost a considerable sum. But, worse still, *un beau matin* her prince vanished; the horses and the carriage vanished too, everything vanished. The bills owing at the hotels were immense. Mlle Selma (she suddenly ceased to be Barberini, and became Mlle Selma) was in the utmost despair. She was shrieking and wailing all over the hotel, and rent her clothes in her fury. There was a Polish count staying here at the hotel (all Polish travellers are counts), and

Mlle Selma, rending her garments and scratching her face like a cat with her beautiful perfumed fingers, made some impression on him. They talked things over, and by dinner-time she was consoled. In the evening he made his appearance at the Casino with the lady on his arm. As usual, Mlle Selma laughed very loudly, and her manner was somewhat more free and easy than before. She definitely showed that she belonged to the class of ladies who, when they go up to the roulette table, shoulder the other players aside to clear a space for themselves. That's particularly *chic* among such ladies. You must have noticed it?'

'Oh, yes.'

'It's not worth noticing. To the annoyance of the decent public they are not moved on here – at least, not those of them who can change a thousand-rouble note every day, at the roulette table. As soon as they cease to produce a note to change they are asked to withdraw, however. Mlle Selma still went on changing notes, but her play became more unlucky than ever. Note that such ladies are very often lucky in their play; they have a wonderful self-control. However, my story is finished. One day the Count vanished just as the Prince had done. However, Mlle Selma made her appearance at the roulette table alone; this time no one came forward to offer her his arm. In two days she had lost everything. After laying down her last louis d'or and losing it, she looked round, and saw, close by her, Baron Burmerhelm, who was scrutinising her intently and with profound indignation. But Mlle Selma, not noticing his indignation, accosted the Baron with that smile we all know so well, and asked him to put down ten louis d'or on the red for her. In consequence of a complaint from the Baroness she received that evening an invitation not to show herself at the Casino again. If you are surprised at my knowing all these petty and extremely improper details, it is because I have heard them from Mr Fider, one of my relations, who carried off Mlle Selma in his carriage from Roulettenburg to Spa that very evening. Now, remember, Mlle Blanche wishes to become the General's wife, probably in order in future not to receive such invitations as that one from the police at the Casino, the year before last. Now she does not play; but that is because, as it seems, she has capital of her own which she lends out at a percentage to gamblers here. That's a much safer speculation. I even suspect that the luckless General is in debt to her. Perhaps des Grieux is, too. Perhaps des Grieux is associated with her. You will admit that, till the wedding, at any rate, she can hardly be anxious to attract the attention of the Baron and Baroness in any way. In short, in her position, nothing could be more disadvantageous than a scandal. You are connected with their party and your conduct might cause a scandal, especially as she appears in public every day either arm-in-arm with the General or in company with Miss Polina. Now do you understand?'

'No, I don't!' I cried, thumping the table so violently that the *garçon* ran up in alarm.

'Tell me, Mr Astley,' I said furiously. 'If you knew all this story and, therefore, know positively what Mlle Blanche de Cominges is, why didn't you warn me at least, the General, or, most of all, most of all, Miss Polina, who has shown herself here at the Casino in public, arm-in-arm with Mlle Blanche? Can such a thing be allowed?'

'I had no reason to warn you, for you could have done nothing,' Mr Astley answered calmly. 'Besides, warn them of what? The General knows about Mlle Blanche perhaps more than I do, yet he still goes about with her and Miss Polina. The General is an unlucky man. I saw Mlle Blanche yesterday, galloping on a splendid horse with M. des Grieux and that little Russian Prince, and the General was galloping after them on a chestnut. He told me in the morning that his legs ached, but he sat his horse well. And it struck me at that moment that he was an utterly ruined man. Besides, all this is no business of mine, and I have only lately had the honour of making Miss Polina's acquaintance. However,' (Mr Astley caught himself up) 'I've told you already that I do not recognise your right to ask certain questions, though I have a genuine liking for you . . . '

'Enough,' I said, getting up. 'It is clear as daylight to me now that Miss Polina knows all about Mlle Blanche, but that she cannot part from her Frenchman, and so she brings herself to going about with Mlle Blanche. Believe me, no other influence would compel her to go about with Mlle Blanche and to beg me in her letter not to interfere with the Baron! Damn it all, there's no understanding it!'

'You forget, in the first place, that this Mlle de Cominges is the General's *fiancée*, and in the second place that Miss Polina is the

General's stepdaughter, that she has a little brother and sister, the General's own children, who are utterly neglected by that insane man and have, I believe, been robbed by him.'

'Yes, yes, that is so! To leave the children would mean abandoning them altogether; to remain means protecting their interests and, perhaps, saving some fragments of their property. Yes, yes, all that is true. But still, still! . . . Ah now I understand why they are all so concerned about Granny!'

'About whom?' asked Mr Astley.

'That old witch in Moscow who won't die, and about whom they are expecting a telegram that she is dying.'

'Yes, of course, all interest is concentrated on her. Everything depends on what she leaves them! If he comes in for a fortune the General will marry, Miss Polina will be set free, and des Grieux . . . '

'Well, and des Grieux?'

'And des Grieux will be paid; that is all he is waiting for here.'

'Is that all, do you think that is all he's waiting for?'

'I know nothing more.' Mr Astley was obstinately silent.

'But I do, I do!' I repeated fiercely. 'He's waiting for the inheritance too, because Polina will get a dowry, and as soon as she gets the money will throw herself on his neck. All women are like that! Even the proudest of them turn into the meanest slaves! Polina is only capable of loving passionately: nothing else. That's my opinion of her! Look at her, particularly when she is sitting alone, thinking; it's something predestined, doomed, fated! She is capable of all the horrors of life, and passion . . . she . . . she . . . but who is that calling me?' I exclaimed suddenly. 'Who is shouting? I heard someone shout in Russian: Alexey Ivanovitch! A woman's voice. Listen, listen!'

At this moment we were approaching the hotel. We had left the café long ago, almost without noticing it.

'I did hear a woman calling, but I don't know who was being called; it is Russian. Now I see where the shouts come from,' said Mr Astley. 'It is that woman sitting in a big armchair who has just been carried up the steps by so many flunkeys. They are carrying trunks after her, so the train must have just come in.'

'But why is she calling me? She is shouting again; look, she is waving to us.'

'I see she is waving,' said Mr Astley.

'Alexey Ivanovitch! Alexey Ivanovitch! Mercy on us, what a dolt he is!' came desperate shouts from the hotel steps.

We almost ran to the entrance. I ran up the steps and . . . my hands dropped at my sides with amazement and my feet seemed rooted to the ground.

CHAPTER NINE

At the top of the broad steps at the hotel entrance, surrounded by footmen and maids and the many obsequious servants of the hotel, in the presence of the *ober-kellner* himself, eager to receive the exalted visitor, who had arrived with her own servants and with so many trunks and boxes, and had been carried up the steps in an invalid chair, was seated – *Granny*! Yes, it was she herself, the terrible old Moscow lady and wealthy landowner, Antonida Vassilyevna Tarasyevichev, the *Granny* about whom telegrams had been sent and received, who had been dying and was not dead, and who had suddenly dropped upon us in person, like snow on our heads. Though she was seventy-five and had for the last five years lost the use of her legs and had to be carried about everywhere in a chair, yet she had arrived and was, as always, alert, captious, self-satisfied, sitting upright in her chair, shouting in a loud, peremptory voice and scolding everyone. In fact, she was exactly the same as she had been on the only two occasions that I had the honour of seeing her during the time I had been tutor in the General's family. Naturally I stood rooted to the spot with amazement. As she was being carried up the steps, she had detected me a hundred paces away, with her lynx-like eyes, had recognised me and called me by my name, which she had made a note of, once for all, as she always did. And this was the woman they had expected to be in her coffin, buried, and leaving them her property. That was the thought that flashed into my mind. 'Why, she will outlive all of us and everyone in the hotel! But, my goodness! what will our friends do now, what will the General do? She will turn the whole hotel upside down!'

'Well, my good man, why are you standing with your eyes starting out of your head?' Granny went on shouting to me. 'Can't you welcome me? Can't you say "How do you do"? Or have you grown proud and won't? Or, perhaps, you don't recognise me?

Potapitch, do you hear?' She turned to her butler, an old man with grey hair and a pink bald patch on his head, wearing a dress-coat and white tie. 'Do you hear? he doesn't recognise me. They had buried me! They sent telegram upon telegram to ask whether I was dead or not! You see, I know all about it! Here, you see, I am quite alive.'

'Upon my word, Antonida Vassilyevna, why should I wish you harm?' I answered gaily, recovering myself. 'I was only surprised... And how could I help being surprised at such an unexpected...'

'What is there to surprise you? I just got into the train and came. The train was comfortable and not jolting. Have you been for a walk?'

'Yes, I've been a walk to the Casino.'

'It's pleasant here,' said Granny, looking about her. 'It's warm and the trees are magnificent. I like that! Are the family at home? The General?'

'Oh, yes, at this time they are sure to be all at home.'

'So they have fixed hours here, and everything in style? They set the tone. I am told they keep their carriage, *les seigneurs russes*! They spend all their money and then they go abroad. And is Praskovya with them?'

'Yes, Polina Alexandrovna, too.'

'And the Frenchy? Oh, well, I shall see them all for myself. Alexey Ivanovitch, show me the way straight to him. Are you comfortable here?'

'Fairly so, Antonida Vassilyevna.'

'Potapitch, tell that dolt, the *kellner*, to give me a nice convenient set of rooms, not too high up, and take my things there at once. Why are they all so eager to carry me? Why do they put themselves forward? Ech, the slavish creatures! Who is this with you?' she asked, addressing me again.

'This is Mr Astley,' I answered.

'What Mr Astley?'

'A traveller, a good friend of mine; an acquaintance of the General's, too.'

'An Englishman. To be sure, he stares at me and keeps his mouth shut. I like Englishmen, though. Well, carry me upstairs, straight to their rooms. Where are they?'

They carried Granny up; I walked up the broad staircase in front. Our procession was very striking. Everyone we met stopped and stared. Our hotel is considered the best, the most expensive, and the most aristocratic in the place. Magnificent ladies and dignified Englishmen were always to be met on the staircase and in the corridors. Many people were making enquiries below of the *ober-kellner*, who was greatly impressed. He answered, of course, that this was a distinguished foreign lady, *une russe*, *une comtesse*, *grande dame*, and that she was taking the very apartments that had been occupied the week before by *la grande duchesse de N.* Granny's commanding and authoritative appearance as she was carried up in the chair was chiefly responsible for the sensation she caused. Whenever she met anyone fresh she scrutinised him inquisitively and questioned me about him in a loud voice. Granny was powerfully built, and though she did not get up from her chair, it could be seen that she was very tall. Her back was as straight as a board and she did not lean back in her chair. Her big grey head with its large, bold features was held erect; she had a positively haughty and defiant expression; and it was evident that her air and gestures were perfectly natural. In spite of her seventy-five years there was still a certain vigour in her face: and even her teeth were almost perfect. She was wearing a black silk dress and a white cap.

'She interests me very much,' Mr Astley, who was going up beside me, whispered to me.

'She knows about the telegrams,' I thought. 'She knows about des Grieux, too, but I fancy she does not know much about Mlle Blanche as yet.' I communicated this thought to Mr Astley.

Sinful man that I was, after the first surprise was over, I was immensely delighted at the thunderbolt that we were launching at the General. I was elated; and I walked in front feeling very gay.

Our apartments were on the third floor. Without announcing her arrival or even knocking at the door, I simply flung it wide open and Granny was carried in, in triumph. All of them were, as by design, assembled in the General's study. It was twelve o'clock and, I believe, some excursion was being planned for the whole party. Some were to drive, others were to ride on horseback, some acquaintances had been asked to join the party. Besides the General and Polina, with the children and their nurse, there were sitting in the study des Grieux, Mlle Blanche, again wearing her riding-habit, her mother, the little Prince, and a learned German traveller whom I had not seen before.

Granny's chair was set down in the middle of the room, three paces from the General. My goodness! I shall never forget the sensation! As we went in the General was describing something, while des Grieux was correcting him. I must observe that Mlle Blanche and des Grieux had for the last few days been particularly attentive to the little Prince, *à la barbe du pauvre général*, and the tone of the party was extremely gay and genially intimate, though, perhaps, it was artificial. Seeing Granny, the General was struck dumb. His mouth dropped open and he broke off in the middle of a word. He gazed at her open-eyed, as though spellbound by the eye of a basilisk. Granny looked at him in silence, too, immovably, but what a triumphant, challenging and ironical look it was! They gazed at each other for ten full seconds in the midst of profound silence on the part of all around them. For the first moment des Grieux was petrified, but immediately afterwards a look of extreme uneasiness flitted over his face. Mlle Blanche raised her eyebrows, opened her mouth and gazed wildly at Granny. The Prince and the learned German stared at the whole scene in great astonishment. Polina's eyes expressed the utmost wonder and perplexity, and she suddenly turned white as a handkerchief; a minute later the blood rushed rapidly into her face, flushing her cheeks. Yes, this was a catastrophe for all of them! I kept turning my eyes from Granny to all surrounding her and back again. Mr Astley stood on one side, calm and polite as usual.

'Well, here I am! Instead of a telegram!' Granny broke the silence by going off into a peal of laughter. 'Well, you didn't expect me?'

'Antonida Vassilyevna . . . Auntie . . . But how on earth . . . ' muttered the unhappy General.

If Granny had remained silent for a few seconds longer, he would, perhaps, have had a stroke.

'How on earth what? I got into the train and came. What's the railway for? You all thought that I had been laid out, and had left you a fortune? You see, I know how you sent telegrams from here. What a lot of money you must have wasted on them! They cost a good bit from here. I simply threw my legs over my shoulders and came off here. Is this the Frenchman? M. des Grieux, I fancy?'

'*Oui, Madame*,' des Grieux responded; '*et croyez, je suis si enchanté . . . votre santé . . . c'est un miracle . . . vous voir ici . . . une surprise charmante . . .* '

'*Charmante*, I dare say; I know you, you mummer. I haven't this much faith in you,' and she pointed her little finger at him. 'Who is this?' she asked, indicating Mlle Blanche. The striking-looking Frenchwoman, in a riding-habit with a whip in her hand, evidently impressed her. 'Someone living here?'

'This is Mlle Blanche de Cominges, and this is her mamma, Madame de Cominges; they are staying in this hotel,' I explained.

'Is the daughter married?' Granny questioned me without ceremony.

'Mlle de Cominges is an unmarried lady,' I answered, purposely speaking in a low voice and as respectfully as possible.

'Lively?'

'I do not understand the question.'

'You are not dull with her? Does she understand Russian? Des Grieux picked it up in Moscow. He had a smattering of it.'

I explained that Mlle de Cominges had never been in Russia.

'*Bonjour*,' said Granny, turning abruptly to Mlle Blanche.

'*Bonjour, madame*.' Mlle Blanche made an elegant and ceremonious curtsey, hastening, under the cover of modesty and politeness, to express by her whole face and figure her extreme astonishment at such a strange question and manner of address.

'Oh, she casts down her eyes, she is giving herself airs and graces; you can see the sort she is at once, an actress of some kind. I'm stopping here below in the hotel,' she said, turning suddenly to the General. 'I shall be your neighbour. Are you glad or sorry?'

'Oh, Auntie! do believe in my sincere feelings . . . of pleasure,' the General responded. He had by now recovered himself to some extent, and as, upon occasion, he could speak appropriately and with dignity, and even with some pretension to effectiveness, he began displaying his gifts now. 'We have been so alarmed and upset by the news of your illness . . . We received such despairing telegrams, and all at once . . . '

'Come, you are lying, you are lying,' Granny interrupted at once.

'But how could you' – the General, too, made haste to interrupt, raising his voice and trying not to notice the word 'lying' – 'how could you bring yourself to undertake such a journey? You must admit that at your age and in your state of health . . . at any rate it is all so unexpected that our surprise is very natural. But I am so pleased . . . and we all' (he began smiling with an ingratiating and delighted air) 'will try our utmost that you shall spend your season here as agreeably as possible . . . '

'Come, that's enough; that's idle chatter; you are talking nonsense, as usual. I can dispose of my time for myself. Though I've nothing against you, I don't bear a grudge. You ask how I could come? What is there surprising about it? It was the simplest thing. And why are you so surprised? How are you, Praskovya? What do you do here?'

'How do you do, Granny?' said Polina, going up to her. 'Have you been long on the journey?'

'Well, she's asked a sensible question – the others could say nothing but oh and ah! Why, you see, I lay in bed and lay in bed and was doctored and doctored, so I sent the doctors away and called in the sexton from St Nicolas. He had cured a peasant woman of the same disease by means of hayseed. And he did me good, too. On the third day I was in a perspiration all day and I got up. Then my Germans gathered round again, put on their spectacles and began to argue. "If you were to go abroad now," said they, "and take a course of the waters, all your symptoms would disappear." And why shouldn't I? I thought. The fools of Zazhigins began sighing and moaning: "Where are you off to?" they said. Well, so here I am! It took me a day to get ready, and the following week, on a Friday, I took a maid, and Potapitch, and the footman, Fyodor, but I sent Fyodor back from Berlin, because I saw he was not wanted, and I could have come quite alone. I took a special compartment and there are porters at all the stations, and for twenty kopecks they will carry you wherever you like. I say, what rooms he has taken!' she said in conclusion, looking about her. 'How do you get the money, my good man? Why, everything you've got is mortgaged. What a lot of money you must owe to this Frenchman alone! I know all about it; you see, I know all about it!'

'Oh, Auntie . . . ' said the General, all confusion. 'I am surprised, Auntie . . . I imagine that I am free to act . . . Besides, my expenses are not beyond my means, and we are here . . . '

'They are not? You say so! Then you must have robbed your children of their last farthing – you, their trustee!'

'After that, after such words,' began the General, indignant, 'I really don't know . . . '

'To be sure, you don't! I'll be bound you are always at roulette here? Have you whistled it all away?'

The General was so overwhelmed that he almost spluttered in the rush of his feelings.

'Roulette! I? In my position . . . I? Think what you are saying, Auntie; you must still be unwell . . . '

'Come, you are lying, you are lying. I'll be bound they can't tear you away; it's all lies! I'll have a look today what this roulette is like. You, Praskovya, tell me where to go and what to see, and Alexey Ivanovitch here will show me, and you, Potapitch, make a note of all the places to go to. What is there to see here?' she said, addressing Polina again.

'Close by are the ruins of the castle; then there is the Schlangenberg.'

'What is it, the Schlangenberg? A wood or what?'

'No, not a wood, it's a mountain; there is a peak there . . . '

'What do you mean by a peak?'

'The very highest point on the mountain. It is an enclosed place – the view from it is unique.'

'What about carrying my chair up the mountain? They wouldn't be able to drag it up, would they?'

'Oh, we can find porters,' I answered.

At this moment, Fedosya, the nurse, came up to greet Granny and brought the General's children with her.

'Come, there's no need for kissing! I cannot bear kissing children, they always have dirty noses. Well, how do you get on here, Fedosya?'

'It's very, very nice here, Antonida Vassilyevna,' answered Fedosya. 'How have you been, ma'am? We've been so worried about you.'

'I know, you are a good soul. Do you always have visitors?' – she turned to Polina again. 'Who is that wretched little rascal in spectacles?'

'Prince Nilsky,' Polina whispered.

'Ah, a Russian. And I thought he wouldn't understand! Perhaps he didn't hear. I have seen Mr Astley already. Here he is again,' said Granny, catching sight of him. 'How do you do?' – she turned to him suddenly.

Mr Astley bowed to her in silence.

'Have you no good news to tell me? Say something! Translate that to him, Polina.'

Polina translated it.

'Yes. That with great pleasure and delight I am looking at you, and very glad that you are in good health,' Mr Astley answered seriously, but with perfect readiness. It was translated to Granny and it was evident she was pleased.

'How well Englishmen always answer,' she observed. 'That's why I always like Englishmen. There's no comparison between them and Frenchmen! Come and see me,' she said, addressing Mr Astley again. 'I'll try not to worry you too much. Translate that to him, and tell him that I am here below – here below – do you hear? Below, below,' she repeated to Mr Astley, pointing downwards.

Mr Astley was extremely pleased at the invitation.

Granny looked Polina up and down attentively and with a satisfied air.

'I was fond of you, Praskovya,' she said suddenly. 'You're a fine wench, the best of the lot, and as for will – my goodness! Well, I have will too; turn round. That's not a false chignon, is it?'

'No, Granny, it's my own.'

'To be sure. I don't care for the silly fashion of the day. You look very nice. I should fall in love with you if I were a young gentleman. Why don't you get married? But it is time for me to go. And I want to go out, for I've had nothing but the train and the train . . . Well, are you still cross?' she added, turning to the General.

'Upon my word, Auntie, what nonsense!' cried the General, delighted. 'I understand at your age . . . '

'*Cette vieille est tombée en enfance*,' des Grieux whispered to me.

'I want to see everything here. Will you let me have Alexey Ivanovitch?' Granny went on to the General.

'Oh, as much as you like, but I will myself . . . and Polina, M. des Grieux . . . we shall all think it a pleasure to accompany you.'

'*Mais, madame, celà sera un plaisir*' . . . des Grieux addressed her with a bewitching smile.

'A *plaisir*, to be sure; you are absurd, my good sir. I am not going to give you any money, though,' she added suddenly. 'But now to my rooms; I must have a look at them, and then we'll go the round of everything. Come, lift me up.' Granny was lifted up again and we all flocked downstairs behind her chair. The General walked as though stunned by a blow on the head. Des Grieux was considering something. Mlle Blanche seemed about to remain, but for some reason she made up her mind to come with the rest. The Prince followed her at once, and no one was left in the General's study but Madame de Cominges and the German.

CHAPTER TEN

At watering-places and, I believe, in Europe generally, hotel-keepers and *ober-kellners*, in assigning rooms to their visitors, are guided not so much by the demands and desires of the latter as by their own personal opinion of them, and, one must add, they are rarely mistaken. But for some reason I cannot explain, they had assigned Granny such a splendid suite that they had quite overshot the mark. It consisted of four splendidly furnished rooms with a bathroom, quarters for the servants and a special room for the maid, and so on. Some *grande duchesse* really had been staying in those rooms the week before, a fact of which the new occupant was informed at once, in order to enhance the value of the apartments. Granny was carried, or rather wheeled, through all the rooms, and she looked at them attentively and severely. The *ober-kellner*, an elderly man with a bald head, followed her respectfully at this first survey.

I don't know what they all took Granny to be, but apparently for a very important and, above all, wealthy lady. They put down in the book at once: '*Madame la générale princesse de Tarasyevichev*,' though Granny had never been a princess. Her servants, her special compartment in the train, the mass of useless bags, portmanteaux, and even chests that had come with Granny probably laid the foundation of her prestige; while her invalid-chair, her abrupt tone and voice, her eccentric questions, which were made with the most unconstrained air that would tolerate no contradiction – in short, Granny's whole figure, erect, brisk, imperious – increased the awe in which she was held by all. As she looked at the rooms, Granny sometimes told them to stop her chair, pointed to some object in the furniture and addressed unexpected questions to the *ober-kellner*, who still smiled respectfully, though he was beginning to feel nervous. Granny put her questions in French, which she spoke, however, rather badly, so that I usually translated. The *ober-kellner's* answers for the most part did not please her and seemed unsatisfactory. And, indeed, she kept asking about all sorts of things quite irrelevant. Suddenly, for instance, stopping before a picture, a rather feeble copy of some well-known picture of a mythological subject, she would ask: 'Whose portrait is that?'

The *ober-kellner* replied that no doubt it was some countess.

'How is it you don't know? You live here and don't know. Why is it here? Why is she squinting?'

The *ober-kellner* could not answer these questions satisfactorily, and positively lost his head.

'Oh, what a blockhead!' commented Granny, in Russian.

She was wheeled on. The same performance was repeated with a Dresden statuette, which Granny looked at for a long time, and then ordered them to remove, no one knew why. Finally, she worried the *ober-kellner* about what the carpets in the bedroom cost, and where they had been woven! The *ober-kellner* promised to make enquiries.

'What asses,' Granny grumbled, and concentrated her whole attention on the bed. 'What a gorgeous canopy! Open the bed.'

They opened the bed.

'More, more, turn it all over. Take off the pillows, the pillows, lift up the feather bed.'

Everything was turned over. Granny examined it attentively.

'It's a good thing there are no bugs. Take away all the linen! Make it up with my linen and my pillows. But all this is too gorgeous. Such rooms are not for an old woman like me. I shall be dreary all alone. Alexey Ivanovitch, you must come and see me very often when your lessons with the children are over.'

'I left the General's service yesterday,' I answered, 'and am living in the hotel quite independently.'

'How is that?'

'A German of high rank, a Baron, with his Baroness, came here from Berlin the other day. I addressed him yesterday in German without keeping to the Berlin accent.'

'Well, what then?'

'He thought it an impertinence and complained to the General, and yesterday the General discharged me.'

'Why, did you swear at the Baron, or what? (though if you had it wouldn't have mattered!)'

'Oh, no. On the contrary, the Baron raised his stick to thrash me.'

'And did you, sniveller, allow your tutor to be treated like that?' she said suddenly, addressing the General; 'and turned him out of his place too! Noodles! you're all a set of noodles, as I see.'

'Don't disturb yourself, Auntie,' said the General, with a shade of condescending familiarity; 'I can manage my own business. Besides, Alexey Ivanovitch has not given you quite a correct account of it.'

'And you just put up with it?' – she turned to me.

'I meant to challenge the Baron to a duel,' I answered, as calmly and modestly as I could, 'but the General opposed it.'

'Why did you oppose it?' – Granny turned to the General again. ('And you can go, my good man; you can come when you are called,' she said, addressing the *ober-kellner*; 'no need to stand about gaping. I can't endure this Nürnberg rabble!')

The man bowed and went out, not, of course, understanding Granny's compliments.

'Upon my word, Auntie, surely a duel was out of the question.'

'Why out of the question? Men are all cocks; so they should fight. You are all noodles, I see, you don't know how to stand up for your country. Come, take me up, Potapitch; see that there are always two porters: engage them. I don't want more than two. I shall only want them to carry me up and down stairs, and to wheel me on the levels in the street. Explain that to them; and pay them beforehand – they will be more respectful. You will always be with me yourself, and you, Alexey Ivanovitch, point out that Baron to me when we are out, that I may have a look at the von Baron. Well, where is the roulette?'

I explained that the roulette tables were in rooms in the Casino. Then followed questions: Were there many of them? Did many people play? Did they play all day long? How was it arranged? I answered at last that she had much better see all this with her own eyes, and that it was rather difficult to describe it.

'Well, then, take me straight there! You go first, Alexey Ivanovitch!'

'Why, Auntie, don't you really mean to rest after your journey?' the General asked anxiously. He seemed rather flurried, and, indeed, they all seemed embarrassed and were exchanging glances.

Probably they all felt it rather risky and, indeed, humiliating to accompany Granny to the Casino, where, of course, she might do something eccentric, and in public; at the same time they all proposed to accompany her.

'Why should I rest? I am not tired and, besides, I've been sitting still for three days. And then we will go and see the springs and medicinal waters; where are they? And then . . . we'll go and see, what was it you said, Praskovya? – peak, wasn't it?'

'Yes, Granny.'

'Well, peak, then, if it is a peak. And what else is there here?'

'There are a great many objects of interest, Granny,' Polina exerted herself to say.

'Why don't you know them? Marfa, you shall come with me, too,' she said, addressing her maid.

'But why should she come?' the General said fussily; 'and in fact it's out of the question, and I doubt whether Potapitch will be admitted into the Casino.'

'What nonsense! Am I to abandon her because she is a servant? She's a human being, too; here we have been on our travels for a week; she wants to have a look at things, too. With whom could she go except me? She wouldn't dare show her nose in the street by herself.'

'But, Granny . . . '

'Why, are you ashamed to be with me? Then stay at home; you are not asked. Why, what a General! I am a General's widow myself. And why should you all come trailing after me? I can look at it all with Alexey Ivanovitch.'

But des Grieux insisted that we should all accompany her, and launched out into the most polite phrases about the pleasure of accompanying her, and so on. We all started.

'*Elle est tombée en enfance*,' des Grieux repeated to the General; '*seule, elle fera des bêtises* . . . ' I heard nothing more, but he evidently had some design, and, possibly, his hopes had revived.

It was half a mile to the Casino. The way was through an avenue of chestnuts to a square, going round which, they came out straight on the Casino. The General was to some extent reassured, for our procession, though somewhat eccentric, was, nevertheless, decorous and presentable. And there was nothing surprising in the fact of an invalid who could not walk putting in an appearance at the Casino; but, anyway, the General was afraid of the Casino; why should an invalid unable to walk, and an old lady, too, go into the gambling saloon? Polina and Mlle Blanche walked on each side of the bath-chair. Mlle Blanche laughed, was modestly animated and even sometimes jested very politely with Granny, so much so that the latter spoke of her approvingly at last. Polina, on the other side, was obliged to be continually answering Granny's innumerable questions, such as: 'Who was that passed? Who was that woman driving past? Is it a big town? Is it a big garden? What are those trees? What's that hill? Do eagles fly here? What is that absurd-looking roof?' Mr Astley walked beside me and whispered that he expected a great deal from that morning. Potapitch and Marfa walked in the background close behind the bath-chair, Potapitch in his swallow-tailed coat and white tie, but with a cap on his head, and Marfa (a red-faced maid-servant, forty years old and beginning to turn grey) in a cap, cotton gown, and creaking goatskin slippers. Granny turned to them very often and addressed remarks to them. Des Grieux was talking with an air of determination. Probably he was reassuring the General, evidently he was giving him some advice. But Granny had already pronounced the fatal phrase: 'I am not going to give you money.' Perhaps to des Grieux this announcement sounded incredible, but the General knew his aunt. I noticed that des Grieux and Mlle Blanche were continually exchanging glances. I could distinguish the Prince and the German traveller at the farther end of the avenue; they had stopped, and were walking away from us.

Our visit to the Casino was a triumph. The porters and attendants displayed the same deference as in the hotel. They looked at us, however, with curiosity. Granny began by giving orders that she should be wheeled through all the rooms. Some she admired, others made no impression on her; she asked questions about them all. At last we came to the roulette room. The lackeys, who stood like sentinels at closed doors, flung the doors wide open as though they were impressed.

Granny's appearance at the roulette table made a profound impression on the public. At the roulette tables and at the other end of the room, where there was a table with *trente et quarante*, there was a crowd of a hundred and fifty or two hundred players, several rows deep. Those who had succeeded in squeezing their way right up to the table, held fast, as they always do, and would not give up their places to anyone until they had lost; for simple spectators were not allowed to stand at the tables and occupy the space. Though there were chairs set round the table, few of the players sat down, especially when there was a great crowd, because standing one could get closer and consequently pick out one's place and put down one's stake more conveniently. The second and the third rows pressed up upon the first, waiting and watching for their turn; but sometimes a hand would be impatiently thrust forward through the first row to put down a stake. Even from the third row people managed to seize chances of poking forward their stakes; consequently every ten or even five minutes there was some 'scene' over disputed stakes at one end of the hall or another. The police of the Casino were, however, fairly good. It was, of course, impossible to prevent crowding; on the contrary, the owners were glad of the rush of people because it was profitable, but eight croupiers sitting round the table kept a vigilant watch on the stakes: they even kept count of them, and when disputes arose they could settle them. In extreme cases they called in the police, and the trouble was over in an instant. There were police officers in plain clothes stationed here and there among the players, so that they could not be recognised. They were especially on the lookout for thieves and professional pickpockets, who are very numerous at the roulette tables, as it affords them excellent opportunity for exercising their skill. The fact is, elsewhere thieves must pick pockets or break locks, and such enterprises, when unsuccessful, have a very troublesome ending. But in this case the thief has only to go up to the roulette table, begin playing, and all at once, openly and publicly, take another person's winnings and put them in his pocket. If a dispute arises, the cheat insists loudly that the stake was his. If the trick is played cleverly and the witnesses hesitate, the thief may often succeed in carrying off the money, if the sum is not a very large one, of course. In that case the croupiers or some one of the other players are almost certain to have been keeping an eye on it. But if the sum is not a large one, the real owner sometimes actually declines to keep up the dispute, and goes away shrinking from the scandal. But if they succeed in detecting a thief, they turn him out at once with contumely.

All this Granny watched from a distance with wild curiosity. She was much delighted at a thief's being turned out. *Trente et quarante* did not interest her very much; she was more pleased at roulette and the rolling of the little ball. She evinced a desire at last to get a closer view of the game. I don't know how it happened, but the attendants and other officious persons (principally Poles who had lost, and who pressed their services on lucky players and foreigners of all sorts) at once, and in spite of the crowd, cleared a place for Granny in the very middle of the table beside the chief croupier, and wheeled her chair to it. A number of visitors who were not playing, but watching the play (chiefly Englishmen with their families), at once crowded round the table to watch Granny from behind the players. Numbers of lorgnettes were turned in her direction. The croupiers' expectations rose. Such an eccentric person certainly seemed to promise something out of the ordinary. An old woman of seventy, who could not walk, yet wished to play, was, of course, not a sight to be seen every day. I squeezed my way up to the table too, and took my stand beside Granny. Potapitch and Marfa were left somewhere in the distance among the crowd. The General, Polina, des Grieux, and Mlle Blanche stood aside, too, among the spectators.

At first Granny began looking about at the players. She began in a half whisper asking me abrupt, jerky questions. Who was that man and who was this woman? She was particularly delighted by a young man at the end of the table who was playing for very high stakes, putting down thousands, and had, as people whispered around, already won as much as forty thousand francs, which lay before him in heaps of gold and banknotes. He was pale; his eyes glittered and his hands were shaking; he was staking now without counting, by handfuls, and yet he kept on winning and winning, kept raking in the money. The attendants hung about him solicitously, set a chair for him, cleared a place round him that he might have more room, that he might not be crowded – all this in expectation of a liberal tip. Some players, after they have won, tip the attendants without counting a handful of coins in their joy. A Pole had already established himself at his side, and was deferentially but continually whispering to him, probably telling him what to stake on, advising and directing his play – of course, he, too, expecting a tip later on! But the player scarcely looked at him. He staked at random and kept winning. He evidently did not know what he was doing.

Granny watched him for some minutes.

'Tell him,' Granny said suddenly, growing excited and giving me a poke, 'tell him to give it up, to take his money quickly and go away. He'll lose it all directly, he'll lose it all!' she urged, almost breathless with agitation. 'Where's Potapitch? Send Potapitch to him. Come, tell him, tell him,' she went on, poking me. 'Where is Potapitch? *Sortez*! *Sortez*!' – she began herself shouting to the young man.

I bent down to her and whispered resolutely that she must not shout like this here, that even talking aloud was forbidden, because it hindered counting and that we should be turned out directly.

'How vexatious! The man's lost! I suppose it's his own doing . . . I can't look at him, it quite upsets me. What a dolt!' and Granny made haste to turn in another direction.

On the left, on the other side of the table, there was conspicuous among the players a young lady, and beside her a sort of dwarf. Who this dwarf was, and whether he was a relation or brought by her for the sake of effect, I don't know. I had noticed the lady before; she made her appearance at the gambling table every day, at one o'clock in the afternoon, and went away exactly at two; she always played for an hour. She was already known, and a chair was set for her at once. She took out of her pocket some gold, some thousand-franc notes, and began staking quietly, coolly, prudently, making pencil notes on a bit of paper of the numbers about which the chances grouped themselves, and trying to work out a system. She staked considerable sums. She used to win every day – one, two, or at the most three thousand francs – not more, and instantly went away. Granny scrutinised her for a long time.

'Well, that one won't lose! That one there won't lose! Of what class is she? Do you know? Who is she?'

'She must be a Frenchwoman, of a certain class, you know,' I whispered.

'Ah, one can tell the bird by its flight. One can see she has a sharp claw. Explain to me now what every turn means and how one has to bet!'

I explained as far as I could to Granny all the various points on which one could stake: *rouge et noir*, *pair et impair*, *manque et passe*, and finally the various subtleties in the system of the numbers. Granny listened attentively, remembered, asked questions, and began to master it. One could point to examples of every kind, so that she very quickly and readily picked up a great deal.

'But what about *zéro*? You see that croupier, the curly-headed one, the chief one, showed *zéro* just now? And why did he scoop up everything that was on the table? Such a heap, he took it all for himself. What is the meaning of it?'

'*Zéro*, Granny, means that the bank wins all. If the little ball falls on *zéro*, everything on the table goes to the bank. It is true you can stake your money so as to keep it, but the bank pays nothing.'

'You don't say so! And shall I get nothing?'

'No, Granny, if before this you had staked on *zéro* you would have got thirty-five times what you staked.'

'What! thirty-five times, and does it often turn up? Why don't they stake on it, the fools.'

'There are thirty-six chances against it, Granny.'

'What nonsense. Potapitch! Potapitch! Stay, I've money with me – here.' She took out of her pocket a tightly packed purse, and picked out of it a friedrich d'or. 'Stake it on the *zéro* at once.'

'Granny, *zéro* has only just turned up,' I said; 'so now it won't turn up for a long time. You will lose a great deal; wait a little, anyway.'

'Oh, nonsense; put it down!'

'As you please, but it may not turn up again till the evening. You may go on staking thousands; it has happened.'

'Oh, nonsense, nonsense. If you are afraid of the wolf you shouldn't go into the forest. What? Have I lost? Stake again!'

A second friedrich d'or was lost: she staked a third. Granny could scarcely sit still in her seat. She stared with feverish eyes at the little ball dancing on the spokes of the turning wheel. She lost a third, too. Granny was beside herself, she could not sit still, she even thumped on the table with her fist when the croupier announced '*trente-six*' instead of the *zéro* she was expecting.

'There, look at it,' said Granny angrily; 'isn't that cursed little *zéro* coming soon? As sure as I'm alive, I'll sit here till *zéro* does come! It's that cursed curly-headed croupier's doing; he'll never let it come! Alexey Ivanovitch, stake two gold pieces at once! Staking as much as you do, even if *zéro* does come you'll get nothing by it.'

'Granny!'

'Stake, stake! it is not your money.'

I staked two friedrichs d'or. The ball flew about the wheel for a long time, at last it began dancing about the spokes. Granny was numb with excitement, and squeezed my fingers, and all at once –

'*Zéro*!' boomed the croupier.

'You see, you see!' – Granny turned to me quickly, beaming and delighted. 'I told you so. The Lord Himself put it into my head to stake those two gold pieces! Well, how much do I get now? Why don't they give it me? Potapitch, Marfa, where are they? Where have all our people got to? Potapitch, Potapitch!'

'Granny, afterwards,' I whispered; 'Potapitch is at the door, they won't let him in. Look, Granny, they are giving you the money, take it!' A heavy roll of printed blue notes, worth fifty friedrichs d'or, was thrust towards Granny and twenty friedrich d'or were counted out to her. I scooped it all up in a shovel and handed it to Granny.

'*Faites le jeu, messieurs*! *Faites le jeu, messieurs*! *Rien ne va plus*!' called the croupier, inviting the public to stake, and preparing to turn the wheel.

'Heavens! we are too late. They're just going to turn it. Put it down, put it down!' Granny urged me in a flurry.' Don't dawdle, make haste!' She was beside herself and poked me with all her might.

'What am I to stake it on, Granny?'

'On *zéro*, on *zéro*! On *zéro* again! Stake as much as possible! How much have we got altogether? Seventy friedrichs d'or. There's no need to spare it. Stake twenty friedrichs d'or at once.'

'Think what you are doing, Granny! sometimes it does not turn up for two hundred times running! I assure you, you may go on staking your whole fortune.'

'Oh, nonsense, nonsense! Put it down! How your tongue does wag! I know what I'm about.' Granny was positively quivering with excitement.

'By the regulations it's not allowed to stake more than twelve roubles on *zéro* at once, Granny; here I have staked that.'

'Why is it not allowed? Aren't you lying? Monsieur! Monsieur!' – she nudged the croupier, who was sitting near her on the left, and was about to set the wheel turning. '*Combien zéro*? *Douze*? *Douze*?'

I immediately interpreted the question in French.

'*Oui, madame*,' the croupier confirmed politely; 'as the winnings from no single stake must exceed four thousand florins by the regulations,' he added in explanation.

'Well, there's no help for it, stake twelve.'

'*Le jeu est fait*,' cried the croupier. The wheel rotated, and thirty turned up. She had lost.

'Again, again, again! Stake again!' cried Granny. I no longer resisted, and, shrugging my shoulders, staked another twelve friedrichs d'or. The wheel turned a long time. Granny was simply quivering as she watched the wheel. 'Can she really imagine that *zéro* will win again?' I thought, looking at her with wonder. Her face was beaming with a firm conviction of winning, an unhesitating expectation that in another minute they would shout *zéro*. The ball jumped into the cage.

'*Zéro*!' cried the croupier.

'What!!!' Granny turned to me with intense triumph.

I was a gambler myself, I felt that at the moment my arms and legs were trembling, there was a throbbing in my head. Of course, this was a rare chance that *zéro* should have come up three times in some dozen turns; but there was nothing particularly wonderful about it. I had myself seen *zéro* turn up three times *running* two days before, and a gambler who had been zealously noting down the lucky numbers, observed aloud that, only the day before, *zéro* had turned up only once in twenty-four hours.

Granny's winnings were counted out to her with particular attention and deference as she had won such a large sum. She received four hundred and twenty friedrichs d'or, that is, four thousand florins and seventy friedrichs d'or. She was given twenty friedrichs d'or in gold, and four thousand florins in banknotes.

This time Granny did not call Potapitch; she had other preoccupations. She did not even babble or quiver outwardly! She was, if one may so express it, quivering inwardly. She was entirely concentrated on something, absorbed in one aim.

'Alexey Ivanovitch, he said that one could only stake four thousand florins at once, didn't he? Come, take it, stake the whole four thousand on the red,' Granny commanded.

It was useless to protest; the wheel began rotating.

'*Rouge*,' the croupier proclaimed.

Again she had won four thousand florins, making eight in all.

'Give me four, and stake four again on red,' Granny commanded.

Again I staked four thousand.

'*Rouge*,' the croupier pronounced again.

'Twelve thousand altogether! Give it me all here. Pour the gold here into the purse and put away the notes. That's enough! Home! Wheel my chair out.'

CHAPTER ELEVEN

The chair was wheeled to the door at the other end of the room. Granny was radiant. All our party immediately thronged round her with congratulations. However eccentric Granny's behaviour might be, her triumph covered a multitude of sins, and the General was no longer afraid of compromising himself in public by his relationship with such a strange woman. With a condescending and familiarly good-humoured smile, as though humouring a child, he congratulated Granny. He was, however, evidently impressed, like all the other spectators. People talked all round and pointed at Granny. Many passed by to get a closer view of her! Mr Astley was talking of her aside, with two English acquaintances. Some majestic ladies gazed at her with majestic amazement, as though at a marvel . . . des Grieux positively showered congratulations and smiles upon her.

'*Quelle victoire*!' he said.

'*Mais, Madame, c'était du feu,*' Mlle Blanche commented, with an ingratiating smile.

'Yes, I just went and won twelve thousand florins! Twelve, indeed; what about the gold? With the gold it makes almost thirteen. What is that in our money? Will it be six thousand?'

I explained that it made more than seven, and in the present state of exchange might even amount to eight.

'Well, that's something worth having, eight thousand! And you stay here, you noodles, and do nothing! Potapitch, Marfa, did you see?'

'My goodness! how did you do it, Ma'am? Eight thousand!' exclaimed Marfa, wriggling.

'There! there's five gold pieces for you, here!'

Potapitch and Marfa flew to kiss her hand.

'And give the porters, too, a friedrich d'or each. Give it them in gold, Alexey Ivanovitch. Why is that flunkey bowing and the other one too? Are they congratulating me? Give them a friedrich d'or too.'

'*Madame la princesse . . . un pauvre expatrié . . . malheur continuel . . . les princes russes sont si généreux . . .* ' A person with moustaches and an obsequious smile, in a threadbare coat and gay-coloured waistcoat, came cringing about Granny's chair, waving his hat in his hand.

'Give him a friedrich d'or too . . . No, give him two; that's enough, or there will be no end to them. Lift me up and carry me out. Praskovya' – she turned to Polina Alexandrovna – 'I'll buy you a dress tomorrow, and I'll buy Mlle . . . what's her name, Mlle Blanche, isn't it? I'll buy her a dress too. Translate that to her, Praskovya!'

'*Merci, Madame.*' Mlle Blanche made a grateful curtsey while she exchanged an ironical smile with des Grieux and the General. The General was rather embarrassed and was greatly relieved when we reached the avenue.

'Fedosya – won't Fedosya be surprised?' said Granny, thinking of the General's nurse. 'I must make her a present of a dress. Hey, Alexey Ivanovitch, Alexey Ivanovitch, give this to the poor man.'

A man in rags, with bent back, passed us on the road, and looked at us.

'And perhaps he is not a poor man, but a rogue, Granny.'

'Give him a gulden, give it him!'

I went up to the man and gave it him. He looked at me in wild amazement, but took the gulden, however. He smelt of spirits.

'And you, Alexey Ivanovitch. Have you not tried your luck yet?'

'No, Granny.'

'But your eyes were burning, I saw them.'

'I shall try, Granny, I certainly shall later.'

'And stake on *zéro* straight away. You will see! How much have you in hand?'

'Only twenty friedrichs d'or, Granny.'

'That's not much. I will give you fifty friedrichs d'or. I will lend it if you like. Here, take this roll – but don't you expect anything, all the same, my good man, I am not going to give you anything,' she said, suddenly addressing the General.

The latter winced, but he said nothing. Des Grieux frowned.

'*Que diable, c'est une terrible vieille!*' he muttered to the General through his teeth.

'A beggar, a beggar, another beggar!' cried Granny. 'Give him a gulden, too, Alexey Ivanovitch.'

This time it was a grey-headed old man with a wooden leg, in a long-skirted blue coat and with a long stick in his hand. He looked like an old soldier. But when I held out a gulden to him he stepped back and looked at me angrily.

'*Was ist's der Teufel*,' he shouted, following up with a dozen oaths.

'Oh, he's a fool,' cried Granny, dismissing him with a wave of her hand. 'Go on! I'm hungry! Now we'll have dinner directly; then I'll rest a little, and back here again.'

'You want to play again, Granny?' I cried.

'What do you expect? That you should all sit here and sulk while I watch you?'

'*Mais, madame* – ' des Grieux drew near – '*les chances peuvent tourner, une seule mauvaise chance et vous perdrez tout . . . surtout avec votre jeu . . . C'est terrible!*'

'*Vous perdrez absolument*,' chirped Mlle Blanche.

'But what is it to do with all of you? I shouldn't lose your money, but my own! And where is that Mr Astley?' she asked me.

'He stayed in the Casino, Granny.'

'I'm sorry, he's such a nice man.'

On reaching home Granny met the *ober-kellner* on the stairs, called him and began bragging of her winnings; then she sent for Fedosya, made her a present of three friedrichs d'or and ordered dinner to be served. Fedosya and Marfa hovered over her at dinner.

'I watched you, ma'am,' Marfa cackled, 'and said to Potapitch, "What does our lady want to do?" And the money on the table – saints alive! the money! I haven't seen so much money in the whole of my life, and all round were gentlefolk – nothing but gentlefolk sitting. "And wherever do all these gentlefolk come from, Potapitch?" said I. May our Lady Herself help her, I thought. I was praying for you, ma'am, and my heart was simply sinking, simply sinking; I was all of a tremble. Lord help her, I thought, and here the Lord has sent you luck. I've been trembling ever since, ma'am. I'm all of a tremble now.'

'Alexey Ivanovitch, after dinner, at four o'clock, get ready and we'll go. Now goodbye for a time; don't forget to send for a doctor for me. I must drink the waters, too. Go, or maybe you'll forget.'

As I left Granny I was in a sort of stupor. I tried to imagine what would happen now to all our people and what turn things would take. I saw clearly that they (especially the General) had not yet succeeded in recovering from the first shock. The fact of Granny's arrival instead of the telegram which they were expecting from hour to hour to announce her death (and consequently the inheritance of her fortune) had so completely shattered the whole fabric of their plans and intentions that Granny's further exploits at roulette threw them into positive bewilderment and a sort of stupefaction seemed to have come over all of them.

Meanwhile this second fact was almost more important than the first; for though Granny had repeated twice that she would not give the General any money, yet, who knows? – there was no need to give up all hope yet. Des Grieux, who was involved in all the General's affairs, had not lost hope. I am convinced that Mlle Blanche, also much involved in the General's affairs (I should think so: to marry a General and with a considerable fortune!), would not have given up hope, and would have tried all her fascinating arts upon Granny – in contrast with the proud and incomprehensible Polina, who did not know how to curry favour with anyone. But now, now that Granny had had such success at roulette, now that Granny's personality had shown itself so clearly and so typically (a refractory and imperious old lady, *et tombée en enfance*), now, perhaps, all was lost. Why, she was as pleased as a child, so pleased that she would go on till she was ruined and had lost everything. Heavens! I thought (and, God forgive me, with a malignant laugh), why, every friedrich d'or Granny staked just now must have been a fresh sore in the General's heart, must have maddened des Grieux and infuriated Mlle de Cominges, who saw the cup slipping from her lips. Another fact: even in her triumph and joy of winning, when Granny was giving money away to everyone, and taking every passer-by for a beggar, even then she had let fall to the General, 'I'm not going to give you anything, though!' That meant that she had fastened upon that idea, was sticking to it, had made up her mind about it. There was danger! danger!

All these reflections were revolving in my mind as I mounted the front stairs from Granny's apartments to my garret in the very top storey. All this interested me strongly. Though, of course, I could before have divined the strongest leading motives prompting the actors before me, yet I did not know for certain all the mysteries and intrigues of the drama. Polina had never been fully open with me. Though it did happen at times that she revealed her feelings to me, yet I noticed that almost always after such confidences she would make fun of all she had said, or would try to obscure the matter and put it in a different light. Oh, she had hidden a great deal! In any case, I foresaw that the *dénouement* of this mysterious and constrained position was at hand. One more shock – and everything would be ended and revealed. About my fortunes, which were also involved in all this, I scarcely troubled. I was in a strange mood: I had only twenty friedrichs d'or in my pocket; I was in a foreign land without a job or means of livelihood, without hope, without prospects, and – I did not trouble my head about it! If it had not been for the thought of Polina, I should have abandoned myself to the comic interest of the approaching catastrophe, and would have been shouting with laughter. But I was troubled about Polina; her fate was being decided, I divined that; but I regret to say that it was not altogether her fate that troubled me. I wanted to fathom her secrets; I wanted her to come to me and say: 'I love you', and if not that, if that was senseless insanity, then . . . well, what was there to care about? Did I know what I wanted? I was like one demented: all I wanted was to be near her, in the halo of her glory, in her radiance, always, for ever, all my life. I knew nothing more! And could I leave her?

In their passage on the third storey I felt as though something nudged me. I turned round and, twenty paces or more from me, I saw coming out of a door, Polina. She seemed waiting: and as soon as she saw me beckoned to me.

'Polina Alexandrovna . . . '

'Hush!' she said.

'Imagine,' I whispered to her, 'I felt as though someone had nudged me just now; I looked round – you! It seems as though there were a sort of electricity from you!'

'Take this letter,' Polina articulated anxiously with a frown, probably not hearing what I had said, 'and give it into Mr Astley's own hands at once. Make haste, I beg you. There is no need of an answer. He will . . . '

She did not finish.

'Mr Astley?' I repeated in surprise.

But Polina had already disappeared behind the door.

'Aha, so they are in correspondence!' I ran at once, of course, to Mr Astley; first to his hotel, where I did not find him, then to the Casino, where I hurried through all the rooms: and at last, as I was returning home in vexation, almost in despair, I met him by chance, with a party of Englishmen and Englishwomen on horseback. I beckoned to him, stopped him and gave him the letter: we had not time even to exchange a glance. But I suspect that Mr Astley purposely gave rein to his horse.

Was I tortured by jealousy? Anyway, I was in an utterly shattered condition. I did not even want to find out what they were writing to one another about. And so he was trusted by her! 'Her friend, her friend,' I thought, 'and that is clear (and when has he had time to become her friend?), but is there love in the case? Of course not,' common-sense whispered to me. But common-sense alone counts for little in such cases; anyway, this, too, had to be cleared up. Things were growing unpleasantly complicated.

Before I had time to go into the hotel, first the porter and then the *ober-kellner*, coming out of his room, informed me that I was wanted, that I had been asked for, three times they had sent to ask: where was I? – that I was asked to go as quickly as possible to the General's rooms. I was in the most disagreeable frame of mind. In the General's room I found, besides the General himself, des Grieux and Mlle Blanche – alone, without her mother. The mother was evidently an official one, only used for show. But when it came to real *business* she acted for herself. And probably the woman knew little of her so-called daughter's affairs.

They were, however, consulting warmly about something, and the doors of the study were actually locked – which had never happened before. Coming to the door, I heard loud voices – des Grieux's insolent and malignant voice, Blanche's shrill fury, and the General's pitiful tones, evidently defending himself about something. Upon my entrance they all, as it were, pulled themselves up and restrained themselves. Des Grieux smoothed his hair and forced a smile into his angry face – that horrid official French smile which I so detest. The crushed and desperate General tried to assume an air of dignity, but it was a mechanical effort. Only

Mlle Blanche's countenance, blazing with anger, scarcely changed. She only ceased speaking while she fixed her eyes upon me in impatient expectation. I may mention that hitherto she had treated me with extraordinary casualness, had even refused to respond to my bows, and had simply declined to see me.

'Alexey Ivanovitch,' the General began in a soft and mollifying tone; 'allow me to tell you that it is strange, exceedingly strange . . . in fact, your conduct in regard to me and my family . . . in fact, it is exceedingly strange . . . '

'*Eh! ce n'est pas ça*,' des Grieux interposed, with vexation and contempt. (There's no doubt he was the leading spirit.) '*Mon cher monsieur, notre cher général se trompe*, in taking up this tone,' (I translate the rest of his speech in Russian) 'but he meant to say . . . that is to warn you, or rather to beg you most earnestly not to ruin him – yes, indeed, not to ruin him! I make use of that expression.'

'But how, how?' I interrupted.

'Why, you are undertaking to be the guide (or how shall I express it?) of this old woman, *cette pauvre terrible vieille*' – des Grieux himself hesitated – 'but you know she'll lose everything; she will gamble away her whole fortune! You know yourself, you have seen yourself, how she plays! If she begins to lose; she will never leave off, from obstinacy, from anger, and will lose everything, she will gamble away everything, and in such cases one can never regain one's losses and then . . . then . . . '

'And then,' the General put in, 'then you will ruin the whole family! I and my family are her heirs, she has no nearer relations. I tell you openly: my affairs are in a bad way, a very bad way. You know my position to some extent . . . If she loses a considerable sum or even (Lord help us!) her whole fortune, what will become of me, of my children!' (The General looked round at des Grieux.) 'Of me.' (He looked round at Mlle Blanche, who turned away from him with contempt.) 'Alexey Ivanovitch, save us, save us! . . . '

'But how, General, how, how can I? . . . What influence have I in the matter?'

'Refuse, refuse, give her up! . . . '

'Then someone else will turn up,' I said.

'*Ce n'est pas ça, ce n'est pas ça*,' des Grieux interrupted again, '*que diable*! No, don't desert her, but at least advise her, dissuade her, draw her away . . . don't let her play too much, distract her in some way.'

'But how can I do that? If you would undertake the task yourself, M. des Grieux,' I added, as naïvely as I could.

Here I caught a rapid, fiery, questioning glance from Mlle Blanche at M. des Grieux. And in des Grieux's own face there was something peculiar, something he could not himself disguise.

'The point is, she won't accept me now!' des Grieux cried, with a wave of his hand. 'If only . . . later on . . . '

Des Grieux looked rapidly and meaningly at Mlle Blanche.

'*O, mon cher M. Alexis, soyez si bon.*' Mlle Blanche herself took a step towards me with a most fascinating smile, she seized me by both hands and pressed them warmly. Damn it all! That diabolical face knew how to change completely in one moment. At that instant her face was so imploring, so sweet, it was such a child-like and even mischievous smile; at the end of the phrase she gave me such a sly wink, unseen by all the rest; she meant to do for me completely, and it was successfully done; only it was horribly coarse.

Then the General leapt up, positively leapt up. 'Alexey Ivanovitch, forgive me for beginning as I did just now. I did not mean that at all . . . I beg you, I beseech you, I bow down before you in Russian style – you alone, you alone can save us. Mlle de Comminges and I implore you – you understand, you understand, of course.' He besought me, indicating Mlle Blanche with his eyes. He was a very pitiful figure.

At that instant there came three subdued and respectful knocks at the door; it was opened – the corridor attendant was knocking and a few steps behind him stood Potapitch. They came with messages from Granny; they were charged to find and bring me at once. 'She is angry,' Potapitch informed me.

'But it is only half-past three.'

'She could not get to sleep; she kept tossing about, and then at last she got up, sent for her chair and for you. She's at the front door now.'

'*Quelle mégère*,' cried des Grieux.

I did, in fact, find Granny on the steps, out of all patience at my not being there. She could not wait till four o'clock.

'Come,' she cried, and we set off again to roulette.

CHAPTER TWELVE

Granny was in an impatient and irritable mood; it was evident that roulette had made a deep impression on her mind. She took no notice of anything else and was altogether absent-minded. For instance, she asked me no questions on the road as she had done before. Seeing a luxurious carriage whirling by, she was on the point of raising her hand and asking: What is it? Whose is it? – but I believe she did not hear what I answered: her absorption was continually interrupted by abrupt and impatient gesticulations. When I pointed out to her Baron and Baroness Burmerhelm, who were approaching the Casino, she looked absentmindedly at them and said, quite indifferently, 'Ah!' and, turning round quickly to Potapitch and Marfa, who were walking behind her, snapped out to them –

'Why are you hanging upon us? We can't take you every time! Go home! You and I are enough,' she added, when they had hurriedly turned and gone home.

They were already expecting Granny at the Casino. They immediately made room for her in the same place, next to the croupier. I fancy that these croupiers, who are always so strictly decorous and appear to be ordinary officials who are absolutely indifferent as to whether the bank wins or loses, are by no means so unconcerned at the bank's losses and, of course, receive instructions for attracting players and for augmenting the profits – for which they doubtless receive prizes and bonuses. They looked upon Granny, anyway, as their prey.

Then just what we had expected happened.

This was how it was.

Granny pounced at once on zèro and immediately ordered me to stake twelve friedrichs d'or. She staked once, twice, three times – *zéro* never turned up.

'Put it down! Put it down!' Granny nudged me, impatiently. I obeyed.

'How many times have we staked?' she asked at last, grinding her teeth with impatience.

'I have staked twelve times, Granny. I have put down a hundred and forty-four friedrichs d'or. I tell you, Granny, very likely till evening . . . '

'Hold your tongue!' Granny interrupted. 'Stake on *zéro*, and stake at once a thousand gulden on red. Here, take the note.'

Red won, and *zéro* failed once more; a thousand gulden was gained.

'You see, you see!' whispered Granny, 'we have gained almost all that we have lost. Stake again on *zéro*; we'll stake ten times more and then give it up.'

But the fifth time Granny was thoroughly sick of it.

'The devil take that filthy *zéro*. Come, stake the whole four thousand gulden on the red,' she commanded me.

'Granny! it will be so much; why, what if red does not turn up!' I besought her; but Granny almost beat me. (Indeed, she nudged me so violently that she might almost be said to have attacked me.) There was no help for it. I staked on red the whole four thousand won that morning. The wheel turned. Granny sat calmly and proudly erect, never doubting that she would certainly win.

'*Zéro*!' boomed the croupier.

At first Granny did not understand, but when she saw the croupier scoop up her four thousand gulden, together with everything on the table, and learned that *zéro*, which had not turned up for so long and on which we had staked in vain almost two hundred friedrichs d'or, had, as though to spite her, turned up just as Granny was abusing it, she groaned and flung up her hands in view of the whole hall. People around actually laughed.

'Holy saints! The cursed thing has turned up!' Granny wailed, 'the hateful, hateful thing! That's your doing! It's all your doing' – she pounced upon me furiously, pushing me. 'It was you persuaded me.'

'Granny, I talked sense to you; how can I answer for chance?'

'I'll chance you,' she whispered angrily. 'Go away.'

'Goodbye, Granny.' I turned to go away.

'Alexey Ivanovitch, Alexey Ivanovitch! stop. Where are you off to? Come, what's the matter, what's the matter? Ach, he's in a rage! Stupid, come, stay, stay; come, don't be angry; I am a fool myself! Come, tell me what are we to do now!'

'I won't undertake to tell you, Granny, because you will blame me. Play for yourself, tell me and I'll put down the stakes.'

'Well, well! Come, stake another four thousand gulden on red! Here, take my pocket-book.' She took it out of her pocket and gave it me. 'Come, make haste and take it, there's twenty thousand roubles sterling in it.'

'Granny,' I murmured, 'such stakes . . . '

'As sure as I am alive, I'll win it back . . . Stake.'

We staked and lost.

'Stake, stake the whole eight!'

'You can't, Granny, four is the highest stake! . . . '

'Well, stake four!'

This time we won. Granny cheered up.

'You see, you see,' she nudged me; 'stake four again!'

She staked – she lost; then we lost again and again.

'Granny, the whole twelve thousand is gone,' I told her.

'I see it's all gone,' she answered with the calm of fury, if I may so express it. 'I see, my good friend, I see,' she muttered, with a fixed, as it were, absent-minded stare. 'Ech, as sure I am alive, stake another four thousand gulden!'

'But there's no money, Granny; there are some of our Russian five per cents and some bills of exchange of some sort, but no money.'

'And in the purse?'

'There's some small change, Granny.'

'Are there any money-changers here? I was told one could change any of our notes,' Granny enquired resolutely.

'Oh, as much as you like, but what you'll lose on the exchange . . . would horrify a Jew!'

'Nonsense! I'll win it all back. Take me! Call those blockheads!'

I wheeled away the chair; the porters appeared and we went out of the Casino.

'Make haste, make haste, make haste,' Granny commanded. 'Show us the way, Alexey Ivanovitch, and take us the nearest . . . Is it far?'

'Two steps, Granny.'

But at the turning from the square into the avenue we were met by our whole party: the General, des Grieux, Mlle Blanche and her mamma. Polina Alexandrovna was not with them, nor Mr Astley either.

'Well! Don't stop us!' cried Granny. 'Well, what do you want? I have no time to spare for you now!'

I walked behind; des Grieux ran up to me.

'She's lost all she gained this morning and twelve thousand gulden as well. We are going to change some five per cents,' I whispered to him quickly.

Des Grieux stamped and ran to tell the General. We went on wheeling Granny.

'Stop, stop!' the General whispered to me frantically.

'You try stopping her,' I whispered.

'Auntie!' said the General, approaching, 'Auntie . . . we are just . . . we are just . . . ' his voice quivered and failed him, 'hiring a horse and driving into the country . . . a most exquisite view . . . the peak . . . We were coming to invite you.'

'Oh, bother you and your peak.' Granny waved him off irritably.

'There are trees there . . . we will have tea . . . ' the General went on, utterly desperate.

'*Nous boirons du lait, sur l'herbe fraîche*,' added des Grieux, with ferocious fury.

Du lait, de l'herbe fraîche, that is the Paris bourgeois notion of the ideally idyllic; that is, as we all know, his conception of *nature et la vérité*!

'Oh, go on with you and your milk! Lap it up yourself; it gives me the bellyache. And why do you pester me?' cried Granny. 'I tell you I've no time to waste.'

'It's here, Granny,' I said; 'it's here!'

We had reached the house where the bank was. I went in to change the notes; Granny was left waiting at the entrance; des Grieux, the General and Blanche stood apart waiting, not knowing what to do. Granny looked wrathfully at them, and they walked away in the direction of the Casino.

They offered me such ruinous terms that I did not accept them, and went back to Granny for instructions.

'Ah, the brigands!' she cried, flinging up her hands. 'Well, never mind! Change it,' she cried resolutely; 'stay, call the banker out to me!'

'One of the clerks, Granny, do you mean?'

'Yes, a clerk, it's all the same. Ach, the brigands!'

The clerk consented to come when he learned that it was an invalid and aged countess, unable to come in, who was asking for him. Granny spent a long time loudly and angrily reproaching him for swindling her, and haggled with him in a mixture of Russian, French and German, while I came to the rescue in translating. The grave clerk listened to us in silence and shook his head. He looked at Granny with an intent stare that was hardly respectful; at last he began smiling.

'Well, get along with you,' cried Granny. 'Choke yourself with the money! Change it with him, Alexey Ivanovitch; there's no time to waste, or we would go elsewhere . . . '

'The clerk says that other banks give even less.'

I don't remember the sums exactly, but the banker's charges were terrible. I received close upon twelve thousand florins in gold and notes, took the account and carried it to Granny.

'Well, well, well, it's no use counting it,' she said, with a wave of her hand. 'Make haste, make haste, make haste!'

'I'll never stake again on that damned *zéro* nor on the red either,' she pronounced, as she was wheeled up to the Casino.

This time I did my very utmost to impress upon her the necessity of staking smaller sums, trying to persuade her that with the change of luck she would always be able to increase her stake. But she was so impatient that, though she agreed at first, it was impossible to restrain her when the play had begun; as soon as she had won a stake of ten, of twenty friedrichs d'ors –

'There, you see, there, you see,' she would begin nudging me; 'there, you see, we've won; if only we had staked four thousand instead of ten, we should have won four thousand, but, as it is, what's the good? It's all your doing, all your doing!'

And, vexed as I felt, watching her play, I made up my mind at last to keep quiet and to give no more advice.

Suddenly des Grieux skipped up.

The other two were close by; I noticed Mlle Blanche standing on one side with her mother, exchanging amenities with the Prince. The General was obviously out of favour, almost banished. Blanche would not even look at him, though he was doing his utmost to cajole her! The poor General! He flushed and grew pale by turns, trembled and could not even follow Granny's play. Blanche and the Prince finally went away; the General ran after them.

'Madame, madame,' des Grieux whispered in a honeyed voice to Granny, squeezing his way close up to her ear. 'Madame, such stakes do not answer . . . No, no, it's impossible . . . ' he said, in broken Russian. 'No!'

'How, then? Come, show me!' said Granny, turning to him.

Des Grieux babbled something rapidly in French, began excitedly advising, said she must wait for a chance, began reckoning some numbers . . . Granny did not understand a word. He kept turning to me, for me to translate; tapped the table with his fingers, pointed; finally took a pencil and was about to reckon something on paper. At last Granny lost patience.

'Come, get away, get away! You keep talking nonsense! "Madame, madame", he doesn't understand it himself; go away.'

'*Mais, madame,*' des Grieux murmured, and he began once more showing and explaining.

'Well, stake once as he says,' Granny said to me; 'let us see: perhaps it really will answer.'

All des Grieux wanted was to dissuade her from staking large sums; he suggested that she should stake on numbers, either individually or collectively. I staked as he directed, a friedrich d'or on each of the odd numbers in the first twelve and five friedrichs d'or respectively on the groups of numbers from twelve to eighteen and from eighteen to twenty-four, staking in all sixteen friedrichs d'or.

The wheel turned.

'*Zéro,*' cried the croupier.

We had lost everything.

'You blockhead!' cried Granny, addressing des Grieux. 'You scoundrelly Frenchman! So this is how he advises, the monster. Go away, go away! He knows nothing about it and comes fussing round!'

Fearfully offended, des Grieux shrugged his shoulders, looked contemptuously at Granny, and walked away. He felt ashamed of having interfered; he had been in too great a hurry.

An hour later, in spite of all our efforts, we had lost everything.

'Home,' cried Granny.

She did not utter a single word till we got into the avenue. In the avenue and approaching the hotel she began to break into exclamations:

'What a fool! What a silly fool! You're an old fool, you are!'

As soon as we got to her apartments –

'Tea!' cried Granny. 'And pack up at once! We are going!'

'Where does your honour mean to go?' Marfa was beginning.

'What has it to do with you? Mind your own business! Potapitch, pack up everything: all the luggage. We are going back to Moscow. I have thrown away fifteen thousand roubles!'

'Fifteen thousand, madame! My God!' Potapitch cried, flinging up his hands with deep feeling, probably meaning to humour her.

'Come, come, you fool! He is beginning to whimper! Hold your tongue! Pack up! The bill, make haste, make haste!'

'The next train goes at half-past nine, Granny,' I said, to check her furore.

'And what is it now?'

'Half-past seven.'

'How annoying! Well, it doesn't matter! Alexey Ivanovitch, I haven't a farthing. Here are two more notes. Run there and change these for me too. Or I have nothing for the journey.'

I set off. Returning to the hotel half an hour later, I found our whole party at Granny's. Learning that Granny was going off to Moscow, they seemed to be even more upset than by her losses. Even though her going might save her property, what was to become of the General? Who would pay des Grieux? Mlle Blanche would, of course, decline to wait for Granny to die and would certainly now make up to the Prince or to somebody else. They were all standing before Granny, trying to console her and persuade her. Again Polina was not there. Granny was shouting at them furiously.

'Let me alone, you devils! What business is it of yours? Why does that goat's-beard come forcing himself upon me?' she cried at des Grieux; 'and you, my fine bird?' she cried, addressing Mlle Blanche, 'what are you after?'

'*Diantre*!' whispered Mlle Blanche, with an angry flash of her eyes, but suddenly she burst out laughing and went out of the room.

'*Elle vivra cent ans*!' she called to the General, as she went out of the door.

'Ah, so you are reckoning on my death?' Granny yelled to the General. 'Get away! Turn them all out, Alexey Ivanovitch! What business is it of yours? I've fooled away my own money, not yours!'

The General shrugged his shoulders, bowed and went out. Des Grieux followed him.

'Call Praskovya,' Granny told Marfa.

Five minutes later Marfa returned with Polina. All this time Polina had been sitting in her own room with the children, and I fancy had purposely made up her mind not to go out all day. Her face was serious, sad and anxious.

'Praskovya,' began Granny, 'is it true, as I learned by accident just now, that that fool, your stepfather, means to marry that silly feather-head of a Frenchwoman – an actress is she, or something worse? Tell me, is it true?'

'I don't know anything about it for certain, Granny,' answered Polina, 'but from the words of Mlle Blanche herself, who does not feel it necessary to conceal anything, I conclude . . . '

'Enough,' Granny broke in vigorously, 'I understand! I always reckoned that he was capable of it and I have always thought him a most foolish and feather-headed man. He thinks no end of himself, because he is a General (he was promoted from a Colonel on retiring), and he gives himself airs. I know, my good girl, how you kept sending telegram after telegram to Moscow, to ask if your old Granny would soon be laid out. They were on the lookout for my money; without money that nasty hussy, what's her name – de Cominges – wouldn't take him for her footman, especially with his false teeth. She has a lot of money herself, they say, lends at interest, has made a lot. I am not blaming you, Praskovya, it wasn't you who sent the telegrams; and I don't want to remember the past, either. I know you've got a bad temper – a wasp! You can sting to hurt; but I'm sorry for you because I was fond of your mother, Katerina. Well, you throw up everything here and come with me. You've nowhere to go, you know; and it's not fitting for you to be with them now. Stop!' cried Granny, as Polina was about to speak; 'I've not finished. I ask nothing of you. As you know, I have in Moscow a palace; you can have a whole storey to yourself and not come and see me for weeks at a time if my temper does not suit you! Well, will you or not?'

'Let me ask you first: do you really mean to set off at once?'

'Do you suppose I'm joking, my good girl! I've said I'm going and I'm going. I've wasted fifteen thousand roubles today over your damned roulette. Five years ago I promised to rebuild a wooden church with stone on my estate near Moscow, and instead of that I've thrown away my money here. Now, my girl, I'm going home to build the church.'

'And the waters, Granny? You came to drink the waters?'

'Bother you and the waters, too. Don't irritate me, Praskovya; are you doing it on purpose? Tell me, will you come or not?'

'I thank you very, very much,' Polina began, with feeling, 'for the home you offer me. You have guessed my position to some extent. I am so grateful to you that I shall perhaps come to you soon; but now there are reasons . . . important reasons . . . and I can't decide at once, on the spur of the moment. If you were staying only a fortnight . . .'

'You mean you won't?'

'I mean I can't. Besides, in any case I can't leave my brother and sister, as . . . as . . . as it may actually happen that they may be left abandoned, so . . . if you would take me with the children, Granny, I certainly would come, and, believe me, I would repay you for it!' she added warmly; 'but without the children I can't come, Granny.'

'Well, don't whimper' (Polina had no intention of whimpering – indeed, I had never seen her cry). 'Some place will be found for the chickens, my henhouse is big enough. Besides, it is time they were at school. Well, so you are not coming now! Well, Praskovya, mind! I wished for your good, but I know why you won't come! I know all about it, Praskovya. That Frenchman will bring you no good.'

Polina flushed crimson. I positively shuddered. (Everyone knows all about it. I am the only one to know nothing!)

'Come, come, don't frown. I am not going to say anything more. Only take care no harm comes of it, understand. You are a clever wench; I shall be sorry for you. Well, that's enough. I should not like to look on you as on the others! Go along, goodbye!'

'I'll come to see you off,' said Polina.

'There's no need, don't you interfere; I am sick of you all.'

Polina was kissing Granny's hand, but the latter pulled it away and kissed her on the cheek.

As she passed me, Polina looked at me quickly and immediately turned away her eyes.

'Well, goodbye to you, too, Alexey Ivanovitch, there's only an hour before the train starts, and I think you must be tired out with me. Here, take these fifty pieces of gold.'

'I thank you very much, Granny; I'm ashamed . . . '

'Come, come!' cried Granny, but so vigorously and angrily that I dared say no more and took it.

'When you are running about Moscow without a job come to me: I will give you some introductions. Now, get along with you!'

I went to my room and lay down on my bed. I lay there for half an hour on my back, with my hands clasped behind my head. The catastrophe had come at last, I had something to think about. I made up my mind to talk earnestly to Polina. The nasty Frenchman! So it was true then! But what could there be at the bottom of it? Polina and des Grieux! Heavens! what a pair!

It was all simply incredible. I suddenly jumped up, beside myself, to look for Mr Astley, and at all costs to make him speak out. No doubt in this matter, too, he knew more than I did. Mr Astley? He was another riddle to me!

But suddenly there was a tap at my door. I looked up. It was Potapitch.

'Alexey Ivanovitch, you are wanted to come to my lady!'

'What's the matter? Is she setting off? The train does not start for twenty minutes.'

'She's uneasy, she can't sit still. "Make haste, make haste!" she says, meaning to fetch you, sir. For Christ's sake, don't delay.'

I ran downstairs at once. Granny was being wheeled out into the passage, her pocket-book was in her hand.

'Alexey Ivanovitch, go on ahead; we're coming.'

'Where, Granny?'

'As sure as I'm alive, I'll win it back. Come, march, don't ask questions! Does the play go on there till midnight?'

I was thunderstruck. I thought a moment, but at once made up my mind.

'Do as you please, Antonida Vassilyevna, I'm not coming.'

'What's that for? What now? Have you all eaten too many pancakes, or what?'

'Do as you please, I should blame myself for it afterwards; I won't. I won't take part in it or look on at it; spare me, Antonida Vassilyevna. Here are your fifty friedrichs d'or back; goodbye!' And, laying the fifty friedrichs d'or on the little table near which Granny's chair was standing, I bowed and went out.

'What nonsense!' Granny shouted after me. 'Don't come if you don't want to, I can find the way by myself! Potapitch, come with me! Come, lift me up, carry me!'

I did not find Mr Astley and returned home. It was late, after midnight, when I learned from Potapitch how Granny's day ended. She lost all that I had changed for her that evening – that is, in Russian money, another ten thousand roubles. The little Pole, to whom she had given two friedrichs d'or the day before, had attached himself to her and had directed her play the whole time. At first, before the Pole came, she had made Potapitch put down the stakes, but soon she dismissed him; it was at that moment the Pole turned up. As ill-luck would have it, he understood Russian and babbled away in a mixture of three languages, so that they understood each other after a fashion. Granny abused him mercilessly the whole time; and though he incessantly 'laid himself at his lady's feet', 'yet he couldn't be compared with you, Alexey Ivanovitch,' said Potapitch. 'She treated you *like a gentleman*, while the other – I saw it with my own eyes, God strike me dead – stole her money off the table. She caught him at it herself twice. She did give it to him with all sorts of names, sir, even pulled his hair once, upon my word she did, so that folks were laughing round about. She's lost everything, sir, everything, all you changed for her; we brought her back here – she only asked for a drink of water, crossed herself and went to bed. She's worn out, to be sure; she fell asleep at once. God send her heavenly dreams. Och! these foreign parts!' Potapitch wound up. 'I said it would lead to no good. If only we could soon be back in Moscow! We'd everything we wanted at home in Moscow: a garden, flowers such as you don't have here, fragrance, the apples are swelling, plenty of room everywhere. No, we had to come abroad. Oh, oh, oh . . . '

CHAPTER THIRTEEN

Now almost a whole month has passed since I touched these notes of mine, which were begun under the influence of confused but intense impressions. The catastrophe which I felt to be approaching has actually come, but in a form a hundred times more violent and startling than I had expected. It has all been something strange, grotesque and even tragic – at least for me. Several things have happened to me that were almost miraculous; that is, at least, how I look upon them to this day – though from another point of view, particularly in the whirl of events in which I was involved at that time, they were only somewhat out of the common. But what is most marvellous to me is my own attitude to all these events. To this day I cannot understand myself, and it has all floated by like a dream – even my passion – it was violent and sincere, but . . . what has become of it now? It is true that sometimes the thought flashes through my brain: 'Wasn't I out of my mind then, and wasn't I all that time somewhere in a madhouse and perhaps I'm there now, so that was all my fancy and still is my fancy . . . ' I put my notes together and read them over (who knows – perhaps to convince myself that I did not write them in a madhouse). Now I am entirely alone. Autumn is coming on and the leaves are turning yellow. I'm still in this dismal little town (oh, how dismal the little German towns are!), and instead of considering what to do next, I go on living under the influence of the sensations I have just passed through, under the influence of memories still fresh, under the influence of the whirl of events which caught me up and flung me aside again. At times I fancy that I am still caught up in that whirlwind, that that storm is still raging, carrying me along with it, and again I lose sight of all order and measure and I whirl round and round again . . .

However, I may, perhaps, leave off whirling and settle down in a way if, so far as I can, I put clearly before my mind all the incidents of the past month. I feel drawn to my pen again. Besides, I have sometimes nothing at all to do in the evenings. I am so hard up for something to do that, odd as it seems, I even take from the scurvy lending library here the novels of Paul de Kock (in a German translation), though I can't endure them; yet I read them and wonder at myself. It is as though I were afraid of breaking the spell of the recent past by a serious book or any serious occupation. It is as though that grotesque dream, with all the impressions left by it, was so precious to me that I am afraid to let anything new touch upon it for fear it should all vanish in smoke. Is it all so precious to me? Yes, of course it is precious. Perhaps I shall remember it for forty years . . .

And so I take up my writing again. I can give a brief account of it to some extent now: the impressions are not at all the same.

In the first place, to finish with Granny. The following day she lost everything. It was what was bound to happen. When once anyone is started upon that road, it is like a man in a sledge flying down a snow mountain more and more swiftly. She played all day till eight o'clock in the evening; I was not present and only know what happened from what I was told.

Potapitch was in attendance on her at the Casino all day. Several Poles in succession guided Granny's operations in the course of the day. She began by dismissing the Pole whose hair she had pulled the day before and taking on another, but he turned out almost worse. After dismissing the second, and accepting again the first, who had never left her side, but had been squeezing himself in behind her chair and continually poking his head in during the whole period of his disgrace, she sank at last into complete despair. The second Pole also refused to move away; one stationed himself on her right and the other on her left. They were abusing one another the whole time and quarrelling over the stakes and the game, calling each other '*laidąk*' and other Polish civilities, making it up again, putting down money recklessly and playing at random. When they quarrelled they put the money down regardless of each other – one, for instance, on the red and the other on the black. It ended in their completely bewildering and overwhelming Granny, so that at last, almost in tears, she appealed to the old croupier, begging him to protect her and to send them away. They were, in fact, immediately turned out in spite of their outcries and protests; they both shouted out at once and tried to prove that Granny owed them something, that she had deceived them about something and had treated them basely and dishonourably. The luckless Potapitch told me all this the same evening almost with tears, and complained that they stuffed their pockets with money, that he himself had seen them shamelessly steal and continually thrust the money in their pockets. One, for instance, would beg five friedrichs d'or for his trouble and begin putting them down on the spot side by side with Granny's stakes. Granny won, but the man shouted that his stake was the winning one and that Granny's had lost. When they were dismissed Potapitch came forward and said that their pockets were full of gold. Granny at once bade the croupier to look into it and, in spite of the outcries of the Poles (they cackled like two cocks caught in the hand), the police came forward and their pockets were immediately emptied for Granny's benefit. Granny enjoyed unmistakable prestige among the croupiers and the whole staff of the Casino all that day, until she had lost everything. By degrees her fame spread all over the town. All the visitors at the watering-place, of all nations, small and great, streamed to look on at '*une vieille comtesse russe tombée en enfance*', who had already lost 'some millions'.

But Granny gained very, very little by being rescued from the two Poles. They were at once replaced by a third, who spoke perfectly pure Russian and was dressed like a gentleman, though he did look like a flunkey with a huge moustache and a sense of his own importance. He, too, 'laid himself at his lady's feet and kissed them', but behaved haughtily to those about him, was despotic over the play; in fact, immediately behaved like Granny's master rather than her servant. Every minute, at every turn in the game, he turned to her and swore with awful oaths that he was himself a '*pan* of good position', and that he wouldn't take a kopeck of Granny's money. He repeated this oath so many times that Granny was completely intimidated. But as this *pan* certainly seemed at first to improve her luck, Granny was not willing to abandon him on her own account. An hour later the two Poles who had been turned out of the Casino turned up behind Granny's chair again, and again proffered their services if only to run errands for her. Potapitch swore that the '*pan* of good position' winked at them and even put something in their hands. As Granny had no dinner and could not leave her chair, one of the Poles certainly was of use: he ran off at once to the dining-room of the Casino and brought her a cup of broth and afterwards some tea. They both ran about, however. But towards the end of the day, when it became evident to everyone that she would stake her last banknote, there were behind her chair as many as six Poles who had never been seen or heard of before. When Granny was playing her last coin, they not only ceased to obey her, but took no notice of her whatever, squeezed their way up to the table in front of her, snatched the money themselves, put down the stakes and made their own play, shouted and quarrelled, talked to the '*pan* of good position' as to one of themselves, while the '*pan* of good position' himself seemed almost oblivious of Granny's existence. Even when Granny, after losing everything, was returning after eight o'clock to the hotel, three or four Poles ran at the side of her bath-chair, still unable to bring themselves to leave her; they kept shouting at the top of their voices, declaring in a hurried gabble that Granny had cheated them in some way and must give them something. They followed her in this way right up to the hotel, from which they were at last driven away with blows.

By Potapitch's reckoning Granny had lost in all ninety thousand roubles that day, apart from what she had lost the day before. All her notes, her exchequer bonds, all the shares she had with her, she had changed, one after another. I marvelled how she could have stood those seven or eight hours sitting there in her chair and scarcely leaving the table, but Potapitch told me that three or four times she had begun winning considerably; and, carried on by fresh hope, she could not tear herself away. But gamblers know how a man can sit for almost twenty-four hours at cards, without looking to right or to left.

Meanwhile, very critical events were taking place all that day at the hotel. In the morning, before eleven o'clock, when Granny was still at home, our people – that is, the General and des Grieux – made up their minds to take the final step. Learning that Granny had given up all idea of setting off, but was going back to the Casino, they went in full conclave (all but Polina) to talk things over with her finally and even *openly*. The General, trembling and with a sinking heart in view of the awful possibilities for himself, overdid it. After spending half an hour in prayers and entreaties and making a clean breast of everything – that is, of all his debts and even his passion for Mlle Blanche (he quite lost his head), the General suddenly adopted a menacing tone and even began shouting and stamping at Granny; cried that she was disgracing their name, had become a scandal to the whole town, and finally . . . finally: 'You are shaming the Russian name,' cried the General, and he told her that the police would be called in! Granny finally drove him from her with a stick (an actual stick). The General and des Grieux consulted once or twice that morning, and the question that agitated them was whether it were not possible in some way to bring in the police, on the plea that an unfortunate but venerable old lady, sinking into her dotage, was gambling away her whole fortune, and so on; whether, in fact, it would be possible to put her under any sort of supervision or restraint . . . But des Grieux only shrugged his shoulders and laughed in the General's face, as the latter pranced up and down his study talking excitedly. Finally, des Grieux went off with a wave of his hand. In the evening we heard that he had left the hotel altogether, after having been in very earnest and mysterious confabulation with Mlle Blanche. As for Mlle Blanche, she had taken her measures early in the morning: she threw the General over completely and would not even admit him to her presence. When the General ran to the Casino in search of her and met her arm-in-arm with the Prince, neither she nor Madame de Cominges deigned to notice him. The Prince did not bow to him either. Mlle Blanche spent that whole day hard at work upon the Prince, trying to force from him a definite declaration. But alas! she was cruelly deceived in her reckoning! This little catastrophe took place in the evening. It suddenly came out that he was as poor as a church mouse, and, what is more, was himself reckoning on borrowing from her on an IOU to try his luck at roulette. Blanche turned him out indignantly and locked herself up in her room.

On the morning of that day I went to Mr Astley – or, to be more exact, I went in search of Mr Astley, but could find him nowhere. He was not at home, or in the park, or in the Casino. He was not dining at his hotel that day. It was past four o'clock when I suddenly saw him walking from the railway station towards the Hôtel d'Angleterre. He was in a hurry and was very much preoccupied, though it was hard to trace any anxiety or any perturbation whatever in his face. He held out his hand to me cordially, with his habitual exclamation: 'Ah!' but without stopping walked on with rather a rapid step. I attached myself to him, but he managed to answer me in such a way that I did not succeed in even asking him about anything. Moreover, I felt, for some reason, ashamed to begin speaking of Polina; he did not ask a word about her. I told him about Granny. He listened attentively and seriously and shrugged his shoulders.

'She will gamble away everything,' I observed.

'Oh, yes,' he answered; 'she went in to play just as I was going away, and afterwards I learnt for a fact that she had lost everything. If there were time I would look in at the Casino, for it is curious.'

'Where have you been?' I cried, wondering that I had not asked before.

'I've been in Frankfort.'

'On business?'

'Yes, on business.'

Well, what more was there for me to ask? I did, however, continue walking beside him, but he suddenly turned into the Hôtel des Quatre Saisons, nodded to me and vanished. As I walked home I gradually realised that if I had talked to him for a couple of hours I should have learnt absolutely nothing, because . . . I had nothing to ask him! Yes, that was so, of course! I could not possibly formulate my question.

All that day Polina spent walking with the children and their nurse in the park, or sitting at home. She had for a long time past avoided the General, and scarcely spoke to him about anything – about anything serious, at any rate. I had noticed that for a long time past. But knowing what a position the General was in today, I imagined that he could hardly pass her over – that is, there could not but be an important conversation about family affairs between them. When, however, I returned to the hotel, after my conversation with Mr Astley, I met Polina with the children. There was an expression of the most unruffled calm on her face, as though she alone had remained untouched by the family tempest. She nodded in response to my bow. I returned home feeling quite malignant.

I had, of course, avoided seeing her and had seen nothing of her since the incident with the Burmerhelms. There was some affectation and pose in this; but as time went on, I felt more and more genuinely indignant. Even if she did not care for me in the least, she should not, I thought, have trampled on my feelings like that and have received my declarations so contemptuously. She knew that I really loved her; she admitted me, she allowed me to speak like that! It is true that it had begun rather strangely. Some time before, long ago, in fact, two months before, I began to notice that she wanted to make me her friend, her *confidant*, and indeed was in a way testing me. But somehow this did not come off then; instead of that there remained the strange relations that existed between us; that is how it was I began to speak to her like that. But if my love repelled her, why did she not directly forbid me to speak of it?

She did not forbid me; indeed she sometimes provoked me to talk of it and . . . and, of course, she did this for fun. I know for certain. I noticed it unmistakably – it was agreeable to her to listen and to work me up to a state of misery, to wound me by some display of the utmost contempt and disregard. And, of course, she knew that I could not exist without her. It was three days since the affair with the Baron and I could not endure our separation any longer. When I met her just now near the Casino, my heart throbbed so that I turned pale. But she could not get on without me, either! She needed me and – surely, surely not as a buffoon, a clown?

She had a secret – that was clear! Her conversation with Granny had stabbed my heart. Why, I had urged her a thousand times to be open with me, and she knew that I was ready to give my life for her. But she had always put me off, almost with contempt, or had asked of me, instead of the sacrifice of my life, such pranks as the one with the Baron!

Was not that enough to make one indignant? Could that Frenchman be all the world to her? And Mr Astley? But at that point the position became utterly incomprehensible – and meanwhile, my God! what agonies I went through.

On getting home, in an access of fury I snatched up my pen and scribbled the following letter to her:

> Polina Alexandrovna, I see clearly that the *dénouement* is at hand which will affect you also. I repeat for the last time: do you need my life or not? If I can be of use in *any way whatever*, dispose of me as you think fit, and I will meanwhile remain in my room and not go out at all. If you need me, write to me or send for me.

I sealed up this note and sent it off by the corridor attendant, instructing him to give it into her hands. I expected no answer, but three minutes later the attendant returned with the message that 'she sent her greetings'.

It was past six when I was summoned to the General.

He was in his study, dressed as though he were on the point of going out. His hat and coat were lying on the sofa. It seemed to me as I went in that he was standing in the middle of the room with his legs wide apart and his head hanging, talking aloud to himself. But as soon as he saw me, he rushed at me almost crying out, so that I involuntarily stepped back and was almost running away, but he seized me by both hands and drew me to the sofa; sat down on the sofa himself, made me sit down in an armchair just opposite himself, and, keeping tight hold of my hand, with trembling lips and with tears suddenly glistening on his eyelashes, began speaking in an imploring voice.

'Alexey Ivanovitch, save, save me, spare me.'

It was a long while before I could understand. He kept talking and talking and talking, continually repeating, 'Spare me, spare me!' At last I guessed that he expected something in the way of advice from me; or rather, abandoned by all in his misery and anxiety, he had thought of me and had sent for me, simply to talk and talk and talk to me.

He was mad, or at any rate utterly distraught. He clasped his hands and was on the point of dropping on his knees before me to implore me (what do you suppose?) to go at once to Mlle Blanche and to beseech, to urge her to return to him and marry him.

'Upon my word, General,' I cried; 'why, Mlle Blanche is perhaps scarcely aware of my existence. What can I do?'

But it was vain to protest; he didn't understand what was said to him. He fell to talking about Granny, too, but with terrible incoherence; he was still harping on the idea of sending for the police.

'Among us, among us,' he began, suddenly boiling over with indignation; 'among us, in a well-ordered state, in fact, where there is a Government in control of things, such old women would have been put under guardianship at once! Yes, my dear sir, yes,' he went on, suddenly dropping into a scolding tone, jumping up from his chair and pacing about the room; 'you may not be aware of the fact, honoured sir,' he said, addressing some imaginary 'honoured sir' in the corner, 'so let me tell you . . . yes . . . among us such old women are kept in order, kept in order; yes, indeed . . . Oh, damn it all!'

And he flung himself on the sofa again, and a minute later, almost sobbing, gasping for breath, hastened to tell me that Mlle Blanche would not marry him because Granny had come instead of the telegram, and that now it was clear he would not come into the inheritance. He imagined that I knew nothing of this till then. I began to speak of des Grieux; he waved his hand: 'He has gone away! Everything of mine he has in pawn; I'm stripped of everything! That money you brought . . . that money – I don't know how much there is, I think seven hundred francs are left and that's enough, that's all and what's to come – I don't know, I don't know! . . . '

'How will you pay your hotel bill?' I cried in alarm; 'and . . . afterwards what will you do?'

He looked at me pensively, but I fancy he did not understand and perhaps did not hear what I said. I tried to speak of Polina Alexandrovna, of the children; he hurriedly answered: 'Yes! yes!' but at once fell to talking of the Prince again, saying that Blanche would go away with him now and 'then . . . then, what am I to do, Alexey Ivanovitch?' he asked, addressing me suddenly. 'I vow, by God! I don't know what to do; tell me, isn't this ingratitude? Isn't this ingratitude?'

Finally he dissolved into floods of tears.

There was no doing anything with such a man; it would be dangerous to leave him alone, too – something might happen to him. I got rid of him somehow, but let nurse know she must look in upon him pretty frequently, and also spoke to the corridor attendant, a very sensible fellow; he, too, promised me to keep an eye on the General.

I had hardly left the General when Potapitch came to summon me to Granny. It was eight o'clock and she had only just come back from the Casino after losing everything. I went to her; the old lady was sitting in an armchair, utterly worn out and evidently ill. Marfa was giving her a cup of tea and almost forcing her to drink it. And Granny's tone and voice were utterly changed.

'Good-day, Alexey Ivanovitch, my good sir,' she said, bending her head slowly, and with dignity; 'excuse me for troubling you once more, you must excuse an old woman. I have left everything behind there, my friend, nearly a hundred thousand roubles. You did well not to come with me yesterday. Now I have no money, not a farthing. I don't want to delay a moment, at half-past nine I'm setting off. I have sent to that Englishman of yours – what's his name, Astley – I want to ask him to lend me three thousand francs for a week. So you must persuade him not to take it amiss and refuse. I am still fairly well off, my friend. I have still three villages and two houses. And there is still some money. I didn't bring it all with me. I tell you this that he may not feel any doubts . . . Ah, here he is! One can see he is a nice man.'

Mr Astley had hastened to come at Granny's first summons. With no hesitation and without wasting words he promptly counted out three thousand francs for an IOU which Granny signed. When this business was settled he made haste to take his leave and go away.

'And now you can go, too, Alexey Ivanovitch. I have only a little over an hour left. I want to lie down: my bones ache. Don't be hard on an old fool like me. Henceforward I won't blame young people for being flighty, and it would be a sin for me now to blame that luckless fellow, your General, either. I won't give him any money, though, as he wants me to, because – to my thinking he is utterly silly; only, old fool as I am, I've no more sense than he. Verily God seeks out and punishes pride, even in old age. Well, goodbye. Marfa, lift me up!'

I wanted to see Granny off, however. What's more, I was in a state of suspense; I kept expecting that in another minute something would happen. I could not sit quietly in my room. I went out into the corridor, even for a moment went for a saunter along the avenue. My letter to her had been clear and decisive and the present catastrophe was, of course, a final one. I heard in the hotel that des Grieux had left. If she rejected me as a friend, perhaps she would not reject me as a servant. I was necessary to her, I was of use to her, if only to run her errands, it was bound to be so!

When the train was due to start I ran to the station and saw Granny into the train. Her whole party were together, in a special reserved compartment. 'Thank you, my good friend, for your disinterested sympathy,' she said, at parting from me; 'and tell Praskovya, in reference to what we were discussing yesterday, I shall expect her.'

I went home. Passing the General's rooms I met the old nurse and enquired after the General. 'Oh, he's all right, sir,' she answered me dolefully. I went in, however, but stood still in positive amazement. Mlle Blanche and the General were both laughing heartily. Madame de Cominges was sitting on the sofa close by. The General was evidently beside himself with delight. He was murmuring incoherently and going off into prolonged fits of nervous laughter, during which his face was puckered with innumerable wrinkles and his eyes disappeared from sight. Afterwards I learnt from Blanche herself that, having dismissed the Prince and having heard how the General was weeping, she had taken it into her head to comfort him by going to see him for a minute. But the poor General did not know that at that time his fate was decided, and that Mile. Blanche had already packed to set off for Paris by the first train next morning.

Stopping in the doorway of the General's study, I changed my mind and went away unnoticed. Going up to my own room and opening the door, I suddenly noticed a figure in the half-darkness sitting on a chair in the corner by the window. She did not get up when I went in. I went up quickly, looked, and – my heart stood still: it was Polina.

CHAPTER FOURTEEN

I positively cried out aloud.

'What is it? What is it?' she asked me strangely. She was pale and looked gloomy.

'You ask what is it? You? Here in my room!'

'If I come, then I come *altogether*. That's my way. You'll see that directly; light the candle.'

I lighted a candle. She got up, went up to the table, and put before me an open letter.

'Read it,' she ordered me.

'It's – it's des Grieux's handwriting,' I cried, taking the letter. My hands trembled and the lines danced before my eyes. I have forgotten the exact wording of the letter, but here is the main drift of it, if not the actual words.

> MADEMOISELLE, [wrote des Grieux] an unfortunate circumstance compels me to go away at once. You have, no doubt, observed that I have purposely avoided a final explanation with you until such time as the whole position might be cleared up. The arrival of your old relation (*de la vieille dame*) and her absurd behaviour have put an end to my doubts. The unsettled state of my own affairs forbids me to cherish further the sweet hopes which I permitted myself to indulge for some time. I regret the past, but I trust that you will not detect in my behaviour anything unworthy of a gentleman and an honest man (*gentilhomme et honnête homme*). Having lost almost all my money in loans to your stepfather, I find myself compelled to make the utmost use of what is left to me; I have already sent word to my friend in Petersburg to arrange at once for the sale of the estates he has mortgaged to me; knowing, however, that your frivolous stepfather has squandered your private fortune I have determined to forgive him fifty thousand francs, and I am returning him part of my claims on his property equivalent to that sum, so that you are now put in a position to regain all you have lost

by demanding the property from him by legal process. I hope, Mademoiselle, that in the present position of affairs my action will be very advantageous to you. I hope, too, that by this action I am fully performing the duty of a man and a gentleman. Rest assured that your memory is imprinted upon my heart for ever.'

'Well, that's all clear,' I said, turning to Polina; 'surely you could have expected nothing else,' I added, with indignation.

'I expected nothing,' she answered, with apparent composure, though there was a tremor in her voice; 'I had made up my mind long ago; I read his mind and knew what he was thinking. He thought that I was trying – that I should insist . . . ' (She broke off without finishing her sentence, bit her lips and was silent.) 'I purposely doubled my scorn towards him,' she began again. 'I waited to see what was coming from him. If a telegram had come telling of the inheritance I'd have flung him the money borrowed from that idiot, my stepfather, and would have sent him about his business. He has been hateful to me for ages and ages. Oh! he was not the same man! a thousand times over, I tell you, he was different! but now, now . . . Oh, with what happiness I could fling that fifty thousand in his nasty face and spit and stamp . . . '

'But the security, the IOU for that fifty thousand, is in the General's hands. Take it and return it to des Grieux.'

'Oh, that's not the same thing, that's not the same thing . . . '

'Yes, that's true, it's not the same thing. Besides, what is the General capable of now? And Granny!' I cried suddenly.

Polina looked at me, as it were absent-mindedly and impatiently.

'Why Granny?' asked Polina, with vexation. 'I can't go to her . . . And I don't want to ask anyone's pardon,' she added irritably.

'What's to be done!' I cried, 'and how, oh, how could you love des Grieux! Oh, the scoundrel, the scoundrel! If you like I will kill him in a duel! Where is he now?'

'He's at Frankfurt, and will be there three days.'

'One word from you and I'll set off tomorrow by the first train,' I said, with stupid enthusiasm.

She laughed.

'Why, he'll say, maybe: "Give me back the fifty thousand francs first." Besides, what should you fight him for? . . . What nonsense it is!'

'But where, where is one to get that fifty thousand francs?' I repeated, grinding my teeth as though it had been possible to pick them up from the floor. 'I say – Mr Astley,' I suggested, turning to her with a strange idea dawning upon me.

Her eyes flashed.

'What, do you mean to say *you yourself* want me to turn from you to that Englishman!' she said, looking in my face with a searching glance and smiling bitterly. For the first time in her life she addressed me in the second person singular.

I believe she was giddy with emotion at the moment, and all at once she sat down on the sofa as though she were exhausted.

It was as though I had been struck by a flash of lightning. I stood up and could not believe my eyes, could not believe my ears! Why, then she loved me! She had come to me and not to Mr Astley!

She, she, a young girl, had come to my room in a hotel, so she had utterly compromised herself by her own act, and I, I was standing before her and still did not understand.

One wild idea flashed through my mind.

'Polina, give me only one hour. Stay here only one hour and . . . I'll come back. That's . . . that's essential! You shall see! Be here, be here!'

And I ran out of the room, not responding to her amazed and questioning look; she called something after me but I did not turn back.

Sometimes the wildest idea, the most apparently impossible thought, takes possession of one's mind so strongly that one accepts it at last as something substantial . . . more than that, if the idea is associated with a strong passionate desire, then sometimes one will accept it at last as something fated, inevitable, predestined – as something bound to be, and bound to happen. Perhaps there is something else in it, some combination of presentiments, some extraordinary effort of will, self-poisoning by one's own fancy – or something else – I don't know what, but on that evening (which I shall never in my life forget) something marvellous happened to me. Though it is quite justified by the laws of arithmetic, nevertheless it is a marvel to me to this day. And why, why had that conviction so long before taken such firm and deep root in my mind? I had certainly thought about it –

I repeat – not as a chance among others which might or might not come to pass, but as something which was absolutely bound to happen!

It was a quarter-past ten. I went into the Casino with a confident expectation and at the same time with an excitement I had never experienced before. There were still a good many people in the gambling hall, though not half as many as in the morning.

Between ten and eleven there are still to be found in the gambling halls the genuine desperate gamblers for whom nothing exists at a spa but roulette, who have come for that alone, who scarcely notice what is going on around them and take no interest in anything during the whole season, but play from morning till night and would be ready perhaps to play all night till dawn, too, if it were possible. And they always disperse with annoyance when at twelve o'clock the roulette hall is closed. And when the senior croupier announces, just before midnight: '*Les trois derniers coups, messieurs*,' they are ready to stake on those last three strokes all they have in their pockets – and do, in fact, lose most at that time. I went up to the very table where Granny had sat that day. It was not crowded, and so I soon took my place at the table standing. Exactly before me was the word '*Passe*' scrawled on the green cloth.

'*Passe*' is the series of numbers from nineteen inclusive to thirty-six.

The first series of numbers from one to eighteen inclusive is called '*Manque*'; but what was that to me? I was not calculating, I had not even heard what had been the winning number last, and I did not ask about it when I began to play – as every player of any prudence would do. I pulled out all my twenty friedrichs d'or and staked them on '*passe*', the word which lay before me.

'*Vingt deux*,' cried the croupier.

I had won and again staked all, including my winnings.

'*Trente et un*,' cried the croupier.

I had won again. I had in all eighty friedrichs d'or. I staked the whole of that sum on the twelve middle numbers (my winnings would be three [sic] to one, but the chances were two to one against me.) The wheel rotated and stopped at twenty-four. I was passed three rolls each of fifty friedrichs d'or in paper and ten gold coins; I had now two hundred friedrichs d'or.

I was as though in delirium and I moved the whole heap of gold to red – and suddenly thought better of it. And for the only time that whole evening, all the time I was playing, I felt chilled with terror and a shudder made my arms and legs tremble. I felt with horror and instantly realised what losing would mean for me now! My whole life was at stake.

'*Rouge*,' cried the croupier, and I drew a breath; fiery pins and needles were tingling all over my body. I was paid in bank-notes. It came to four thousand florins and eighty friedrichs d'or (I could still keep count at that stage).

Then, I remember, I staked two thousand florins on the twelve middle numbers, and lost: I staked my gold, the eighty friedrichs d'or, and lost. I was seized with fury: I snatched up the two thousand florins I had left and staked them on the first twelve numbers – haphazard, at random, without thinking! There was, however, an instant of suspense, like, perhaps, the feeling experienced by Madame Blanchard when she flew from a balloon in Paris to the earth.

'*Quatre*!' cried the croupier:

Now with my stake I had six thousand florins. I looked triumphant already. I was afraid of nothing – nothing, and staked four thousand florins on black. Nine people followed my example and staked on black. The croupiers exchanged glances and said something to one another. People were talking all round in suspense.

Black won. I don't remember my winnings after, nor what I staked on. I only remember as though in a dream that I won, I believe, sixteen thousand florins; suddenly three unlucky turns took twelve thousand from it; then I staked the last four thousand on '*passe*' (but I scarcely felt anything as I did so; I simply waited in a mechanical, senseless way) – and again I won; then I won four times running. I only remember that I gathered up money in thousands; I remember, too, that the middle twelve won most often and I kept to it. It turned up with a sort of regularity, certainly three or four times in succession, then it did not turn up twice running and then it followed three or four times in succession. Such astonishing regularity is sometimes met with in streaks, and that is what throws inveterate gamblers who calculate with a pencil in their hands out of their reckoning. And what horrible ironies of fate happen sometimes in such cases!

I believe not more than half an hour had passed since I came into the room, when suddenly the croupier informed me that I had won thirty thousand florins, and as the bank did not meet claims for a larger sum at one time the roulette would be closed till next morning. I snatched up all my gold, dropped it into my pockets, snatched up all my notes, and at once went into the other room where there was another roulette table; the whole crowd streamed after me; there at once a place was cleared for me and I fell to staking again haphazard without reckoning. I don't understand what saved me!

At times, however, a glimmer of prudence began to dawn upon my mind. I clung to certain numbers and combinations, but soon abandoned them and staked almost unconsciously. I must have been very absent-minded; I remember the croupiers several times corrected me. I made several gross mistakes. My temples were soaked with sweat and my hands were shaking. The Poles ran up, too, with offers of their services, but I listened to no one. My luck was unbroken! Suddenly there were sounds of loud talk and laughter, and everyone cried 'Bravo, bravo!' some even clapped their hands. Here, too, I collected thirty thousand florins, and the bank closed till next day.

'Go away, go away,' a voice whispered on my right.

It was a Frankfurt Jew; he was standing beside me all the time, and I believe sometimes helped me in my play.

'For goodness' sake go,' another voice whispered in my left ear.

I took a hurried glance. It was a lady about thirty, very soberly and quietly dressed, with a tired, pale, sickly face which yet bore traces of having once been beautiful. At that moment I was stuffing my pockets with the notes, which I crumpled up anyhow, and gathering up the gold that lay on the table. Snatching up the last roll of notes, I succeeded in putting it into the pale lady's hands quite without attracting notice; I had an intense desire to do so at the time, and I remember her pale slim fingers pressed my hand warmly in token of gratitude. All that took place in one instant.

Having collected quickly all my winnings I went quickly to the *trente et quarante.*

Trente et quarante is frequented by the aristocratic public. Unlike roulette, it is a game of cards. Here the bank will pay up to a hundred thousand thalers at once. The largest stake is here also four thousand florins. I knew nothing of the game, and scarcely knew how to bet on it, except the red and the black, upon which one can bet in this game too. And I stuck to red and black. The whole Casino crowded round. I don't remember whether I once thought of Polina all this time. I was experiencing an overwhelming enjoyment in scooping up and taking away the notes which grew up in a heap before me.

It seemed as though fate were urging me on. This time, as luck would have it, a circumstance occurred which, however, is fairly frequent in the game. Chance favours red, for instance, ten or even fifteen times in succession. I had heard two days before that in the previous week red had turned up twenty-two times in succession; it was something which had never been remembered in roulette, and it was talked of with amazement. Everyone, of course, abandoned red at once, and after the tenth time, for instance, scarcely anyone dared to stake on it. But none of the experienced players staked on black either. The experienced gambler knows what is meant by this 'freak of chance'. It would mean that after red had won sixteen times, at the seventeenth time the luck would infallibly fall on black. Novices at play rush to this conclusion in crowds, double and treble their stakes, and lose terribly.

But, noticing that red had turned up seven times running, by strange perversity I staked on it. I am convinced that vanity was half responsible for it; I wanted to impress the spectators by taking a mad risk, and – oh, the strange sensation – I remember distinctly that, quite apart from the promptings of vanity, I was possessed by an intense craving for risk. Perhaps passing through so many sensations my soul was not satisfied but only irritated by them and craved still more sensation – and stronger and stronger ones – till utterly exhausted. And, truly I am not lying, if the regulations had allowed me to stake fifty thousand florins at once, I should certainly have staked them. People around shouted that it was madness – that red had won fourteen times already!

'*Monsieur a gagné déjà cent mille florins*,' I heard a voice say near me.

I suddenly came to myself. What? I had won during that evening a hundred thousand florins! And what more did I want? I fell on my banknotes, crumpled them up in my pockets without counting them, scooped up all my gold, all my rolls of notes, and ran out of the Casino. Everyone was laughing as I went through the room, looking at my bulging pockets and at the way I staggered under the weight of gold. I think it weighed over twenty pounds. Several hands were held out to me; I gave it away in handfuls as I snatched it up. Two Jews stopped me at the outer door.

'You are bold – you are very bold,' they said to me, 'but be sure to go away tomorrow as soon as possible, or else you will lose it all – you will lose it all . . . '

I didn't listen to them. The avenue was so dark that I could not see my hand before my face. It was half a mile to the hotel. I had never been afraid of thieves or robbers even as a small boy; I did not think of them now either. I don't remember what I thought of on the road; I had no thoughts. I was only aware of an immense enjoyment – success, victory, power – I don't know how to express it. Polina's image hovered before my mind too; I remembered her and was conscious I was going to her; I should be with her in a moment, should be telling her and showing her . . . But I hardly remembered what she had said to me earlier, and why I had gone, and all the sensations I had felt, not more than an hour and a half before, seemed to me something long past, transformed, grown old – something of which we should say no more because everything now would begin anew. Almost at the end of the avenue a sudden panic came upon me. What if I were robbed and murdered at this instant? At every step my panic grew greater. I almost ran. Suddenly, at the end of the avenue there was the glare of our hotel with its many windows lighted up – thank God, home!

I ran up to my storey and rapidly opened the door. Polina was there, sitting on the sofa with her arms crossed, with a lighted candle before her. She looked at me with amazement, and no doubt at that moment I must have looked rather strange. I stood before her and began flinging down all my piles of money on the table.

CHAPTER FIFTEEN

I remember she fixed a very intent look on my face, but without even moving from her seat or changing her position.

'I've won two hundred thousand francs!' I cried, as I flung down the last roll of notes.

The huge bundles of notes and piles of gold filled up the whole table; I could not take my eyes off it. At moments I completely forgot Polina. At one moment I began arranging the heap of banknotes, folding them up together, at the next I began undoing the rolls of gold and heaping them up in one pile; then I abandoned it all and strode rapidly up and down the room, lost in thought, then went up to the table, counting the money again. Suddenly, as though coming to myself, I ran to the door and locked it with two turns of the key. Then I stood pondering before my little portmanteau.

'Shall I put it in the portmanteau till tomorrow?' I said, suddenly remembering Polina and turning towards her.

She was still sitting in the same place without stirring, but watching me attentively. Her expression was somehow strange; I did not like that expression. I am not mistaken if I say that there was hatred in it.

I went up to her quickly.

'Polina, here are twenty-five thousand florins – that's fifty thousand francs – more, in fact. Take it, throw it in his face tomorrow.'

She did not answer me.

'If you like I will take you away early in the morning. Shall I?'

She suddenly burst out laughing. She laughed for a long time.

I looked at her with wonder and a mortified feeling. That laugh was very much like sarcastic laughter at my expense, which had always been so frequent at the times of my most passionate declarations.

At last she ceased laughing and frowned; she looked at me sternly from under her brows.

'I won't take your money,' she declared contemptuously.

'How? What's this?' I cried. 'Polina, why?'

'I won't take money for nothing.'

'I offer it you as a friend; I offer you my life.'

She looked at me with a long, penetrating look, as though she would pierce me through with it.

'You give too much,' she said, with a laugh; 'des Grieux's mistress is not worth fifty thousand francs.'

'Polina, how can you talk to me like that!' I cried, reproachfully. 'Am I a des Grieux?'

'I hate you! Yes . . . yes! . . . I love you no more than des Grieux,' she cried, her eyes suddenly flashing.

Then she suddenly covered her face with her hands and went into hysterics. I rushed to her.

I realised that something had happened to her while I was away. She seemed quite out of her mind.

'Buy me! Do you want to? Do you want to? For fifty thousand francs, like des Grieux?' broke from her with convulsive sobs.

I held her in my arms, kissed her hands, her feet, fell on my knees before her.

Her hysterics passed off. She put both hands on my shoulders, and looked at me intently; she seemed trying to read something in my face. She listened to me, but evidently did not hear what I was saying to her. Some doubt and anxiety betrayed itself in her face. I was anxious about her; it seemed to me that her brain was giving way. Then she began softly drawing me to her; a trustful smile began straying over her face; but she suddenly pushed me away, and again fell to scanning me with a darkened look.

Suddenly she fell to embracing me.

'You love me, you love me, don't you?' she said. 'Why, you . . . why, you . . . wanted to fight the Baron for my sake!'

And suddenly she burst out laughing – as though she had recalled something sweet and funny. She cried and laughed all at once. Well, what was I to do? I was in a fever myself. I remember she began saying something to me – but I could scarcely understand anything. It was a sort of delirium – a sort of babble – as though she wanted to tell me something as rapidly as possible – a delirium which was interrupted from time to time with the merriest laughter, which at last frightened me. 'No, no; you are sweet, sweet,' she repeated. 'You are my faithful one!' And again she put her hand on my shoulders, again she looked at me and repeated, 'You love me . . . love me . . . will love me?' I could not take my eyes off her; I had never seen her before in such a mood of love and tenderness; it is true this, of course, was delirium, but . . . noticing my passionate expression, she suddenly began smiling slyly; apropos of nothing she began suddenly talking of Mr Astley.

She talked incessantly of Mr Astley, however (she talked of him particularly when she had been trying to tell me of something that evening), but what she meant exactly I could not quite grasp; she seemed to be actually laughing at him. She repeated continually that he was waiting and that, did I know, he was certainly standing under the window?

'Yes, yes, under the window; come, open it: look out: look out: he certainly is here!' She pushed me to the window, but as soon as I made a movement to go she went off into peals of laughter and I remained with her, and she fell to embracing me.

'Shall we go away? Shall we go away tomorrow?' The question suddenly came into her mind uneasily. 'Well . . . ' (and she sank into thought). 'Well, shall we overtake Granny; what do you think? I think we might overtake her at Berlin. What do you think she will say when she sees us? And Mr Astley? . . . Well, he won't leap off the Schlangenberg – what do you think?' (She burst out laughing.) 'Come, listen, do you know where he is going next summer? He wants to go to the North Pole for scientific investigations, and he has asked me to go with him, ha-ha-ha! He says that we Russians can do nothing without Europeans and are incapable of anything . . . But he is good-natured, too! Do you know he makes excuses for the General? He says that Blanche . . . that passion – oh, I don't know, I don't know,' she repeated, as though she didn't know what she was talking about. 'They are poor – how sorry I am for them, and Granny . . . Come, listen, listen, how could you kill des Grieux? And did you really imagine you could kill him? Oh, silly fellow! Can you really think I would let you fight with des Grieux? Why, you did not even kill the Baron,' she added, suddenly laughing. 'Oh, how funny you were then with the Baron. I looked at you both from the seat; and how unwilling you were to go then, when I sent you. How I laughed then, how I laughed,' she added, laughing.

And suddenly she kissed and embraced me again. Again she pressed her face to mine passionately and tenderly. I heard nothing and thought of nothing more. My head was in a whirl . . .

I think it was about seven o'clock in the morning when I woke up. The sun was shining into the room. Polina was sitting beside me and looking about her strangely, as though she were waking from some darkness and trying to collect her thoughts. She, too, had only just woken up and was gazing at the table and the money. My head ached and was heavy. I tried to take Polina by the hand: she pushed me away and jumped up from the sofa. The dawning day was overcast. Rain had fallen before sunrise. She went to the window, she opened it, put out her head and shoulders and with her face in her hands and her elbows on the window-sill, stayed for three minutes looking out without turning to me or hearing what I said to her. I wondered with dread what would happen now and how it would end. All at once she got up from the window, went up to the table and, looking at me with infinite hatred, with lips trembling with anger, she said to me: 'Well, give me my fifty thousand francs now!'

'Polina, again, again?' I was beginning.

'Or have you changed your mind? Ha-ha-ha! Perhaps you regret it now.'

Twenty-five thousand florins, counted out the evening before, were lying on the table; I took the money and gave it to her.

'It's mine now, isn't it? That's so, isn't it? Isn't it?' she asked me, spitefully holding the money in her hand.

'Yes, it was always yours,' I answered.

'Well, there are your fifty thousand francs for you!'

With a swing of her arm she flung the money at me. It hit me a stinging blow in the face and the coins flew all over the table. After doing this Polina ran out of the room.

I know that at that moment she was certainly not in her right mind, though I don't understand such temporary insanity. It is true that she is still ill, even now, a month later. What was the cause of her condition, and, above all, of this whim? Was it wounded pride? Despair at having brought herself to come to me? Had I shown any sign of priding myself on my happiness, and did I, like des Grieux, want to get rid of her by giving her fifty thousand francs? But that was not so; I know that, on my conscience. I believe that her vanity was partly responsible; her vanity prompted her to distrust and insult me, although all that, perhaps, was not clear, even to herself. In that case, of course, I was punished for des Grieux and was made responsible, though I was not much to blame. It is true that all this was almost only delirium; it is true, too, that I knew she was in delirium and . . . did not take that fact into consideration; perhaps she cannot forgive me for that now. Yes, but that is now; but then, then? Why, she was not in such a delirium and so ill then as to be utterly oblivious of what she was doing; when she came to me with des Grieux's letter she knew what she was doing.

I made haste to thrust all my notes and my heap of gold into the bed, covered it over and went out ten minutes after Polina. I made sure she would run home, and I thought I would slip into them on the sly, and in the hall ask the nurse how the young lady was. What was my astonishment when I learnt from nurse, whom I met on the stairs, that Polina had not yet returned home and that nurse was coming to me for her.

'She only just left my room about ten minutes ago; where can she have gone?'

Nurse looked at me reproachfully.

And meanwhile it had caused a regular scandal, which by now was all over the hotel. In the porter's room and at the *ober-kellner's* it was whispered that Fraülein had run out of the hotel in the rain at six o'clock in the morning in the direction of the Hôtel d'Angleterre. From what they said and hinted, I noticed that they all knew already that she had spent the night in my room. However, stories were being told of the whole family: it had become known all through the hotel that the General had gone out of his mind and was crying. The story was that Granny was his mother, who had come expressly from Russia to prevent her son's marriage with Mlle de Cominges, and was going to cut him out of her will if he disobeyed her, and, as he certainly would disobey her, the Countess had purposely thrown away all her money at roulette before his eyes, so that he should get nothing. '*Diese Russen*!' repeated the *ober-kellner*, shaking his head indignantly. The others laughed. The *ober-kellner* was making out his bill. My winning was known about already. Karl, my corridor attendant, was the first to congratulate me. But I had no thought for any of them. I rushed to the Hôtel d'Angleterre.

It was early; Mr Astley was seeing no one; learning that it was I, he came out into the corridor to me and stopped before me, turning his pewtery eyes upon me in silence, waiting to hear what I should say. I enquired about Polina.

'She is ill,' answered Mr Astley, looking at me as fixedly as before.

'Then she really is with you?'

'Yes, she is.'

'Then, what do you . . . do you mean to keep her?'

'Yes.'

'Mr Astley, it will make a scandal; it's impossible. Besides, she is quite ill; perhaps you don't see it?'

'Oh, yes, I notice it, and I've just told you she is ill. If she had not been ill she would not have spent the night with you.'

'Then you know that?'

'Yes, I know it. She came here yesterday and I would have taken her to a relation of mine, but as she was ill, she made a mistake and went to you.'

'Fancy that! Well, I congratulate you, Mr Astley. By the way, you've given me an idea: weren't you standing all night under our window? Miss Polina was making me open the window and look out all night to see whether you were standing under the window; she kept laughing about it.'

'Really? No, I didn't stand under the window; but I was waiting in the corridor and walking round.'

'But she must be looked after, Mr Astley.'

'Oh, yes, I've sent for the doctor, and, if she dies, you will answer to me for her death.'

I was amazed.

'Upon my word, Mr Astley, what do you want?'

'And is it true that you won two hundred thousand thalers yesterday?'

'Only a hundred thousand florins.'

'Well, do you see, you had better go off to Paris this morning!'

'What for?'

'All Russians who have money go to Paris,' Mr Astley explained, in a tone of voice as though he had read this in a book.

'What could I do now in Paris, in the summer? I love her, Mr Astley, you know it yourself.'

'Really? I am convinced you don't. If you remain here you will certainly lose all you have won and you will have nothing left to go to Paris with. But, goodbye, I am perfectly certain you will go to Paris today.'

'Very well, goodbye, only I shan't go to Paris. Think, Mr Astley, what will be happening here? The General . . . and now this adventure with Miss Polina – why, that will be all over the town.'

'Yes, all over the town; I believe the General is not thinking about that: he has no thoughts to spare for that. Besides, Miss Polina has a perfect right to live where she likes. In regard to that family, one may say quite correctly that the family no longer exists.'

I walked away laughing at this Englishman's strange conviction that I was going to Paris. 'He wants to shoot me in a duel, though,' I thought, 'if Mlle Polina dies – what a complication!' I swear I was sorry for Polina, but, strange to say, from the very moment when I reached the gambling tables the previous evening and began winning a pile of money, my love had retreated, so to speak, into the background. I say this now; but at the time I did not realise all this clearly. Can I really be a gambler? Can I really . . . have loved Polina so strangely? No, I love her to this day. God is my witness! And then, when I left Mr Astley and went home, I was genuinely miserable and blaming myself. But . . . at this point a very strange and silly thing happened to me.

I was hurrying to see the General, when suddenly, not far from his rooms, a door was opened and someone called me. It was Madame *la veuve* Cominges, and she called me at the bidding of Mlle Blanche. I went in to see Mlle Blanche.

They had a small suite of apartments, consisting of two rooms. I could hear Mlle Blanche laugh and call out from the bedroom.

She was getting up.

'*A, c'est lui! Viens donc, bête!* Is it true, *que tu as gagné une montagne d'or et d'argent? J'aimerais mieux l'or.*'

'Yes, I did win,' I answered, laughing.

'How much?'

'A hundred thousand florins.'

'*Bibi, comme tu es bête*. Why, come in here. I can't hear anything. *Nous ferons bombance, n'est ce pas*?'

I went in to her. She was lying under a pink satin quilt, above which her robust, swarthy, wonderfully swarthy, shoulders were visible, shoulders such as one only sees in one's dreams, covered to some extent by a batiste nightgown bordered with white lace which was wonderfully becoming to her dark skin.

'*Mon fils, as-tu du coeur*?' she cried, seeing me, and burst out laughing. She laughed very good-humouredly, and sometimes quite genuinely.

'*Tout autre*,' I began, paraphrasing Corneille.

'Here you see, *vois-tu*,' she began babbling; 'to begin with, find my stockings, help me to put them on; and then, *si tu n'es pas trop bête, je te prends à Paris*. You know I am just going.'

'Just going?'

'In half an hour.'

All her things were indeed packed. All her portmanteaux and things were ready. Coffee had been served some time before.

'*Eh bien*, if you like, *tu verras Paris. Dis donc qu'est ce que c'est qu'un uchitel*? *Tu étais bien bête, quand tu étais uchitel*. Where are my stockings? Put them on for me!'

She thrust out some positively fascinating feet, little dark-skinned feet, not in the least misshapen, as feet that look so small in shoes always are. I laughed and began drawing her silk stockings on for her. Meanwhile Mlle Blanche sat up in bed, prattling away.

'*Eh bien, que feras-tu, si je te prends avec*? To begin with, I want fifty thousand francs. You'll give them to me at Frankfurt. *Nous allons à Paris*: there we'll play together: *et je te ferai voir des étoiles en plein jour*. You will see women such as you have never seen before. Listen . . . '

'Wait a minute – if I give you fifty thousand francs, what will be left for me?'

'*Et cent cinquante mille francs*, you have forgotten: and what's more, I consent to live with you a month, two months: *que sais-je*! In those two months we shall certainly get through that hundred and fifty thousand francs, you see, *je suis bonne enfant*, and I tell you beforehand, *mais tu verras des étoiles*.'

'What! all in two months!'

'Why! does that horrify you? *Ah, vil esclave*! But, do you know? one month of such a life is worth your whole existence. One month – *et après le déluge*! *Mais tu ne peux comprendre*; *va*! Go along, go along, you are not worth it! *Aie, que fais tu*?'

At that moment I was putting a stocking on the other leg, but could not resist kissing it. She pulled it away and began hitting me on the head with the tip of her foot. At last, she turned me out altogether.

'*Et bien*! *mon uchitel, je t'attends, si tu veux*; I am starting in a quarter of an hour!' she called after me.

On returning home I felt as though my head were going round. Well, it was not my fault that Mlle Polina had thrown the whole pile of money in my face, and had even yesterday preferred Mr Astley to me. Some of the banknotes that had been scattered about were still lying on the floor; I picked them up. At that moment the door opened and the *ober-kellner* himself made his appearance (he had never deigned to look into my room before) with a suggestion that I might like to move downstairs to a magnificent suite of apartments which had just been vacated by Count V.

I stood still and thought a little.

'My bill – I am just leaving, in ten minutes,' I cried. 'If it's to be Paris, let it be Paris,' I thought to myself; 'it seems it was fated at my birth!'

A quarter of an hour later we were actually sitting in a reserved compartment, Mlle Blanche, Madame *la veuve* Cominges and I. Mlle Blanche, looking at me, laughed till she was almost hysterical. Madame de Cominges followed suit; I cannot say that I felt cheerful. My life had broken in two, but since the previous day I had grown used to staking everything on a card. Perhaps it is really the truth that my sudden wealth was too much for me and had turned my head. *Peut-être, je ne demandais pas mieux*. It seemed to me for a time – but only for a time, the scenes were shifted. 'But in a month I shall be here, and then . . . and then we will try our strength, Mr Astley!' No, as I recall it now, I was awfully sad then, though I did laugh as loudly as that idiot, Blanche.

'But what is the matter with you? How silly you are! Oh! how silly you are!' Blanche kept exclaiming, interrupting her laughter to scold me in earnest. 'Oh well, oh well, we'll spend your two hundred thousand francs: but in exchange *mais tu seras heureux comme un petit roi*; I will tie your cravat myself and introduce you to Hortense. And when we have spent all our money, you will come back here and break the bank again. What did the Jews tell you? The great thing is – boldness, and you have it, and you will bring me money to Paris more than once again. *Quant à moi, je veux cinquante mille francs de rentes et alors* . . . '

'And the General?' I asked her.

'Why, the General, as you know, comes to see me every day with a bouquet. This time I purposely asked him to get me some very rare flowers. The poor fellow will come back and will find the bird has flown. He'll fly after us, you will see. Ha-ha-ha! I shall be awfully pleased to see him. He'll be of use to me in Paris; Mr Astley will pay his bill here . . . '

And so that was the way in which I went to Paris.

CHAPTER SIXTEEN

What shall I say about Paris? It was madness, of course, and foolery. I only spent a little over three weeks in Paris, and by the end of that time my hundred thousand francs was finished. I speak only of a hundred thousand. The other hundred thousand I gave to Mlle Blanche in hard cash – fifty thousand at Frankfurt and three days later in Paris I gave her an IOU for another fifty thousand francs, though a week later she exchanged this for cash from me. '*Et les cent mille francs, qui nous restent, tu les mangeras avec moi, mon uchitel.*' She always called me an *uchitel*, i.e., a tutor. It is difficult to imagine anything in the world meaner, stingier and more niggardly than the class of creaures to which Mlle Blanche belonged. But that was in the spending of her own money. As regards my hundred thousand francs, she openly informed me, later on, that she needed them to establish herself in Paris, 'as now I am going to settle in decent style once for all, and now no one shall turn me aside for a long time; at least, that is my plan,' she added. I hardly saw that hundred thousand, however; she kept the money the whole time, and in my purse, into which she looked every day, there was never more than a hundred francs, and always less and less.

'What do you want money for?' she would say, sometimes, in the simplest way, and I did not dispute with her. But she furnished and decorated her flat very nicely with that money, and afterwards, when she took me to her new abode, as she showed me the rooms, she said: 'You see what care and taste can do even with the scantiest means.' These 'scanty means' amounted to fifty thousand francs, however. With the second fifty thousand she provided herself with a carriage and horses. Moreover, we gave two balls, that is, two evening parties at which were present Hortense, Lizette and Cléopatra, women remarkable in very many respects and even quite good-looking. At those two evenings I had to play the very foolish part of host, to receive and entertain the stupidest rich tradesmen, incredibly ignorant and shameless, various army lieutenants and miserable little authors and journalistic insects, who appeared in the most fashionable swallow-tails and straw-coloured gloves, and displayed a vanity and affectation whose proportions were beyond anything conceivable in Petersburg – and that is saying a great deal. Many of them thought fit to jeer at me; but I got drunk with champagne and lolled at full length in a back room. To me it was all loathsome to the last degree. '*C'est un uchitel,*' Blanche kept saying about me, '*il a gagné deux cent mille francs.* Without me he wouldn't have known how to spend it. And afterwards he will be an *uchitel* again; don't you know of a place for one? We ought to do something for him.'

I had recourse to champagne very often, because I was often sad and dreadfully bored. I lived in the most bourgeois, in the most mercenary surroundings in which every *sou* was reckoned and accounted for. Blanche disliked me for the first fortnight: I noticed that; it is true, she dressed me like a dandy, and tied my cravat for me every day, but in her soul she genuinely despised me. I did not pay the slightest attention to that. Bored and dispirited, I used to go usually to the Château de Fleurs, where regularly every evening I got drunk and practised the *cancan* (which they dance so disgustingly there), and acquired in the end a kind of celebrity.

At last Blanche gauged my true character. She had for some reason conceived the idea that I should spend all the time we were together walking after her with a pencil and paper in my hand, and should always be reckoning how much she had spent, how much she had stolen, how much she would spend and how much more she would steal. And she was, of course, convinced that we should have a regular battle over every ten-franc piece. She had an answer in readiness for every attack that she anticipated from me; but when she found I did not attack her, she could not at first refrain from defending herself, unprovoked. Sometimes she would begin with great heat, but seeing that I remained silent as a rule, lying on a sofa gazing at the ceiling – at last, she was surprised. At first she thought I was simply stupid, '*un uchitel*', and merely cut short her explanations, probably thinking to herself: 'Why, he's a fool. There's no need to lay it on for him, since he doesn't understand.' She would go away but come back again ten minutes later (this happened at a time when she was spending most ferociously, spending on a scale quite out of proportion to our means: she had, for instance, got rid of the horses first bought and bought another pair for sixteen thousand francs).

'Well, so you are not cross, bibi?' she said, coming up to me.

'N–n–n–no! You weary me!' I said, removing her hands from me, but this seemed to her so curious that she immediately sat down beside me.

'You see, I only decided to pay so much because they could be sold later on if need be. They can be sold again for twenty thousand francs.'

'No doubt, no doubt; they are splendid horses, and you have a fine turn-out now; it suits you; well, that's enough.'

'Then you are not cross?'

'Why should I be? You are sensible to provide yourself with things that are necessary to you. All that will be of use to you afterwards. I see that it is quite necessary for you to establish yourself in such a style; otherwise you will never save up your million. Our hundred thousand francs is only a beginning; a drop in the ocean.'

Blanche had expected from me anything but such reflections (instead of outcries and reproaches). She seemed to drop from the clouds.

'So that's what you are like! *Mais tu as l'esprit pour comprendre. Sais-tu, mon garçon*, though you are an *uchitel* you ought to have been born a prince. So you don't grudge the money's going so quickly?'

'Bother the money! the quicker the better!'

'*Mais sais-tu . . . mais dis donc*, are you rich? *Mais sais-tu*, you really despise money too much. *Qu'est ce que tu feras après, dis donc*?'

'*Après*, I shall go to Homburg and win another hundred thousand francs.'

'*Oui, oui, c'est ça, c'est magnifique*! And I know you will certainly win it and bring it here. *Dis donc*, why you will make me really love you. *Eh bien*, I will love you all the time for being like that, and won't once be unfaithful to you. You see, I have not loved you all this time, *parceque je croyais que tu n'étais qu'un uchitel* (*quelque chose comme un laquais, n'est-ce pas*?), but I have been faithful to you all the same, *parce que je suis bonne fille*.'

'Come, you are lying! How about Albert, that swarthy-faced little officer; do you suppose I didn't see last time?'

'*Oh, oh, mais tu es . . .*'

'Come, you are lying, you are lying; why, do you suppose I should be angry? Why, it's no matter; *il faut que la jeunesse se passe.* And there's no need for you to send him away if you had him before me and are fond of him. Only don't give him money, do you hear?'

'So you are not angry about it? *Mais tu es un vrai philosophe, sais-tu? Un vrai philosophe*!' she cried enthusiastically. '*Eh bien! je t'aimerai, je t'aimerai – tu verras, tu seras content*!'

And from that time she really did seem to be attached to me, to be really affectionate; and so our last ten days passed. The 'stars' promised me I did not see. But in some respects she really did keep her word. What is more, she introduced me to Hortense, who really was a remarkable woman in her own way, and in our circle was called *Thérèse philosophe* . . .

However, there is no need to enlarge upon that; all that might make a separate story, in a different tone, which I do not want to introduce into this story. The fact is, I longed above everything for this episode to be over. But our hundred thousand francs lasted, as I have mentioned already, almost a month – at which I was genuinely surprised; eighty thousand of that, at least, Blanche spent on things for herself, and we lived on no more than twenty thousand francs – and yet it was enough. Blanche, who was in the end almost open with me (or, at any rate, did not lie to me about some things), declared that, anyway, the debts she had been obliged to make would not fall upon me: 'I have never given you bills or IOUs to sign,' she said, 'because I was sorry for you; but any other girl would have certainly done it and got you into prison. You see, you see how I loved you and how good I am! Think of what that devil of a wedding alone is going to cost me!'

We really were going to have a wedding. It took place at the very end of my month, and it may be assumed that the last remains of my hundred thousand francs went upon it; that was how the thing ended; that is, my month ended with that, and after it I received my formal dismissal.

This was how it happened: a week after our arrival in Paris the General suddenly turned up. He came straight to Blanche, and from his first call almost lived with us. He had a lodging of his own, it is true. Blanche received him joyfully, with shrieks of laughter, and even flew to embrace him; as things had turned out, she was unwilling to let him go: and he had to follow her about everywhere, on the boulevards, and to the theatres, and to call on her acquaintances, and to take her for drives. The General was still of use for such purposes; he was of rather imposing and decorous appearance – he was above the average in height, with dyed whiskers and moustaches (he had once served in the Cuirassiers); he was still presentable-looking, though his face was puffy. His manners were superb; he looked well in evening dress. In Paris he began wearing his decorations. The promenade on the boulevard with a man like this was not only possible, but *advantageous*. The good-natured and senseless General was immensely delighted with all this; he had not reckoned upon it at all when he came to see us on arriving in Paris. He had come, then, almost trembling with terror; he was afraid that Blanche would make an uproar and order him to be turned out; and so he was highly delighted at the changed aspect of the position, and spent the whole month in a sort of senseless rapture: and he was in the same state when I left him. I learnt that on the morning of our sudden departure from Roulettenburg he had some sort of a fit. He had fallen insensible, and had been all that week almost like a madman, talking incessantly. He was being nursed and doctored, but he suddenly threw up everything, got into the train and flew off to Paris. Of course, Blanche's reception was the best cure for him; but the traces of his illness remained long after, in spite of his joy and his enthusiastic condition. He was utterly incapable of reflection or even of carrying on a conversation on any serious subject; when any such topic was brought forward, he confined himself to nodding his head and ejaculating, 'H'm!' at every word. He often laughed, but it was a nervous, sickly laugh, as though he were giggling; another time he would sit for hours looking as black as night, knitting his bushy brows. Of many things he had no recollection whatever; he had become absent-minded to an unseemly degree, and had acquired the habit of talking to himself. Blanche was the only person who could rouse him; and, indeed, his attacks of gloom and depression, when he hid himself in a corner, meant nothing but that he hadn't seen Blanche for a long time, or that Blanche had gone off somewhere without taking him, or had not been nice to him before going. At the same time he could not say what he wanted, and did not know why he was depressed and miserable. After sitting for two or three hours (I noticed this on two or three occasions when Blanche had gone out for the whole day, probably to see Albert), he would suddenly begin to look about him in a nervous fluster, to stare round, to recollect himself, and seem to be looking for something; but seeing no one and not remembering the question he meant to ask, he sank into forgetfulness again till Blanche reappeared, gay, frisky, gorgeously dressed, with her ringing laugh; she would run up to him, begin teasing him, and even kissing him – a favour which she did not often, however, bestow upon him. Once the General was so delighted to see her that he even burst into tears – I really marvelled at him.

From the very first, Blanche began to plead his cause before me. Indeed, she waxed eloquent in his behalf; reminded me that she had betrayed the General for my sake, that she was almost engaged to him, had given him her word; that he had abandoned his family on her account, and, lastly, that I had been in his service and ought to remember that, and that I ought to be ashamed . . . I said nothing while she rattled away at a terrific pace. At last I laughed, and with that the matter ended; that is, at first, she thought I was a fool: and at last came to the conclusion that I was a very nice and accommodating man. In fact, I had the good fortune to win in the end the complete approval of that excellent young woman. (Blanche really was, though, a very good-natured girl – in her own way, of course; I had not such a high opinion of her at first.) 'You're a kind and clever man,' she used to say to me towards the end, 'and . . . and . . . it's only a pity you are such a fool! You never, never, save anything!'

'*Un vrai russe, un calmouk*!' Several times she sent me to take the General for a walk about the streets, exactly as she might send her lapdog out with her footman. I took him, however, to the theatre, and to the Bal-Mabille, and to the restaurants. Blanche gave me the money for this, though the General had some of his own, and he was very fond of taking out his pocket-book before people. But I had almost to use force to prevent him from buying a brooch for seven hundred francs, by which he was fascinated in the Palais Royal and of which he wanted, at all costs, to make Blanche a present. But what was a brooch of seven hundred francs to her? The General hadn't more than a thousand francs altogether. I could never find out where he had got that money from. I imagine it was from Mr Astley, especially as the latter had paid their bill at the hotel. As for the General's attitude to me all this time, I believe that he did not even guess at my relations with Blanche. Though he had heard vaguely that I had won a fortune, yet he probably supposed that I was with Blanche in the capacity of a private secretary or even a servant. Anyway, he always, as before, spoke to me condescendingly, authoritatively, and even sometimes fell to scolding me. One morning he amused Blanche and me immensely at breakfast. He was not at all ready to take offence, but suddenly he was huffy with me – why? – I don't know to this day. No doubt he did not know himself. In fact, he made a speech without a beginning or an end, *à bâtons-rompus*, shouted that I was an impudent boy, that he would give me a lesson . . . that he would let me know it . . . and so on. But no one could make out anything from it. Blanche went off into peals of laughter. At last he was somehow appeased and taken out for a walk. I noticed sometimes, however, that he grew sad, that he was regretting someone and something, he was missing something in spite of Blanche's presence. On two such occasions he began talking to me of himself, but could not express himself clearly, alluded to his times in the army, to his deceased wife, to his family affairs, to his property. He would stumble upon some phrase – and was delighted with it and would repeat it a hundred times a day, though perhaps it expressed neither his feelings nor his thoughts. I tried to talk to him about his children: but he turned off the subject with incoherent babble, and passed hurriedly to another topic: 'Yes, yes, my children, you are right, my children!' Only once he grew sentimental – we were with him at the theatre: 'Those unhappy children!' he began suddenly. 'Yes, sir, those un–happy children!' And several times afterwards that evening he repeated the same words: 'unhappy children!' Once, when I began to speak of Polina, he flew into a frenzy. 'She's an ungrateful girl,' he cried. 'She's wicked and ungrateful! She has disgraced her family. If there were laws here I would make her mind her p's and q's. Yes, indeed, yes, indeed!' As for des Grieux, he could not bear even to hear his name: 'He has been the ruin of me,' he would say, 'he has robbed me, he has destroyed me! He has been my nightmare for the last two years! He has haunted my dreams for whole months! It's, it's, it's . . . Oh, never speak to me of him!'

I saw there was an understanding between them, but, as usual, I said nothing. Blanche announced the news to me first – it was just a week before we parted: '*Il a du chance*,' she babbled. 'Granny really is ill this time, and certainly will die. Mr Astley has sent a telegram. You must admit that the General is her heir, anyway, and even if he were not, he would not interfere with me in anything. In the first place, he has his pension, and in the second place, he will live in a back room and will be perfectly happy. I shall be "Madame la Générale". I shall get into a good set,' (Blanche was continually dreaming of this) 'in the end I shall be a Russian landowner, *j'aurai un château, des moujiks, et puis j'aurai toujours mon million*.'

'Well, what if he begins to be jealous, begins to insist . . . on goodness knows what – do you understand?'

'Oh, no, *non*, *non*, *non*! How dare he! I have taken precautions, you needn't be afraid. I have even made him sign some IOUs for Albert. The least thing – and he will be arrested; and he won't dare!'

'Well, marry him . . . '

The marriage was celebrated without any great pomp; it was a quiet family affair. Albert was invited and a few other intimate friends. Hortense, Cléopatra and company were studiously excluded. The bridegroom was extremely interested in his position. Blanche herself tied his cravat with her own hands, and pomaded his head: and in his swallow-tailed coat with his white tie he looked *très comme il faut*.

'*Il est pourtant très comme il faut*,' Blanche herself observed to me, coming out of the General's room, as though the idea that the General was *très comme il faut* was a surprise even to her. Though I assisted at the whole affair as an idle spectator, yet I took so little interest in the details that I have to a great extent forgotten the course of events. I only remember that Blanche turned out not to be called 'de Cominges', and her mamma not to be *la veuve* 'Cominges', but 'du Placet'. Why they had been both 'de Cominges' till then, I don't know. But the General remained very much pleased with that, and 'du Placet' pleased him, in fact, better than 'de Cominges'. On the morning of the wedding, fully dressed for the part, he kept walking to and fro in the drawing-room, repeating to himself with a grave and important air, 'Mlle Blanche du Placet! Blanche du Placet, du Placet! . . . and his countenance beamed with a certain complacency. At church, before the *maire*, and at the wedding breakfast at home, he was not only joyful but proud. There was a change in both of them. Blanche, too, had an air of peculiar dignity.

'I shall have to behave myself quite differently now,' she said to me, perfectly seriously: '*mais vois-tu*, I never thought of one very horrid thing: I even fancy, to this day, I can't learn my surname. Zagoryansky, Zagozyansky, Madame la Générale de Sago-Sago, *ces diables de noms russes, enfin madame la générale a quartorze consonnés*! *Comme c'est agréable, n'est-ce pas*?'

At last we parted, and Blanche, that silly Blanche, positively shed tears when she said goodbye to me. '*Tu étais bon enfant*,' she said, whimpering. '*Je te croyais bête et tu en avais l'air*, but it suits you.' And, pressing my hand at parting, she suddenly cried, '*Attends*!' rushed to her boudoir and, two minutes later, brought me a banknote for two thousand francs. That I should never have believed possible! 'It may be of use to you. You may be a very learned *uchitel*, but you are an awfully stupid man. I am not going to give you more than two thousand, for you'll lose it gambling, anyway. Well, goodbye! *Nous serons toujours bon amis*, and if you win, be sure to come to me again, *et tu seras heureux*!'

I had five hundred francs left of my own. I had besides a splendid watch that cost a thousand francs, some diamond studs, and so on, so that I could go on a good time longer without anxiety. I am staying in this little town on purpose to collect myself, and, above all, I am waiting for Mr Astley. I have learnt for a fact that he will pass through the town and stay here for twenty-four hours on business. I shall find out about everything: and then – then I shall go straight to Homburg. I am not going to Roulettenburg; not till next year anyway. They say it is a bad omen to try your luck twice running at the same tables; and Homburg is the real place for play.

CHAPTER SEVENTEEN

It is a year and eight months since I looked at these notes, and only now in sadness and dejection it has occurred to me to read them through. So I stopped then at my going to Homburg. My God! With what a light heart, comparatively speaking, I wrote those last lines! Though not with a light heart exactly, but with a sort of self-confidence, with undaunted hopes! Had I any doubt of myself? And now more than a year and a half has passed, and I am, to my own mind, far worse than a beggar! Yes, what is being a beggar? A beggar is nothing! I have simply ruined myself! However, there is nothing I can compare myself with, and there is no need to give myself a moral lecture! Nothing could be stupider than moral reflections at this date! Oh, self-satisfied people, with what proud satisfaction these prattlers prepare to deliver their lectures! If only they knew how thoroughly I understand the loathsomeness of my present position, they would not be able to bring their tongues to reprimand me. Why, what, what can they tell me that I do not know? And is that the point? The point is that – one turn of the wheel, and all will be changed, and those very moralists will be the first (I am convinced of that) to come up to congratulate me with friendly jests. And they will not all turn away from me as they do now. But, hang them all! What am I now? Zero. What may I be tomorrow? Tomorrow I may rise from the dead and begin to live again! There are still the makings of a man in me.

I did, in fact, go to Homburg then, but . . . afterwards I went to Roulettenburg again, and to Spa. I have even been in Baden, where I went as valet to the councillor Gintse, a scoundrel, who was my master here. Yes, I was a lackey for five whole months! I got a place immediately after coming out of prison. (I was sent to prison in Roulettenburg for a debt I made here.) Someone, I don't know who, paid my debt – who was it? Was it Mr Astley? Polina? I don't know, but the debt was paid; two hundred thalers in all, and I was set free. What could I do? I entered the service of this Gintse. He is a young man and frivolous, he liked to be idle, and I could read and write in three languages. At first I went into his service as a sort of secretary at thirty guldens a month; but I ended by becoming a regular valet: he had not the means to keep a secretary; and he lowered my wages; I had nowhere to go, I remained – and in that way became a lackey by my own doing. I had not enough to eat or to drink in his service, but on the other hand, in five months I saved up seventy gulden. One evening in Baden, however, I announced to him that I intended parting from him; the same evening I went to roulette. Oh, how my heart beat! No, it was not money that I wanted. All that I wanted then was that next day all these Gintses, all these *ober-kellners*, all these magnificent Baden ladies – that they might be all talking about me, repeating my story, wondering at me, admiring me, praising me, and doing homage to my new success. All these are childish dreams and desires, but . . . who knows, perhaps I should meet Polina again, too, I should tell her, and she would see that I was above all these stupid ups and downs of fate . . . Oh, it was not money that was dear to me! I knew I should fling it away to some Blanche again and should drive in Paris again for three weeks with a pair of my own horses, costing sixteen thousand francs. I know for certain that I am not mean; I believe that I am not even a spendthrift – and yet with what a tremor, with what a thrill at my heart, I hear the croupier's cry: *trente et un*, *rouge*, *impair et passe*, or: *quatre*, *noir*, *pair et manque*! With what avidity I look at the gambling table on which louis d'or, friedrichs d'or and thalers lie scattered: on the piles of gold when they are scattered from the croupier's shovel like glowing embers, or at the piles of silver a yard high that lie round the wheel. Even on my way to the gambling hall, as soon as I hear, two rooms away, the clink of the scattered money I almost go into convulsions.

Oh! that evening, when I took my seventy gulden to the gambling table, was remarkable too. I began with ten gulden, staking them again on *passe*. I have a prejudice in favour of *passe*. I lost. I had sixty gulden left in silver money; I thought a little and chose *zéro*. I began staking five gulden at a time on *zéro*; at the third turn the wheel stopped at *zéro*; I almost died of joy when I received one hundred and seventy-five gulden; I had not been so delighted when I won a hundred thousand gulden. I immediately staked a hundred gulden on *rouge* – it won; the two hundred on *rouge* – it won; the whole of the four hundred on *noir* – it won; the whole eight hundred on *manque* – it won; altogether with what I had before it made one thousand seven hundred gulden – and that in less than five minutes! Yes, at moments like that one forgets all one's former failures! Why, I had gained this by risking more than life itself, I dared to risk it, and – there I was again, a man among men.

I took a room at the hotel, locked myself in and sat till three o'clock counting over my money. In the morning I woke up, no longer a lackey. I determined the same day to go to Homburg: I had not been a lackey or been in prison there. Half an hour before my train left, I set off to stake on two hazards, no more, and lost fifteen hundred florins. Yet I went to Homburg all the same, and I have been here for a month . . .

I am living, of course, in continual anxiety. I play for the tiniest stakes, and I keep waiting for something, calculating, standing for whole days at the gambling table and watching the play; I even dream of playing – but I feel that in all this, I have, as it were, grown stiff and wooden, as though I had sunk into a muddy swamp. I gather this from my feeling when I met Mr Astley. We had not seen each other since that time, and we met by accident. This was how it happened: I was walking in the gardens and reckoning that now I was almost without money, but that I had fifty gulden – and that I had, moreover, three days before paid all I owed at the hotel. And so it was possible for me to go once more to roulette – if I were to win anything, I might be able to go on playing; if I lost I should have to get a lackey's place again, if I did not come across Russians in want of a tutor. Absorbed in these thoughts, I went my daily walk, across the park and the forest in the adjoining principality.

Sometimes I used to walk like this for four hours at a time, and go back to Homburg hungry and tired. I had scarcely gone out of the gardens in the park, when suddenly I saw on one of the seats Mr Astley. He saw me before I saw him, and called to me. I sat down beside him. Detecting in him a certain dignity of manner, I instantly moderated my delight; though I was awfully delighted to see him.

'And so you are here! I thought I should meet you,' he said to me. 'Don't trouble yourself to tell me your story; I know, I know all about it; I know every detail of your life during this last year and eight months.'

'Bah! What a watch you keep on your old friends!' I answered. 'It is very creditable in you not to forget . . . Stay, though, you have given me an idea. Wasn't it you bought me out of prison at Roulettenburg where I was imprisoned for debt for two hundred gulden? Some unknown person paid it for me.'

'No, oh no; it was not I who bought you out when you were in prison at Roulettenburg for a debt of two hundred gulden. But I knew that you were imprisoned for a debt of two hundred gulden.'

'Then you know who did pay my debt?'

'Oh, no, I can't say that I know who bought you out.'

'Strange; I don't know any of our Russians; besides, the Russians here, I imagine, would not do it; at home in Russia the orthodox may buy out other orthodox Christians. I thought it must have been some eccentric Englishman who did it as a freak.'

Mr Astley listened to me with some surprise. I believe he had expected to find me dejected and crushed.

'I am very glad, however, to find that you have quite maintained your independence of spirit and even your cheerfulness,' he pronounced, with a rather disagreeable air.

'That is, you are chafing inwardly with vexation at my not being crushed and humiliated,' I said, laughing.

He did not at once understand, but when he understood, he smiled.

'I like your observations: I recognise in those words my clever, enthusiastic and, at the same time, cynical old friend; only Russians can combine in themselves so many opposites at the same time. It is true, a man likes to see even his best friend humiliated; a great part of friendship rests on humiliation. But in the present case I assure you that I am genuinely glad that you are not dejected. Tell me, do you intend to give up gambling?'

'Oh, damn! I shall give it up at once as soon as I . . . '

'As soon as you have won back what you have lost! Just what I thought; you needn't say any more – I know – you have spoken unawares, and so you have spoken the truth. Tell me, have you any occupation except gambling?'

'No, none . . . '

He began cross-examining me. I knew nothing. I scarcely looked into the newspapers, and had literally not opened a single book all that time.

'You've grown rusty,' he observed. 'You have not only given up life, all your interests, private and public, the duties of a man and a citizen, your friends (and you really had friends) – you have not only given up your objects, such as they were, all but gambling – you have even given up your memories. I remember you at an intense and ardent moment of your life; but I am sure you have forgotten all the best feelings you had then; your dreams, your most genuine desires now do not rise above *pair*, *impair*, *rouge*, *noir*, the twelve middle numbers, and so on, I am sure!'

'Enough, Mr Astley, please, please don't remind me,' I cried with vexation, almost with anger, 'let me tell you, I've forgotten absolutely nothing; but I've only for a time put everything out of my mind, even my memories, until I can make a radical improvement in my circumstances; then . . . then you will see, I shall rise again from the dead!'

'You will be here still in ten years' time,' he said. 'I bet you I shall remind you of this on this very seat, if I'm alive.'

'Well, that's enough,' I interrupted impatiently; 'and to prove to you that I am not so forgetful of the past, let me ask: where is Miss Polina now? If it was not you who got me out of prison, it must have been her doing. I have had no news of her of any sort since that time.'

'No, oh no, I don't believe she did buy you out. She's in Switzerland now, and you'll do me a great favour if you leave off asking about Miss Polina,' he said resolutely, and even with some anger.

'That means that she has wounded you very much!' I laughed with displeasure.

'Miss Polina is of all people deserving of respect the very best, but I repeat – you will do me a great favour if you cease questioning me concerning Miss Polina. You never knew her: and her name on your lips I regard as an insult to my moral feelings.'

'You don't say so! you are wrong, however; besides, what have I to talk to you about except that, tell me that? Why, all our memories really amount to that! Don't be uneasy, though; I don't want to know your private secret affairs . . . I am only interested, so to say, in Miss Polina's external affairs. That you could tell me in a couple of words.'

'Certainly, on condition that with those two words all is over. Miss Polina was ill for a long time; she's ill even now. For some time she stayed with my mother and sister in the north of England. Six months ago, her grandmother – you remember that madwoman? – died and left her, personally, a fortune of seven thousand pounds. At the present time Miss Polina is travelling with the family of my married sister. Her little brother and sister, too, were provided for by their grandmother's will, and are at school in London. The General, her stepfather, died a month ago in Paris of a stroke. Mlle Blanche treated him well, but succeeded in getting possession of all he received from the grandmother . . . I believe that's all.'

'And des Grieux? Is not he travelling in Switzerland, too?'

'No, des Grieux is not travelling in Switzerland: and I don't know where des Grieux is; besides, once for all, I warn you to avoid such insinuations and ungentlemanly coupling of names, or you will certainly have to answer for it to me.'

'What! in spite of our friendly relations in the past?'

'Yes, in spite of our friendly relations in the past.'

'I beg a thousand pardons, Mr Astley. But allow me, though: there is nothing insulting or ungentlemanly about it; I am not blaming Miss Polina for anything. Besides – a Frenchman and a Russian young lady, speaking generally – it's a combination, Mr Astley, which is beyond your or my explaining or fully comprehending.'

'If you will not mention the name of des Grieux in company with another name, I should like you to explain what you mean by the expression of "the Frenchman and the Russian young lady". What do you mean by that "combination"? Why the Frenchman exactly and why the Russian young lady?'

'You see you are interested. But that's a long story, Mr Astley. You need to understand many things first. But it is an important question, however absurd it may seem at first sight. The Frenchman, Mr Astley, is the product of a finished beautiful tradition. You, as a Briton, may not agree with this; I, as a Russian, do not either, from envy maybe; but our young ladies may be of a different opinion. You may think Racine artificial, affected and perfumed;

probably you won't even read him. I, too, think him artificial, affected and perfumed – from one point of view even absurd; but he is charming, Mr Astley, and, what is more, he is a great poet, whether we like it or not. The national type of Frenchman, or, rather, of Parisian, had been moulded into elegant forms while we were still bears. The Revolution inherited the traditions of the aristocracy. Now even the vulgarest Frenchman has manners, modes of address, expressions and even thoughts, of perfectly elegant form, though his own initiative, his own soul and heart, have had no part in the creation of that form; it has all come to him through inheritance. Well, Mr Astley, I must inform you now that there is not a creature on the earth more confiding, and more candid than a good, clean and not too sophisticated Russian girl. Des Grieux, appearing in a peculiar rôle, masquerading, can conquer her heart with extraordinary ease; he has elegance of form, Mr Astley, and the young lady takes this form for his individual soul, as the natural form of his soul and his heart, and not as an external garment, which has come to him by inheritance. Though it will greatly displease you, I must tell you that Englishmen are for the most part awkward and inelegant, and Russians are rather quick to detect beauty, and are eager for it. But to detect beauty of soul and originality of character needs incomparably more independence and freedom than is to be found in our women, above all in our young ladies – and of course ever so much more experience. Miss Polina – forgive me, the word is spoken and one can't take it back – needs a long, long time to bring herself to prefer you to the scoundrel des Grieux. She thinks highly of you, becomes your friend, opens all her heart to you; but yet the hateful scoundrel, the base and petty money-grubber, des Grieux, will still dominate her heart. Mere obstinacy and vanity, so to say, will maintain his supremacy, because at one time this des Grieux appeared to her with the halo of an elegant marquis, a disillusioned liberal, who is supposed to have ruined himself to help her family and her frivolous stepfather. All these shams have been discovered later on. But the fact that they have been discovered makes no difference: anyway, what she wants is the original des Grieux – that's what she wants! And the more she hates the present des Grieux the more she pines for the original one, though he existed only in her imagination. You are a sugar-boiler, Mr Astley.'

'Yes, I am a partner in the well-known firm, Lovel & Co.'

'Well, you see, Mr Astley, one one side – a sugar-boiler, and on the other – Apollo Belvedere; it is somewhat incongruous. And I am not even a sugar-boiler; I am simply a paltry gambler at roulette, and have even been a lackey, which I think Miss Polina knows very well, as I fancy she has good detectives.'

'You are exasperated, and that is why you talk all this nonsense,' Mr Astley said coolly, after a moment's thought. 'Besides, there is nothing original in what you say.'

'I admit that! But the awful thing is, my noble friend, that however stale, however hackneyed, however farcical my statements may be – they are nevertheless true! Anyway, you and I have made no way at all!'

'That's disgusting nonsense . . . because, because . . . let me tell you!' Mr Astley, with flashing eyes, pronounced in a quivering voice, 'let me tell you, you ungrateful, unworthy, shallow and unhappy man, that I am come to Homburg expressly at her wish, to see you, to have a long and open conversation with you and to tell her everything – what you are feeling, thinking, hoping, and . . . what you remember!'

'Is it possible? Is it possible?' I cried, and tears rushed in streams from my eyes.

I could not restrain them. I believe it was the first time it happened in my life.

'Yes, unhappy man, she loved you, and I can tell you that, because you are – a lost man! What is more, if I were to tell you that she loves you to this day – you would stay here just the same! Yes, you have destroyed yourself. You had some abilities, a lively disposition, and were not a bad fellow; you might have even been of service to your country, which is in such need of men, but – you will remain here, and your life is over. I don't blame you. To my mind all Russians are like that, or disposed to be like that. If it is not roulette it is something similar. The exceptions are very rare. You are not the first who does not understand the meaning of work (I am not talking of your peasantry). Roulette is a game pre-eminently for the Russians. So far you've been honest and preferred serving as a lackey to stealing . . . But I dread to think what may come in the future. Enough, goodbye! No doubt you are in want of money? Here are ten louis d'or from me. I won't give you more, for you'll gamble it away in any case. Take it and goodbye! Take it!'

'No, Mr Astley, after all you have said.'

'Ta–ake it!' he cried. 'I believe that you are still an honourable man, and I give it as a true friend gives to another friend. If I were sure that you would throw up gambling, leave Homburg and would return to your own country, I would be ready to give you at once a thousand pounds to begin a new career. But I don't give you a thousand pounds: I give you only ten louis d'or just because a thousand pounds and ten louis d'or are just the same to you now; it's all the same – you'll gamble it away. Take it and goodbye.'

'I will take it if you will let me embrace you at parting.'

'Oh, with pleasure!'

We embraced with sincere feeling, and Mr Astley went away.

No, he is wrong! If I was crude and silly about Polina and des Grieux, he was crude and hasty about Russians. I say nothing of myself. However . . . however, all that is not the point for the time: that is all words, words, and words; deeds are what are wanted! Switzerland is the great thing now! Tomorrow . . . Oh, if only it were possible to set off tomorrow! To begin anew, to rise again. I must show them . . . Let Polina know that I still can be a man. I have only to . . . But now it's too late – but tomorrow . . . oh, I have a presentiment and it cannot fail to be! I have now fifteen louis d'or, and I have begun with fifteen gulden! If one begins carefully . . . and can I, can I be such a baby? Can I fail to understand that I am a lost man, but – can I not rise again? Yes! I have only for once in my life to be prudent and patient and – that is all! I have only for once to show willpower and in one hour I can transform my destiny! The great thing is willpower. Only remember what happened to me seven months ago at Roulettenburg just before my final failure. Oh! it was a remarkable instance of determination: I had lost everything, then, everything . . . I was going out of the Casino, I looked, there was still one gulden in my waistcoat pocket: 'Then I shall have something for dinner,' I thought. But after I had gone a hundred paces I changed my mind and went back. I staked that gulden on *manque* (that time it was on *manque*), and there really is something peculiar in the feeling when, alone in a strange land, far from home and from friends, not knowing whether you will have anything to eat that day – you stake your last gulden, your very last! I won, and twenty minutes later I went out of the Casino, having a hundred and seventy gulden in my pocket. That's a fact! That's what the last gulden can sometimes do! And what if I had lost heart then? What if I had not dared to risk it? . . .

Tomorrow, tomorrow it will all be over!